the POPPING CORK MURDER

A St. James City, Florida Mystery

BY MITCH GRANT

ISBN: 1484847989
ISBN 13: 9781484847985
Library of Congress Control Number: 2013908654
CreateSpace Independent Publishing Platform
North Charleston, South Carolina

CHAPTERS

Prologue   xi
Chapter One   Of Boats and Beer   1
Chapter Two   The Perfect Small Town   3
Chapter Three   We Find a Home   7
Chapter Four   Javier Asks to Go Fishing   17
Chapter Five   A Labor Day Tradition   21
Chapter Six   Big Ed Lowder   27
Chapter Seven   Fun in the Afternoon   35
Chapter Eight   Javier Comes to Town   39
Chapter Nine   Javier Goes Fishing   47
Chapter Ten   Javier Gets to Know the Locals   55
Chapter Eleven   Javier Moves Out   63
Chapter Twelve   Javier Rents a Boat   69
Chapter Thirteen   A Late-Night Visit   73
Chapter Fourteen   A Wake at Woody's   83
Chapter Fifteen   Lieutenant Collins's Visit   87
Chapter Sixteen   A Dead End   93
Chapter Seventeen   Spanish Gold   103
Chapter Eighteen   An Encounter at the Waterfront   107
Chapter Nineteen   A Beautiful Day on the Water   117
Chapter Twenty   One Suspect Cleared   127
Chapter Twenty-One   Frustration   131
Chapter Twenty-Two   A New Rumor   137
Chapter Twenty-Three Crime from the Past,
                     Fear from Today   145

Chapter Twenty-Four	An American Tycoon— a Florida Legend	153
Chapter Twenty-Five	A Glorious Morning	163
Chapter Twenty-Six	The Island Telegraph	175
Chapter Twenty-Seven	Let's Make a Deal	183
Chapter Twenty-Eight	Appreciation Day	185
Chapter Twenty-Nine	Lunch with a Collier	193
Chapter Thirty	An Evening in Madrid	199
Chapter Thirty-One	Some Cuban History	203
Chapter Thirty-Two	A Night at the Tiki Hut	211
Chapter Thirty-Three	A Call from Spain	221
Chapter Thirty-Four	The Knot Begins to Unravel	229
Chapter Thirty-Five	A Cuban Crime of Passion	239
Chapter Thirty-Six	Old Blue Cools Off	245
Chapter Thirty-Seven	The Joy of Fishing	251
Chapter Thirty-Eight	On the Deck at Woody's	259
Chapter Thirty-Nine	The Sheriff Says No	269
Chapter Forty	A Soldier Volunteers	275
Chapter Forty-One	Putting a Plan in Place	281
Chapter Forty-Two	A Late-Night Pizza Party	291
Chapter Forty-Three	An Early Start	309
Chapter Forty-Four	A Surprise	317
Chapter Forty-Five	Kneeling and Praying	325
Chapter Forty-Six	Jalapeno Vienna Sausage	337
Chapter Forty-Seven	A Matter of Family Pride	345
Chapter Forty-Eight	Being Dead Is Not So Bad	363
Chapter Forty-Nine	Processing the Scene	367

Chapter Fifty   In Search of a Little Peace   373
Chapter Fifty-One   A Party in Saint James City   385
Notes on Visiting Pine Island and Saint James City   393
About the Author   417

LIST OF MAJOR CHARACTERS

Jim Story	Retired banker
Jill Story	Jim Story's wife and retired banker
Eddie	The local electrician
Carl Perez	Real estate agent
Javier Hernandez	Spanish banker
Anna	Bartender at Woody's
Chesley, Kimberly, and Sunny	Servers at Woody's
Ed Lowder	Wealthy Sanibel resident
Tim	Dock master at Sanibel Island Marina
Sea Tow Sammy	Local Sea Tow captain
Cue Ball	New York banker
Lieutenant Mike Collins	Lee County sheriff detective
Rich Samuelson	Human resources executive
Lester	Local friend of Javier Hernandez
D.W. and Jamie	Owners of the Waterfront
Arantxa Garcia-Myer	Spanish banker
Senora Hernandez	Javier Hernandez's mother
Steve Fairchild	Retired military officer
Katie Fairchild	Steve Fairchild's wife
Colin Collier	Great-grandson of Barron Collier
Hector Sanchez	Fishing guide
Randy Sanchez	Hector's wife

With love and appreciation to my wonderful wife, Sherry, for her support and understanding throughout the process of writing this novel. I want to recognize and thank Randy Wayne White for providing the inspiration that motivated me to undertake this project. In addition, I wish to especially recognize my banker friends after whom I have modeled many of the key characters in this book. Finally, I want to thank my neighbors in Saint James City, Florida for their encouragement and support, as well as for providing many of the book's ideas, tales and characters.

PROLOGUE

"I was heading north with a charter client this morning. We were running along the east side of Cayo Costa, up on the tower, looking for redfish, heading on up towards Cape Haze. As I came around the point I saw him on his boat, anchored off the back side of Punta Blanca. I waived, and he waived back. It looked like he was having the time of his life. He gave me two thumbs up. But, I don't think he was fishing. He was just sitting there, like he was waiting on something to happen, or maybe waiting to meet somebody. Then, about 3:00 p.m., as we were headed back home, we ran by there again. His boat was anchored in the same place, although it had turned around with the tide. But, what was strange was that he was still sitting in the boat where he had been earlier- but now he was leaning back against the front of the console. I figured he must have been taking a nap. But, that didn't look right, him sleeping out in the hot sun like that. So I slowed down and we went over to check on him. I stopped about twenty yards away, and yelled. He didn't move, or say anything. So we came alongside to take a look. It was obvious then why he hadn't responded. Jim, damn it, I hate to tell you this, but he had a bullet hole right between his eyes. Somebody had blown his brains out!"

Chapter One
OF BOATS AND BEER

"The first two words that Carolina ever learned to say were boat and beer!" Eddie, the electrician, was describing his two-year-old daughter as we talked in the kitchen of the old house that my wife and I had recently purchased. While Eddie had described his kid, I thought that he had also perfectly described the community to which we had moved. Saint James City, one of five small towns on Southwest Florida's Pine Island, is sometimes referred to as "a quaint fishing village with a drinking problem." Without question, boats and beer are both very important here.

Eddie was repairing a short in the wiring to the kitchen's garbage disposal. We had gotten to know Eddie well during the first weeks that we lived in the house. After the purchase, and despite the glowing, pre-purchase inspection, we had learned a few things about our house—and about our new community. We knew the house was old, but on the surface, it had appeared to be extremely well maintained. What we didn't know was that the home's previous owner, Delmar O'Riley, had performed most of the maintenance himself; and that Delmar, while a great guy, apparently was the type who was reluctant to spend good money to fix something properly if there was any way it could be done more cheaply. This seemed to be especially true when it came to electrical repairs. Hence, our close and growing relationship with Eddie. As they say, live and learn. And find a good electrician.

My name is Jim Story. My wife is Jill. She's the long-suffering one who has followed me around for decades as we pursued the American dream. We started our banking careers in Florida, and then moved to Georgia, where we worked for a long time with a giant banking company that really didn't know what it wanted to be when it grew up. Finally, we had a pleasant and rewarding stint in Birmingham, where I worked with a well-managed regional bank that did know what it wanted to be—it wanted to be sold at an attractive multiple of the book value of its shares. And that eventually happened when a large, aggressive (and somewhat arrogant) Spanish bank was willing to pay four times the book price for the company. As a result, Jill and I found ourselves at a point where we could afford to stop working, move back to Florida, lie in the sun, and enjoy retirement.

At least, that's what we thought we would be doing. Life here has proven to be somewhat different. Never could we have imagined that in our quiet, little town, one of our best friends would be murdered, and that as we tried to find out who had killed him, we, too, would almost lose our lives.

Chapter Two

THE PERFECT SMALL TOWN

Given the game plan of the company we worked for, we knew that employment with the Alabama bank would come to an end, and probably sooner rather than later. Having spent almost forty years of getting up and going to work every day, neither of us looked forward to starting over with another firm. We were ready to retire. Being prudent banker types, several years earlier we had begun to think about where we might want to live when the paychecks and bonuses were replaced with pensions and Social Security payments. How then, you might ask, did we end up here—in a tiny fishing village, literally at the end of the road on one of Florida's most remote and least-known islands?

I had grown up in Florida, descended from cracker clans whose Florida history stretched back to the 1820s. Jill was from Grover, North Carolina, a small mill town near the South Carolina border—so near, in fact, that the border between the two Carolinas actually ran right through her grandparent's backyard. We both had grown up in small towns. In many ways, we were the better for it. We both had been well educated, had developed self-confidence, and had learned the work ethics necessary to enjoy successful and rewarding professional careers. In our business lives, we had been blessed to travel to, and live in, many of the larger cities in the United States. We also were fortunate to have seen enough of the rest of the world to know that we weren't missing anything there. In short, we had pretty much "been there, done that." It was time for us to move back to Florida.

Our formative years in small towns were in places where we knew just about everyone in town. Not only did we know the kids in each family, but we also knew their moms and dads. And there was a very good chance that we were even on speaking terms with each family's dog or cat. That's the kind of place to which we were looking to retire.

The only problem was that for the most part, those kinds of places don't exist in Florida anymore. When I was a kid, Florida (excluding Miami and Fort Lauderdale) was truly a backwater. But now, Florida is not like that at all. The small, pleasant towns like the one in which I had grown up were no longer small. Or, if they were, they weren't as pleasant as I remembered them to be. They had become suburbia, largely populated by old folks who had moved from somewhere up North—from someplace where, in the winter, the sun only comes out when the temperature is below freezing. Like us, they had come to Florida seeking to spend their final years in the sun. I don't really have anything against old folks, and, in fact, I am slowly coming to grips with being one. But that doesn't mean I want to surround myself with them.

The makeup of the population isn't the only thing that has changed in these towns. Their economies have also changed. When I was growing up, citrus, cattle, and phosphate were the leading industries in much of the state. But hard freezes wiped out the trees; the phosphate was depleted, and soaring land prices have put an end to the cowboys' way of life. When I was child, I could stand on top of a hill in Central Florida and gaze out at rolling hills covered with citrus trees as far as I could see. Now, if you were to look from the same place, you would see mile after mile of nearly identical houses, with scarcely a tree of any type in sight. This was not the Florida we were seeking.

With these givens, we started to look around, and stumbled upon Saint James City. I tell people now that if you were to combine a dash of each of the towns that had been important to me as I grew up in Florida, throw them in a blender, add in some mango slices, let a mullet jump around in this mix for a while, process the concoction, and pour it out to bake in the hot, Florida sun, when it dried what you would be left with would be something a lot like Saint James City. As we researched the area, we learned that Pine Island is quiet, out-of-the-way, flat, and only slightly above sea level. We also learned that there are no beaches on the island, but there are plenty of mosquitoes. Consequently, it has, for the most part, been overlooked during Florida's periodic development frenzies. Unsurprisingly, there are few permanent residents here, and property values are reasonable. For most people, this type of place would not sound all that attractive. But for us, it looked and felt just right. We did more research. Liked what we learned. And made plans to go down to have a look. The next step was finding a real estate agent with whom to work.

Chapter Three
WE FIND A HOME

"Paradise Island Realty. My name is Jeri. How may I help you?"

"Hello," I responded. "My name is Jim Story. My wife and I are interested in buying a house in Saint James City. Is there someone with whom I could speak about this?"

"Certainly," answered Jeri. "Our firm is very active in that market. If you will hold, I will have one of our brokers with you shortly."

In less than a minute, I heard a professional-sounding voice say, "Hello. My name is Carl Perez. How may I be of service?"

My research had shown that Paradise Island Realty was the leading real estate firm operating in the Sanibel, Captiva, and Pine Island markets. My perusal of several other websites confirmed that this firm had more listings than all the other firms on the islands combined. But I have to admit that I was surprised when Carl Perez took my call. Paradise Island Realty is a large firm, and I knew that Mr. Perez was its sole owner and CEO. I also had learned that his interests were far broader than that of just running a residential real-estate business. He also controlled a subsidiary that was the major player in Southwest Florida's commercial real-estate industry. It had developed many of the most successful and prestigious shopping malls, office complexes, and multifamily residential projects in the area. I knew he was on the board of directors of the largest bank in the area. In addition, my research had shown that he was very civically active, serving on the boards of the local state university, the area's Industrial Development Board, the Lee County Tourist Development Commission, and the Southwest Florida Aviation Authority. He was also on the executive boards of several of the area's most important charities, including serving as the executive chairman of the Sanibel-Captiva Islands Environmental Conservancy. In short, Carl Perez was an influential businessman—a true mover and shaker. You don't expect men like him to want to get involved with a routine retail home transaction—especially a modest home purchase like we were looking to make in quiet Saint James City.

"Yes, Carl. My name is Jim Story. My wife and I are interested in buying a small retirement home in Saint James City." I emphasized "small "and "retirement "to make sure he knew that I wasn't a high roller looking for some palatial estate on Sanibel. I went on to explain a little more about what we were looking for, and about how much money we were willing to spend. I fully expected for him to offer to have a more "suitable" (i.e. junior) broker work with us on this transaction. So you can imagine my surprise when I heard him say, "Mr. Story, I would love to help you and your wife find the perfect home in Saint James City.

Thus began our relationship with Carl. We were, needless to say, impressed, and once we worked with him, our admiration only grew.

A few weeks later, we were standing in the baggage claim area of the sparkling Southwest Florida International airport, shaking hands with Carl Perez. When we had confirmed our travel plans, I was surprised and pleased that Carl had offered to have a car pick us up at the airport. That was certainly a classy move. But there was no way I expected Carl himself to be there to meet us. In my experience, that just doesn't happen.

But there he was, in the flesh. And a nicer guy you could not ask to meet. He gave Jill a friendly kiss on the cheek and greeted me with a warm, welcoming handshake. He asked how our flight had been, and, despite our protests, grabbed our bags. Needless to say, he was making a very good impression.

He loaded our bags into his Cadillac SUV and we began the forty-five-minute drive to the island. After the usual pleasantries, we began to get to know each other. He asked about our families, our careers, our plans, and how we had found Pine Island. As is our custom, I let Jill do most of the talking. When it comes to social networking, she is the master and I'm more like Ned in the third grade. I'm far better at listening. Jill and Carl got along fabulously. But I think it would be fair to say that despite Jill's best efforts, by the time we neared the island, Carl knew a lot more about us than we knew about him. It wasn't that he was pushy or evasive, or that he seemed to ask a lot of questions. Rather, it was just that he was able, in a friendly way, to ask questions that somehow got us to talk about ourselves. And he listened in such an interested manner that we felt we really needed to tell him more, rather than less. Clearly, this was not the first time he had dealt with the buying public. The man was a pro. But throughout the drive, I couldn't help but wonder why he was going out of his way to deal with us. Finally, I broke my silence and asked.

"Carl, I know how large your firm is and I know about the types of deals that your firm does. Our search for a modest, little, retirement home in Saint James City doesn't seem like the kind of transaction that someone like you would normally have the time to be involved with. I would have thought you would have assigned this to one of your more junior associates. Please don't take this the wrong way—and I'm not complaining—but I'm just wondering why you are willing to work with us."

Carl laughed. "Jim, that's a very reasonable question. I get that a lot. There are several reasons I'm doing this—several reasons that to me are very important. First, I like to stay involved with what goes on at the grassroots level of my firm. That way, I can relate to what my employees are having to deal with. So I always try to work with a few retail clients each month. Secondly, I grew up in Saint James City. My family goes back in the Pine Island Sound area for over a hundred years. Because of that, it's important to me to stay in touch with what is going on in this area. It's true that I can't handle many clients, but I've found that if I limit what I do only to buyers interested in Saint James City, it all seems to work out about right. Of course, if I'm too busy, I can have one of my associates handle the case. But I've found over the years that I can handle the Saint James City market by myself—especially, this time of the year. Besides, I have a house in Saint James City. My 'primary' residence is on

Sanibel, but I only really only use that when I want to impress and entertain. Truthfully, I prefer to stay in Saint James City as often as possible. I learn more from spending an evening at the bar at Froggy's than I ever learn at the Sanibel Island Yacht Club. I commute from Saint James City to my Sanibel office, whenever I need to, by boat. I hope this makes sense. But if you're worried that I won't have enough time or won't be able to focus properly on your transaction, please let me know. I can easily ask one of my associates to work with you on this."

"No, no," I replied. "Carl, what you've told me makes perfect sense. I just wanted to make sure we weren't imposing. And I have to say, I'm very impressed that you want, and are able, to spend time down in the trenches of your business. That's important. It's something we always tried to do at the bank, but, honestly, were seldom able to do well. We look forward to working with you."

And work we did. We got to Carl's office in Saint James City a little before 6:00 p.m., and sat down at his conference table while he pulled up on his computer a list of the key features that we had said were important. We were looking for properties with three bedrooms and pool, located on a canal, with a dock and a boat lift. The property needed to be in good condition, with attractive, low-maintenance, tropical landscaping. We reviewed this list together to make sure Carl understood what we wanted. Then, using this list of features and the budget we had suggested, Carl brought up on the computer a list of properties that he thought might be of interest. When we had finished going over the list, Carl said, "Great! We've got a really good group of properties to look at in the morning. I'm confident that you are going to find a place you will love. Now, let me take you to your hotel so you can get settled in. I'll pick you up there at nine in the morning. By the way, there's a great little restaurant across the street from where you're staying. It serves an excellent grouper sandwich. And just down the street is a super place for breakfast. Just don't let the name of the place, Hobo's, turn you off. The omelets and the pancakes there are really something special."

Carl dropped us in front of the Two Fish Inn, a pleasant, if slightly funky, six-room, canal-front motel that caters to fishermen. There are docks right out back. I suspect it may also appeal to couples wanting to disappear for the weekend. It has that sort of vibe. We checked in, unpacked, and went to eat. Carl was right about the sandwich.

In the morning, we discovered he was also correct about breakfast. We were off to a great start.

Carl was prompt, pulling into the shell driveway right on time. By noon we had seen eight of the properties, and to be honest, we were getting somewhat discouraged. Some of the houses looked great from the outside but needed a lot of work on the inside; some looked great on the inside but weren't so nice on the outside. Some were small and felt claustrophobic. Some had challenging locations. Truthfully, we had not seen anything yet that either Jill or I felt really good about. Finally, we stopped for lunch at a canal-side café that featured a tiki hut with a genuine thatched roof. I loved the name of the place: the Low Key Tiki (note that Saint James City is on the southern tip of Pine Island). As the waitress brought us our drinks, Carl asked how we were feeling. He listened intently as we expressed our frustrations.

Once we were through venting, Carl told us to relax. He said he had led us through a variety of challenging properties all morning just so that he could judge firsthand what we were really looking for. He said that we would see several properties right after lunch that he felt would suit us much better. He sounded so confident as he said this that we couldn't help but relax and begin to look forward to the afternoon.

Once we had finished our sandwiches, we loaded up and headed back on the road.

The first house that we looked at was a delightful, older home that had started life as a stilt house. It had been remodeled at some point so that it now featured three stories of living space. The house showed signs of having been very carefully decorated and landscaped. The top floor featured a lovely—and very private—master bedroom. The lower level featured an office, a den, a full bath, and a kitchen, and opened through sliding doors onto a screened pool. The second level featured two bedrooms, a bath, a wonderful kitchen, and a delightful living area with French doors that opened onto a screened porch overlooking the pool, and the canal. The house had a delightful, quirky, funkiness to it that let you know it had been lived in, and that the living there had been good. Along the canal, the property featured what looked to be a well-constructed dock; a large, covered boat lift; a fish-cleaning station; running water; lights; and electricity. And the property featured amazing landscaping. The driveway was lined with beautiful queen palms. The pool cage was surrounded by areca palms that had been carefully placed to provide seclusion, while still allowing unobstructed views down the canal. I counted at least five other types of palms on the property. And there were a host of different varieties of tropical trees, most that I didn't even know the names of. It was all just gorgeous. The yard was covered in rocks, so there was no grass to worry about. There was even a fish pond next to the stone pathway that wound down to the dock. And, to top it all off, the property had an occupied osprey nest in the top of a tall Norfolk pine alongside the canal. It was just what we were looking for.

We went through the exercise of looking at a number of other properties that Carl had selected. While they were nice, they just didn't excite us. Finally, we told Carl that we were ready to stop looking, that we loved the stilt house, and that we would like to make an offer. While he was happy, he cautioned that we should think about the decision overnight. He suggested that we select the three properties that we were most interested in, and then look at all three again in the morning. We agreed that sounded like good advice. But in the morning, after having looked at the three properties again, we still felt the same.

So, in short order, Carl drafted an offer and presented it to the owners. By early afternoon, after some minor negotiations, we had a deal. We now knew where we would be spending our final days in the sun. It felt great to have that uncertainty removed from our lives.

Looking back on the experience as we flew home, we were very impressed with the way that Carl had led us through the buying process. He clearly knew the market, and he clearly knew how to deal with people. The secret to what had made him such a success was obvious. He had a knack for getting people to talk to him, and more importantly, when they did talk, he listened to what they were saying. From my experience as a banker, I knew that was always the mark of a great salesman. I liked Carl a lot. I was hoping that we would be able to spend more time with him in years to come.

With our home purchase out of the way, we began preparing to move to Florida.

Chapter Four
JAVIER ASKS TO GO FISHING

Back at the bank, I announced my plans to retire, and began to say my good-byes. If you've had a career, you understand how important all the people you've worked with are to you. To succeed, there's very little that you can do by yourself. Most, if not all, of your success is due to the efforts of the people who actually do what needs to get done. Over time, those people become very dear to you. It's tough saying good-bye, knowing full well that once you move away, you'll likely never see them again. The emotions you experience in this situation are a little bit like the emotions you feel when someone dies. Except in this case, you're supposed to be happy. And we were. Jill and I were absolutely delighted to be able to make our big move.

One of the final things I did at the bank was to send a note to all of the people who were important to me. I wanted to thank them for their help over the years. In the note, I also extended an invitation to please look us up should they ever come to Southwest Florida. I promised to take them fishing, if they should find their way out to Pine Island. I understood that it was a near certainty that none of them would ever take us up on the offer, but I was hopeful that we might stay in touch in some way.

So I was absolutely delighted when, as I was packing up my office, Javier Hernandez popped in and said, "Hey, boss, when can we go fishing?"

Javier was one of the good guys at the office. He had been sent from Spain a year earlier to implement the company's model for managing risk. While he was in a position where he could have dictated to the Americans what needed to get done, that wasn't the way he approached the task. He explained carefully to his staff what needed to be done, discussed why it needed to be done in that fashion, and outlined how it fit together into the bigger risk-management efforts of the company. He assured everyone that the changes to come would be evolutionary, rather than revolutionary. He approached this task in a very patient way, listened to the concerns that his staff had about the implementation, and tried to incorporate their suggestions about how things might be done better. Over time, he built a team of loyal employees who capably performed their risk-management responsibilities. As I said, he was one of the good guys.

And I wasn't the only one who thought Javier was a good guy. If you were to think of a guy who is tall, dark, and handsome, you would likely envision someone who looks much like Javier. His features were clearly that of an aristocratic Spaniard, but he lacked any of the cruel, haughty features that oftentimes goes with that breed.

As you can imagine, Javier had plenty of female admirers in the office. Whenever he ate lunch in the bank's break room, his table had more than its proportionate share of attractive female bankers. I always assumed that they were just trying to learn more about risk management. Right!

"Hey, Javier! I didn't know you liked to fish."

"Are you kidding? I'm a great fisherman," he answered. "And I've read a lot about Pine Island Sound. It's one of America's best fishing spots. I've always wanted to fish there. Jim, I really am serious about coming to see you and Jill. When do you think would be a good time for me to visit?"

"Great! We'd love to have you. We'll need about a month to get settled in, but after that we'll be open for visitors. Will that work for you?"

"That will be perfect. Look, Jim. As you know, we Spaniards have lots more holiday time than you Americans. And I've taken very little of what I've earned since I've been over here. I was thinking I might come down and stay with you for a week. Would that be too long?"

"Heck, no! We'd love to have you with us. When do you want to come?"

"What do you say if I come down in about six weeks—right after your Labor Day? Will the fishing be good then?"

"Javier, that would be a perfect time for us! From what I've read, the fishing then is great. We'll be settled in, and by then I will have discovered where some of the best fishing spots are. This sounds like a plan to me."

"All right, boss! I'm excited. I'm really looking forward to fishing that area with you. I can't wait to set my hook into some trout, redfish, snook, and lots of mullet! I'll be there." With that, Javier walked out the door, and I returned to cleaning out my desk.

I was genuinely pleased that Javier was going to stay with us in our new home. I looked forward to showing him Saint James City and Pine Island Sound. We had fallen in love with both, and were excited to share them with as many of our friends as we could. Now, I was really looking forward to Labor Day.

I was also happy to learn that Javier liked to fish. I had not known that about him in the year that we had worked together. But I suppose he hadn't had much time or opportunity in Birmingham to wet a hook. I have to admit, though, that I wasn't quite sure how to take his comment about hooking lots of mullet. We should be able to hook plenty of trout, snook, and redfish. But, apart from using a cane pole and a snatch hook, I have never heard of anyone ever actually hooking a mullet. But maybe they do things differently in Spain. I looked forward to fishing with Javier.

Chapter Five
A LABOR DAY TRADITION

Time flew as we settled into our new life. Before we knew it, we were celebrating Labor Day. In Saint James City, celebrating Labor Day means finding your way to Woody's Waterside for the afternoon and staking out choice seats on the patio under the shade of a coconut palm. From such a spot, you will enjoy a great view of the day's entertainment—both that provided by the local musician who plays his unique blend of zydeco, rock, and polka on keyboard and accordion (no one ever said that things in Saint James City were normal!), and that provided by the people coming and going in boats. For some reason, the goings always seem to be the most fun—the skippers and crews having been well served for several hours by the attentive wait staff at Woody's. It's a fun way to spend a Labor Day afternoon.

Everyone who is anyone in town usually makes an appearance at this event. This year was no different. We soon found ourselves chatting with one of the local celebrities, Sea Tow Sammy. Sammy skippers the Saint James City Sea Tow boat, and today he was making the rounds from table to table, exchanging pleasantries with the ladies and giving high fives to the guys. Sammy was in especially fine form today since he had recently appeared on local TV newscasts, discussing how he had rescued a boat offshore that mysteriously had developed a sizeable hole in its hull. Sammy shared with everyone that, in his opinion, the hole in the hull really wasn't that much of a mystery. To him, it appeared that the boat had likely run into a buoy—possibly while the skipper was operating under the influence!

Soon, Sammy stopped by our table, and we said hello. I had recently met Sammy at the Sanibel Island Marina fuel dock. We had introduced ourselves and discovered that we were neighbors. So at Woody's, we were now chatting like old chums. As we talked, a local named Andy untied his bay boat, pushed it away from the dock, and motored down the canal. As he left, Sammy shared with us a story about Andy. It seems that Andy and a buddy recently had spent a day drinking at the pool bar of the Tween Waters hotel, which is located on Captiva. Tween Waters is a large, pleasant resort that fronts on the gulf and opens on the back to Roosevelt Channel. The channel is well marked, which is a very good thing, since some extremely shallow sandbars border it. These bars lie in wait for any unwary boaters seeking a direct path into Pine Island Sound. The most critical marker is market number four. Miss it and you will likely end up high and dry. According to Sammy, it seems that Andy and his friend, having been at the bar nearly all day and well into the night, may have become somewhat impaired. In any case, it appeared to Sammy that they must have been in a hurry to get home—possibly because, in Sammy's opinion, they had discovered that there was no more beer on their boat. Regardless, Andy decided that it would be a good idea to take a shortcut back to the sound. This, as it turned out, was not a particularly wise decision. Andy's bay boat reportedly was going nearly fifty miles per hour when it hit the sandbar that borders marker number four. Needless to say, at that speed, the boat ended very, very far up on the sandbar. With the tide going out, Andy and his friend were not going anywhere on their own.

It was time to call Sea Tow. Apparently, since Andy and Sammy are friends, Andy specifically requested that Sammy come out to rescue them. As soon as they were communicating by cell phone, Andy said, "Sammy, you got to come pull me off the sandbar at number four. The tide's going out, and I'm so far up that damn bar that if you don't get here pretty soon, I'm going to be able to build a sand castle." And here's the good part. "And Sammy," Andy added, "when you come, make sure you bring us a case of beer. We're getting thirsty."

Sammy, wanting to keep his clients happy, did as requested. St. James City!

When Sammy finished his story, he moved on to regale the next table—one populated by several admiring older females. Jill and I resumed enjoying the music.

It wasn't long, however, before we noticed another familiar face in the crowd. Sitting at the bar was none other than Carl Perez, our favorite Realtor. Soon, he spied us and came over to say hello. We were, of course, delighted to see Carl, and asked him to join us at our table, which he gladly did.

We fell into conversation, with Carl being particularly interested in how we liked the house, and how we were finding life in Saint James City. We assured him we were ecstatic on both fronts. One topic led to another, and soon we were talking about how life on the island had changed since he was a youngster. We were fascinated to learn some of the history of the city, and to discover some personal information about Carl and his ancestors. We learned that his early relatives in Florida had all been commercial fisherman. His great-grandfather on his father's side apparently had been a man of competence and vision. Somehow, he managed to save enough money from what he earned fishing to buy almost half of Sanibel and Captiva. He could do that because, at that time, the islands were considered to be nothing more than worthless sandbars. In those days, there was no bridge, no electricity, and crucially, no fresh water. The only plentiful things on the islands were sand gnats and mosquitoes. He must have been a man of vision, indeed. Carl's great-grandfather accumulated the property gradually. Surprisingly, he had told no one about these acquisitions—not even his wife. So when he died, it came as a great surprise to Carl's grandfather to learn, at the reading of the will, that he had inherited all of this property. Carl's grandfather proved to be a good shepherd for this estate, maintaining it and even adding small parcels as they became available. And he never sold any of it. Carl's father, in turn, also managed these holdings well. By this time, though, the bridge to Sanibel had been completed and the islands had been "discovered." Still, for many years, Carl's father sold almost none of the family's property. He did manage to generate a nice annuity stream of revenue, however, by leasing the choicest locations to the hotels and other businesses that were moving onto the islands. Toward the end of his life, back in the 1970s, there was a huge explosion in real estate prices. Only then did the family cash in, as Carl's father disposed of the majority of his holdings. The vast amount of cash from selling these properties eventually passed to Carl, and he had managed to multiply it many times over through his various real estate ventures.

In fact, I already knew that Carl actually controlled one of the state's greatest modern-day fortunes. Carl, of course, didn't mention that. But he did tell us how proud he was of his ancestors for what they had been able to accomplish. Over the past century, there have been some remarkable rags-to-riches success stories in the Florida. Today, the names of those families are legendary. Lykes, Griffin, McNulty, and Perez are some of the old names that people think of when they think of folks who started here with nothing and amassed great fortunes. It was clear, as Carl spoke, that he was immensely proud of his family's history.

We found this story to be fascinating. It was almost beyond belief that a poor, commercial fisherman—most of whom barely lived at a subsistence level—had had the foresight and discipline to save and invest in this fashion. It was easy to see why Carl's family story was revered as one of Florida's most remarkable. We certainly were impressed and our respect for Carl only grew.

Carl again expressed his delight that we had fit in so well in Saint James City. He said he'd thought that we would, but it was always good when his intuition about someone buying property proved to be on the mark. He told us that in many cases, when he didn't think that the island would be a good fit for someone who was looking to buy property here, he would tell the client not to proceed with the transaction until after he'd spent at least a week living on the island. In many cases, the seclusion and isolation of island life would convince these potential buyers that Pine Island wasn't what they were looking for. It certainly does take a special type to enjoy living here.

As we concluded our conversation, Carl confided in us that he would be making a big announcement soon, and he asked us to keep this to ourselves for a few days. We, of course, agreed. Carl went on to explain that the governor had selected him to complete the remaining term of Florida's recently deceased US senator. He said that he had never had much interest in political office, but he had always contributed generously to politicians who he felt had the best interest of the state in mind. Despite his traditional antipathy toward serving in political office, this opportunity was just too good to pass up. He said he was look-ing forward to being able to use his experience as a businessper-son to do a lot of good for the state, and for Southwest Florida, in particular. Knowing Carl the way we did, we didn't doubt for a minute that he would be able to accomplish both of these aspirations. We genuinely felt good for Carl and looked forward to the announcement to come.

Eventually, the musician's contracted performance period came to an end. He played one last, rousing encore. With that, the crowd gradually started to disperse. We said our good-byes, got on our bicycles, and peddled happily (if a little unsteadily) the five blocks to our house. We arrived without incident and decided that a nice dip in the pool would be in order. It had been another really great day on the island.

Chapter Six
BIG ED LOWDER

Sanibel Island Marina lies two miles across the bay from the canal on which we live. It primarily caters to the yachts of Sanibel. But this marina does sell ethanol-free gasoline at the same price that you can buy it in Saint James City, and it's a lot quicker for me to just run across the bay than to idle all the way up Monroe Canal. Plus, the dock master, Tim, is a great guy. When we first met, he really went out of his way to make us—and our little bay boat—feel at home among the towering yachts.

We had spent the week boating on the sound, and enthusiastically burning up a tank of the Arab states' finest hydrocarbons. So it was that I needed to head toward Tim's fuel dock. I ran the boat to the Sanibel bridge, throttled down to idle under it, and then planed over to the entrance to the marina's canal. I slowed, obeyed the no-wake restrictions, and idled into the narrow channel. Coming in, I hailed the fuel dock on the radio, and, after switching to his working channel, asked Tim for permission to dock. He was his usual jovial self. He told me the dock was unoccupied and to come on in. To get into the marina, you idle up a narrow cut between two sea-walled peninsulas, each of which is home to a lot of high-priced real estate. This little channel is only one hundred yards long and twenty yards wide. It has good depth on its northern side, but it features a shallow sandbar on the southern edge. Therefore, effectively, the channel is only ten yards wide. It never fails to amaze me that the enormous yachts that frequent the marina are able to get through this narrow and shallow passageway.

But this gap certainly was not an issue for my little boat, and I was soon tied up at the fuel dock, having a pleasant chat with Tim. As he handed me the fuel hose, I heard a call come in over the radio.

"Sanibel Island Marina, this is the *Florida Blanca*. I saw Tim roll his eyes and go inside to answer the call. The marina's radio is connected to an outside speaker so that staffers can monitor it when they are on the dock. I wasn't really trying to listen to the conversation between Tim and the *Florida Blanca*, but I couldn't help but hear—particularly since they were talking about me.

"Tim, it's about time you got off your lazy ass and answered the fucking radio! What the hell are they paying you to do? Maybe I ought to talk to your boss about the service you give your best customer!"

"*Florida Blanca*, this is Sanibel Island Marina," I heard Tim reply. "How may we be of service to you today?"

"Tim, I need to refuel. The tide's going out. I'm coming in now."

Tim replied, *"Florida Blanca* this is Sanibel Island Marina. The tide just turned and you've still got plenty of water. The fuel dock is currently occupied. Stand off for a couple of minutes and it will be available."

"Shit, Tim, I can see what's at your dock. You going to let that little piss pot keep me from coming in? You know I'll buy more fuel when I get there than that whole damn boat is worth. Tell the little motherfucker to get the hell off the dock and make room for a real boat!"

"Florida Blanca, this is Sanibel Island Marina. If you wish to purchase fuel at this dock today, you will follow my instructions. The fuel dock will be available in a few minutes. Stand off and wait until you receive my permission to approach," Tim replied tersely.

The last word from the *Florida Blanca* was, "Asshole!"

As Tim came out to the dock, I apologized and said that I would move immediately.

Tim said, "Stay where you are. When you get full, we'll settle up the bill, chat a little bit more, and then you can leave—if you're ready."

"Man, is that how all your clients over here behave?" I asked.

Tim laughed and replied, "No! Most of the folks here are as nice as they can be—rich, for sure—but still good folks. This fellow is just a special little nutcase that I put up with because he's got so damn much money. His name is Ed Lowder but he likes to be called Big Ed. When you see him, you'll understand why. He had the good fortune to inherit his daddy's company about four years ago, and his advisors were smart enough to convince him to sell it at the market's peak. Now he's got more money than he knows what to do with. For some reason, he thinks that makes him special."

We finished with the fuel, and Tim went in to run my card. When he came out, he continued, "Big Ed's got all this money and doesn't know what to do with himself. He's now decided that he's going to find the pirate treasures that are supposedly buried around these islands. He's bought himself a beautiful Viking and named it after Jose Gaspar's flagship. Now he spends his time running up and down the sound, occasionally stopping to drag a magnetometer around looking for wrecks, and cussing at his crew when he doesn't find anything. He's a screwball. He's not right. Watch out for him. Now, Jim, is there anything else I can do for you?"

"No, Tim. Thanks for the gas and thanks for the warning. Now, I think it's time for me to get out of the way. Good luck with Big Ed."

With that, I cast off and began to head toward the entry channel, going as fast as I could to get out of Big Ed's way, but making sure I didn't create too much of a wake.

I had just entered the cut when I saw a sports-fisherman coming around the seawall on the left. The big boat was running on a plane, going through the slow-speed zone as if the rule didn't apply to it. The boat was solid black. Its hull was black, its superstructure was black, and even all the windows and railings were blacked out. The boat was unlike anything I had ever seen. It looked sinister, but at the same time it was gorgeous. The boat was well over sixty feet long, and was moving at over thirty miles per hour. It continued to turn right. Soon it was headed straight for the channel to the marina—and straight at me!

A boat that big, going that fast, throws out a hell of a wake. When you see something like that coming right at you, trust me, it will scare you. There was no way that my boat could survive that kind of wake, particularly in this narrow channel. It would swamp the boat, and wash it—and me—over the seawall. My first thought was to accelerate to get out of the canal before I met the incoming boat. But there just wasn't enough time for that. My only real option was to spin the steering wheel to the left, put the throttle down hard, and hope that the Sailfish could get up onto a plane fast enough to outrun the approaching jug-gernaut. If this worked, I would have enough time to turn out of the yacht's way. But if this didn't work, my boat would be run over in a flash. There wouldn't be much left of it or me when the Viking's props passed over.

Thankfully, the Sailfish responded like I had hoped. The propeller cavitated as the boat turned, but it took a bite once we were going straight, and it jumped the boat onto a plane just in time. The sinister black Viking had never slowed. By the time my boat was moving, the Viking was only a few feet behind. Together, we flew out of the narrow channel and into the marina's basin. Once clear of the cut, I turned the steering wheel hard to port. My boat dove to the left, and the Viking flew past, miss-ing me by maybe a foot. Then, the big boat's wake hit. It threw the Sailfish forward violently, but since my boat was moving in the same direction as the wake, it was able to surf along until the wake passed.

As we slowed, I looked back. The name on the Viking's stern was *Florida Blanca*. Standing in the elevated steering station and looking back at me was a skinny, middle-aged man. He had one hand on the wheel. With the other, he was giving me a vigorous middle-finger salute. This had to be Big Ed Lowder. Funny thing was, Big Ed couldn't have been more than five foot four. Figures.

The commotion in the basin was something to behold. Every boat in the marina was bouncing like crazy as wakes ricocheted between the surrounding seawalls. A lot of expensive and carefully polished gel coat was being gouged against barnacle-encrusted pilings.

My initial reaction was to confront the asshole who had almost wrecked my boat and who had almost killed me. To put it mildly, I wanted to go kick the bejesus out of him. But as I approached the Viking, I counted four deckhands standing between me and the short little prick I wanted to strangle. I noted that none of these hired hands showed much fat, and that all of them displayed a lot of muscles, many of which were bulging out of their tight-fitting, matching black shirts. I quickly deduced that these well-built lads had not been hired solely on the basis of their nautical skills. It also dawned on me that the type of act I was contemplating was exactly what the little asshole wanted me to do. He would love to see me try to climb aboard his boat and get by his bodyguards, while he was thirty feet up in the air in his damn tuna tower. I didn't see much enthusiasm for their jobs on the faces of the deckhands, and I doubted that Big Ed's gorillas would really want to hurt me, but still I was sure that they couldn't afford to let me get past them, either. All in all, there would be little upside for me in such an encounter. It might make me feel better to yell and scream, but there was no way I would be able to board the Viking to get my hands around Big Ed's scrawny little neck.

So reluctantly, I backed off while taking one last long look at Big Ed. I wanted to make sure I would recognize this idiot if I ever came across him alone. All the while, Big Ed was yelling insults at me, knowing full well that he was perfectly safe. There was nothing for me to do at this point but let Tim deal with this jerk. I touched the brim of my cap to give Tim a salute, turned the boat around, and calmly idled out the channel, making sure to not create even the smallest wake.

All the way home, all I could do was shake my head and marvel at what I had just experienced. I told myself that I needed to let this go and just stay away from the *Florida Blanca*. But at the same time, I vowed that if Big Ed's path and mine should ever cross in a situation where he was not shielded by his goon squad, I would do my best to put several sizeable bumps on his ugly little head.

So much for enjoying a peaceful and quiet retirement. My blood pressure was pegged!

Chapter Seven

FUN IN THE AFTERNOON

By the time I reached my dock, I had stopped shaking. Now, I was more amazed at what had just happened than really angry about it. I like to think that I am basically a nice guy. At least, that's how I try to act. I guess you never really know how others see you. Who knows? Big Ed's probably convinced he's a nice guy, too. The fucking asshole! But really, I do genuinely try to treat people in a nice way. Probably comes from growing up in a small town.

After putting the boat on the lift, I ran up the stairs to find Jill so I could tell her what had just happened. She was in the master bedroom, deeply involved in a project to hang new tropical-themed drapes. Jill is the type of person who is never really happy unless she's doing something. She can't sit still. Consequently, she's still as slender as a fashion model. She's able to maintain this weight despite having a ravenous appetite for cheeseburgers and beer. Her secret is that she is almost always on the move. Gardening, decorating, cleaning, and cooking are all things she loves to do. And if she's not doing one of the above, then she's jogging, biking, or doing Pilates. Even when she talks on the phone she's standing up and moving. All this activity must burn up a ton of calories. She's in great shape—there's no question that she looks better than most thirty-year-olds do, even though she's nearly my age. Hey, it works for me.

Unfortunately, I don't share the same hyperactivity gene. I would rather sit and think about the best way to do a project, while she is much happier actually doing it. This different approach usually works out pretty well. Together, we are usually able to get things done.

"Babe," I shouted. "You're not going to believe what just happened! This asshole just tried to kill me!"

"What?" she screamed. "What do you mean someone tried to kill you? Are you OK?"

I told her the whole story.

"Oh, my God! I'm so sorry," she said. "Are you sure you're OK?" And, being ever practical, she then inquired, "Is the boat OK?"

"Yeah, the boat's fine. It really saved my life. If it hadn't performed like it did, I wouldn't be here. They'd be dragging the bottom of the channel looking for pieces of me. Thank God for that Yamaha engine—it reacted instantly. I just can't believe the way that idiot acted!"

"How do you figure someone like that?" Jill said. "You wouldn't think a guy with that much money would act that weird. I read a story in the *News Press* last week about him. He claims to be the richest guy on Sanibel. But I'm pretty sure, from the tone of the article, that the reporter didn't buy that claim. But you also got the sense that Big Ed thinks he's the smartest guy on the island, too. The story said that now that he has retired, he is working to document, once and for all, the true pirate history of Southwest Florida. He's supposedly engaged historians and cryptologists from the University of Florida and from a university in Spain to go through the original documents and archives from the pirate period. He claims that his team has already deciphered a previously unbroken pirate code and, as a result, has solved the mystery of where Gasparilla's treasures are buried. Supposedly, he's now in the process of assembling a team to recover it."

"Yeah, well," I interjected. "I've seen the guy operate, and I think he'd be lucky to find himself with himself, if you know what I mean. This guy's a complete jerk."

"Without a doubt," Jill agreed. "Honey, I think we just need to stay out of his way. You know, there's really no reason for us to have to go to Sanibel. It's not our kind of place anyway. We'll be a lot better off to just stay close to home. If we do that, we should be able to avoid those kinds of people and that kind of trouble."

"Agreed," I replied. "Now, why don't we go down by the pool, lie in the sun, and have a few drinks? I'll even let you rub my shoulders for a while, just to help me relax and forget that any of this ever happened," I joked.

"I know if I start rubbing you, then you'll want to start rubbing me back," she said. "And you know where that leads."

"I most certainly do," I replied with a grin on my face. "You want to meet me by the pool?"

"I'll be there in a couple of minutes. I need to put my bathing suit on."

"You don't need to do that on my account," I replied. "And the neighbors can't see through the arecas."

With that, we went down to the pool, lay in the sun, got great tans (without tan lines), shared gentle, therapeutic massages (just to help each other relax, you understand), and spent a fantastic Florida afternoon. Not a bad way to kill time for a couple of old retirees—one of whom had almost been killed earlier in the day.

Chapter Eight
JAVIER COMES TO TOWN

A few days later, I was sitting in the office studying a navigation chart for the sound, trying to decipher where I should go to secure my day's limit of trout, when the phone rang. The phone ringing is now a pretty unusual event. About the only people who call are the kids, who check in occasionally, or solicitors. So I looked at the caller ID before I answered. The number looked familiar, but I couldn't immediately place it. So I answered, "Hello, Story residence."

To my surprise and delight, I heard, "Hey, boss! How are those mullet biting?"

That could only be one person: Javier Hernandez, my pleasant, Spanish, former banking compatriot.

"Hey, Javier," I answered. "How the heck are you? It's good to hear your voice."

"I'm great. And I am ready to go fishing. I was thinking about coming to see you soon. Wanted to check in with you and see when might be a good time. I've got lots of holiday saved up, and was thinking I might come down for a week and let you introduce me to your beautiful island."

"That would be great! We've got nothing coming up this month. You just name it, and I'll pick you up at the airport. You, of course, will stay with us. We will really be delighted to have the company. I can't wait to take you fishing. We'll go out on the boat every day. And when we're not fishing, we'll explore the whole sound from one end to the other. There's lots of great stuff to show you."

"Perfect! How about if I were to come down a week from this Saturday?" Javier asked.

"Couldn't be better," I responded. "Bring your shorts and flip-flops. Just get me your flight details, and I'll pick you up right in front of the airport when you get in."

When we finished, I ran upstairs to tell Jill. In my excitement, I had completely forgotten to check with her to make sure this would be OK. Fortunately, she was as excited as I was about having Javier come down.

We could hardly wait for him to arrive. We set about making sure that the guest room was in perfect shape, and Jill, always wanting to be the perfect hostess, began to make a list of things that needed to be done around the house to spruce it up for our guest. Together, we excitedly chatted about what we would like to do while Javier was with us.

We soon had a list of things to share with Javier. The days seemed to fly by as we anticipated his arrival, and on the agreed-upon day, I was parked in front of the Southwest Florida International Airport. And right on schedule (he was flying Southwest, not Delta!), he came through the sliding-glass doors.

He had a huge smile on his face, his white teeth gleaming in the bight Florida sun, and his dark olive skin serving notice of his Spanish heritage. He was as handsome as I remembered, and I couldn't help but notice that as he came out, several flight attendants heading in through the same set of doors gave him admiring glances. He was dressed perfectly for Southwest Florida in a white, Columbia fishing shirt, Polo khaki shorts, and a pair of Sperry flip-flops. That didn't surprise me. Javier always dressed well. But I was surprised by how much luggage he had brought. I would have expected a man going fishing for a week to have only one, or at the most, two small bags. But the luggage cart pulled by a porter behind Javier was loaded with three good-sized pieces of luggage. I know the Spanish like to dress, but this seemed to be taking things a little too far. Regardless, there was plenty of room in the SUV for the bags.

I may have been surprised by Javier's luggage, but not half as much as he was surprised when he saw me. The last time we had seen each other, I was still a banker. My hair had been neatly trimmed, my Brooks Brothers suit neatly pressed, and my wingtips nicely shined. I guess Javier must have expected to see me looking about the same. I had forgotten to tell him that the "banker was dead" and that he had been replaced by an aspiring pirate look-alike. I have not cut my hair since I retired, and it is now "styled" in a short, but promising, ponytail. The suit and shoes had been replaced by T-shirt, shorts, and flip-flops. And both of my ears now feature small, gold, hoop earrings. Javier looked right past me as he was looking for his ride. Only when I called his name did he put it all together. When he did, he burst out laughing, and exclaimed "Hey, boss, you don't look like the boss anymore! I like it! I like it! Hold still! Let me get your picture so I can send it back to everyone in the office. He whipped out his smartphone, pushed a button or two, and nabbed my new likeness for dissemination among the troops. I knew it would get a laugh back at the bank.

The drive from the airport to Saint James City takes about an hour, more during the "season." So I thought we would have plenty of time to catch up. But Javier was so excited about what he was seeing that it was hard to stay on that conversational track. He admitted that he had never before been to Florida, but had heard a lot about it. As we drove, it was clear how excited he was about finally getting to the Sunshine State. He asked question after question about what he was seeing. "What kind of bird is that?"

"An osprey."

"What kind of palm tree is that?"

"A cabbage palm. That's the state tree of Florida."

"What body of water is that?"

"That's the Caloosahatchee River. It flows into San Carlos Bay, very near Saint James City."

"What are those old buildings?"

"Those are part of the Thomas Edison-Henry Ford Estates."

"What is that land mass way over there?"

"That's Sanibel Island."

"How far is it from here?"

"Maybe ten miles."

"How far is it from your house?"

"By boat, it's about a mile. But by car, it's a forty-five mile trip each way."

"What kind of bird is that?"

"A pelican. An amazing bird, the pelican. His beak can hold more than his belly can."

"Did you see that fish jump? What kind of fish is that?"

(As I had expected, Javier didn't have a clue about what a mullet was!) On and on. "What kind of trees are those growing in the water?"

"Those are mangroves. They are called the trees that walk on water."

"Did you see that boat? What kind of boat is that?"

"That is a shrimp boat."

"Look at all those people fishing right off of the bridge! What kind of fish will they catch?"

"They will probably catch snapper, grunts, or sheepshead. But they might get lucky and catch a snook or even hook into a tarpon!"

"Wow! Look at those cute little buildings! Can we come back and visit them?"

"Sure. You and Jill can do that. She's very well acquainted with all those shops."

"Did you see that big bird? Was that an eagle?"

"Yes. We have fifteen mating pairs of eagles on the island." He was obviously excited to be here, and it was great for me to be a part of his excitement. When you live somewhere for a while, even in Southwest Florida, it's easy to get accustomed to what you are seeing and overlook the wonder of the natural beauty that's around you. Being with Javier as he saw Florida for the first time helped to bring that wonder back. I think I loved our trip back to Pine Island as much as he did.

As we neared Saint James City, Javier confided, "I can't tell you how excited I am to finally get to see this part of Florida. When I was a kid, I used to talk with my grandfather about Southwest Florida. He had never been here, but he had learned about it from his father. He had always wanted to come see it, but he wasn't able to get here before he died. I guess, in some ways, I'm here now on his behalf. I want to see and do everything while I'm here. I feel like I owe it to my father and my grandfather."

"Don't you worry, Javier," I replied. "We've got nothing but time. It's not like Jill and I have anything else to do. We will be delighted to help you see everything there is to see. We really love this place, and nothing could make us happier than to share it all with you."

A few minutes later, we were at the house. Javier and I managed to get the bags up the stairs and into the guest room. Jill and Javier exchanged kisses on each cheek in the Spanish tradition and soon were engaged in conversation about the trip, about the bank, about how we liked the area, etc. I couldn't help but smile as I noticed that Jill seemed to be just a tiny bit enlivened by seeing Javier again. I assumed that this was due to his good looks and his Continental charm. I've observed that Javier seems to have that effect on many females. Or maybe it was just that Jill was excited to meet anyone who wasn't old and didn't smell like fish. In Saint James City, that's what she normally encounters. I guess it's fair to say that she hasn't gotten to meet many guys like Javier lately. I noticed that Javier also seemed to enjoy meeting her. I was glad on both counts.

Once we got Javier settled in, we had drinks and snacks by the pool and talked about life on Pine Island. We then headed into "town" for dinner at Woody's. By car, we were there in two minutes. As is customary on a Saturday night, Woody's was happening. The place was packed. A talented singer-guitarist was belting out covers of Seger, Dylan, the Stones, the Allman Brothers, you name it—the kind of stuff I like. Seemed like everyone else liked it, too. As he played more and more requests, the tip jar was starting to get full. And so was the dance floor. The bar was tended, as is customary, by Anna. She waved at us when we came in, but it was clear that she was far too busy to chat. She was slinging beer and booze at a furious pace.

We were fortunate to snag a round table in the main room when its previous tenants left just as we came in. Soon a waiter was over to bus our table.

"Hey, Sunny! How's it going?" I said. Sunny is one of our favorite waiters at Woody's. He's quick to let you know that Sunny—with a "u," not an "o"— is not his real name, but that's what he wants his friends to call him. Sunny has a couple of characteristics that make him unique. First, he's one of the islands few Afro-American residents. In fact, he may be the island's only Afro-American resident. And, second, in addition to waiting tables, Sunny makes the restaurant's famous key lime pies. In my opinion, these pies are about the best you'll ever put into your mouth. They are the real deal. Whenever his pies are on the menu, we always order at least one piece. Usually, since we're so full, we order the pie to go. It's just as good when we get home. That's what we did tonight.

Javier loved Woody's. He said it reminded him a lot of the cafes in Spain. Everybody in town seemed to be there. And there was great music, loud conversation, lots of drinking, and some really good food. He noted one big difference between the Spanish cafes and Woody's, however: Woody's closes its doors at 10:00 p.m., which is about when the Spanish clubs open theirs. But this is Saint James City. Here, the average age is way, way past sixty!

Tonight, we were there until they closed the place down. Just another night of old folks behaving badly. We safely made the short drive home and followed up with dessert and coffee on the lanai. The night had been a fun start to what we all hoped would be a fun week.

Chapter Nine
JAVIER GOES FISHING

We were up at seven. Jill and Javier had several cups of extra-strong K-cup coffee. It looked like they badly needed the caffeine. I enjoyed my customary pot of black tea. I needed that, too. But, it wasn't long before the boat was in the water and loaded with rods, tackle, and coolers. By eight thirty, we were ready to go. Before we untied the boat, we made sure to spray Javier with SPF 30 sunscreen. Jill and I have been out in the sun enough now that we rarely need to put it on, but we knew that Javier had not, and we didn't want him to fry his first day on the water. That's very easy to do and it's a sure way to screw up your vacation. We didn't want that to happen to Javier.

The canal that we live on connects to a mangrove-lined bay. The channel through this bay winds for about a half mile to the sound. The ride to the sound is a little longer than we might like, but the wildlife we see more than compensates. I especially like it when we're coming in from fishing and a white egret hitches a ride on the boat's bow. I swear that somehow these birds seem to know which boats are likely to have fish on board. Once they join us on the boat, they usually stay all the way to the dock. I guess they want to know exactly where the fish will be cleaned. I really admire this ingenuity, and I always make sure to reserve some prime fish scraps for my hitchhiking, feathered passengers.

Our plan today was to do a little trout fishing in the morning, and then boat into the Waterfront for a late lunch. After that, we'd run the boat back to the house, clean the fish, put the boat in order, jump in the pool, and chill out during the hottest part of the day. Then, a little before the sun set, we'd head up to the north end of the island to show Javier around.

As we idled through the mangroves, Javier seemed to have reverted to being the calm, happy, laid-back Javier that I remembered from when we worked together in Alabama. But, once we exited the mangroves, and I pointed the boat out into the sound, he again became just as curious as he had been in the car..

"What is that?" he asked, pointing straight ahead as we idled through the markers out into the bay. "That's the south end of Sanibel Island," I answered. "You can see the bridges and causeways that connect it to Fort Myers. If you look down beyond the third bridge, you can see the old Sanibel Lighthouse."

"Wow! That is so cool! I wish my grandfather could have seen this!"

Once we cleared the slow-speed manatee zone, I put the boat on a plane, and we headed up the channel toward one of my favorite fishing spots.

In about ten minutes, we had run to one of my favorite grass flats. I baited the hooks for Jill and Javier, since I was playing fishing guide. Now, Jill is a pretty good fisherwoman. She loves to fish and generally knows what to do. I've even seen her land some very large sharks. It's not unusual for her to out-fish me. I hate it when it happens—male pride and all of that—but when she does, I'm still happy for her.

I looked forward to seeing what kind of a fisherman Javier was. When we had talked in Birmingham, it sounded as if he was pretty experienced. But it didn't take long to see that his claim was more than a little exaggerated. We use spinning reels, loaded with fifteen-pound test line, mounted on medium-light, seven-foot rods. When a right-handed person uses a spinning reel, he holds the rod in his right hand with the reel hanging down below the rod. The handle on the reel is on the left side of the reel. You use your left hand to turn the handle.

But Javier quickly established that he had never before used a spinning reel. Initially, he couldn't cast the bait. Jill finally got him straight on how to do that, and shortly he was able to fling the bait out about thirty feet. That's not so good—you want to get it out about a hundred feet—but it was a start. We knew he'd get better.

Then he wanted to reel the bait back in and try again. But rather than positioning the reel under the rod, he did the opposite. He turned the rod over, putting the reel on top of the rod so he could use his right hand to turn the handle. While many first-timers want to use this method, it won't work, since turning the handle in a forward direction when the reel is in this position will simply unscrew the handle from the reel. And that's what Javier was in the process of doing before we got him properly oriented.

Once we got the basics out of the way, it didn't take long for Javier to get up to speed. Fishing for trout is really pretty simple. As the boat drifts slowly over the grass, you cast out your popping cork and bait, letting it drift along behind the boat. Then, about every minute or so, you give the rod a short twitch to make the cork pop. When a trout hits, the cork will go under in a big way, and you jerk the rod back to set the hook. Most times, when the cork goes under you catch a fish.

It didn't take long for Javier to have his first bite. The first several times it happened, he overreacted, setting the hook so aggressively that he actually snatched the bait right out of the surprised fish's mouth. But with a little coaching, he was soon in the game. After an hour of fishing, Jill had caught eight fish and had three "keepers" in the box; Javier had caught five and had boxed two. The game was on.

We had a great breeze for drift fishing, and an incoming tide that complemented the wind. All in all, it was a nearly perfect morning for fishing. The sun was bright and we had just enough wind to keep us comfortable. And, clearly, we were on the fish. Periodically, we drifted out of them, but all we had to do was move the boat back to where we started and do it all over again. It wasn't long before Jill and Javier had their combined limit of eight fish (Jill, five; Javier, three). But Javier had the biggest fish. He had boated what we like to call a "gator trout." This one was twenty-three-and-a-half inches long. It was an impressive fish. It's quite a sight when you reel in a fish like that. Not only does it put up a good fight, but the edges of the mouth on a fish that age are bright yellow in color. It's not something that one soon forgets—especially someone like Javier, who obviously had never been fishing before in his life!

Early in the day, I had called him on his claim of being an experienced fisherman. He readily admitted that he had never been fishing, but said that he had made that claim because he was afraid that I wouldn't have invited him to visit if he said he didn't know how to fish, and he so badly wanted to see this area. He said that it was important that he come because of the stories his grandfather had told him about Southwest Florida.

I assured him that we were delighted that he was here, and that we could care less if he could fish or not. It didn't matter a bit to us. We were just glad he had come.

With the live well full, we headed to the Waterfront. As usual, the place was packed, but we were lucky to squeeze into a slip as another boat left. A few minutes later, our boat was neatly tied up. Our first order of business was to use the restroom, but it wasn't long before we were all relaxing at our table enjoying some frosty beverages, while the grouper and conch we had ordered was frying. Since none of us had eaten breakfast, we were starved. When the food came, conversation stopped and we made pigs out of ourselves.

Once lunch was over, it was back to the house, where Javier and I spent an hour cleaning fish and washing the boat. Honestly, I did most of the work, but Javier stayed with me and helped when he could. Throughout, he kept up the questions. He wanted to know about all of the barrier islands, and I told him as much as I knew. Truthfully, most of what I knew came from reading, since, to date, we had spent very little time actually visiting them. But I told him what I could, and tried to remember to differentiate what I believed to be fact from what may have been only pirate fiction.

It was a good way to spend an hour. We soon had the boat shipshape and secured on the lift. We retired to the house, washed off the salt, sweat, bait scent, and fish scales, put on our bathing suits, and gratefully submerged ourselves in the pool's chilly water. An hour or so later, we were much refreshed. Then we cleaned up properly, put on fresh clothes, and, as promised, loaded into the SUV and headed up island toward Bokeelia.

We gave Javier a thorough tour of the island's highlights, including the museum, the library, the curvy drive over to Pineland, the tiny Pineland post office, a look at the Indian mounds upon which much of Pineland sits, the Randall Research Center, the house where Randy Wayne White used to live, and Tarpon Lodge, where we stopped for a drink and to admire the view. As we had by now come to anticipate, Javier was again extremely excited about all the new sights that he was seeing, especially so as we stood together on the dock at Tarpon Lodge. He wanted to know the names of the various islands that you can see from there. I told him what I knew, but to be honest, I wasn't 100 percent certain about some of what I told him.

Eventually, we moved on up the island looking at other sights, such as the huge mango trees that grow in what appear to be somewhat casually tended groves. Soon we were in the tiny little town of Bokeelia. It's beautifully located on the northern tip of the island, with great views of Charlotte Harbor, Boca Grande, and many of the islands in the northern sound.

When you come into town, you pass over a small bridge that spans what is now known as Jug Creek. Of course, we had to explain to Javier the origin of that name. The story goes that back in the days of Prohibition, a lot of illegal liquor was distilled in this area. To hide the product until it could be shipped to the mainland, the liquor was poured into jugs that were then tied to the roots of the mangrove trees in the creek. Supposedly, that's all in the past. Jug Creek is now home to several condo complexes, a restaurant, a commercial marina, and a marine dry-storage facility.

We crossed the bridge and eventually ran out of road after it bent around to the west. At that point, there's a simple, slightly dilapidated building that is home to a well-known restaurant, Captain Con's. By this time, lunch had pretty much worn off, so we agreed it would make sense to have dinner at this fine establishment.

The food at Captain Con's pretty much matches the exterior of the building: it's simple. There's nothing fancy about how it's prepared or how it's served. It's just good, basic seafood, but the portions are "ginormous!" I should mention that Jill is a huge fan of the restaurant's seafood chowder. It's a cream-based concoction, loaded with potatoes and no end of seafood. When we eat here, we always order a cup with our meal and usually order a quart to take home. Tonight was no exception.

After dinner, we felt the need to walk a bit to help the meal settle. So we slowly ambled across the street to the restaurant's fishing pier. Walking on a pier with active fishing going on is always a fun way to kill some time. And tonight did not disappoint. Every few minutes, someone would catch something. Whenever that happened, all of the kids on the pier would run over to see what was being landed, while the other anglers would sneak a quick peek to try to discover what tackle or bait the lucky angler had used.

The highlight of the evening, however, was the view to the west. The sun was setting out in the gulf, while lights were starting to appear on some of the islands. It was a spectacular ending to a great day.

Chapter Ten

JAVIER GETS TO KNOW THE LOCALS

By the time we got back to Saint James City, Jill and I were beat. As we've gotten older, our bedtime has gotten earlier. Even though we're retired and have nothing to do, we're usually in bed by ten.

But Javier is significantly younger. He's also very Spanish, which, if you don't know, means that the evening doesn't officially get started until ten p.m..So after we had reviewed our plans for the next day, Javier spoke up. "Hey, boss. You know about the Spanish lifestyle—we stay up very late. It's just who we are and how we live. There is no way that I can go to bed now. My body just won't let me do it. Not two nights in a row! How about if I use your bike to pedal into to town so I can see if anything is going on? I promise not to damage it."

"Sure. That sounds like a great idea to me," I said. "There're lights on the bike, so make sure you turn those on. I'm not sure what will be open this late, but you are welcome to go find out. We'll leave the front door unlocked and the lights on. Just remember—the boat leaves at eight o'clock sharp in the morning! Have a good night."

Jill and I went upstairs and turned in. We didn't hear Javier when he came in, but when we went downstairs at seven in the morning, there he was. He was dressed for fishing, looking none the worse for wear.

"Javier, how was your night out?"

"It was fabulous," Javier answered. "I first tried Woody's, but it was getting ready to close down. I had one drink there and then pedaled to Low Key Tiki. There were several guys still at the bar, so I joined them. I think a couple may have been fishermen who had just come in off the water. I started talking with a fellow named Lester, and we had a great time. He shared some great information about the town. Seems he came here from the Midwest right out of high school. He came with nothing but a duffel bag that contained a couple of T-shirts and one extra pair of jeans. He's been here ever since. Seems like he's happy as he can be. I bought him some beers and we had a great evening. We're going to try to meet again this evening. He promised to introduce me to some of the other locals tonight."

Soon enough, we were underway. The day's schedule called for visiting the manatees in Tarpon Bay and then taking a tour of the whole sound, with Cabbage Key being our destination for lunch. As you come out of our channel, it's a straight shot to the mouth of Tarpon Bay. It is a large body of water, completely surrounded by land, except for one small channel that connects with the sound. It would be hard to design a more perfect shelter from the wind. I guess that is why it was reportedly the home of Black Caesar, one of history's most notorious pirates. I don't know if that's true or not, but this bay certainly would be a perfect place to anchor and rest from a voyage of raping and pillaging.

Today, Tarpon Bay is part of the National Park System; it's called the Ding Darling National Wildlife Refuge. Consequently, all of the waters within the boundary of the park are a restricted, slow-speed zone. Getting into the bay can be time consuming, but once inside, if you ease over onto the grass flats on either side of the channel, shut off your engine, and listen, you will be able to locate manatees pretty quickly.

They are large, slow-moving creatures. They are usually about ten feet in length and weigh close to a thousand pounds. They are warm-blooded and have lungs rather than gills. Consequently, they must periodically surface to breathe. On average, they surface every three to four minutes. When they come up, they exhale noticeably. You can easily hear them from a long distance away. On this day, they were easy to find. We could see a pod several hundred feet up the northern side of the bay. To approach as quietly as possible, I put down the trolling motor and slowly eased toward the pod. As we got close, I turned off the motor and electronically lowered the Talon shallow-water anchor. Soon enough, the curiosity of the manatees took over, and they swam over to investigate us.

There are few sights in the world as cool as seeing a manatee surface right next to your boat and look you straight in the eye. I don't care what anyone says; creatures like this are intelligent beings—and not too much different from human beings. Today, they were certainly interested in learning more about us. Some people feed lettuce to manatees. Reportedly, they love iceberg lettuce and will eat it right out of your hand. Reportedly, they also love to drink fresh water and even have been known to sip it directly from a bottle. But these practices are discouraged, since they tend to make manatees less wary of boats and humans than they should be. We always limit our interaction to talking to them, taking their pictures, and reaching down to scratch their snouts. This pod seemed to enjoy all of these things.

Javier was absolutely beside himself. He had never seen a manatee before. Every time one would surface, he would lean over the edge of the boat to get as close as he could, and then reach out to touch it. After a while, he decided that this just wasn't close enough. He wanted to swim with them.

I knew that this was safe enough. I swam with them many times when I was a kid in Central Florida. What I wasn't sure about was the legality of swimming with them in the confines of the park. I hadn't seen any signs that said you couldn't do it, but somehow it didn't seem like the kind of activity upon which a park ranger would look favorably. I explained this to Javier, but he was not to be dissuaded. He said he had to do it. So, reluctantly, I agreed—as long as he agreed to pay any fines we might incur. With a last warning from me that he should not, under any circumstances, touch any of the manatees, Javier jumped in.

Fortunately, no one took exception to what we were doing that day. Javier quietly kicked over toward the creatures, and was soon swimming in the middle of the pod. They actually seemed to enjoy his company. I think they were as curious about him as he was about them. Eventually their curiosity seemed to wear off, and they eased away from the boat. I guess they were in search of their next source of amusement, or maybe just their next meal. In any case, it was time for Javier to come back to the boat.

"Wow! I can't believe that! It was so much fun. I can't wait to tell all the people back in Spain. They are not going to believe this. You took lots of pictures, didn't you?"

Jill assured him that she had taken many, many shots, and that there were certainly some very excellent pictures. But she ribbed him a little by saying that in the water, it wasn't always easy to tell which creature was the manatee."In the water, you all seemed to be about the same size!" she said, laughing.

At first, Javier wasn't sure how to take this. But as we laughed, he caught on and joined in."Jill, if I keep eating grouper sandwiches and drinking so much beer, it won't be long before I am the same size as a manatee," he agreed.

"Speaking of lunch," I interjected, "I think it's time for us to start heading toward Cabbage Key. I figure that if we take our time and do a little exploration on the way, we should arrive right about noon."

"Sounds good to me! Let's go!"

So we idled out of the bay, taking great care to not hit any of our new friends. Soon we were outside the park boundary. I brought the boat onto a plane and fine-tuned the engine's tilt to achieve the right balance for the day's conditions. The weather was absolutely perfect for a run to the north. The sun was bright and there were only a few fluffy clouds to the west. There was the slightest breeze from the south, which was producing barely noticeable ripples on the water. A perfect day for boating up the sound.

Our first detour was a run up into Blind Pass, the smallest of the openings between the sound and the gulf. It serves as the dividing line between Sanibel to the south, and Captiva to the north. From there, we eased up into Roosevelt Channel (remember Andy?), and slid past the hotels, restaurants, marinas, and mansions that line its shores. Once we were back in the sound, we ran up to Redfish Pass. This pass is much larger and deeper than Blind Pass. It generally stays open without dredging, but the entry channel from the gulf is constantly shifting as beach sand gets moved about with storms. When we cleared Redfish Pass, we continued up the sound to the north. Our next stop was Safety Harbor. To get into this sheltered basin, you have to head into Captiva Pass to find the very small, marked channel that meanders off to the south. And it runs almost underneath a very cool, old fish shack. Seeing this old house on stilts excited Javier to no end. He took pictures from every angle as we passed it. Leaving Safety Harbor, we swung over to the east side of the sound. We headed to an area known as Captiva Shoal so that Javier could get a good look at the "fish shacks" that still stand in this area. When I first mentioned these buildings to Javier, he'd gotten a strange look on his face. I guessed that he may have thought I was talking about shacks in which fish live. Or maybe it was something else. I wasn't sure.

The six buildings we were looking at had originally been fish shacks, serving as dormitories for fishermen. Now they were all brightly painted and well maintained, with self-contained sanitary sewage systems, and served as retreats for the few families fortunate enough to own one.

When Javier saw these houses, he became extremely animated. He was clearly fascinated by them. I did my best to explain the history and significance of these houses. He said he had heard about them from his grandfather.

He wanted to know if we could tie up to one of the houses so that he could climb the ladder to the house's deck. I explained that we could not do that since these were all private homes now. If we climbed onto a house, we would be trespassing, and we could be arrested. I was more insistent about this than I had been about swimming with the manatees. For a while, I thought Javier might simply jump into the water and swim to one of the houses. But after I mentioned the size of the bull sharks in these waters, I think he reconsidered that plan. Eventually, he gave up and resigned himself to simply taking more pictures of each house.

When the photo session was completed, we motored back to the channel and ran the remaining few miles up the sound to Cabbage Key.

By this time, we were hungry and ready for a good lunch. From experience, I knew that the food at the Key would be good, but the choices would be limited. The menu at Cabbage Key is simple, since there is no bridge from the mainland. All ingredients have to be brought in by boat. The kitchen, in what had once been a private home, is also basic. For example, there are no facilities for deep frying—a rarity in this part of the world.

But, despite these limitations, Cabbage Key is a really cool place to visit. The island, and the buildings on it, are a throwback to the Florida of a different era. It's a great place to stroll around the grounds, and visit for a while.

Another neat thing about Cabbage Key is the collection of autographed dollar bills that adorn the inside of the restaurant. Almost everyone that visits has to tape their signed bill to the wall. Javier, of course, had to do this too. But, I noticed that he had written his message in Spanish. I had no clue what it said, but I could tell from the 'smiley face' that he included on the bill that he had enjoyed himself.

Eventually, we made our way down the sound and back to the house. This time we had no fish to clean, but we did need to wash the salt off the boat and flush the engine. But, within twenty minutes, we were all three floating in the pool, cooling off, and discussing the next day's expedition. Later, Jill cooked a delicious dinner of Caribbean-marinated chicken breasts, topped with mango salsa, and accompanied by savory, saffron-infused, Spanish yellow rice. We finished with home-made key lime pie, that nestled in Jill's famous short-bread cookie crust. As I said, it was all delicious. By that time Jill and I were ready to turn in. We were whipped! But, when Javier asked to borrow the bike again, we were not surprised. Those Spaniards sure do like to party! More power to them.

Chapter Eleven
JAVIER MOVES OUT

In the morning, we again came down at seven. Once again, we found Javier looking chipper, and drinking coffee. We asked how his evening had been. If anything, he seemed even happier than he had been the morning before.

"I had a wonderful time. I met Lester at Low Key Tiki and then we moved on to Froggy's. I met so many nice people while I was there. I had a really, really good time. When I wasn't talking with folks at the bar, I was either playing pool or throwing darts. I guess I probably should have told them that when I was at the university in Spain, darts were my specialty. I actually won the university's pub championship three years running. I may have taken advantage of the nice folks at Froggy's. But just a little. Honestly, I don't think they minded very much. In fact, I bought them so much beer that I think they thought they had won!"

"Wow! That's great," I said. "Who did you meet at Froggy's? Anyone we might know?"

"Well, let's see. I met the folks you bought your house from—Delmar and Carolyn, I think?"

"Yeah, that's right. How were they?" I asked.

"Oh, they were great. Every time we talked about the house they had big smiles on their faces."

"I bet they did," I replied. "Who else was there?"

"Well, later in the evening I met your Realtor, Carl. He seemed like a really great guy. We talked a long time. I was really interested in learning about his family's history on the islands. I wondered if his great-grandfather and my great-grandfather might have crossed paths in Cuba. But Carl didn't know anything about that."

"I didn't know that your great-grandfather had been in Cuba," I said.

"Yes. He wasn't there long, only a couple of years. But as a young man, he was there in what today we would call a consulting role. Cuba and this part of the world really made a big impression on him. That's where all the stories came from that my grandfather passed along to me. I am so excited to finally be able to see these stories come to life!"

Javier went on, "I can never thank you and Jill enough for what you've done for me. This is really like a dream come true. I've seen so much and done so much. And I have met so many nice people. This trip has exceeded all my expectations. In fact, I'm having such a great time that I've decided I want to stay another week."

Perhaps he saw my face turn white, or maybe he would have said what he said next anyway. "Don't worry; I've booked an apartment at the Buccaneer. I'm going to rent a boat and a car, too. I really want to see so much more of this area, and I don't want to impose on you and Jill. You have both been so great. What do you say we go fishing one more time today, and then I'll move in the morning? Let's go out today and catch lots of fish. When we get back, we'll clean them, and I bet if we take them to Woody's tonight, they'll cook them for us for dinner. And all the drinks will be on me!"

I could see by the look on Javier's face that this is really what he wanted to do, and that it would be a waste of time to try to convince him otherwise. And, besides, it sounded like a good idea to me. I was really happy that he was having such a great time and that he wanted to spend even more time here. Many people who visit Pine Island have had enough after a day or two, and are more than ready to get back to 'civilization.' But not Javier. And, quite honestly, I wondered if this might not have been his plan all along. That would explain his three suitcases. So I replied, "Makes sense to me. Now, let's go fishing!"

And fishing we went. It was another successful day. I was fishing, too. We had our combined limits by 11:00 a.m. To change things up a little, we decided to have lunch at the Green Flash restaurant, which is a really nice place on Captiva Island, facing Roosevelt Channel. The food is first class. The ambiance is, as you would expect on Captiva, several giant steps up from that of the Waterfront—white tablecloths, folded and stiffly starched cotton napkins, picture windows looking out onto the bay, and a wait staff in matching, upscale, tropical-casual uniforms. The restaurant has ample dockage and there was no problem tying up. We were soon sitting at a table, enjoying something cool and frosty. Somehow, it seemed a little like we were celebrating

Javier's happiness and his decision to extend his stay. We were genuinely pleased for him.

As we finished dessert (key lime pie that was very good, but not as good as Sunny's, or Jill's), I excused myself to go to the restroom. As you may have noticed already, there are a lot of things down here that are a little quirky. The restrooms at the Green Flash certainly fall into this category. Jill had earlier returned from the ladies' room and related that there was a life-sized statue of a fully dressed man standing in the corner. It had given her quite a shock.

As I entered the men's room, I looked around to make sure there were no women present. I didn't see any, so I turned to the row of urinals on the right. Imagine my surprise, as I began to take a whiz, to realize that I was looking through a window and staring directly at the bar. It soon dawned on me, however, that none of the patrons there was looking back at me. I realized that I was looking through one-way glass—I could see out, but from the bar, all you could see was a mirror. As I said, things are different here. Without question, this feature made the men's room quirky and cool, too!

But what was not cool was who I saw walk into the bar as I stood there taking a leak: none other than one of my least-favorite people from my old banking company! This onetime head of the New York office came in and took a seat at the bar, facing me directly. I pretty much put all of the old bank crap behind me when I retired. After all, as I tell anyone who wants to know, the banker is dead. But seeing the smug face and neatly shaved head of this world-class jerk brought me up short. There was probably no one in the world I wanted to see less than I wanted to see this guy. He had personally cost me—and the bank—a lot of money. Using what he considered to be his superior intellect, he had ruined several good businesses, and in the process, caused a lot of good people—people whom I admired and respected—to quit the bank rather than continue to work with him. I truly thought and hoped that when I'd retired, I'd seen the last of this guy.

My quandary was what to do. If I went out the restroom door, he would be looking straight at me, and there was no way we could avoid speaking. I really didn't relish that thought. And quite honestly, I'm not sure I wouldn't have thrown a punch at him, just for fun. While I was thinking this over, I went over to the sink to wash my hands. I gave them a really, really good scrub, trying to buy some time. When I looked back at the bar, he was still there. "Shit! Now what?"I thought. Of course, a shit! Why hadn't I thought of that before? So into an empty stall I went. I came out in about five minutes and my "friend" was gone. Where to, I didn't know, but I hoped he had left the restaurant. When I came out of the bathroom, I told the bartender that I had seen a friend of mine sitting there and I wanted to say hello. I asked where he had gone.

"He met a guy and walked out. Just a couple of minutes ago."

"Thanks. I'll catch him next time."

When I returned to our table, Jill saw the concern on my face and gave me a questioning look. I apologized for having taken so much time and explained that something at lunch must not have agreed with me. I looked around. "Cue Ball" was nowhere to be found. We paid our bills and strolled back to the boat.

Once underway, with Javier sitting beside me on the boat's leaning post, I told him who I had seen at the restaurant.

His jaw dropped. "Damn! I'm sure glad I didn't see him. That would have ruined my whole trip. I wonder what he's doing down here?"

"Beats me," I replied. "I never knew him to have any interest in this part of the world. Only thing I ever knew him to be interested in was how to screw people out of money while sucking up to his bosses to make himself look good. Seeing him was like a rerun of a nightmare from the distant past."

"I know exactly how you feel," Javier answered. "I hope he stays on Captiva. I don't want to run into him, either."

Later that night, several rounds of drinks at Woody's (on Javier's tab), and a large platter of our delicious, freshly caught fish, helped to put this encounter out of our minds.

One thing I did notice, however, was how many folks at the bar now seemed to be very friendly with Javier. His nightly visits apparently had made him a popular guy. I suspected that Jill and I weren't the only folks for whom he had been buying drinks.

Despite the shock at lunch, it was another very good day.

Chapter Twelve
JAVIER RENTS A BOAT

Early the next morning, I helped Javier move to the Buccaneer. It's a small, two-story apartment building located on Monroe Canal, just down from Woody's. With the apartment rental, he also gained access to a boat slip. Once we checked him in and moved his bags inside, we drove into Cape Coral to rent a car. That went smoothly. Soon we were back in Saint James City. We left our cars at the Buccaneer, and walked down Stringfellow to the Monroe Canal Marina for Javier to rent a boat.

I explained to George, who owns the place, what we wanted. He said he had just what Javier needed, and took him over to look at a used, nineteen-foot, center console that was tied up in a nearby slip. The neat, clean, little boat was powered by what looked to be a fairly new 115-horsepower Yamaha.

After Javier had looked the boat over, George asked him, "How does this one suit you?"

Javier replied, "It looks good to me. But I'll have to see what Jim says. He's the expert. Boss, what do you think about this one?"

It may not have been the flashiest or fastest boat on the flats, but I thought it would be sturdy, safe, and reliable. I was pretty sure that Javier had never piloted a boat before. I figured these characteristics would be just what Javier needed.

"It looks perfect to me."

Javier went inside the office with George to sign the necessary forms.

When he returned, we climbed on board the boat. The first thing I did was to explain the controls. Then, I told him that driving a boat is a lot like driving a car. You turn the wheel to the right, it goes to the right; turn to the left, it goes to the left. But the biggest difference, and the most important thing to remember, is that a boat doesn't have any brakes. It's critical that you allow for that. Granted, if you're moving slowly, you can put the engine in reverse to help slow down, but that only goes so far. Trust me, it may not be impressive, but my personal tactic when approaching a dock is to coast to a stop well before I get there, and then use the engine to gently bump the boat into the dock at a very slow speed. I know that a lot of guys prefer to come in at speed, and then, right before they ram the dock, throw the engine into reverse and let the boat settle down at the dock. That approach is impressive, for sure. But I think my approach will eventually save on fiberglass-repair bills. "When you dock a boat, always take it slow and easy, and think ahead."

I noticed the boat had a VHF radio. I suspected there was a good chance that Javier might need to use that at some point.

So, as George worked to get the boat ready, I gave him a quick course in marine radio protocol. I was pretty sure he didn't take it all in. I figured, however, that he now knew enough to turn it on, put it on Channel Sixteen, and transmit a message. If he needed help, I was confident that he now knew enough to ask for it.

The boat came with a chart of the sound. We spent a fair amount of time looking this over. I wanted to make sure that Javier understood how to read it. With all the shallow water in the sound, he was going to need to pay close attention to where he could, and could not, go safely. We stayed at this until I was sure that Javier understood the concept. Next, we spent time on maritime rules of the road. It's easy to get lost in this stuff, but it all boils down to one thing: don't run into another boat.

Once the instruction was out of the way, George untied us and wished us well. Javier was at the controls. Without too much drama, we were soon idling out of Monroe Canal. He seemed reasonably comfortable at the wheel. Granted, initially he was overcorrecting, causing us to veer from one side of the canal to the other. But with a little instruction on how to anticipate what the boat would do when you turned the wheel, and about the importance of steering toward a point in the distance, he was soon able to steer in a reasonably straight line.

As we were leaving the canal, I explained how to use navigational markers. He especially liked the "red on right, returning" navigational reminder. As soon as we were in open water, I told him to open her up. After a few attempts, he seemed comfortable with getting the boat up onto a plane, and with the feel of slowing it down to return to an idle. Once we started going fast, you should have seen the smile on his face. He was having a great time.

Once in the open bay, I asked him to steer the boat to a couple of different spots in the lower sound. I was glad to see that he stayed on the proper side of the markers as we headed up the channel. Apparently, he had listened to what I had told him. We must have spent a good hour on the water. Finally, I felt confident that Javier would be able to safely take the boat out on his own. We headed back up the canal to the Buccaneer. All the way back in, he had a huge smile on his face. I had never seen anyone as happy as Javier looked to be. When we went by the marina, he pressed the horn button and gave George an ear-shattering salute. George laughed, and waved back. Then, when we reached the Buccaneer's dock, Javier laid it in slowly and gently, just like I had told him. As far as I was concerned, he was good to go.

Chapter Thirteen
A LATE-NIGHT VISIT

Jill and I had both enjoyed Javier's stay. But we had to admit that once he was gone, we welcomed the return to the relative peace, quiet, and routine of our normal life. We had a good night's sleep. In the morning we slept in, and when we finally got up, we spent a couple of hours drinking coffee and tea and reading the paper. Just relaxing. It was good to have the house to ourselves and nowhere to go.

The next day, though, we got back to work addressing the old house's never-ending list of projects. As the week went by, I was somewhat surprised that we rarely ran into Javier. But I wasn't concerned, since I noted when we drove by the Buccaneer that he seemed always to be out on the boat. Good for him! I was delighted he was having such a good time.

I was a little more surprised that we didn't run into him at Woody's—which isn't to say, however, that he hadn't been there. Every time we went in, one of the girls (Chesley, Kimberly, or Anna) would bring us up to date on Javier's most recent visit.

They reported that he came in every night at nine o'clock and stayed until they closed the place down. From there, he either went to Low Key or to Froggy's, depending upon which place had music. They said he seemed to be having a great time. Anna noted that the previous night he had seemed especially happy. He told her that he had accomplished something his grandfather had always wanted to do. She asked him what that was, but he just smiled and said he couldn't tell her—like it was some big secret, or something. But he sure seemed pleased.

"All he would tell me was that it was something that had been very important to his grandfather. But," she added, "whatever it was, I think it must have involved something on Sanibel. He had mentioned earlier that he had spent the day over there."

Another couple of quiet days passed. On my end, the latest project involved staining the dock. I guessed it had been a number of years since it was last done. It was starting to look a little worse for wear. A couple of trips to the hardware store and I was ready to get started. The first step involved cleaning the dock thoroughly with a weak oxalic-acid solution. That took most of the first day. The second day, it was time to break out the long-handled paint roller and actually apply the stain.

Jill took one look at what I was up to with the paint roller, and decided it was a good time for her to drive to Cape Coral to get her nails done. Without question, women and men have different perspectives on what should take priority. For example, when we first arrived in Saint James City, my highest priority was to find out where to buy bait. Hers was to find out where to get her hair and nails done. I guess there must be some kind of fundamental biological difference between the sexes that guides these kinds of decisions. But I certainly don't mind. I really, really appreciate that she looks great all the time.

Or maybe she just had the good sense to get out of my hair, which I kind of appreciated. Truthfully, if she had been there, she would have been unable to resist giving some well-intentioned advice on things that I needed to do differently. I wouldn't have appreciated that. All in all, it was probably a good thing that she had a nail appointment.

Applying the stain proved to be a little more time-consuming than cleaning the dock had been the day before. I guess it had been so long since any stain had been applied that when I laid down a coat, the boards sucked it right in. Took a couple of coats to get it looking right. I wrapped up the project late in the afternoon. After getting everything cleaned up and put away, I celebrated with a quick plunge in the pool. It always feels good when you get a project completed. I like it when you can step back and look at a job well done.

I was feeling pretty proud of my accomplishment, even though my neighbor across the canal had made a point of telling me that in six months time, my dock would once again look just like everyone else's. Didn't matter. This project was checked off the list.

Later that evening, we were enjoying our favorite libations when the doorbell rang.

It's true that we have a doorbell. But we have heard it ring only a few times, and those were when repairmen came to the house to discuss projects. We had never yet heard it ring in the evening.

Our first reaction was surprise. But then I decided that it was probably just Javier coming to give us an update on his travels.

"Hey, babe. I'll get the door. I bet it's Javier. I hope so. It'll be good to see him."

But when I opened the door, it wasn't Javier. Rather, it was Hector and his cute little wife, Randy, our neighbors from down the street. Her real name is Duranda, but everyone calls her Randy. We like them. They are hard-working folks. Hector is, without question, the best commercial fishing guide in Saint James City. He's on the water almost every day.

I asked them to come right in. I was happy to see them. They had never come to the house before. I assumed they had come to welcome us to the neighborhood. I invited them into the living room where Jill was sitting. But as they came in, I began to get the first inkling that maybe this wasn't a social call since neither of them looked especially happy. I knew that Hector was a little shy, so I hoped that this was the reason for the long faces. In my gut, though, I knew it had to be something else.

Randy started to speak as soon as we were all seated. "We hate to come here like this, but someone has to tell you. Hector was out on the water today, and he saw something that ya'll need to know about. Honey, tell Jim and Jill what happened."

"Guys, I'm so damned sorry! But I found your friend Javier this afternoon up by Punta Blanca. It...it...it was just terrible."

"Hector, what do you mean that you found him? Had his boat broken down or run out of gas?"

"No! Oh, I wish it had only been that. Jim, I really hate to tell you this, but I found Javier this afternoon in his boat, and he..."

I could tell that Hector was having trouble telling me what he wanted to me to know."Hector, take a deep breath. Now, tell us what you need to tell us."

I saw him take a breath, hold it, and close his eyes. Then, as he slowly exhaled, he opened his eyes and looked directly into mine. "Jim, when I found him, he was dead!"

Jill and I looked at Hector as if he were an alien from outer space. It was like he was speaking a language that we couldn't understand. Our mouths were hanging open and we were both blinking our eyes like we couldn't see. We tried to say something, but nothing would come out.

He continued, "I was heading north with a charter client this morning. We were running along the east side of Cayo Costa, up on the tower, looking for redfish, heading on up towards Cape Haze. As I came around the point I saw him on his boat, anchored off the back side of Punta Blanca. I waived, and he waived back. It looked like he was having the time of his life. He gave me two thumbs up. But, I don't think he was fishing. He was just sitting there, like he was waiting on something to happen, or maybe to meet somebody. Then, about 3:00 p.m., as we were headed back home, we ran by there again. His boat was anchored in the same spot, although it had turned around with the tide. But, what was strange was that he was still sitting in the boat where he had been earlier- but now he was leaning back against the front of the console. I figured he must have been taking a nap. But, that didn't look right, him sleeping out in the hot sun like that. So I slowed down and we went over to check on him. I stopped about twenty yards away and yelled. He didn't move, or say anything. So we came alongside to take a look. It was obvious then why he hadn't responded. Jim, damn I hate to tell you this, but he had a bullet hole right between his eyes. Somebody had blown his brains out! We didn't go on board his boat. It was clear that there wasn't anything that we could do to help him. But we looked around the boat. I couldn't see any sign of a gun to indicate that he had shot himself. And it didn't look to me like he had been in a fight. His clothes were neat, his shirttail was tucked in, and his flip-flops were still on his feet. Like I said, it looked like he was simply sleeping, but he wasn't. At that point, I backed away a little bit, and called the coast guard. Apparently, they called the Lee County Sheriff's Department. The sheriff's boat got there in a little less than an hour, and the deputies took charge of the scene. They asked us to hang around. Eventually, they questioned me and my client separately on their boat. I guess they were satisfied with what we told them, since they told us we could go on home. Jim, I can't tell you how much seeing Javier like that upset my client and me. When we got to the mouth of Monroe, I asked him if he wanted me to clean the fish we had in the live well. I've got to tell you, I was glad when he said he didn't. He said he had seen enough death for one day. I agreed, and slipped the fish overboard. I was happy to see that they were all able to swim away. As soon as I got the boat put up, I came home and told Randy what had happened. We agreed that we needed to come tell you. It just didn't seem right that you didn't know. We didn't want you to hear about this later from the sheriff's department, or maybe down at Woody's."

"Damn! Damn, damn, damn, damn! He was having such a great time down here. I have never seen him happier. I can't believe he's dead. That's just not right!"

Hector said, "Man, you've got that right. I really liked Javier."

"I guess the sheriff's got his boat, and by now, they will have sealed off his hotel room. I guess I should call the sheriff's department and tell them everything I know. Hector, do you have any idea who I should call?"

"Yeah, I do. The investigator gave me his card and said I should call him if there was anything else that I could think of. Here it is. His name is Lieutenant Mike Collins. I agree that it would be a good idea for you to give him a call. It'll save him having to track you down."

Jill and I thanked Randy and Hector, and told them how much we appreciated their letting us know about Javier. I told Hector that I would call Lieutenant Collins as soon as they left. Which I did.

I dialed the lieutenant's cell number. After a couple of rings, a clipped male voice answered, "Collins." I told him my name and why I was calling. When I had finished, he thanked me for calling and said he'd like to talk with me first thing in the morning. We agreed to meet at our house, at 10:00 a.m. I gave him the address.

Jill and I discussed what else we needed to do and whom we needed to call. But, in truth, we didn't really know anyone else that we could call at this hour. The only thing we could think to do was to get in touch with the bank's human resources department and bring them up to speed. They would know how to contact Javier's family. Fortunately, the head of HR at the bank was a friend, and I had his personal cell number. Although it was getting late, I went ahead and dialed the number. A familiar voice answered, "This is Rich Samuelson. How may I help you?"

"Rich," I said. "This is Jim Story. Man, I'm sorry to disturb you, but I've got some really bad news that you need to know about! This is terrible!"

"Jim, calm down. Take a deep breath. I can hardly understand a word you're saying. What's happened? What's going on?"

"Rich, you know Javier Hernandez, the Spaniard who works in Risk Management. He's been down at my place for a couple of weeks, on vacation. I hate to tell you this, but I just heard that he was found dead this afternoon out on Pine Island Sound. Rich, that's bad enough, but from what I've been told, it looks like he was fucking murdered. I don't know who else to tell, but I figured you could get in touch with his family."

"Shit! He's such a nice guy. What in the hell happened?"

I told Rich what I knew, which wasn't very much. He said that he would contact Javier's family. I made sure he had my contact information in Florida. I also gave him Lieutenant Collins's number. We agreed to talk further the next day. I clicked off.

Jill and I just looked at each other.

"Oh, my God!" Jill said. "I can't believe this. He was such a great guy! Everyone who met him just fell in love with the man! I feel terrible."

"I agree. You know, I feel like this is all our fault. If he hadn't come down here, this never would have happened. Shit, if we had never moved here, this never would have happened. This is just terrible. What do you think caused this? I wonder if he pissed somebody off in a bar. Maybe he fucked some fisherman's girlfriend!"

"No," Jill said. "I don't think so. This doesn't feel like that kind of thing. If he pissed off the wrong guy here in Saint James City, he might have gotten his face kicked in. Or a fisherman might have sliced him up with his filet knife. But shooting him in his boat with no sign of a struggle! That doesn't feel like a crime of passion. There's more to this, for sure."

"I agree. There's more to this story. And I'm not going to rest until the bastard who did this is put away, or better yet, is fucking killed. I feel responsible. Now I've got to make sure that whoever did it is caught and strung up by his nuts."

"I agree. Where do we start?"

"Fuck if I know. I don't know about you, but I certainly don't want anything to eat now. And there's no way that I can sleep. What do you say we go down to Woody's and see if anyone down there has heard anything?"

"Sounds like a plan."

Chapter Fourteen
A WAKE AT WOODY'S

As I waited in the car, I turned off the radio. My mood was as black as the night was dark. The last thing I wanted to hear was Jimmy Buffet or Bob Marley—or anyone else, for that matter—singing about how great things are in the tropics. Things were certainly not great that night in Saint James City.

The parking lot was surprisingly crowded for a weekday night, especially for a night with no scheduled entertainment. As we approached the door, we could hear the low murmur of people talking. I guessed they had heard the news, too. But as soon as we entered the room, everyone stopped talking and just looked at us. Clearly, they didn't know what to say.

Anna quickly came out from behind the bar and put her arm around Jill's shoulders. "Have ya'll heard about Javier?" she asked.

"Yes, Anna. We've heard. We thought we'd come down to see if anyone has any more information."

"Ya'll come right on over to the bar. Kenny, get your fat ass up off that stool and make room for Jill and Jim," she commanded.

Kenny did as directed and made room for us to sit in the middle of the bar.

"Listen up! Jim and Jill have just heard about Javier. They came down here to see if anyone has any more news. If you know anything, let them know."

Then, to us, she said, "Tonight the drinks are on me. Jill, you want a pitcher of Ultra? Jim, Johnny Red?"

We nodded and thanked her.

Immediately, a crowd surrounded us. It looked like most of the people we knew in town were there. They all wanted to tell us how sorry they were about what had happened to Javier. To a person, they all said how much they had come to like Javier. They said that he had fit in well and that he seemed to be having a great time. No one could come up with any reason why anyone might have wanted to hurt him. They all said he was a great guy.

The men came to talk to me, while the women gathered around Jill. I asked each of the guys I talked with if he had heard any more news or had any idea about what might have happened. Most said they had not heard anything other than that Javier had been found shot up around Punta Blanca. But a couple of guys, I don't remember who, said they had heard that a gold doubloon had been found in the boat along with Javier's body.

After about an hour, we thanked Anna, said our good-byes, and left. We were anxious to talk with the sheriff's investigator in the morning. As we drove home, I asked Jill if she had gotten any news from the ladies. She said a couple of the women had mentioned that they had heard there might be some kind of connection with pirate treasure. One of them even wondered if, having come from Spain, Javier might have had some information about Spanish gold that had been buried on the barrier islands.

"That's funny. A couple of the guys mentioned that someone told them that a gold doubloon had been found on Javier's boat. Maybe there is some connection to pirates or to gold. We know, for sure, that there was some reason he wanted to be here. He kept talking about information he had gotten from his father and his grandfather. You know, I don't think he really came down here to see us. I think that was just an excuse so that he could come down and go exploring on his own. He was looking for something."

We were silent as we drove the few blocks to the house. As we parked in our garage, we turned to each other and simultaneously said, "Big Ed Lowder! That miserable son of a bitch!"

Chapter Fifteen
LIEUTENANT COLLINS'S VISIT

The next morning, promptly at ten o'clock, the doorbell rang. I opened the door to find a tall, good-looking, middle-aged man dressed in civilian clothes. He introduced himself as Lieutenant Mike Collins, senior investigator with the Lee County Sheriff's Gulf Islands Division. He asked if he could come in.

"Of course, Lieutenant. We've been expecting you. Come on in. Let's go sit in the living room."

Mike Collins made a good impression. I would guess he was about forty years old, and he looked like he worked out regularly. I'd guess he was a man whom women would find attractive. At first glance, I gauged him to be intelligent and competent. My immediate impression was that he knew what he was about.

I introduced Jill. As we sat down, she offered Lieutenant Collins something to drink."Would you like coffee? I can make you a K-cup in a flash."

I was somewhat surprised when he answered that he would very much like a cup.

"It'll take just a second. How would you like it?"

"Black will be fine. Thank you."

As we waited for the coffee to brew, he started to talk.

"I want to express condolences on behalf of the sheriff's department to you and your wife. I understand you and Mr. Hernandez were good friends."

"Thank you," I replied. "Javier and I worked together a couple of years before I retired at the end of June. He was a good guy. As far as I know, everyone at the bank liked him. He and I worked together well, but we didn't socialize out of the office. He was a good manager. I think he did a good job. I respected him, and I think he respected me. When he first came to the United States from Spain, I tried, as much as I could, to help him get his bearings around the bank. I think he appreciated that. We got along well. When I retired, he bought a great bottle of single malt, and we shared that after work one afternoon with a couple of other guys from the office. I liked Javier. I think you'll find that as you talk to people who met him down here, they liked him too."

"I guess at least one person didn't like him," Lieutenant Collins reminded me.

"Yeah. I guess so."

"So, you got along well, but you weren't really close friends. How did he come to be visiting you in Saint James City?"

I explained that I had extended an invitation to visit to a lot of people at the bank. Javier had surprised me somewhat when he said that he really wanted to come down to go fishing.

Jill returned with the coffee, and joined me on the couch. I briefed the investigator on what had transpired since I had picked Javier up at the airport. Jill filled in what I had forgotten. I made a point of emphasizing how well Javier had seemed to fit in with the town, and how he had gotten to know so many folks in such a short time.

Whenever our answers slowed, Lieutenant Collins would ask a simple but well reasoned question to keep us talking. It was soon apparent that he was doing a very professional job of eliciting everything we knew about Javier and what he had been doing while he was here.

I made sure to tell Lieutenant Collins how excited Javier had appeared to be about being in this area. I also said he seemed to be on some kind of mission on behalf of his father, grandfather, and great-grandfather—even though they were all dead now. I told him everything I knew, which wasn't much.

Eventually, he got around to asking what we had been doing the morning before. At first, I was shocked that he had the audacity to consider us suspects, but I quickly realized that it was a question he had to ask.

I asked the lieutenant to walk with me over to the French doors that overlook the canal."How do you like my freshly stained dock?" I asked."That's what I was doing yesterday. I painted the whole damn thing. I got started at nine, and finished about three thirty."

"Is there anyone who can verify that?" Collins asked.

"Well, Jill was here when I started. And I spoke with my neighbor across the canal for a few minutes. I think that was at about ten o'clock."

"And how about you, Mrs. Story?"

"I was here until nine thirty. Then I drove into Cape Coral to have my nails done at the Tropical Islands Salon and Spa on Pine Island Road. I got there a little before ten o'clock. I'm sure they will verify that I was there. After that, I did a little shopping at Target and at Bealls. Then I stopped by Publix at the corner of Burnt Store. I think I've still got receipts from all those places, if you need to verify this information. They'll probably have the time I checked out on them."

"That won't be necessary. Let's get back to Javier. As far as you know, did he get into any trouble while he was here?"

"Not that I know of. He seemed to visit all the bars in town on a nightly basis, usually starting at about 9:00 p.m. I think he got to be buddies with several folks doing that. You might ask Lester MacDonald. I think they hit it off. I know that they met up a couple of nights to do some pub visits. I suspect that Javier was buying beer for Les, and in return, Les was introducing him to others in the bars. But I never heard that Javier had been in any kind of trouble. As far as I know, everyone seemed to like him. My impression was that he used these nightly pub crawls to learn more about the area and the people who live here. Like I told you, he seemed to be on some kind of mission—something related to something his grandfather had told him. But I don't have a clue what that was about."

"Anything else you can tell me?"

"Well, I don't know if this is related, but I'll pass it along for what it might be worth. Jill heard last night at Woody's—from a couple of different ladies—that there might be some connection between Javier's murder and buried treasure. I heard from a couple of the guys that a Spanish doubloon was found on Javier's boat. When we heard about treasure, and about the doubloon, it led us to think about an incident I had a couple of weeks ago with a fellow over on Sanibel. I was gassing up my boat at the Sanibel Island Marina when this jackass named Ed Lowder tried to run me over with his Viking. He damn near killed me. The folks at the marina had told me that this Lowder guy is hunting pirate treasure. They also told me that he has teams of folks going through archives related to the pirate period in Gainesville and even in Spain. Now, I know for a fact that Javier was out on his boat all the time during the past week. I heard last night from a couple of guys that he was spending a lot of time on the boat up around Cayo Costa and around Punta Blanca. I don't know, but maybe he was hunting for treasure, too, and got sideways with Big Ed while he was up there. In my opinion, that guy is nuts. I wouldn't put it past him to kill someone he thought was getting in his way of finding treasure. I know that sounds far-fetched. But, believe me, this guy could do anything. I wanted you to know just in case there might be some connection."

"Thanks for telling me about your run-in with Lowder. That's interesting. I hadn't heard about your incident, but we've had reports about a couple of others recently. We're familiar with him and what he's up to. Do you know if Javier ever met Lowder?"

"I don't have a clue. But I do know that he mentioned that he needed to go to Sanibel to meet with someone. He wanted to know if it would be faster to go by boat or by car. But I've no idea who he planned to meet or if he actually went."

"Jill, anything else you can tell me?"

"I guess the only thing I'd suggest is that you should talk with the ladies who work down at Woody's. I know Javier spent a lot of time there at night. I think he especially liked to talk with Anna and Chesley. They'll know who else Javier was hanging out with, and they'll probably know what they were talking about."

"We'll follow up on that. Any idea who we can talk with so that we can contact his family?"

"Sure." I gave Collins the phone number for Rich Samuelson, and suggested that he give him a call. "He was going to tell Javier's family this morning. He'll know for sure how to get in touch with them."

"OK. Thank you both for your help. And Jill, thanks for the coffee. I want you to know that we are as anxious as you are to find who killed your friend. If you can think of anything I should know, or if something else comes up, give me a call."

I responded, "We'll do that. I'd appreciate it if you could keep us posted on the progress you're making. I know you probably won't be able to tell us much, but I feel responsible for Javier being down here, and I guess in some way, responsible for him being killed. It's very important to me that the bastard who did this is caught and dealt with appropriately."

"It's important to us, too."

Chapter Sixteen
A DEAD END

There was, for about a week, a flurry of activity associated with the investigation into Javier's death. The sheriff's department spent the first couple of days talking with everyone in town who had ever crossed paths with Javier. They sealed his motel room, and spent a whole day analyzing it. They also examined his boat, his car, and his phone. I never knew what, if anything, these searches uncovered.

The bank arranged to have Javier's body shipped to Spain. Reporters from the Fort Myers newspaper and television stations came to Saint James City to interview locals. Nothing like a mysterious murder—especially one that involves a foreign banker—to bump up your ratings. To hear the evening news, you would have thought that Javier was the glamorous and mysterious leader of a secret, international, money-laundering organization. Of course, nothing could be further from the truth. Javier's mid-level role in the bank had been to measure and control risk. He was anything but a risk taker. Regardless, over the next several days, our little town was the featured story in every station's news broadcast. But by the end of the week, the media's excitement had noticeably diminished. I guess they had run out of anything new to say about Javier's murder. Besides, by the end of the week they had moved on to a new sensation—the arrest of a high-profile Lee County commissioner for possession of cocaine while in the company of a transvestite! One thing about living in Florida: there's never a shortage of entertaining news.

I think most of us in town were glad to see the media leave. Maybe the owners of the bars and restaurants were not as pleased. I'm sure they were probably quite happy for the business the newshounds brought to town. Normally, reporters only come to town once a year—for the opening of stone crab season—and even then, they only spend a couple of hours here. Truthfully, having a bunch of them in town for days had not been an altogether pleasant experience, as they had tried to find the town's most colorful characters to interview for their stations' nightly newscasts. It's been my experience that it's hard enough being a colorful character without having to worry about making a fool of yourself on TV. I was glad when they finally left so that we could, once again, drink in peace.

While the town was beginning to calm down, I was not. In fact, I was getting more and more agitated about what I perceived to be the lack of progress in the investigation. I wanted someone caught—and hanged! And I wanted it done now! I was beyond frustrated that nothing seemed to be happening. I know that real-life police work is not like what you see on television. But still!

I was also pissed off that I wasn't being kept in the know about what was happening with the investigation. Granted, I'm not part of the sheriff's department. But Javier was my friend, and I felt responsible for his death. Damn it! I felt that I deserved to be kept updated on the investigation. But no one was telling me anything.

Jill kept telling me that I was being unreasonable. She kept telling me to calm down. "These things take time. You have to let them work through their processes," she said. I knew she was right. Nevertheless, I was anything but happy with the apparent pace of the investigation.

So, a few days later, when Jill and I were having lunch at the Waterfront and Lieutenant Collins and several deputies came in, I couldn't resist going over to ask him how the investigation was going.

"Mr. Story, good to see you." Collins introduced me to the others at the table. "The investigation is proceeding well. We have a number of leads that we are pursuing, but I'm afraid that there is nothing definitive that I can share with you at this time. It really is fortunate, however, that you are here. I was planning to come by to see you this afternoon. How about if you and I step outside for a minute?"

"Sure, Lieutenant. Just give me a second." I walked over to our table and told Jill what was up. I asked her to order me a grouper Reuben with extra sauerkraut.

I then followed Lieutenant Collins outside. We crossed the deck, took the stairs down to the boat dock, and walked away from the building.

When we were far enough away so that no one would be able to hear, he said, "Jim—I hope you don't mind me using your first name. And please drop the lieutenant crap. I'm Mike.

Jim—I think I'm going to need your help. I've talked with Javier's mother. She is, of course, devastated by his death. I think she loved her son very much. Now, I had been told that she speaks English well, and for the first part of our conversation we had no trouble communicating. But when I asked her about the 'mission' that Javier was here to pursue, it seemed like she suddenly forgot all of the English she ever knew. Despite my best efforts, she would not share any information with me about what Javier's interest in this area might have been."

Collins and I walked along the dock where the construction barge was tied up. "I got the clear impression she knows why he was here," he continued. "When we moved on to other topics, amazingly enough, she could once again carry on a conversation. The police in Spain are working on this, too, and they're not getting anywhere with her, either. But to get to the bottom of this, we need to know what she knows. I know that you know a lot of the other Spaniards at your bank. Some of them had to have been good friends with Javier. I was hoping that you might ask one of them to talk to Javier's mother, and convince her that she can trust us and that she needs to help us so that we can find the person who killed her son."

"That's really interesting," I said. "Look, I don't know much about the Spanish, but I do know that there's a lot to their culture that we Americans can't even begin to comprehend—things like relationships between families going back centuries, titles, protocols, rules...you name it, all that matters to them. Maybe she won't talk to you because of a status thing or something. Or maybe it's something else entirely. It wasn't that long ago that they had a civil war there. Who knows who trusts whom?"

I thought for a moment about the bank staff. "I know a couple of people who might be willing to talk to her. I'll let you know how I get on."

"Jim, I appreciate it. I think we need this. Otherwise, I wouldn't have asked."

"Yeah. I can understand that. Now, what else can you tell me? Was there really a doubloon on the boat? And have you checked out Big Ed?"

"Jim, I'm sorry. I can't really share that kind of information with you. At this point, we have ruled out some suspects, and we haven't ruled out others. I can't really tell you which category anyone is in. I will tell you, however, that we did find what appeared to be an old coin in the boat. We're checking that out now. Let me know if you're able to get any information from the Spaniards about why Javier was so interested in being here. Now, let's get back to our lunches before they get cold."

Once we were back at home, I told Jill about my conversation with Mike Collins. We agreed that it would be worthwhile to go down the path he had suggested. I mentally ran through the list of Spaniards I knew in the bank, and tried to decide which one would be able to get close to Javier's mother. I ruled out the bank's CEO. He's a really good guy, but his position and status would probably prevent Javier's mom from feeling comfortable enough to confide anything of a sensitive nature. I ruled out the other Spanish males in the bank, as well. I just didn't think that a man, any man, would be able to get close enough to Mrs. Hernandez. I also ruled out most of the women. Some of them just seemed a little too cold, and too haughty, for this kind of mission. Most of the Spanish women at the bank were from Madrid. I remembered that Javier and his family were from Salamanca, an ancient city in western Spain, about half-way between Madrid and Portugal. I didn't think it would be likely that a Madrileno would play well in Salamanca. (Just a guess, but it seemed to me that this might be a lot like a New Yorker going to Birmingham). So, given these considerations, I placed a call to the one person who might be able to befriend Mrs. Hernandez.

"Arantxa, this is Jim Story. How are you?" I asked. Arantxa Garcia-Myer is not her complete name. Best as I can make out, they include both maternal and paternal lineages in their formal names. Sometimes they're hyphenated; sometimes they're not. All I know for sure is that they are usually long. Most Spaniards develop a shortened version to use when they have to deal with us ignorant Americans. Arantxa works in the policies and procedures area at the bank. In this role, she deals with just about everyone. Her demeanor is friendly, fun, and just a little self-deprecating. She's definitely not the type who takes herself too seriously. But I do know that behind this persona, she is very competent and intelligent. She's the type who knows how to use her personality and talent to get the job done. She quickly and easily used those abilities to make friends with most of the Americans she worked with in Birmingham. I thought those skills might be useful in trying to get close to Mrs. Hernandez.

"Jim! It has been so long! We've missed you so much. The place isn't the same without you!"

"I'm sure it's not," I replied. "Arantxa, look, it's really good to talk with you. I've missed you, too. But I didn't call to catch up. You've heard, I'm sure, about Javier's death?"

"Yes, of course. It is so sad. We are all just devastated! He was such a great guy. We miss him so very much. Every time I think of him, I start to cry."

Yeah. Me, too. I am working with the police here to find out who killed him. They have asked me if I know a Spaniard at the bank who might be able to help them. I thought of you."

"I will be glad to help in any way I can. You know that, Jim. But I don't see what I can do."

I told Arantxa what Javier had been up to while he was visiting. I told her about how excited he seemed to be here. I told her what he had said about his great-grandfather. And, finally, I told her about Lieutenant Collins's experience with Javier's mother. I told her that we both suspected there was a connection between the family mission that Javier was on and his murder. I told her that we both believed that if we could understand why he was here, then we might be able to understand why he was killed. Whatever the secret was, it appeared to be something that Mrs. Hernandez was unwilling to share with the police—especially with an American law enforcement officer. I asked Arantxa if she thought she might be able to get close enough to Javier's mom to find out what that link was.

Arantxa was silent for quite some time. At first, I thought that I may have insulted her, and that she had hung up.

When I asked if she was still on, she said, "Yes. Yes, I'm here. I've just been thinking about what you have suggested. This will be very difficult, but I can see why it is important. I certainly don't think this is something that I can do over the phone. I do not know Senora Hernandez, and she would never share something like this with me in such a manner. The only way she might get comfortable enough to discuss this would be if I met with her in person. As it happens, I'm leaving for Spain on Friday. I'll be there at least three weeks. I'll find time to visit with Javier's mom while I am there. I certainly want to visit to pay my respects anyway. So, my visit will not appear to be out of line. I can't promise that I will be able to get you this information, but I promise I will try."

"Thanks, Arantxa. I appreciate that."

"Jim, how familiar are you with the town Javier was from?"

"I know where it is, and I know that there is a university there. That's about all I know."

"Jim, this is not just any university! The University of Salamanca is the oldest university in Spain. It was founded in 1218. It's the third-oldest university in all of Europe. In the middle of the thirteenth century, Pope Alexander acknowledged it as one of the world's four greatest universities. I believe the others were the universities in Oxford, Paris, and Bologna. But that's not what's important about what I want to tell you. This university is where all the famous explorers studied. Christopher Columbus studied there. So did, Cortes. This is where they all went to school. And this is where much of the gold that they brought back from South America ended up. The grand buildings of the university that help to make it so famous today were financed with this gold. The university has always been linked closely to the exploration—and exploitation—of the Americas. As you would expect, the university's archives contain most of the original records from that period. I know that this is a reach at this point, but do you think that there could be a link between Javier's murder and buried treasure? Maybe that was why he was so excited to be there. Probably just a coincidence. But who knows? Jim, I will see what I can find out. But it will take me some time. At least a couple of weeks. I will let you know what I learn. What is the best way to reach you?"

We exchanged phone numbers and e-mail addresses. I promised to touch base with her in a week, once she had arrived in Spain. I assured her that I would update her on any developments on my end, and she promised to do the same.

Chapter Seventeen
SPANISH GOLD

I was delighted that Arantxa had agreed to help. I knew that if anyone could get close to Javier's mom, she could. And it was really exciting to learn about the connection between Javier's hometown and the Spanish explorers. It was not too far-fetched to believe that Javier's family had found information in the university's archives, or possibly had been given information by someone within the university, and that that information was tied to treasure in the Southwest Florida area.

Pine Island Sound and the surrounding area have been linked in both fact and fable with some of the most famous characters of piracy's golden age. For example, it is a fact that Calico Jack and Jill Bonny, the most romantic of all pirates, spent their honeymoon encamped on what is now known, appropriately enough, as Lovers Key. It's located just south of Fort Myers Beach. A lot of today's pirate lore is actually based upon the lives of these famous lovers. For example, Jack Sparrow, the main character in Disney's *Pirates of the Caribbean* was modeled, in part, on Calico Jack.

Another pirate linked to this area was Black Caesar. This famous Haitian pirate based his operation on the south end of Sanibel Island. He is known to have been the cruelest of all pirates, his life view colored by his childhood as a slave on a French plantation on Haiti. During the revolution that overthrew the French, he was able to escape his job in the plantation's sawmill, and subsequently used the mill's crosscut saw to cut his overseer in half! Eventually, he was able to steal a ship and turn to piracy. In time, he became quite successful in this role. He is said to have buried a portion of his treasure on Pine Island.

Bru Baker was an English pirate. He is known to have operated out of Saint James City and Bokeelia.

But legend says that the most famous Spanish pirate of all, Jose Gaspar—now known more commonly as Gasparilla—operated his hugely successful enterprise from Boca Grande. This quaint little city, more recently the vacation retreat of some of the nation's wealthiest citizens, sits on the southern end of what is now called Gasparilla Island.

Most of the barrier islands in Southwest Florida are tied, in some fashion, to Gasparilla's legend. For example, Captiva Island is said to have been where Gasparilla held his female guests captive as they waited, if they were lucky, for ransoms to be paid. And Useppa Island is thought to have been named after Joseffa, a beautiful Spanish princess whom Gasparilla took prisoner when he seized a Spanish treasure ship sailing from Mexico. Joseffa was said to have been especially beautiful, very intelligent, and witty. She is said to have quickly become Gaspar's favorite. He was so taken with her that he made her the subject of his most earnest romantic overtures. To locate her closer to Boca Grande, he gave her a private island of her own, Joseffa's Island. Ultimately, Joseffa spurned Jose's offer of marriage. That refusal led, shortly thereafter, to her decapitation. Reportedly, she was buried on the island.

In 1920, the island's name was changed to Useppa. Barron Gift Collier, one of America's wealthiest men, had purchased it for $100,000,intendingto develop it and several surrounding islands into the world's most exclusive sporting club. He also envisioned developing the west coast of Florida, much as Henry Flagler was developing Florida's east coast. The name change from Joseffa to Useppa is said to have been made because of his wife's squeamishness over the legend of the Spanish princess's demise. She convinced Collier that the association with such a bloody legend would detract from the island's appeal to vacationers and investors. Eventually, the Great Depression defeated Collier's development plans, but he and his wife made Useppa Island their home. He and his family lived there until his death in 1939.

Gaspar himself was said to have been a disgraced Spanish nobleman. As a young man, he was handsome, dashing, headstrong, and more than a little hot headed. His eventual career as a pirate may have been foretold when, as a young boy, he kidnapped a rich man's daughter and held her for ransom. He, of course, was found out. Given the choice of being executed or joining the Spanish navy, he logically enough, chose the navy. Gaspar proved to be very adept at sea and at battle. Eventually, he became a highly decorated captain. With this recognition, and given his family's position in the aristocracy, he became a fixture in the royal court. Ultimately, however, he insulted the queen in too public a fashion—apparently, he had deflowered one of her favorite nieces and bragged about it in public. Her majesty "suggested" that he should do the honorable thing and marry the young lady. He refused. To avoid execution, he commandeered a Spanish ship of war. He rechristened the vessel *Florida Blanca,* and sailed to the Caribbean and into history. He is acknowledged to have been the most successful Spanish pirate. Some claim that he was the most successful pirate of all. He used his base in Southwest Florida to attack Spanish galleons heavily laden with treasure. Twice a year, ships from across Spain's North American empire met in Havana, where they would be combined into vast convoys, or armadas, to sail together across the Atlantic. To reach Havana, the ships sailing from Mexico and elsewhere in Latin America would sail the great loop current that flows through the Gulf of Mexico. This current frequently put these ships within easy reach of Southwest Florida. As a result, Gaspar's fortune was said to have been worth forty million dollars at the time of his death in 1823. Some say that this fortune is still buried somewhere in Southwest Florida. None of it has ever been recovered.

This was the treasure that Big Ed Lowder hoped to find. Was that treasure also what had brought Javier Hernandez to this area? Was Gaspar's treasure what had caused his excitement? Was it what had caused his death? And the bottom line: Was Big Ed responsible for Javier's death?

I had no way of knowing. All I could do was hope that Arantxa would find information that Lieutenant Collins could use to answer these questions.

Chapter Eighteen
AN ENCOUNTER AT THE WATERFRONT

The days crept past with, from what I could tell, no additional developments. I had no idea how long it would be before Arantxa could visit with Javier's mother. It could easily be a week before she could get back to us with any news. In the meantime, I was sitting in Saint James City, feeling totally out of the loop with respect to the investigation. I was simply waiting for something to happen. It was driving me nuts! My friend had been murdered, and I knew that in some minor way, I had contributed to his death. The only thing I could do for him now was to make sure his killer was caught. I wanted the bastard hanged! And if that bastard was Big Ed Lowder, then so much the better, as far as I was concerned. But other than wishing and praying, I had no idea what I could do to help move the investigation forward.

Who knows? Maybe there is something to this prayer stuff. I guess that's the thing about prayer—you never know what caused what to happen. All I know is that a few days later, Big Ed and I got to know each other a lot better.

Jill had driven upstate to spend some quality time with grandchild number three. She would be gone for five days, so I would have to fend for myself with respect to meals. Now, I'm a pretty fair country cook. I can whip up just about anything, and it usually turns out to be edible. Heck, I can even make something fancy. All I have to do is find a cookbook and follow the instructions. But when you're cooking for yourself, who wants to spend time whipping up something special? Not me. So, when Jill is visiting one of the kids, I usually fall back on a few reliable standbys. For instance, I love to fry up a few trout filets, stuff them in a hoagie roll, add a few condiments, and voila, a trout po'boy. Add a handful of sea-salt potato chips and you have a meal fit for a king. When I run out of trout, Bubba Burgers are a specialty of the house. Beyond that, I can live for a couple of days off a pack of quality hot dogs. Yeah, when Jill is away, I eat pretty damn well. But after a few days of eating this kind of gourmet food, I sometimes need to step down the food pyramid and visit one of the local restaurants. So it was that I ended up at the Waterfront at a little after eight o'clock on Wednesday evening.

As I've mentioned before, this great little place is only a couple of blocks from the house. It makes for an easy bike ride. And if I should have a few too many drinks, well, a BUI (bicycling under the influence) is probably going to be a less serious offense than a DUI. I have heard of the occasional DUI arrest in Saint James City, but I've never heard of a BUI. So, the bike it was.

As I coasted up to the restaurant's bike rack, I noticed a couple of boats docked in the Waterfront's slips. One, in particular, caught my eye. I'm a real fan of boats, and, in most cases, I consider them to be things of beauty. Even as a kid, I studied their lines carefully and developed what I thought was a pretty good sense of what a boat should look like. To guys, I guess boats are a lot like women. Some guys like blondes, while some are turned on by redheads. In the same fashion, some guys like a classic-looking hull, while some are more attracted to the modern go-fast style. Clearly, whoever owned this boat fell in the latter category. It had to be nearly forty feet long, and multiple 300-horsepower Mercury Verados hung off the stern. Every part of the boat, even including its darkly tinted windows, was black. The only exception was the boat's name, *Infidel,* which was emblazoned in gaudy gold leaf on each side of the hull. The cockpit was outfitted with every high-tech radar and night-vision gadget that a civilian could buy. The seats looked as if they were developed with some kind of military or tactical law-enforcement purpose in mind. Same for the empty gun racks that were carefully located around the cockpit. And, I swear, there was even a rack on the bow to hold a machine gun. Whoever owned this boat must have some kind of unfulfilled fantasy. I looked forward to seeing who that was.

I went in the front door, and scanned the main dining room. It was empty except for two groups. One was a man and woman whom I tagged as being the owners of the other boat tied up out front. It looked as if they were trying to settle up their tab so they could get out of the restaurant as quickly as possible. The other table was occupied by a group of four guys, all of whom seemed to be vying for the restaurant's "Asshole of the Year Award." It was clear from the number of empty beer pitchers on the table that they had been drinking for a while. And from the way they were harassing the worried waitress, they had no intention of going anywhere any time soon.

I started toward the bar when I noticed that one of the drunken idiots was noticeably smaller than the others. He was also the loudest, and clearly, the most obnoxious. Could it be? It had to be! I looked more closely as the little guy turned to reach for the one pitcher that still had beer in it. I was right: it was none other than my dear friend, Big Ed Lowder.

Now, that was interesting. This situation presented a number of possibilities. In order to consider them appropriately, I ventured into the bar area off to the side of the main room, and took a seat at a table, with my back to the group. I knew they had not seen me, and I was pretty sure they would not have recognized me even if I had walked right up to them. But this way I could think about my options while they continued to enjoy their five-dollar pitchers. I noticed, as I waited, that another four pitchers had just been delivered to their table. One thing was certain: they would all be visiting the men's room frequently, and probably pretty soon.

The label, "men's room," at the Waterfront is a slight exaggeration. Hell, it's actually a huge exaggeration. To put this in perspective, I note that, in order to satisfy government regulations that restrooms be wheelchair-accessible, management had set up a double-wide Port-a-Potty outside in a corner of the parking lot. There was simply no way the existing building could be modified to accommodate the extra space required for wheelchairs.

The hallway that leads to the men's room can't be more than eighteen inches wide. A good-size guy, like me, actually has to turn sideways to go down the hall. Since the women's room is off to the side of this hallway, interesting encounters frequently take place in this space. I presume that most male and female patrons needing to pass one another in this hall would try to do so with a minimum of body-to-body contact. But depending upon how attractive the person you need to pass is, that may not always be the case. In fact, the hall is so narrow that most returning visitors quickly learn that it's better to queue up in the corner anteroom that leads to the hall and simply wait for it to clear. And besides, this is really not such a bad place to stand. The walls are covered from floor to ceiling with some of the most humorous bumper stickers you can imagine. At this inter-section you can find such classics, as "Ten Reasons Cucumbers are Better Than Men," "If You're Going to Act Like a Turd, Go Out and Lie in the Yard," and my personal favorite, "Nuke the Gay Whales for Jesus." That one offends just about everyone. I love it!

Once the path is clear, you can see that the hallway ends with a small, blue-painted, louvered door featuring a brass plaque that proclaims, "Men's." The door can't be more than fifteen inches wide. It's obviously handmade—there is no way you could buy one at the Home Depot. I'm pretty sure that the only way this facility can possibly meet building code is that it's registered as an historic building.

The men's room can't be more than five feet long. It's maybe four feet wide. To your right, as you enter, area commode and a urinal. Straight ahead is a simple sink with an unframed mirror mounted over it. The distance between the closed door and the sink can't be more than a couple of feet. This is one tight, little space. While, in theory, it might be able to accommodate more than one person at a time, in practice, it's definitely made for one. This situation presented an interesting opportunity.

It was not hard to anticipate that Big Ed was going to need to visit this space soon. I could guess that his companions knew they would have to wait for anyone using the facility to return before they would be able to make use of it themselves. In other words, it seemed likely that I was going to have an opportunity in the near future to reintroduce myself, in private, to Big Ed Lowder. That sounded like too good an opportunity to pass up!

Sure enough, in a few minutes, Big Ed stumbled past my table and down the hall. As he rounded the corner, I headed that way, too. When he saw me coming, he looked up and gave me his best, albeit sloppy, go-fuck-yourself sneer. This is what I had anticipated. And I was pretty sure that, even if he had been sober, he wouldn't have known me from Adam. He didn't.

Now, I would bet that it was Big Ed's intention to make me wait outside while he took all in the time in the world to take a piss, wash his hands twice, comb his hair, etc. In other words, I'm pretty sure he planned to do everything he could to make me uncomfortable as I waited outside with my legs crossed. But I'm also pretty sure that Big Ed never expected what happened next.

Just as he turned to push the door open, I leapt forward, and, using all of my 250 pounds, shoved him through the doorway and into the men's room. My momentum was more than enough to propel his 150 pounds backward and upward onto the sink. That and my left hand around his throat. I actually had not intended to break the mirror behind the sink with his head, but those things happen. When it did, I think it helped to focus Big Ed's attention more clearly on what was happening to him.

He kick and squirmed, but my body was pressed up against him so tightly that he couldn't generate enough leverage to do any damage. That, and the rather deliberate way I was gripping his throat convinced him that further struggle might not be in his best interest. "What the fuck do you want?" was about all that he could croak.

"Hi, Big Ed. You tried to run me over a couple of weeks ago over at Sanibel Island Marina. You almost killed me! Is it coming back to you now?"

At that point, I saw a flicker of recognition in his eyes. I think I also saw him start to reason that maybe he could buy his way out of this situation. There was probably some relief in his brain that there was a purpose for my attack, and that I wasn't just some crazy, drunk, redneck who wanted to beat his little ass to a pulp just for the fun of it. But I don't think that relief lasted very long.

"Look," Ed said. "I...I...I...I do remember when that happened. And I felt really bad about that, but it was...it was...it was...it was just a simple mistake. I had a new captain at the controls, and he didn't know how to handle that situation. I'm very sorry for the problem he caused. I'll be glad to pay you to clear this up."

That was certainly not what Big Ed should have said. Of course, I had seen him at the wheel with my own eyes, so I knew that he was lying. Unfortunately for Big Ed, there are not many things in the world that I hate more than a liar.

Processing this information must have caused some kind of adrenaline rush in my body. The next thing I knew, my right fist had somehow come into contact with his face. Apparently, it did this with quite a bit of force. I say that because I swear that I heard, at the instant of contact, something rattle inside his head. Whether it was his teeth, his brain, or something else, I can't say for sure. But I can definitely say that, for some reason, a fair amount of bright, red blood now began to gush from his nose, and fall onto his expensive, white, linen shirt.

"Big Ed, you're a fucking liar! You were at the controls of your damned Viking. I saw you myself! You even shot me the bird as you went past. Do you remember that? It wasn't a fucking accident!"

Along about then, I started to note the effect that squeezing my left hand was having on Big Ed's face. When I got angry and squeezed harder, I noticed that he seemed to stop breathing. And that his face turned purple. When I eased up, he would start to breathe again, and his color looked less like that of an eggplant. I tried it a couple more times just to make sure I could replicate the effect. I could. I knew then that if I had wanted to, I could have killed him by simply maintaining my grip for a couple of minutes.

But I certainly didn't want to kill him. In fact, now that I was in the middle of this, I wasn't really sure what I wanted. I guess all I really wanted was to make sure that Big Ed didn't try to run me over again. Also, it would be nice to find out if he was involved in Javier's murder. I decided that to further the above objectives, I could use my newfound knowledge about the effect of squeezing the larynx and the jugular vein.

"Big Ed, whether I kill you tonight depends on two things. First, let me show you how easily I could kill you if I wanted to." With that, I squeezed hard for about ten seconds. That was enough to get my point across.

I guess it also was more than enough to remind Ed's body that he really did need to go to the bathroom. I suppose all that beer needed some place to go. And, apparently, it couldn't wait any longer, since the blood coming out of his nose now wasn't the only fluid escaping from his body.

I let him breathe for a second before squeezing again. Then, in my best Clint Eastwood voice, I said, "Let me make myself perfectly clear. I haven't yet decided if I'm going to kill you. But just on the small chance that I decide to let you live, I want you to remember one thing. If you ever try to run me down again, or to run anyone else over, for that matter, I'll come back and finish this job. In fact, if I ever see you so much as creating a wake in a slow-speed zone, I'll finish this job. Do you understand?"

I released my grip enough for Ed to breathe again, and to whisper a hoarse, "Yes."

At that point, I gripped his throat harder than I had squeezed up to this point. I could see the terror swell in his eyes.

"Did you kill Javier Hernandez?"

Big Ed shook his head from side to side. His eyes got bigger than I had yet seen them. I looked deeply into those eyes, trying to look deeply into his soul. At that moment, I don't know how I knew, but I knew that he was telling me the truth. In fact, at that instant, I swear I saw a look in his eyes that let me know that the joke was, somehow, on me. From that moment on, I no longer believed that Big Ed was Javier's killer.

"There's no reason I should believe you. All the evidence says you blew his brains out over some silly gold coins. Know this,

Ed: if you had anything to do with his death, I will find you, and you will pay. When I get though with you, all they'll find is your bloody carcass, gutted and filleted. It'll be feeding the redfish and crabs out on some fucking oyster bar in the sound."

By this time, all the adrenaline in my body had gone, and my anger had disappeared. In fact, the whole experience of beating up this pathetic, drunken, little asshole was just making me feel disgusted. All I wanted to do now was to stop, leave him alone, and go home.

I gently let him sink down into the bowl, and paused a minute to make sure that he wasn't going to try to retaliate. But it was clear that his fight was gone for this evening. With that, I backed out the door, walked out the side door of the restaurant, and into the parking lot. I retrieved my bike from the rack and pedaled off into the night. I previously had left twenty bucks on the table to pay my tab. I'd come back to settle up for the mirror in a couple of days.

When I got home, I climbed off the bike, stumbled onto the rocks that serve as our lawn, and threw up. Clearly, I wasn't cut out for violence.

I knew I'd really need some Scotch that night before I'd be able to sleep.

Chapter Nineteen
A BEAUTIFUL DAY ON THE WATER

The next morning, I got up early. My first task was to walk the dog. Once we returned, and the dog was fed, I loaded the boat with a cooler and rods, and headed out onto the sound. I seriously needed peace, quiet, and some time to process what had happened the previous night. I also wanted to make myself scarce, just in case the sheriff was looking for me.

It was one of those beautiful, subtropical mornings for which Southwest Florida is famous. The sun was shining, and the sky was pale blue. There were only a few cumulus clouds to enliven the view. The humidity had dropped a few points—just enough to mark the passage of a cold front during the night. Down here, cold is a relative term. That morning, the temperature was about seventy-six degrees and heading to ninety; versus the summertime norm of eighty degrees, heading to ninety-four. A drop of a few degrees and a little less humidity can make a world of difference. That morning felt great.

I wanted to try a new fishing spot. In truth, I really needed to break out of some fishing habits that I had fallen into. Recently, all I had been doing was putting on a popping-cork rig, baiting it with a Gulp shrimp, and then dragging it along behind the boat as I drifted across shallow grass flats. It's an effective technique for catching trout. But the downside is that you rarely catch anything other than trout. To me, part of the magic of saltwater fishing is that you never know what you may hook. I needed to find that magic again.

I had studied the charts of the sound, and decided to run well up north. I wanted to try an area I had heard the guides talk about, but that I had never actually fished. The area was on the east side of the sound, near marker number forty-eight. On the chart, it showed depths of two to six feet. The bottom looked to be grassy. I was particularly intrigued by what looked to be significant variations in depth across the flats. My experience is that deviations in depth like this can create some really exciting fishing.

Running up the sound on a beautiful day is one of the most pleasant experiences I know. The visual imagery alone can be mind-blowing. In the morning, the rising sun often creates all kind of colors on the clouds—both those back to the east over Okeechobee and those way out over the gulf. And there is no telling what wildlife you may see. It's not at all unusual this time of the year to see tarpon jump. I almost always see sea turtles popping up to breathe and pelicans diving, creating geysers of spray. Ospreys skim the surface, looking to grab unsuspecting fish in their talons. In the early morning I sometimes see dolphins working together in pods to round up a breakfast of mullet. And, of course, mullet are jumping everywhere. It's always an amazing spectacle.

Being out in a boat on a day like this does wonders to help me relax and forget about what's bothering me. It wasn't long before I stopped thinking about Big Ed, and about what I had done to him. Instead, I had simply started to focus on navigating the boat up the sound.

The easy way to go north is to simply follow the channel markers. It's also the safest way to get there. Parts of Pine Island Sound can be scarily shallow, with depths of less than a foot at normal low tide. And that's not considering that oyster bars and sand flats actually stick out of the water when the tide is negative (below dead mean tide level). So, you can't just head out across the bay and feel secure that you won't end up high, dry, and missing the lower unit of your outboard. But on the other hand, simply following the channel adds a considerable distance to the journey. With ethanol-free gasoline costing five bucks a gallon, it makes sense to take a shortcut whenever possible.

As you leave Saint James City heading north, there are at three ways to shorten the journey. You can cut inside marker number eighteen. Or, the really adventurous may try the Old Mail Boat channel, but if you screw that up you can end up high and dry. To me, the best alternative, if there's enough water, is to stay right of the channel until you pick up the manatee-zone buoys. Then, just follow them around to the north until you come to the sign that announces the slow-speed zone. You give that sign a miss to the west by about twenty yards and head straight out into the main channel. This route will put you out between markers number twenty and twenty-two, and it works as long as the tide is not more than half low. From there, if you draw three feet or less, you can proceed straight north under the power lines, avoiding the long run to the west toward marker twenty-six. Staying on this course, you've got plenty of water, as long as you stay to the west of Red Light Shoal, which extends to the northeast, just past marker number thirty. Be warned, it gets seriously shallow there.

If you take this path, you'll knock off at least a mile, which isn't bad. Plus, it makes you feel a little superior to those who don't know this shortcut and stick to the middle of the channel as they proceed up to Cabbage Key for their obligatory cheeseburgers.

That day, there was plenty of water, so I took my shortcut. But I really wasn't concerned with saving time or distance; I simply wanted to be outside, on the water. Twenty minutes later, I arrived where I wanted to fish. Since the water was a little deeper than where I had been fishing, I needed to change up my approach. I still threw out one popping-cork rig, but I also threw out another rig that was nothing more than a simple, free-lined jig, baited with a three-inch-long Gulp shrimp.

You know it's going to be a good day when on your first cast you connect with a keeper trout. That's what happened that day. Wouldn't you know it, on the popping cork. No sooner had the cork hit the water than it was slammed under in that aggressive way that announces a strike by a big, hungry fish. When you see the cork disappearing under the water like this, all you have to do is jerk the rod a little to set the hook, hold the end of the rod up, and, if the fish isn't stripping line off the spool, start to reel.

If it starts to take line, you stop winding, and just let it run until it's tired itself out. Once it's made that run, and stopped, you can begin to reel it in. But if it's still got some fight, simply repeat the process until it's done.

When fishing on the flats, you can tell almost immediately what kind of creature is on the end of the line. If it's a trout, it'll always come to the surface and roll. If it's a catfish, it fights to stay on the bottom. And you can clearly feel the different way that a catfish struggles against the line. The pulses that come up the line from a trout are slower and less frantic. A catfish, on the other hand, pulls down more aggressively, sending quick pulses through the line as it tries to swim down toward the safety of the bottom. Or, you may have a jack on the other end. These dive, too, but less deeply than catfish, and they put up one heck of a fight. A ten-pound jack will give you all the fight you can handle. One of the most spectacular fish you can hook on the flats is a ladyfish. These are beautiful, slender fish that somewhat resemble small barracuda. They are bright silver in color, and consequently, are desired by anglers as great cut bait. You will know, without a doubt, when a ladyfish hits your line, since it will immediately jump in an incredibly acrobatic fashion. It's common for them to leap clear of the water by four or five feet, and then keep fighting in this fashion all the way to the boat. They are fun to catch. It's too bad they aren't bigger. If they were larger, they'd be the greatest sports fish in the world. But they're not, and since you can't eat them, they usually end up being sliced into cut bait.

But on the first cast that day, I had connected with a good-size trout. When I got it in the boat, it measured eighteen inches, right in the middle of the slot. It went into the live release well. The day was off to a good start.

For the next couple of hours, the action was great. I caught a huge number of juvenile trout, and still managed to get my limit of keepers. In addition, I was besieged by hungry jacks that kept me entertained. One of the problems with fishing two poles by yourself is that it's hard to give either one the proper amount of attention. If you let the bait settle toward the bottom, and if you don't keep moving it, you can count on having a catfish on the line soon.

As they day wore on, I completely forgot about the night before. And about all the other issues that had been on my mind. I was so busy tending the lines in the water that I simply didn't have time to think about anything else. Once I had my limit of trout in the live well, I started to up-size my catch. If I caught a fish that was bigger than one of those swimming in the well, I released the smaller one, and replaced it with the bigger one.

All of this action kept me entertained. But it was nothing compared with what was to come. I had a strike on the free-lined jig when I saw something huge heading toward the popping cork. That something turned out to be a bull shark—it must have been at least six feet in length, maybe more.

When you see one of these brutes in action, it's obvious why they are called bull sharks. They are big, broad across the chest, strong, and aggressive—just like a bull. There is no question that this fish is the apex predator on the flats. There is nothing else out there that could stand up to an attack by a bull shark. There are a lot of dangerous sharks in Florida's waters, but the one most feared up and down the coast is the bull shark. Every year, there are dozens of shark attacks along the beaches of Florida. The state actually leads the country, and the world, in reported shark attacks. Most are minor, and don't make the headlines. They are really more like bites than attacks. Usually, these result from accidental contact between a human and a small black tip or some other type of less aggressive shark. In these encounters, the shark is usually chasing bait in the murky water of the surf zone. Being unable to see clearly, it simply bites a human by mistake. As soon as the shark realizes what it has bitten, it lets go and tries to get away as quickly as possible. These encounters may result in a nasty wound, require a lot of stitches, and leave an ugly scar. But most victims survive. The victims who don't survive are likely the ones who encounter a feeding bull shark. These predators don't care what they eat. To them, a human is just as appetizing as a mackerel. And when a bull shark bites, the hole that's left is usually so big that all the sutures in the world couldn't repair it—assuming the victim doesn't bleed to death first. Usually, that's what happens. Most victims of bull shark attacks are dead before they can be brought to the beach.

This was the type of shark that I saw. In the blink of an eye, this giant swam around my popping cork before diving to the shrimp below it. There was no doubt that it intended to eat the bait. While this was going on, I was dealing with the other rod. When I was able to put that rod down, and turned back to the rod with the popping cork, I was surprised to see that the line had only moved a couple of dozen feet to the side. I'd expected the shark to immediately race off once it felt the hook in its mouth, or to cut the line. That had not happened. But once I set the hook, all hell broke loose. The shark took off like a Saturn

5 over at the Cape. This brute was headed somewhere else, and he wasn't going to stop, regardless of how much pressure I put on the reel's drag. I tried briefly to fight the shark, but line was being stripped from the reel like the drag didn't even exist. It was clear that if I persisted, I was going to lose every inch of line on my reel. Not wanting that to happen, and knowing that, even if I could have caught the fish, there was no way I wanted to deal with a mad, six-foot bull shark along the side of my boat, I cupped the reel to keep it from turning. In the blink of an eye, the line popped, and the monster was gone.

That was one of the most amazing experiences I had ever had on the flats—and I had been fishing Florida for a very long time. An encounter like that helps to put everything in perspective. I reeled in what was left of my line, and tied it off. What I had just witnessed had left me drained—there would be no more fishing that day. I was spent. It was time to head home.

I put the boat on an easy plane back to the south. There would be no short cuts for me on the way back home. Even if the tide had allowed (which it didn't), I don't think I would have taken the short cut. That would have required more involvement than I wanted to give and a degree of impatience that I simply wasn't feeling. What I was feeling was a sense of awe about the fearsomeness of what I had just witnessed.

I was thinking about just two things. One, there was no way in hell that I was ever going to go swimming in the sound. And, two, I couldn't help but think about how that predator had behaved before the hook was set. It had struck, killed its prey, and moved off as calmly as if nothing had happened. But once the hook was set, that killer had exploded!

Thinking about this encounter brought me back to Javier's murder. He had been killed by an apex predator of the human kind. And I knew that so far, that predator was moving among us just as calmly as he or she did on any normal day. Another thing I now knew was that Big Ed Lowder wasn't the apex predator who had taken Javier's life. Big Ed was more like a catfish—an annoyance for sure, but nothing more than a bottom feeder. He wasn't the killer we were after. When I had seen the bull shark, I had felt awe, respect, and fear for that killer's capability. Big Ed Lowder brought out none of those emotions. He wasn't the guy we were after.

The person who had killed Javier was strong, aggressive, calculating, fearless, and, so far, calm. Somehow, we would have to find a way to bait a hook that would draw that shark in, and then set the hook to make him run. Once we were able to do that, we'd better make sure our tackle was strong enough to land him. That bull shark was a fearless killer—and so was the human being for whom we were fishing. For the first time, the reality of what we were trying to do dawned on me. Finding this murderer wasn't like some kind of game—we were in a life and death struggle. If anyone was ever able to get this murderer to the boat, he'd better be prepared to defend himself. And be prepared to kill in order to keep from being killed.

I didn't pay much attention to the scenery the rest of the way home.

Chapter Twenty
ONE SUSPECT CLEARED

I got to the dock about three o'clock, and set about accomplishing the chores that I have to get done whenever I return from fishing. When the boat's safely on the lift, I unload the cooler with the iced-down fish that I have transferred from the live well before heading in for the day. Depending on the number of fish that need to be cleaned, it can take twenty to thirty minutes to get the fish into the freezer. Then, it takes about thirty minutes to wash down the boat, flush the engine, and wash off the reels. Finally, I move all the gear back to the house.

That day, I had finished cleaning the fish, and had just started on the boat, when Lieutenant Collins walked down the path toward to the dock.

"Hey, Mike. How're you doing?"

"Jim. I'm good. How was fishing? You catch anything?"

"Yeah, I had a great day. Got my limit of some really nice trout. The weather was splendid, and nobody bothered me all day! Just the way I like it."

"Glad to hear it. But I'm going to bother you right now. There's a rumor going around that you might have had a run in with Big Ed last night."

"Might have. Is he pressing charges?"

"He might, if he knew who you were."

"So, now that I've confessed, are you going to arrest me?"

"Not yet. I figure he probably had it coming. The folks at the restaurant were actually pretty happy that you dealt with him. The way they tell it, Big Ed and his crew were drunk and obnoxious. If D.W. had been there, he'd have kicked their asses out a long time before you did. But it was his night off, and just the ladies were working. They didn't want to cause a scene. So they were glad that someone took the problem off their hands. But, look, Jim, one get-out-of-jail-free card is all you get. Make a habit of this kind of thing, and you'll get to be our guest in downtown Fort Myers at the county's bed and breakfast."

"Don't worry. First fight I've been in since I was a kid. I hope it's the last. And, just so you know, I didn't enjoy it. But I came away from our little chat convinced that Big Ed's not the guy who killed Javier. He's not a killer. There's someone else out there. And, whoever that is, is someone to be scared of."

Collins laughed. "I agree that Lowder's not the killer. And we didn't need you to tell us that. He and his entire crew were in custody in Charlotte County the day Javier was killed. They had spent the previous couple of nights acting out their pirate fantasies in some of the waterfront bars in Boca Grande. Finally, some of the local fishing guides decided that they'd had enough. Generally, the guys up there leave the tourists alone. It just makes good economic sense. But if you manage to get those fishermen mad at you, the outcome's not going to be pretty. I heard that the bar at Miller's Marina was busted up pretty good, and apparently, so were Ed and his buddies. Fortunately, everyone kept their knives and guns in their pockets, and there was no serious bloodshed. By the time the deputies got there, it was pretty much all over. Charlotte County ended up hauling everyone into Punta Gorda for the night. The locals were released early the next morning on their own recognizance. But for some strange reason, it took a couple of days before Ed and crew were able to work through the process to post bail. It's funny how things sometimes can work out for the best when you've got the right judge on the case. In this case, old Ben Daniel was presiding. He grew up in Boca Grande, and knew, on a first-name basis, everyone of the guys who had invited Big Ed and his boys to leave town. That's the reason Big Ed's clown show was at the Waterfront last night—Boca Grande is now off-limits. They show up in Boca Grande again, and they'll likely become tarpon bait. I think that was explained to them pretty clearly. I think it's been a rough week for Big Ed."

"So, Mike," I asked. "If it wasn't Big Ed, then who did do it?"

"I wish the fuck I knew. Truthfully, at this point, we don't have a clue. Have you heard anything yet from your friend in Spain? We really need a lead on why Javier was down here."

"No. I haven't heard from her yet. I know she's working on it, but I don't know how long it might take for her to get any information. If I don't hear anything in the next couple of days, I'll give her a call. I'll let you know what I learn. What about the doubloon?"

"I never said it was a doubloon, did I?"

"No. But that's what everyone in town is saying."

"Yeah, I know. Shit, I might as well tell you. It was a doubloon. It was a genuine, two-escudo coin, minted in Mexico. Those things are rare. Almost a quarter ounce of pure gold! Today, it's worth three times more than the value of the gold just due to its historical significance. You have to wonder why anyone would just leave that lying around."

"Don't suspect one would," I opined. "Maybe the killer dropped it by mistake. Or, maybe Javier had it in his hand, and dropped it when he died."

"Or, maybe," Lieutenant Collins added, "the killer left it there to lead us in the wrong direction. I'm guessing that as soon as we understand why that coin was on the boat, we'll have a good start on figuring this out. Stay in touch."

Chapter Twenty-One
FRUSTRATION

Jill still wasn't back. Seems like she was well on her way to getting the grandbaby to say "Grandma." At least that's the reason she gave for needing to stay. As if she actually needed, or wanted, an excuse. When it comes to her grandchildren, she's all in.

By this point, I had exhausted my culinary repertoire. One day, I had even resorted to whipping up a batch of tuna salad for lunch. I actually thought it was delicious. But a man can only eat so much of his own cooking. Or maybe I just needed a little human interaction. It was starting to get pretty lonely around the house with just the dog to talk to. Or rather, just the dog to talk at. It's been my experience that dogs are generally pretty good companions. The best dogs always seem to understand what you're saying, and can communicate back in some fashion. Maybe it's a look, or a raised ear, or a shake of the tail. Now, our dog is a pleasant enough companion. But she's well past her prime. She's fifteen years old , and she's as deaf as the proverbial doorknob. She can't hear a thing! But her eyesight is still pretty good. So she can stay in touch with what's going on (at least as long as she's awake), but these days she's really not much of a conversationalist.

I decided to bike down to Woody's for lunch. When I walked in, I saw that there were only a couple of other customers. As my eyes adjusted to the dark, I saw none other than our soon-to-be US senator, Carl Perez, sitting at the bar. He turned, recognized me, and waved me over to sit on a stool next to him.

"Hey, Senator. It's good to see you!"

Carl smiled. "Let's keep that quiet for now. It hasn't been officially announced yet. But just between you and me, the announcement is scheduled for next week when the governor returns from his trade mission to Asia.

"It's about time," I exclaimed. "We need to get some common sense up there. The sooner, the better."

"Thanks. I appreciate your confidence in me. Hope I can live up to those expectations. Jim, what's going on with the investigation? I try to keep my ear close to the ground, but it seems to have gone pretty quiet. Last thing I heard was that there might be some connection with buried treasure. You heard anything new?"

"Carl, truth is, I'm starting to get pretty frustrated. From what I understand, there's probably not a connection with buried treasure. I'd be surprised if the sheriff's going down that path anymore. I like Mike Collins a lot, but I don't think he has a clue about where to look next."

"That's too bad. I thought they found a gold coin on the boat."

"Yeah. I think they did find a coin. But the prime suspect they had in mind if the murder was related to pirate treasure has now been cleared. Just my guess, but I suspect the line of inquiry related to the doubloon has come to an end."

I told Carl about the recent fracas up in Boca Grande. He got a big laugh over that.

"I wish I could have been there to see that! Sounds like the local boys haven't forgotten how to deal with a situation that needs dealing with. That kind of thing used to happen around here all the time. But now, not so much. Today, most folks just call the sheriff's office. I probably shouldn't be saying this as a US senator, but I'm glad to hear they've still got it in them! That really makes my day."

I agreed that I, too, would have liked to have seen Big Ed and his boys get their butts kicked."But," I added, "now I don't have any idea who killed Javier. It just seems too far-fetched to believe that anyone from around here would have anything against him. He simply wasn't the type to make enemies. Especially since he had only been here a few days. As far as I could tell, he was everyone's friend."

"There must be something," Carl replied. "Was there anything out of the ordinary while he was here? Did anything happen that was unusual? Was there anyone here that shouldn't have been here? There has to have been some clue that's being overlooked."

"Well, now that you mention it. There was one thing that seemed a little weird. I had almost forgotten about it." I went on to tell Carl about seeing our coworker from New York through the mirror at the Green Flash. "Him being down here at the same time as Javier—that just never made any sense to me. Maybe it was just coincidence. But I know Javier thought it was kind of strange, too. I think I'll start to look into why he was down here."

Carl nodded. I took this as tacit agreement that this should to be looked into.

About that time, Anna came over to see if I was ready to order. "You betcha! I'm starved. Let me have a Perez. But let's substitute a side salad with blue cheese dressing for the fries. And bring me an unsweetened tea."

"That sounds good. You must be hungry. You know how big the Perez is?"

"Indeed, I do. And it's about the best Cuban sandwich I've ever tasted. I love that smoked pork you guys put on it. I don't know anywhere else that actually cooks the pork for a Cuban sandwich right out front in a wood-fired smoker! But don't worry! My plan is to only eat half of it here. I'm going to have you wrap up the other half so I can take it home for lunch tomorrow. I'm swearing off tuna salad and hot dogs.

By the time Anna returned with my tea, Carl had finished his lunch. "Jim, I've got to be running. I need to meet a client in two minutes down at the office. He's in the market for a big house down on the bay. I don't want to be late for that. But let's try to stay in touch about what's going on in the investigation. If you don't think it's getting the attention it deserves, let me know. I'm sure I can help fix that."

"Thanks, Carl. I appreciate it. I'll certainly let you know if I think it needs any attention from the top."

As I ate, Anna waited on a couple of other guys who had come in and taken seats at the other end of the bar. I didn't recognize them, but I pegged them as out-of-town fishermen. When she had their orders, and had brought them a couple of drafts, she came back down to chat with me.

"So, when's Jill coming back? She needs to be here to keep an eye on you. Now that you're starting to hang out at the bar, there's no telling who might try to pick you up."

"Yeah, right. Which of the septuagenarian honeys around here should I be concerned about?"

"You never know. Maybe one of the chicks from the garden club will have one too many and decide to make a pass! I've seen stranger things than that happen here."

"I bet you have," I said, laughing.

"You know Jim, I sure am sorry about Javier. Not a day goes by that I don't think about what a nice guy he was. All of us here miss him."

"Thanks, Anna. I miss him, too. I sure do wish we could figure out who was responsible. I'm not going to rest until we know who did it. But, right now, it sure is frustrating. From what I can tell, the investigation is at a dead end. All that pirate treasure stuff just didn't pan out."

"That's what I heard. A couple of deputies were in late last night, and that's the gist of what I overheard them discussing. Didn't seem like they knew where to look next."

"Yeah. That's the feeling I'm getting, too. We've got someone in Spain trying to figure out why Javier wanted to be here. But, so far, we've gotten nothing. Anna, do me a favor. If you hear anything at the bar that might relate to this, I don't care how insignificant it might seem, I'd very much appreciate it if you would pass it along."

"Jim, you know I will. I want the bastard caught as badly as you do."

"Thanks. Now, what day of the week does the garden club meet?"

"Get out of here, you horny old fool!"

Chapter Twenty-Two
A NEW RUMOR

I piddled around the house the next day, washing the white deck around the house, trimming the trees, picking up fallen palm fronds, and watering the hanging plants. Once that was done, I turned to the important stuff, and made sure that I had the right tackle on each rod. Basically, I was just killing time, but still trying to stay productive, while waiting for Jill to return.

She pulled in about five o'clock. I know she hates to leave the grandchildren. She hadn't been able to spend as much time with them—or with the kids—as she would have liked while we were working in Birmingham. Now she was making up for lost time. I was happy for her. I know the role of grandmother is something she enjoys immensely. And seeing her this happy was something that I enjoyed just as immensely.

Which isn't to say that I wasn't very happy to see her when she got home. Trust me, I was. And it wasn't just so that I could eat her cooking instead of mine. We've had a special relationship for a long time, and it just keeps getting better and better.

When she's away, it's like a part of me is missing. When she's back, I feel complete. I'm pretty sure she feels the same way.

I know for a fact that she loves our house in Saint James City. She knows it's going to be our home for the rest of our lives, and she wants it to be as special as it can be. She's put up pictures of the kids and grandkids, and decorated the house with all kinds of Pine Island stuff and many of the relics that we collected over the years on dozens of vacation trips to the Bahamas, with and without the kids. For example, she framed a chart of the waters around Exuma because that area is special to both of us. On every trip we made to that area, she acquired a unique, hand-made, Bahamian figurine. Now, those colorful artworks are on display throughout the house. They look right here, too. And they certainly remind us of the many unbelievably happy hours we enjoyed in the Bahamas, especially at the Club Peace and Plenty in Georgetown, Exuma.

In my mind, the P&P (as it's called in Georgetown) is the quintessential old Bahamian resort. I'm convinced that the inside bar, located in what was the original house's slave kitchen, is the best bar in the world. It's small, dark, quaint, cozy, old-fashioned, cooled only by trade winds blowing in through wooden shutters, and full of interesting people from all over the world. In the resort's glory days, you would have found celebrities like Ted Williams bellied up in that crowded little space, sharing stories after dinner about the day's catch. Today, you don't find as many celebrities, but you may still find some of the world's most colorful characters. On any given night you may chat with yachtsmen waiting to connect with their boats to make the run south to the islands, or with helicopter pilots ferrying aircraft to the banana republics. We've shared drinks with artists, scientists, drug runners, you name it. The bar is also where all the prominent locals gather every evening. There is simply no telling who you'll meet. It's a great place, for sure. We miss it a lot.

One of the reasons we decided to move to Saint James City is that it reminds us so much of the Bahamian Out Islands—Exuma, Eleuthera, Cat Island, Abaco, Long Island, all places we visited and loved. Anywhere but Nassau—once there was enough. Now we're in Florida's version of the Out Island. We love it here, too.

And I was so happy that Jill was back!

As I helped her carry her bags in, she brought me up to speed on the grandbaby's most recent accomplishments. The child is now sixteen months old and walking everywhere. As her daddy says, "She only has two speeds: on and off." Keeping up with her and monitoring what she is up to is a full time job. A job for a grandmother! Jill was happy to have been able to spend time with her. But she was also happy to be back to our special little place. And I'm pretty sure she was happy to see me, too. At least, the hug she gave me made me think so.

As soon as she was settled, we went out by the pool, Jill with her beer and me with my Scotch. I quickly brought her up to speed on everything that had transpired in the investigation. When I finished, she was as puzzled as I was about where we should look next.

An hour (and several cocktails) later, we decided that neither of us felt like cooking. Consequently, we decided to bike down to Woody's for a quick bite. Once there, it didn't take long for each of us to become involved in conversations with different groups of locals. Anna and Chesley gave Jill big hugs to welcome her back to town, and were soon talking about grandbabies. It wasn't long before she was pulling up pictures on her iPhone, with a whole crowd of ladies gathered around, oohing and ahhing.

I cornered several fishing buddies, and they were soon catching me up on their recent exploits. Hector; Jerry; Bobby, the stone-crab guy; and Grady were all there. Before long, Sea Tow Sammy and Eddie, the electrician, came in as well. Eddie clearly had the evening's top yarn. Just the night before, he had caught almost a dozen of the biggest snook any of us had ever seen. And he had the pictures on his phone to prove it! The biggest of these brutes was over forty-five inches long—that's one hell of a snook! He had used a heavy grouper rod spooled with sixty-pound line and a hundred-pound leader to handle these fish. He told us that he'd simply free-lined palm-sized pin fish under the mangroves, just as the tide was turning out. He told us everything except the exact location he'd fished. And, there are some things you just can't ask.

I had contributed the account of my short-lived battle with the bull shark. It wasn't much of a story, but I did my best to make it sound impressive.

Several of the guys had been down at Froggy's before showing up at Woody's for dinner, as is the custom among many of the locals. (Did I mention that Saint James City is sometimes referred to as "a quaint fishing village with a drinking problem"?) When the locals get off work, Froggy's starts to fill up. The bar does its part by featuring an attractively priced happy hour. And without question, it's where most of the island's gossip is exchanged.

It's really true what they say about the "island telegraph." On small islands, where everyone knows everyone else, and where bars and beverages in the afternoon help to offset the boredom and monotony of island routine, it's normal for news to be passed from person to person in an extremely short period of time. We had observed it in the Bahamas, and it's just as true in Saint James City. Here, Froggy's is the island's switchboard though which any rumor, story, or gossip worth its salt is quickly passed. From there, who knows where the news would travel?

That night, some of it had traveled to Woody's. It wasn't long before the talk of fishing turned to news about the investigation into Javier's murder. I contributed what I knew, and everyone nodded solemnly.

As soon as I finished, Eddie, the electrician, said, "I guess it makes sense that the treasure story really didn't pan out. What I'm hearing now is that Javier's murder may have had something to do with gold that was hidden up on Punta Blanca Island by Barron Collier just before he died. I heard that down at Froggy's. I don't remember who told me, but I think the guy who told me said that the guy who told him said that he had heard it earlier in the night from someone over at Low Key. Anyway, the story I heard was that Javier knew about a bunch of gold that Collier had buried on Punta Blanca. But then he got crossed up with a group that was down from New York trying to recover it. According to this guy, that's who killed him."

"Whoa," I said. "What the hell is this about? First, it was gold buried by pirates, and now it's gold buried by a long-dead tycoon? This is fucking weird! Has anyone else heard about this?"

Hector spoke up. "I wasn't at Froggy's, but I did hear the same thing while I was at the marina cleaning my boat. Old Will Yearty stopped by to gas up his boat, and we talked. I think he might have also been at Low Key for a while. He usually goes up there to have a couple of beers when he finishes with a charter. He told me that someone there said that he'd heard that Javier's death might have had something to with gold on Punta Blanca."

"Hector, what made him think there could be something behind this?"

"Well, Will's a pretty smart guy. And he likes history a lot. I know that he hangs around at the Island Museum whenever he doesn't have a charter. According to him, it's pretty well known that Old Man Collier was stashing away gold before he died. You know, at one time, he was one of the richest men in the world. But in the Great Depression, having invested in Florida real estate during the land boom and being heavily invested in the stock market before the crash, he lost a ton of money. According to Will, Collier was scared to death that the government wasn't going to be able to save the economy. He was worried that all the banks were going to fail, and consequently, he was putting away as much as he could in gold, just in case that happened. I don't know any more than that. But I do know that Collier once owned all of Punta Blanca. I don't remember if I told you, but that's where I found Javier's body."

"Yeah, that's right. He was anchored about halfway between Punta Blanca and Cayo Costa, wasn't he?"

"Yep. You know, this is getting to be kind of strange."

"Yeah. It sure is."

With that, conversation stopped. I guess the reality of Javier's death and the realization that a killer was still roaming among us made fish stories seem inappropriate.

We all settled our tabs, and went home.

Chapter Twenty-Three

CRIME FROM THE PAST, FEAR FROM TODAY

The next morning, I phoned Mike Collins. When he answered, he already knew who was calling. Made sense that he'd have caller ID.

"Hey, Jim! What's up? You got any news yet from Spain?"

No. Wish I did, but my source hasn't called. When we get through, I'll give her a call. I'll let you know what I find out. But that's not why I'm calling. I want to pass along the latest rumor that's going around Saint James City. Jill and I were at Woody's last night, and some of the guys who'd been at Froggy's came in and started telling us that they'd heard from various sources that Javier's death is somehow related to gold that Barron Collier buried on Punta Blanca Island. Supposedly, Javier got crossways with some folks from New York who were down here trying to find that gold, and they took him out."

"Jeez. First it's pirate treasure, and now it's Collier's long-lost hidden fortune! Can this get any more fucking bizarre?

Used to be, all I had to solve were simple gang-banger disputes over drug territory, or maybe clean up love triangles where the aggrieved party decided to settle the score. In any case, it wasn't hard to figure out the motive, and decide who had pulled the trigger. Might make you sick at your stomach occasionally, but nothing that caused a lot of stress. Just, simple plodding, "Book 'em, Dano," kind of crime-solving. Now, I've got a case where someone from the other side of the world is rubbed out in the middle of the frickin bay with no witnesses because he's pursuing something his long-dead relatives may or may not have known about something that we don't even have a clue about! If this story gets out, I'll have CNN, Fox, you name it, all down here demanding updates. Hell, it wouldn't surprise me if we didn't get Geraldo, himself, down here. He'd probably hire the *Pieces of Eight* over at Matanzas Pass, dress up like a pirate, and do nightly newscasts from the poop deck while sailing around the fucking bay! Damn. We've got to get this thing solved. Jim, you get on the line to Spain. I'm going to do some research on Collier, and in the meantime, I'll get some of the boys out to Punta Blanca. Shit, at least it'll give them something to do, other than harassing poor guys that are just trying to go fishing, while they're waiting to have lunch at the Waterfront. Speaking of the Waterfront, why don't we meet there at noon tomorrow? That'll give you time to touch base with Spain, and give me time to dig up some information about Collier and Punta Blanca."

"Sounds like a plan. I'll see you there."

Once we hung up, I called Arantxa in Spain. Through the miracle of cell phones she answered immediately.

I took the portable phone outside to the pool deck, and settled into a wicker chair for what I hoped would be a pleasant and productive conversation.

"Jim! It is so good to hear from you. I was just getting ready to call you. I drove back a few hours ago from visiting Javier's mother in Salamanca. I actually spent a couple of days with her. She is a lovely lady, so traditional in her manners and customs. In some ways, it was like taking a step back in time to spend a few days with her in that beautiful, old city. I absolutely adored her, and I feel so sorry for her. Javier was her only son, and it's obvious that he meant the world to her. It's clear where Javier got his demeanor and his manners. I let her know that many others also miss him. It obviously meant a lot to her to hear that. I didn't like that I was really there to pry information out of her that she clearly was reluctant to share with the police."

"Arantxa, I'm sorry. I know that could not have been easy for you. But we need help to find out who killed Javier. So far, nothing is making sense. To get to the bottom of why he was killed, we need to know why he came here."

"I know, I know. I decided after meeting Senora Hernandez that I couldn't try to deceive her. I decided, instead, that I should simply tell her the truth, tell her who you are and why we need the information. I don't know if that was the best thing to do or not. But she was the kind of lady that I could never have felt good about trying to deceive. I think she appreciated me being upfront with her. In the end, she gave me some information that I think may be helpful, but I'm convinced that she did not tell me everything she knows about why Javier was with you."

"Damn. Why do you think she won't come forward with information that might help us find her son's killer? That just doesn't make sense."

"I know. It didn't make sense to me either, at first. But I'm pretty sure that she does not trust law enforcement in the United States. I believe she even thinks that the police may have been involved in Javier's murder."

"Arantxa, that's crazy! Why on earth would she think that?"

"Let me start from the beginning. Javier's great-grandfather was a very important person in the Spanish Guardia Civil, that's our national police system. When he retired, he held the rank of general, and had responsibility for policing the entire Region of Leon, the district of Northwestern Spain that includes Salamanca. In his younger years, he was a rising star in the Spanish gendarmerie. He graduated with honors from the University of Salamanca, and joined the force upon graduation. He rose through the ranks quickly, and was so highly thought of that he was sent to Cuba in 1910 at the age of thirty to work as a consultant with the American authorities who were then helping the Cubans establish a new national police system. His job was to serve as a liaison between the Americans and the Cubans, to help the Americans understand the subtleties of the Latin culture, to help the Cubans put up with the Americans, and, all the while, to keep an eye on things for Madrid. It was a very prestigious assignment. His selection to fill this role came from the very top of the Guardia Civil, and it was personally approved by the king. He was clearly a man destined for bigger, and better, things. His assignment in Cuba lasted four years. He returned in 1914, after what was reportedly a successful mission.

Upon his return, he was recognized by the Crown for his contributions, and promoted to the rank of major. He married in 1916, and their first son was born in 1918—Javier's grandfather. According to Senora Hernandez, Javier's great-grandfather avoided the periodic scandals that plagued the organization, and managed to stay on the right side of Spanish politics, which certainly wasn't easy. He retired shortly before the Civil War, and moved with his wife to a villa outside Salamanca. It was there that he died in his sleep, at the age of seventy-six. An honorable life, and a life well lived."

"OK, Arantxa. That's interesting, but where's the connection? I don't see anything there that links to treasure, or, for that matter, to anything else that would have gotten Javier killed."

"Hold on, Jim. Quit acting so much like a silly American. You Americans are always so impatient to get to the point. Let me tell the story my way. Apparently, when Senor Hernandez was in Cuba, there was a sensational murder of an important American businessman. One of the things that made this murder so sensational was that a considerable amount of gold was rumored to have been stolen when the businessman was murdered. That gold was never recovered. Apparently, Javier's great-grandfather suspected an American of committing the murder. However, he was overruled by the authorities, who did not want an American to be blamed for the murder. Mrs. Hernandez said that she never knew for sure why the American police wanted a Cuban national to be found guilty of the crime. She did say, however, that the political situation in Cuba at that time was very unstable. According to her, at that time there were some in the United States who wanted to make Cuba an American state, and others who wanted nothing to do with Cuba and who wanted the United States to withdraw from the island as soon as possible. Still others liked things just the way they were. They were delighted to take advantage of the turmoil on the island so that they could profit by developing Cuba as they saw fit, without having to be overly concerned with abiding by America's laws. To many, Cuba was the next great frontier. In Cuba, too, people were on all sides of these issues. And everyone, on every side, suspected the Spanish of trying to destabilize the situation so they could find a way to take back their former colony. After all, it was a place that the Spanish still felt rightfully belonged to them.

"With respect to the murder, despite the best efforts of Captain Hernandez, a Cuban fisherman was eventually convicted of the crime, and executed by firing squad just a few days later. The appeals process for capital crimes that was specified in Cuba's constitution was not followed in this case. But this wasn't so unusual then, given that the judicial system was in such a state of turmoil. The fisherman was quietly laid to rest, and the crime was soon forgotten.

"But, according to Senora Hernandez, Javier's great-grandfather never forgot this crime, and he never forgave those who had been responsible for convicting the fisherman. To him, it was always clear that the wrong man had intentionally been accused and convicted. He passed this story along to his son, who passed it on to Javier's father, who eventually told it to Javier. Javier's mother said that the dying wish of General Hernandez was that the true killer would be brought to justice. And on his death bed, he had warned the family to never, ever, trust the American police. He thought they had, at the very least, badly botched the investigation. But Senora Hernandez thinks that what he really believed was that the Americans had intentionally covered up the crime and sent an innocent man to his death, just to keep America from getting a black eye. Now, as a result, Senora Hernandez does not trust the American criminal justice system. She suspects that even after all these years, the American authorities might have been responsible for Javier's death. Therefore, she will not cooperate with the authorities.

"Jim, that is all I know. I will keep working to see what more I can learn, and I'll let you know if I find out anything else. I'm sorry I don't have any more information, but hopefully, this will be a start. Jim, I don't want to offend you, but I think that you need to be very careful. Senora Hernandez is convinced that there are important people in the American government who will kill to keep the truth about this crime from coming out. And, clearly, if they'd kill Javier, there's no reason they wouldn't kill you, too. I don't want to lose another good friend. Please be careful."

"Arantxa, this is great information. Thanks for your help. Look, I promise, I'll keep my head down. You need to be careful, too. I'll keep your name out of this. I won't let the sheriff's office here know where this information is coming from. Who knows who might be keeping an eye of both of us? I'll give you a call in a couple of days to see if you've been able to learn anything else."

I hung up, set the phone down, and stared at it. What the heck was going on? What had we stumbled into? A century-old murder that our government had covered up—and possibly was still covering up? Was this somehow connected with the Collier family and with the gold supposedly buried on Punta Blanca? A cold chill gradually spread up my spine. I gave my shoulders a good shake, and turned my head from side to side, trying to get rid of the sensation. I only partially succeeded. This was starting to get really spooky! Whose side was the sheriff really on? Was the federal government involved? Were Jill and I being targeted? Were the Colliers behind this? They are still one of the most powerful families in Florida. Was there something that they didn't want everyone to know about their past? Whoever, and whatever, it was clear that someone was willing to go to any length to keep this quiet.

That cold chill was still with me. I went inside, and locked all the doors. It was definitely time for a Scotch, and, not just any Scotch. Rather than my usual inexpensive, pre-dinner blend, I needed something stronger, something more bracing, something with some heat in it to warm the cold fear that was lodged in my spine. This called for a Lagavulin—sixteen years old when I bought it eight years ago—in a tumbler half full of liquor with only one cube of ice. A proper drink to think over. I opened the Scotch cabinet.

Chapter Twenty-Four

AN AMERICAN TYCOON—
A FLORIDA LEGEND

Sitting on the screened porch, savoring the last of the bracing drink, I told Jill what Arantxa had learned. We agreed it was time we do some research on Punta Blanca Island and on the Collier family. We retired to the little office that overlooks the pool, and fired up the computer.

The Internet is truly an amazing thing. It didn't take long for us to find some fascinating information about the Colliers. All Americans have heard of Rockefeller. They know about Carnegie, Mellon, Morgan, Edison, and Ford. But relatively few know the story of Barron Gift Collier, and that is our loss. Today, if you mention Barron Collier, most people would think that he was a displaced European aristocrat who somehow found his way to Florida in the early days of the last century. But they would be wrong. In his day, Collier was one of America's greatest success stories. He was a man who made millions, but unlike some of the robber barons of the Gilded Age, he was a man who enjoyed a reputation for fairness, for even-dealing, for being law abiding, and for going out of his way to treat his employees with kindness and respect. He was a common man who built a hugely successful company, not by coming up with a unique invention, or by using an advantageous monopoly position. Rather, he had prospered by looking at what already existed in plain sight, and then transforming it from mediocrity into a hugely successful money-making machine. In the process, he developed what today is one of our largest industries: mass marketing. He was a plain man, but a man blessed with common sense and vision. He had the ability to peer through the dust of commerce and find the nugget of value that was obscured within. By the time he was twenty-six years old, he was already a millionaire—and that was when a million dollars was real money! A million then would be worth over fifty million dollars today. Collier was not just a successful businessman. Far from it. His interests, and his energies, were aimed beyond the daily routine of buying and selling. He was a founding member of the Boy Scouts of America. He was also a founding member of INTERPOL, the international police organization, and he was responsible for getting America to agree to join it. He served as deputy commissioner for the New York City Policy Department. He advised many US presidents, and, before his death, he had received the highest honors from all of the most important countries in the world. Barron Gift Collier was indeed a remarkable man.

He was born in 1873 in Memphis, Tennessee. As a boy, he was bright and ambitious. At sixteen, he quit school to go to work for the Illinois Central Railroad, selling advertising. Four years later, on one of his journeys, he ran into a man who had invented a gasoline-powered streetlight system. He liked the idea, returned home, and sold the system to his hometown of Memphis. He used the capital raised from this sale to finance his next venture, the purchase of a struggling printing plant in Memphis. He used his energy and vision to transform this company, and in a short period of time, he had turned it into one of the country's greatest marketing enterprises. Prior to Collier's ownership, the printing company had pursued a limited business model—printing advertising placards to be displayed on the sides of horse-drawn trolleys in the Memphis area. Collier used the company as a springboard for creating a truly unified marketing model. His vision was that his company would control all aspects of the advertising process: he would sell the ads, print the placards, and place them on streetcars across the country. He understood that by combining all aspects of marketing under one umbrella, he could charge the companies that were advertising, and pay streetcar companies for the use of the space on the sides of their cars. This unified approach revolutionized the marketing model. Soon he had franchises in seventy large US cities, as well as in major cities in Canada and Cuba. As time went on, he expanded his enterprise beyond just advertising. Eventually, his empire included hotels, banks, bus lines, newspapers, a telephone company, and a steamship line. In addition, and of relevance to our inquiry, he purchased over a million acres in Southwest Florida.

In 1911, he and his wife visited Fort Myers. They fell deeply in love with the area. His first Florida purchase was Useppa Island in the northern part of Pine Island Sound. Collier purchased the island from a business acquaintance, a man who owned a streetcar company in Chicago where Collier had placed advertising. This friend had developed the island as a winter retreat for his family. Collier's idea was to open up Southwest Florida more broadly. His vision was to start by creating on Useppa Island the world's most exclusive sporting club and resort. In typical Collier fashion, he spared no expense in bringing his vision to reality. Soon, he had transformed the island from a simple vacation retreat into a world-class destination for privileged sportsmen. He dredged deepwater channels that led to a harbor that he dug out of shallow, grass flats. In the harbor, he built first-class dockage to accommodate even the largest yachts of his expected guests. To give his clients something to do when they were not fishing, he carved a professional quality golf course out of the island's mangrove swamps. For guest accommodations, he constructed dozens of beautiful, luxurious, tropical-style homes. For his own residence, he built a beautiful manor with unobstructed views of the island's harbor and the sound. This mansion also served as the clubhouse for the Izaak Walton Fly Fishing Club, named after the seventeenth-century British author of *The Compleat Angler*. Collier also purchased most of the surrounding islands, and configured them to provide services and supplies for the Useppa resort and its guests. For example, on neighboring Punta Blanca Island, he dredged a sheltered, deep-water harbor, and constructed boat-maintenance facilities of sufficient size and capability to overhaul yachts of any size. To get those yachts out of the water and into the maintenance buildings, he built three marine railways, each big enough to accommodate the largest yachts of the day. To support this marine works, he even constructed his own foundry, and installed a complete machine shop. He wanted to ensure that any parts needed to repair a boat could be manufactured on site, if necessary.

He knew that he would need workers, and that it would not be practical for them to commute from the mainland. He also knew that they would not be happy if forced to live in temporary housing away from their families. Therefore, on his islands he built complete towns, providing not only housing but the key services his employees would need to live comfortably. On Punta Blanca, for instance, he built a large school to serve the children on all of the surrounding islands, whether or not their parents were his employees. There was also a church, a post office, and a general store.

Collier purchased Patricio Island, about a mile northeast of Useppa, and transformed it from a barren, scrub-covered wasteland into a farm to provide fruit, vegetables, chickens, and milk for the resort's use.

Of Collier, it was said, "He was not a man that dreamed small dreams!"

Useppa and the surrounding complex was only the start of Collier's transformative plans for Southwest Florida. It wasn't long before he owned over one million acres of land in the area, becoming Florida's largest landowner- by far. His vision was to develop Southwest Florida so that people from all walks of life, not just the wealthy, would be able to visit and live there, enjoying the same beauty and weather that he and his wife loved so much. To this end, he developed the town of Everglades City from scratch. Not only did he build the town, he even dug a ten-mile long channel to the gulf to ensure that the city could be conveniently reached by water. The buildings he constructed included a hotel, a marina, a bank, a church, a municipal building, a store, a water plant, an ice plant, and an electricity-generating facility.

But he didn't stop there. He knew that for his vision to be fulfilled, there would need to be easy access to the area, not only by boat, but by rail, and later, by automobile. He knew he would eventually need transportation from the relatively small and remote city of Tampa, and more importantly from the east coast of Florida, across the very heart of the Everglades. In short order, he arranged to have the Atlantic Coast Line Railroad extend its tracks sixty miles south from Punta Gorda to Everglades City. Then, he rescued Florida's financially strapped Tamiami Trail project, and, at his own expense, completed construction of the highway across the Everglades. This project took five years to complete. At the time it was hailed as one of the world's greatest engineering accomplishments. This highway made it possible for one to drive all the way from Tampa to Miami. It literally opened Southwest Florida to the world. No other individual did as much to put Southwest Florida on the map, and to make it accessible, than Barron Collier. Even today, his descendants are still among the state's most prominent residents, and their companies are among the state's most important and profitable.

As gifted and as visionary as Collier was, however, he couldn't escape the ravages of the Great Depression. Eventually, the cash flow from his advertising empire began to dry up as business ground to a halt across the country in the early 1930s. By the middle of the decade, his companies were deeply in debt and unable to service their obligations. He spent the last five years of his life negotiating with creditors. It was rumored that Collier was reduced to relying on the pennies from his gumball franchise in the subways of New York City for his family's personal cash flow. Eventually, he was forced to close the Useppa Island resort and all of the supporting islands. Characteristically, rather than displacing the staff who lived on those islands, he allowed them the choice of continuing to live there or moving the houses in which they lived to the mainland. He, his wife, and their three sons retired to the big house on Useppa Island. But rather than being able to enjoy a well-earned retirement, Collier died of a heart attack in 1939. Given the complexity of his vast holdings, it took many years for the affairs of his estate to be settled. Many surmised that, given the debt-servicing issues of his companies, Collier died nearly destitute. But when the estate was finally closed, he'd left a considerable fortune and huge land holdings to his heirs.

There was never a question that Collier was blessed with great vision. He was a consultant to presidents, kings, and prime ministers around the world. He certainly was a man who could understand what was going on around the world, and a man who could anticipate what that would mean in years to come. He did not shrink from taking action when action was required. Without doubt, he would have understood that Roosevelt's passage of the Gold Reserve Act of 1934, which unlinked the US dollar from the value of gold, and which required that all private gold holdings in the United States be exchanged for Federal Reserve gold certificates, was a precursor to the eventual devaluation of the dollar. Collier was a man who would have understood what was to come, and would have taken action to protect his family's wealth from inevitable erosion. His property holdings were one hedge against that outcome. But these holdings were not liquid. He would have understood that, at a minimum, it would take decades before it would be possible to realize their true value. He was the type of man who would have taken the steps necessary to hedge the value of his financial assets by transforming them from US dollars into gold. But would he have stockpiled that gold on a remote island? Did that explain why he and his family abandoned New York, and moved to Useppa? Did that explain some of his severe cash-flow problems toward the end of his life?

If he had taken these steps, was that gold still buried on Punta Blanca Island? And did that explain why someone had killed Javier? Had Javier somehow gotten in the way of a group, rumored to have been from New York, that was on Punta Blanca searching for this gold? And was our mutual acquaintance from my bank's New York office, the guy whom I had seen at the Green Flash, involved? Was he, in fact, responsible for Javier's murder?

Or was something else going on? At this point, the chill returned to my spine. Javier's great-grandfather apparently had suspected that an American had murdered another American businessman in Cuba, and had stolen a fortune in gold. Collier had business interests in Cuba at that time. Was he, or a member of his family or his company, involved in this murder? Was that why the US government wanted the blame shifted to a Cuban fisherman? Was that why the fisherman was convicted and executed so quickly? Was the connection to the Colliers the knowledge that Javier had brought with him from Spain? Was this what had gotten him killed? Was the most important and powerful family in Florida involved in Javier's murder?

At this point, my appreciation for the second glass I had poured of that wonderful, old Lagavulin disappeared. I could no longer appreciate its warmth, its smokiness, and its subtle tang of sea salt. It might as well have been a cheap, bottom-shelf blend. The chill in my spine would not go away no matter how many times I turned my head and shrugged my shoulders. No matter how many sips of Scotch I had. Quite simply, I was scared. Jill and I looked at each other, and simultaneously said, "Oh, shit!"

She was scared, too.

Chapter Twenty-Five
A GLORIOUS MORNING

The next morning, we awoke to what I can only describe as a glorious day. After our scare the night before, we were glad just to wake up. Beyond that, this particular morning was one of those Southwest Florida days that must have enticed Collier and his wife to fall in love with the area. During the night, a weak cold front had passed through, and the morning temperature was a pleasant sixty-five degrees. The sky was a perfect light blue, and from horizon to horizon, there were no clouds to be seen. The breeze was slightly stronger than normal, and during the night it had swung around to come from the northwest, but it never blew stronger than ten miles per hour. The sun was bright, and the water sparkled. You couldn't imagine a more beautiful day.

I took Cody out for her morning stroll, fortified by my customary cup of black tea, and armed with an ample supply of doggie bags. We ran into many of the canine/human pairs that we commonly encounter on similar missions. Without fail, we exchange cheerful "good mornings," and always wish each other a nice day. Saint James City is, indeed, a pleasant place to walk your dog.

Given that fall was approaching, the first of our winter residents were trickling into town. Each day, as we walked around our neighborhood, we'd notice another house with the hurricane shutters removed and a car parked outside. Occasionally, we would encounter these new arrivals. Many were walking their animals, as well. This influx of new neighbors allowed our greeting ritual to be varied. With new folks (and dogs), the routine invariably involved standing at a slight distance as we allowed the dogs to decide whether they liked each other. If their tails were wagging, then we'd walk a little closer, and chat. If all was still going well, we would then introduce the dogs. "Hi! This is Cody."

"Hi, Cody. This is Harvey."

Usually, we would chat for a few minutes, talking about the dogs and how they were doing. I know it sounds funny, but only rarely would we introduce ourselves. I guess that just seems too intrusive—getting to know each other's dogs is a safer first step in getting to know each other. After a few meetings, if we liked each other as humans, we might exchange names—or not. Somehow, it just doesn't seem important down here.

I just couldn't get over how beautiful the morning was. Normally, on a day like that, we might be packing the boat, and heading out on the sound. We'd get in four hours of fishing, and then head to a local restaurant for lunch. Which restaurant depended mostly on which fishing area we had decided to try, a decision in turn influenced by the direction of the wind.

The sound generally runs north to south, and in the summer our winds normally blow from the east in the morning (a land breeze), and from the west in the afternoon (a sea breeze). Only when a front approaches, or has passed, does that pattern change. Normally, these changes persist for only a few days. As a front approaches, the wind direction moves in clockwise around the compass. Just before the front arrives, the wind will normally be out of the southwest, and it will be gaining speed. But as the front comes through, the wind begins to blow strongly out of the northwest. Then, as the front passes to the east, the wind direction will gradually move back to our usual east/west wind pattern. Therefore, absent a front coming through, I try to fish the east side of the sound in the morning, and the west side in the afternoon. Normally, I'm out there just drifting over the grass flats and jerking on my rods to make the popping corks pop. That's what makes me happy.

That day, we didn't take the boat out. Since I had to meet Lieutenant Collins at the Waterfront, we needed to stay close to home. So, rather than loading the boat, I was sitting on the porch deck, drinking a second cup of tea and reading the paper. About the time I got to the sports section, one of my neighbors came by in his boat. We waved at each other, and joked about how many fish he was going to catch as he motored slowly on down the canal. Man, I envied him. It was going to be a glorious day on the sound.

But, I wasn't going fishing. After the tea was gone, I headed outside to tend to some yard work that I had neglected. In our yard, about the only type of work we have to do involves palm trees. Our yard has no grass, only rocks. But we've got about palm trees. Best I can tell, we have eight different varieties. There are a couple of coconut palms, several royal palms, at least eight queens that line the drive, a fox tail, several clusters of king palms, two types I haven't been able to identify yet, and a bunch of pigmy date palms. Speaking of pigmy date palms, I hate those things. If you ever get the chance, carefully take a look at the base of the fronds of those palms. There, you will find thorns at least two inches long and as sharp as hypodermic needles. Dealing with them requires care. That was the task I had assigned myself for the day. The ones in our yard badly needed pruning. One of the things that make this type of palm attractive is that when it is neatly pruned, you can see its twisting, curved trunk covered in what looks like course hair. But to be able to see the trunk, you've got to keep the dead leaves trimmed off, and that requires dealing with those damn thorns. As far as I know, the only way to get the job done is to stick your head under the tree, and use a pruning shear to cut them off, one by one. If you're lucky, you won't puncture yourself in the process. Today, the pruning went fairly well. I only suffered two needle wounds in my arms—relatively minor, as these things go, and the blood flow was minimal. The toughest part, though, is having to pick these nasty things up to take them to the refuse pile at the street. You need great gloves, and you have to hold the dead fronds well away from your body. A couple of hours later, after some sweat and quite a few loud curses, the pigmies were finally looking good.

I then moved on to removing ripe coconuts from the coconut palms. In Florida, you need to take care that you don't allow a coconut to fall from a tree and hit something, or someone. Those darned things are heavy—husk and all, they must weigh about five pounds. If a coconut falls on something, it's going to leave a mark. Therefore, it's a good idea to prune them before they get ripe enough to fall.

Mature coconut palms can be very tall. To remove the potentially lethal nuts from tall trees, you'll probably need some type of mechanical lift, or crane. Fortunately, my trees haven't gotten that large yet. I'm still able to use a ladder and a twelve-foot, extendable pole with a pruning saw attached to the end. With this, I'm just barely able to reach the nuts at the crown of the tree. That day, after twenty minutes of diligent sawing, I had managed to get all the ripe nuts on the ground, along with associated leaves, stalks, and other debris. All was going well until I started to pick up this stuff to take it to the street. As I lifted one especially large clump of nuts, out crawled a large snake, obviously upset that I had interrupted its siesta in the tree. Fortunately, it went one way, while I went the other. I hate snakes. In this case, I think it was clear that I was a lot more frightened of it than it was of me. It calmly turned, wiggled back to the palm, and began to climb the trunk, heading upward absolutely vertically. It beats me how they can do that. As far as I know, the snake is still in that tree. At least I hope so, and I hope it stays there. I hate snakes.

Snakes aside, I think it's fair to say that the morning's labors had helped to get my mind off of the previous evening's research. I normally don't enjoy yard work, but with the weather as beautiful as it was, I was glad, despite my encounter with the snake, to have been outside. On a day like that, time passes quickly. So I was surprised and a little disappointed when I looked at my watch and saw that it was time to clean up to have lunch with Lieutenant Collins.

A few minutes before twelve, I pushed off on my bike, pedaling slowly. Reflecting upon the remote possibility that my life might actually be in danger, I took care to slow down before I ran through the few stop signs on the streets I have to cross to get to the restaurant. Take all possible precautions—what else was there for me to do?

Collins was leaning against the rail on the back deck when I arrived. He waved me over, and we went to the end table, far away from the other guests who had arrived for their daily grouper fix.

"Story, you OK?" Collins asked. "What's with all the Band-Aids? Big Ed didn't have a go at you with a knife, did he?"

"Oh, those. I was trimming pigmy date palms this morning. They got their licks in, but I eventually prevailed," I explained.

"I hate those damn things," Collins agreed. "Once I learned what they were about, I had everyone of them pulled out of my yard. But I'm not very bright. Guess what I replaced them with? Bougainvillea! How can anyone be that stupid? At least they look great when they bloom. Just don't try to prune them."

"I know," I replied. "I've got them all over my yard, too. My strategy with them is to prune them regularly and often, so that the thorns I have to deal with are small. You don't want to wait until you have to wade into a thicket of those things. That might be fatal."

"Yeah, you're right about that. Speaking of fatal, you learn anything yet from Spain?"

"I sure did. I learned a lot of really interesting stuff, including the fact that Javier's mother suspects the sheriff's department of having killed her son!"

"Oh, fuck! Just when I thought this deal couldn't possibly get any more bizarre. Why the hell would she think we were in the business of whacking vacationing Spaniards? I don't even want to put that in the damn report! The sheriff reads that, and he'll make me the laughing stock of the whole damned department. I'd never live that down."

"Let me start from the beginning."

I quickly summarized what I had learned from Arantxa, taking care not to mention her name. "My source is going to keep working with Javier's mother to see if she can find out more about this. But we're not sure that Senora Hernandez actually knows much more. It sounded to me like this story may have been pretty much kept to the men in the family, and she simply wasn't privy to many details."

"Wow! That's pretty interesting. That sure could be a reason why Javier was killed. He comes over here, starts poking around, and somebody gets nervous, and decides to shut him up. But come on! We're talking about something that happened a century ago. Everyone involved has been dead a long time. Why would anyone care after all this time?"

"I don't know. But it must still be important today to someone. I know this is pretty far-fetched, but do you think this might be connected with the gold that was supposedly hidden on Punta Blanca? Do you think the Colliers might be involved, somehow? Would they be willing to have someone killed to keep their family's name from being dragged through the mud? Or could it have something to do with the group from New York?"

"Fuck if I know. But I do know one thing. It's not going to be me who goes down to Naples, knocks on the Colliers' front door, and asks if they recently killed someone. That would likely result in my very quick return to the rank of junior patrol officer, assigned to pulling over drunks on the midnight shift. Besides, it's just not possible that the Colliers killed someone. These are the most respectable people in the whole damn state. No, there's got to be something else."

Lieutenant Collins continued, "Let me tell you what I've learned. First, we had a couple of our guys out on Punta Blanca. You're not going to believe this. First, they took their boat out to the island, and just drove around it. It didn't take them long to find tracks on the southwest side of the island that led from the water up into the middle of what must have been the old settlement. They followed the tracks, and eventually found signs that someone had recently dug a hole. And you'll never guess what was lying on the ground right next to the frickin hole!"

"Don't tell me," I said, laughing. "I bet it was another doubloon!"

"Close. It wasn't a doubloon. But it was another gold coin. This time, a 1910 American Indian Head Eagle. These were only minted between 1907 and 1916. It's almost a half an ounce of pure gold."

"Wow. This keeps getting crazier and crazier," I said.

"Couldn't agree more. But it's starting to get real interesting, too. I asked the folks at the Lee County Library system if they could get me a report on the Colliers and their connection with

Punta Blanca. They sent it to me this morning, and I was reading through it before you came. I'll give you the highlights."

Collins went through a lot of the same information that Jill and I had found the night before on the web. I could tell, though, that a lot of what he learned was as new to him as it had been to us. He had a little more information on Punta Blanca Island than what Jill and I had been able to discover. Specifically, he had learned what happened to it after Collier died.

"With the Great Depression, Collier quickly closed the boat works on the island. The school and the homes were still there, and the little town continued to exist. It actually wasn't until 1949, ten years after Collier died, that Lee County made the decision to close the school and start transporting students to the mainland by boat. The island has pretty much been left undisturbed since then. I'm not sure yet when the Collier family sold the island. I do know that in the late 1970s, the south end of the island was sold by a Matt Hughes to the state. The north end of the island was given to the state by the federal government in 1985."

"That's not a lot to go on," I said.

"Yeah. I know. But it's all we've got. The way I see it, if the Colliers sold the island fifty or sixty years ago, it's unlikely that they would suddenly become interested in a fortune supposedly buried out there."

"I have to agree with you on that one. That doesn't seem very likely. But where does that leave us?"

"It looks to me like we've only got three possibilities. One, maybe someone from New York somehow stumbled across an old record, maybe in a bank vault, that showed there was gold buried on Punta Blanca. Maybe Javier knew something about this, too. And maybe he got killed for getting in the way. Two, maybe the Colliers were involved years ago in the deal in Cuba, and decided they had to shut Javier up to keep him from ruining the family name. Or three, maybe there is something else—something that we don't yet know anything about. I don't like the first two choices. The first one just seems too damn convenient. The second one seems too unlikely, and certainly out of character. If I were a betting man, which I'm not, I'd put my money on the last option."

"That makes sense to me," I said. "But, for what it's worth, let me tell you about something strange that happened over on Captiva when Javier, Jill, and I were having lunch there shortly before he was killed. Do you know about the one-way mirror over the urinals in the Green Flash men's room?"

"Yeah. I laugh every time I go in there to take a whiz. It reminds me of all the trick glass we've got over at the Justice complex. But what does this have to do with who killed Javier?"

"Well. It was like this. I was taking a piss when I saw a guy come in and take a seat at the end of the bar. It surprised the heck out of me because this guy's an acquaintance who works for the same bank I used to work for. And, I might add, not one of my favorite people. He's a guy who, over the years, screwed over a lot of people, and made a lot of bad decisions. Javier didn't care for him, either. Frankly, he's not a guy I ever want to shake hands with again. So, I hid out in a stall for a couple of minutes. A few minutes later, when I looked through the mirror again, he was gone."

"That's it?"

"Yeah. Not much, but it sure seemed strange to bump into this guy down here like that. I never knew him to come down this way. It's probably just a coincidence. But I never like to assume away things like this. Maybe he was part of the group from New York that was down here looking for gold. I wouldn't put it past him. I think I know a way to check up on why he was really here. It should only take me a day or two."

"OK. Why don't you run that down? I'm going to have our guys keep poking around out on Punta Blanca. We're also checking on that coin, but I don't expect much from that. Things like that are impossible to trace. What I really want to look into is what happened in Cuba a century ago. There have to be records somewhere. Maybe the old Havana newspaper files would have something. We may even need to get the State Department's help. Regardless, we still need to try to find out what happened back then. Once we understand that, maybe we'll know how all this tied back to Javier. I'm also going to touch base with the Colliers to see what they can tell me. I actually went to school with one of the great-grandsons. Nice guy. He and I were pretty good friends back then."

"I like the plan. I'll touch base with you tomorrow, and let you know if I've learned anything from either New York or Madrid."

"Sounds good. Talk to you tomorrow."

Chapter Twenty-Six
THE ISLAND TELEGRAPH

One of many great things about living in Saint James City is that nothing is very far away. Jill and I had agreed to meet at Woody's when I got through with Lieutenant Collins. I walked out the front door, pulled my bike from the rack in the palms, and headed north on Oleander. Two and a half minutes later, I pedaled into the parking lot at Woody's. Jill's SUV was already there.

Another great thing about Saint James City is that it doesn't take long to recognize the vehicles that the folks around town drive. For example, as I pedaled into the parking lot, I noticed the golf cart that belongs to Barbee, a mildly handicapped woman who operates a small produce stand a couple of hundred yards up the road. Everyone in town knows her and likes her—not only for her produce, but also for the singing act she performs at Woody's every other Friday night. The musician who has been playing that gig for over twenty years always invites Barbee to join him for a rendition of Sam the Shams' "Hey There, Little

Red Riding Hood." She even dresses for her part by draping a shawl over her head. The act always brings the house down, and Barbee enjoys it immensely. I looked forward to saying hello to Barb.

There were a couple of other cars and trucks of folks that I knew, but not any folks that I really needed to speak with. When I walked in, I saw Jill sitting at the bar next to Barb. They were talking with Anna.

"Hello, ladies! Am I interrupting anything?"

"Yes, you are," Jill joked. "Why don't you ride your bike up to the Center, and then come back. By then, we'll probably have caught up on everything that's happening in town."

"The heck with that nonsense! It's an eight-mile trip each way. The last time I rode a bike that far—probably the only time I've ridden a bike that far—was when we coasted down Haleakala in Maui, but that was downhill all the way! Tell you what, when you get caught up, I'll be sitting under a palm tree on the deck, just watching the mullet jump. Anna, would you please see if Chesley would be kind enough to bring me a Ketel One salty dog? Ya'll just take your time."

I had to smile as I walked outside. Jill can get more information sitting at that bar chatting for a few minutes than I could find out in a month of diligent effort. If she's chatting with another woman, she'll know all about their kids, their relatives, and where they are all from. And who knows what else she'll might learn. If she's sitting at the bar alone, it's not unusual for a visiting fisherman to strike up a conversation. What woman wouldn't enjoy being flirted with? And in the process of letting him down easy, she would find out all kind of stuff from him, too—where to fish, what bait to use, where to visit on Sanibel or Captiva. I guess all guys have a tough time keeping secrets from an attractive woman. Heck, one time she even came home with the recipe for a homemade mosquito repellent that some of the locals concoct. There's just no telling what she'll learn at that bar.

Me? When I sit at a bar, I'll probably end up talking about college football, or something equally useful, while steadily getting drunk. I'm just not that much of a gossiper, and I am always pretty linear in my thinking. In my mind, if I'm sitting at a bar, then I should be consuming an alcoholic beverage. I usually don't get too far beyond that. Consequently, I don't normally learn much information. That's why I was happy for Jill to stay inside. I knew she'd know something interesting when she finally joined me.

When she came outside, I wasn't disappointed.

"That was so much fun. I always enjoy talking with them. They are both so nice. Did you order me a pitcher yet?"

"No, Dear. I didn't want it to get warm. But I will when Chesley brings me a refill. So, did you learn anything interesting today?"

"I'll say. You know Katie and Steve, who live around the corner from us, right beside Carlos's house? They were in the bar having lunch when I go there. We talked a long time. They left right before you came in. I bet you didn't know that Katie used to play golf for the Gators. And when she was in high school, she used to ski in Sea World's water ski show. And here's the best part: she actually grew up in Windermere, the same town where your sister lives now. We really should get to know them better."

"Yeah, we should. But, you know, I've really already gotten to know Steve pretty well. When you're out of town on the weekends, sometimes I come down here to watch college football. Steve's usually here, doing the same thing. Did you know that he played football in college?"

"I didn't know that."

"Yeah, he did. He played strong safety at West Point. He started his last three years."

"Wow. I didn't know that. He must have been pretty good."

"I think he was. He said that he might have even been able to play in the pros, but instead he went into the army, and trained as an officer in some kind of elite, special-forces unit. He was in Desert Storm in Iraq, and did two tours in Afghanistan. Unfortunately, during his last tour, he was seriously wounded by an IED. That's why he walks with a cane."

"Yeah. Katie told me about that. She said that he really had a rough time. Not only were his legs messed up, but he had a traumatic brain injury, too. And, of course, his military career was over. She said that he's had a pretty rough time dealing with that. He was kind of lost for a while. But you can tell they are really happy together."

"Yeah, you're right. I saw you talking with Anna, also."

"Yeah. I like her so much. I told Anna that once all of this stuff with Javier is resolved, we'll have her and Grady over for dinner. She said that sounded like a good idea. But then, when I told her about the snook that live in the canal behind our house, she got really excited. She loves to fish!"

"Wow, I didn't know that. From what I hear, Grady knows just about all there is to know about boats and outboard engines.

I think he also loves to sail. I hope we can make that dinner happen pretty soon. Did you hear anything about the Punta Blanca rumor?"

"Well, kind of. We talked about it some. But neither Anna nor Barbee had ever heard anything about there being gold up there. In fact, Anna said that if there had ever even been a hint about gold being on that island, the locals would have sifted every grain of sand a long time ago. And with respect to there being a group in the area from New York looking for it, she didn't buy that, either. She definitely hadn't seen a group matching that description at Woody's. And she said that Grady hadn't seen them at the marina, either. Anna's got a sister who works the bar at the Tarpon Lodge. She said her sister hadn't noticed any folks at that bar with those kinds of accents, either. And her best friend has a friend who waits tables at Cabbage Key. They all got together a couple of nights ago up at Froggy's after Woody's closed, and they talked about this. Her friend's friend said that it's very slow out there this time of the year, and, as far as she could remember, there hadn't been any New Yorkers hanging around for at least a month. I know that's not conclusive, but if there were newcomers in that part of the sound, chances are they would have visited one or both of those locations. Everyone does."

"That's interesting. I think the bartender network would certainly know if something like that was going down."

"I agree. Especially if anyone in the group was a jackass. And, from what I've heard about your friend from New York, there's a better than even chance that he might have made himself noticeable in that way."

"It's been known to happen. But who knows? They could have been staying on Sanibel or on Captiva. Lots of hotels and lots of bars over there."

"That's true. But we're talking about folks exploring Punta Blanca Island. What's that? A half mile, at the most, from Cabbage Key? And remember, everyone who visits up that way has to go to Cabbage Key at least once. That's a rite of passage. And if they did, you would find a dollar bill on the wall with their names on it. But I'm betting there was no group from New York down here looking for gold. Anna says that rumor just doesn't feel right to her. As you know, she hears about everything that goes on around here, and she has a good nose for what makes sense and what doesn't. She says that this story smells kind of contrived. She thinks someone may be making these rumors up and spreading them all over town. She wonders if someone is just trying to mislead the investigation."

"That's what Anna said?"

"Exactly."

"How could someone do that? How could someone start a rumor, and then get it spread like that?"

"That's what I asked her. She said, 'Jill, you've been here long enough to understand that Froggy's is where the locals meet every afternoon after work. If anyone there at four thirty were to tell someone at the bar a juicy piece of information, I'd bet that by five, everybody in the bar would have heard the same information. By five thirty, most of the ladies go home to get dinner ready, but a lot of their husbands migrate over to the Low Key to have a beer or three with the locals who favor that side of the road. By six o'clock, any rumor would be well on its way to having been heard by everyone in town. It's just the way it is here. Once it starts going around, you might hear it from three of four different people. No way to sort out where it started.'"

"That's making a lot of sense to me," I said. "There's someone here in town who's trying to keep the Sheriff's Office from getting to the truth. I would bet the plan is to keep doing this long enough that the deputies get frustrated enough to quit looking. But we just can't ignore the possibility that what we heard about Punta Blanca may be true."

I told Jill about the gold coin that the deputies found up there.

"Oh, come on! There's too much gold showing up. That's just a little too damn convenient."

"I agree. But until we get a better plan, all I know to do is to run down the lead I've got, and let Mike Collins do the same."

I told her what he was planning to do, and then added: "I'm glad he's talking with the Colliers. Maybe they will be able to shed some light on this. And I'm excited that he's trying to get some information out of Cuba. If he can do that, or if Arantxa can get us some more information, I think we'll be a lot closer to knowing what this is all about."

"What lead are you going to run down?"

"You remember Frank Tranh? He worked in Risk Management in Birmingham with Javier."

"Yeah. Wasn't he, like, American-Vietnamese, or something? He's such a nice guy. Didn't they have a couple of really cute kids?"

"That's him. One of Frank's traits is that he always has to know what's going on around the company. If someone was out of town, as soon as he noticed, he'd be chatting with that person's admin assistant to find out where he went and why. It's just the way he is. Doesn't mean any harm by it. I guess it's just his innate sense of curiosity. Probably why he's such a good risk manager. So, it wouldn't be at all out of character for him to do some snooping for me about why our follicularly challenged friend was in Captiva a few days before Javier was killed. When we get home, I'm going to give him a call."

"I like it," Jill said. "Now, pay the bill and let's get out of here. The sun is very nice today. I think I'm going to go lay out in the sun while you make that call."

"Sounds like a plan. Just make sure you stay behind the palms so that I won't be able to see you. If I have to look at you in your bikini, there's no way I'd ever be able to get that phone call made."

"Shut up, you dirty old man. Let's get out of here before you get any more ideas. See you at home. And try not to fall off your bike!"

Chapter Twenty-Seven
LET'S MAKE A DEAL

"Frank, this is Jim Story. Have I got a deal for you!"

"Jim Story! I heard you'd fallen off your boat, and been eaten by a hungry shark. Nobody's heard from you since Javier died. You OK?"

"Yeah. I'm fine. Just frustrated as hell that we can't figure out who killed Javier. That's why I'm calling. I need your help."

"Hey, you name it. Javier was my friend, too. I'll do anything I can to find that bastard. What do you want me to do?"

"A few days before Javier was killed, we were over on Captiva—that's a barrier island just across the bay from us—and I saw in a restaurant bar none other than your friend and mine, Cue Ball. Thankfully, he didn't see me. You know damn well that I didn't want to have to say hello to him. Fortunately, he was only there a few minutes. But here's where I need your help. There's a rumor going around down here that maybe Javier's death was somehow related to a group from New York that had come down to look for gold buried on a nearby island. That island is near where Javier was killed. Long story short, I want to know why Old Cue Ball was here, and whether he was still here when Javier was killed. I know you've got some sources in the New York office that can get you that information."

"Piece of cake. I'll be back to you in the morning. You really think he might have killed Javier?"

"No, I don't. We all know that he can be a prick when he puts his mind to it. But I can't really imagine that he would want to have anything to do with killing someone. And especially not with killing Javier. He's too smart for that. I'm actually thinking that you will be able to clear him. But I just need to know one way or the other."

"I understand. I'll go to work. Now, what was the deal you mentioned?"

"Here's the deal. You get that information by tomorrow, and I'll buy you a bottle of single malt, your choice. As long as it costs less than a hundred bucks."

"Hey! I like that deal. I'll take it. And I'll make you a deal in return."

"What's that?"

"You just hold that bottle down there. And when you find out who killed Javier, I'll come down and we'll drink that bottle together, and celebrate justice for our friend."

"You've got a deal. I'll be waiting for your call."

Chapter Twenty-Eight
APPRECIATION DAY

During the night the wind had kicked up. By morning, it was blowing out of the northwest, twenty to twenty-five knots, with gusts near gale force. It was certainly not a day to venture out on the sound. Way too much wind for fishing. That much wind would churn up some serious chop. No thanks. It was a far better day to keep the boat on the lift, and stay close to home.

After taking care of the usual chores, Jill and I put on our jogging shoes. At least that's what we call them. She still runs, but those days are now behind me. Too much weight, and too many miles. Regardless, we like to walk around town. It's always interesting to see which houses have been opened up by returning snowbirds. And we always enjoy saying hello to the people we meet. Saint James City is such a nice town.

It's also a great time for Jill and me to talk. As is our custom, we walk a few blocks, and then start to chat. Today we were commenting on the ospreys and eagles that were flying over, and wondering when they would start to build their nests.

We also tried to identify several types of birds that we had not seen over the past few months. I'm guessing they, too, had just migrated from colder climes. All this is new to us, and we're still trying to understand the patterns of life down here. Eventually, we got around to the subject that I really wanted to talk with her about.

"Hey, babe," I started. "I think the investigation into who killed Javier is starting to move into its critical phase. It seems to me we're starting to get beyond the red herrings that have been laid in our path, and that as we do that, things will start to get a lot more serious. It's just my guess, but I think the killer is someone here in town. And, once the search starts to focus here, I'm worried about what might happen. There's no reason the killer wouldn't kill again if he thought that would help him avoid being discovered. Bottom line, I think it's going to get dangerous around here, and I don't want you getting hurt. I want you out of town so no one can take a shot at you."

Jill went silent. I know from experience that it's best not to interrupt that silence. It normally signifies that she is processing deep emotions, and that some keen intellectual analysis is taking place at the same time. Over the years, I've learned that whenever this process if going on, it is best to keep quiet and wait until she is ready to reengage.

So, we continued to walk along our normal route, neither of us saying a thing. Finally, as we made the turn back to the house, the dam broke. She turned to look at me, and I could see that there were tears running down her face.

"I am not going to leave you here. Sir Galahad, in case you haven't noticed, I'm not the one who is really in danger here.

You are! How do you think I'd feel if I went to stay with the kids, just to get out of harm's way, only for you to end up being killed? You think I could live with that? Nice try, but no dice. I haven't followed your ass around for forty years just so that, once we finally retired, you can go and get shot. We're in this together. Always have been. I've got your back, and you've got mine. If either of us is going to get shot, then they'll damn sure have to shoot both of us! That's just the way it is."

"OK. OK. You win. But I want to go on record that I don't like it."

"Your objection's noted, and overruled. Now, let's get practical. What do we need to do to make sure that neither of us actually gets whacked?"

"I guess we'd better start by being a little more careful. For example, I don't think we ought to ride our bikes around town anymore. That might be making it a little too convenient for someone to run us over in a car. Beyond that, we ought to limit the amount of time we spend out after dark. And, as much as I hate it, and I know this is getting pretty extreme, we probably need to start thinking about possibly locking the doors of the house."

"Shit!"

"I agree with that sentiment. But it looks like reality may have finally caught up with us in Saint James City."

"Do you think we should buy a gun?"

This time it was my turn to be quiet. We've never owned a gun. Never really had a reason to."We'll need to think about that."

When we got back to the house, I noticed that we had a voice message. I punched the button, and heard Frank's voice.

"Jim, you can cross our friend off the list of suspects. He was back in New York by the time Javier was killed. But that's not all. I found out why he was down there. You'll love this. Supposedly, he flew down to participate in the Sanibel Triathlon. I guess he did, as far as that goes. But here's the good part: rumor has it that he really went down there to rendezvous with his 'partner.' Anyway, you can cross him off your list. Now, I've upheld my end of the deal. You think you can find a really nice bottle of Glenmorangie? Maybe an eighteen-year-old? If I remember right, Glenmorangie was the last malt that you, Javier, and I drank together. Would seem fitting that, if you find out who killed him, we should toast Javier with some of the same. You just keep the bottle there, and let me know when I need to come down and drink it. Jim, I'm serious; call me if you need me. If there's anything I can do up here, let me know. And, if you need me down there, I can be there in a couple of hours. I want the bastard that killed Javier caught as badly as you do."

I erased the message, picked up the phone, and called Mike Collins. I was disappointed that I got his voice mail. I left a message outlining what I had learned from Frank, and asked him to call.

Jill had already gone upstairs to clean up, and I decided to do the same. We had decided earlier that it would be a good day to have lunch at the Waterfront. We hadn't been there together in a while, and I still needed to talk with D.W. about the matter of a broken mirror in the men's room. At a quarter to twelve, we backed out the car, and drove the few blocks to the restaurant.

Usually, we try to sit outside on the deck, looking at the canal. But today, given how hard the wind was blowing, we asked to sit inside by a window. Once we sat down, I looked outside. I couldn't help but laugh. The wind was blowing a gale—literally. But, despite that, there were three die-hard fishermen sitting in a boat anchored in the middle of the canal. Their backs were hunched against the wind, and they were fishing for all they were worth. I guess they had decided that while it was too rough to be on the bay, they were not going to be denied their chance to go fishing. I hoped they caught something.

Jamie came over to wait on us, and to say hello. She gave me a nice hug, and said: "I want to thank you for what you did to help our girls out the other night. We really appreciate you taking care of that situation."

"Jamie, what the heck are you talking about?" I asked as I smiled and gave her my best wink and nod. "Say, is D.W. cooking today?"

"Of course. And he is so excited about today's menu. He's got some really nice trigger fish in this morning."

"Wow! That sounds good. Pretty sure that's what I'm going to have. But, before we order, do you think I might be able to trouble him for a second? I need to talk with him for just a minute."

"You bet. Come on over to the bar, and I'll go drag him out of the kitchen."

"Hey, Jim! Long time no see," D.W. said, wiping his hands on a towel as he came out of the kitchen.

"Too long, D.W., too long. I'm badly in need of some good seafood. I understand that you've got trigger fish on the menu today?"

"Sure do. Fresh off the boat this morning. That what you wanted to talk about?"

"No, not really. I heard through the grapevine that someone busted up your bathroom last week. I felt bad that someone would treat your place like that. In fact, it's been bothering me so much that I wanted to make a contribution toward getting it repaired. You think $200 would cover the cost?"

D.W. laughed."Yeah, but that's not all that got busted up. An obnoxious customer was giving Chris and the other girls a hard time. But fortunately, the customer got so drunk that when he went to use the bathroom he apparently passed out. And when he fell, he must have hit his head on the mirror. However he did it, he sure busted the heck out of it. I guess when he fell he must have also busted his nose. He sure bled all over the place. And, not only that, but I think he pissed his pants, as well. But you know what? When he came out of the restroom, he told his crew to pay the bill, and to tip the ladies 100 percent. That knock on the head must have done him some good! Thanks for the offer to fix the mirror. But I've already taken care of it. I found a fine used one down at the Beacon of Hope thrift shop. It cost me five bucks. So, don't offend me anymore by offering to pay for it. Seriously, it's a good thing that ya'll came in today. 'Cause, today just happens to be the official Jim and Jill Story Appreciation Day. Your meals are on us!"

I looked D.W. in the eye. He gave me a wink. But I could see he was serious. I laughed. "Wow! Then, it is a good thing we came in. You guys never fail to amaze. Thanks for lunch."

"Thank you."

When I returned to the table, Jill had already ordered our lunches. We're so predictable. We were starting with an order of D.W.'s freshly made mullet dip. You can't go wrong with that. She was having her usual conch and grouper basket, fried, with onion strings, a Shock Top, and a glass of water. For me, she had ordered a Greek salad topped with broiled triggerfish, and an unsweetened iced tea. Perfect!

"Hey, babe. Guess what? It looks like today's Jim and Jill Story Appreciation Day. Good thing we stopped by."

"What are you talking about?"

"Just what I said. D.W. told me that today had been designated on their calendar as our day, and since we stopped by, we would get our lunches for free. Not only that, I think he really appreciated some help I gave him recently with a little remodeling that he was doing in the bathroom."

Her eyebrow arched up in that familiar way that signifies she doesn't know what I'm talking about, and that, even if she did, she knew better than to believe a word of it.

"Yeah, I helped him replace the mirror. No big deal. Hey, here comes the dip. It sure looks good!"

Chapter Twenty-Nine
LUNCH WITH A COLLIER

When we returned to the house, the answering machine was blinking. Mike Collins returning my call.

"Jim, thanks for the information on your friend from New York. That makes sense. I don't think there's anything at all to this rumor about gold on Punta Blanca. And certainly, there's nothing to the theory of there being a gang of bad guys from New York. We checked with all the hotels out that way. When you get back, give me a call. I'll fill you in on what else I've learned."

I dialed his number.

"Collins. What's up?"

"Hey, Mike. I'm returning your call."

"Yeah, thanks. I appreciate you running to ground the information about the guy from New York. That fits with what we've learned. Our guys scoured Punta Blanca and could find nothing on the island other than the one recently dug hole that I told you about. There were no other tracks. Nothing. We talked with all the hotels, restaurants, and bars in the area. Nothing tied back to a group of New Yorkers working on Punta Blanca Island. I think that was just a story to take our eye off the ball."

"Yeah. I'm thinking the same. Were you able to get anything from the Colliers?"

"Yeah. I got in touch with the guy that I had known in high school. He's Barron Collier's great-grandson. We agreed to meet for lunch in Ave Maria. Do you know about Ave Maria?"

"Do you mean Anna Maria?"

"No, Jim. You think I don't know the difference between Anna Maria and Ava Maria?"

"Sorry. I think I've heard of it. Isn't that the official Catholic town?"

"Well, not exactly. But it's a pretty amazing place. Back in 2002, Tom Monaghan, the founder of Domino's Pizza and owner of the Detroit Tigers, decided that he wanted to leave a legacy that people would remember him for. I guess he was a very religious guy. Either that, or he had a big guilt complex. For whatever reason, he decided to found and endow a Catholic university. Somehow, he knew the Collier family, and they got together. It seems like the Collier vision of town building was still alive. Monaghan endowed the university with a donation of $250 million, and the Colliers kicked in 5,000 acres of land. Together, they've built a fully accredited university, and a complete city around it. It's located way out on the east side of Collier County. Ave Maria, the town, has all the amenities, including roads, utilities, police, fire, post office, gas station, bank, retail space, and a K-through-twelve school—everything you need to live.. It's really a beautiful place. I had never been out there. But I'm glad I went. Frankly, it's a pretty amazing place."

"So, it is an official Catholic town?"

"Not exactly. They claim that all religions, all faiths, all life-styles, are welcome. But I suspect that invitation may be more about avoiding any constitutional issues than anything else. I would bet that a survey would show that close to 100 percent of the population is Catholic. But everyone else is, of course, welcome."

"Wow, that's cool." I couldn't help asking, "You see any Baptist churches out there? How about family- planning clinics?"

Mike laughed. "Come on! I'm serious. This place is something else. I was impressed."

"Sorry. So how was your lunch? You learn anything?"

"It was good getting back together with Colin. I hadn't seen him in almost twenty years. But he still seems to be the same, level-headed, smart, polite guy I remember. I'm not sure, but I gather that he now has overall responsibility for the Colliers' portion of the Ave Maria project. Everyone in the restaurant certainly knew who he was. And I did note that service at lunch was very attentive!"

"What did he think about the Punta Blanca gold story?"

"He actually thought it was a very interesting story, but then he quickly threw cold water on it. He said the idea of the old man secretly hiding gold from the government was just not in his character—at least based on what he's been told about him. From everything he's ever heard, Barron Sr. was about as honest and straight-laced, as you could be. But he told me that the idea of him having a gold hoard was not off base. Family history says that Collier was, in fact, very concerned about the Great Depression, and specifically, about what Roosevelt was doing to address it. Supposedly, he and Roosevelt got along well. But, privately, Collier didn't like the New Deal. He'd seen enough of socialism in Europe to understand what it was all about. To minimize the impact of Roosevelt's inflationary policies, he converted a sizeable chunk of his remaining fortune into gold bullion, and stored it in banks in London and Zurich. Once the old man's estate was settled, control of this gold eventually found its way to his family. According to him, there's still a lot of gold sitting there. It's been a damn good investment, just like the old man thought it would be. But he's sure there never was a secret hoard stashed out on Punta Blanca. Besides, the old man shut down everything out there way back in the early thirties. Family history says he never went there again. Colin thinks that was probably because it reminded him about how much money he'd pissed away out there on his boats. He got rid of that island as soon as he could."

"So, you don't think there's anything to this Collier gold stuff?"

"No. I never really did. That just never made much sense to me. After Collier abandoned the place, there was no way he could have safeguarded any gold that was buried out there. Back then, the place was overrun with mullet fisherman, bootleggers, and who knows what other kinds of down-on-their luck islanders. I'm pretty sure they would have stripped the island bare of anything of value."

"Yeah. I buy that. But what about the murder in Cuba? We do know that Collier's company had an operation in Cuba back then. They certainly must have had influence there. Could

Collier have been involved in the murder or the cover-up? Would that have given the family reason to knock off Javier? Hell, I wouldn't think that being descended from a lying murderer would do home sales in the Catholic town any good."

"No. Don't expect that would help. But I don't have any more information about that murder. The State Department is not being particularly helpful. But it's hard to believe that anyone would have any reason to be concerned, after all this time, with covering up a cover-up. My gut tells me that the delay is just due to normal bureaucratic inefficiency. Unless there's an important politician making a public stink about something, things like this just don't get immediate staff attention. I really don't have much faith that we're going to get what we need in a reasonable time from Foggy Bottom. So, instead, I sent one of our smart, Spanish-speaking interns to the Lee County Public Library with a laptop. I told her not to bring her intelligent, ambitious little butt back to the office until she's got a list of every murder of an American that was reported in the Havana newspapers between 1910 and 1914."

"I like that plan. It would help a lot if we knew who the victim was."

"I agree. Look, I know you're worried, but I don't think there's anything to be concerned about regarding the Colliers organizing a hit squad. That's not the way they do things. I'm certainly not going to use up any more of my brain cells thinking about that possibility. But, clearly, there is someone out there who might want to hurt you, or your wife. Have ya'll talked about getting out of town for a while? Maybe a trip to the Bahamas for a couple of weeks?"

"Yeah. We've talked about it. But we're not going to run. That's not the way *we* do things. We're going to stay right here, and do everything we can to help you find out who killed our friend. And, besides, we've got all the faith in the world that you will keep us safe while you seek out the killer."

Mike laughed. "I hate to be the bearer of bad news, but I'm just a government employee. Haven't you heard? All the smart guys work in the private sector. You might want to think twice about that faith you just mentioned."

"Let's just find this bastard. I'll contact my source in Spain. Maybe she's got some more information."

"Good idea," Mike said. "Say hello to Arantxa for me." With that, he hung up.

Chapter Thirty
AN EVENING IN MADRID

A familiar chill in my spine made me start to shiver even before the line went dead. How in the hell did he know Arantxa's name? For sure, I hadn't mentioned it to him. Shit! Had I, somehow, managed to put her in danger? Was there really something to the theory that the authorities were covering something up? Was this something so big that the Spaniards and the Americans were in it together? Was it so big that both governments were willing to kill to keep their secrets safe? Damn, just when I thought we were getting somewhere!

I immediately dialed Arantxa in Spain. I didn't care what time it was there. I wanted her to know, as soon as possible, that her identity had been compromised. I also wanted her to know that I had not done it.

As I dialed, I guessed it was around 10:00 p.m. in Madrid. While that was certainly too late to call someone in Saint James City, in Madrid, people would just be getting ready for dinner. I knew she would have her phone with her—all Spaniards are connected to their technology much more intimately than even the most savvy American teenagers are. They are years ahead of us in how they use smart phones. I just hoped she would answer hers.

"Jim, it is wonderful to hear from you. I miss you so much! Do you have news? Have you arrested Javier's killer?"

"Arantxa, listen to me. This is serious. I am really worried about you. The police here have somehow identified that you are helping me. I did not tell them. They may be watching you. You need to be careful. I don't know who is responsible for Javier's death. But maybe there really is something to his mother's concerns. Maybe the police are involved."

I could hear her giggling. My blood started to boil. Didn't she realize how much danger she was in?

"Arantxa, please stop laughing. This is serious. Have you been drinking?"

"Of course, I've been drinking! This is Spain, and it's almost ten o'clock at night. That is what we do here! You know that. We go from bar to bar, sipping wine and eating our wonderful tapas. We have so much fun here. It's not like Birmingham, where everyone drinks tea over ice, eats a huge meal in their homes at 6:00 p.m., and goes to bed early so they can get up at five to go to work. This is Spain! Here, we love the evenings! We all go out every night."

"Arantxa, did you hear what I said about the police? Your life may be in danger!"

"Jim, please stop worrying. Of course the police know that I am your source. I told them."

I was dumbfounded. "You told them?"

"Yes. I did. Let me tell you how this happened. I have been visiting Senora Hernandez quite often. But I am not the only one who has been visiting. The police have also been asking for her help. One day last week, the police officer who has been calling on her happened to come to her home while I was there. You're not going to believe this, but this officer was actually a great friend of mine from when we were in school. His name is Jamie de la Cruz. We went to school together from the time we were babies. I said good-bye to Senora Hernandez, and Jamie went in to talk with her. I waited outside. When he came back outside, we talked. He was as surprised to see me as I was to see him. I told him that Javier had been a good friend of mine, and that we had worked together both in Spain and in Birmingham. I also told him that I was trying to help you by getting information from Senora Hernandez. He said that he was trying to do the same for the authorities in Florida. I'm sure that's how your sheriff knew my name."

I could feel myself exhaling, almost like a balloon being deflated. I didn't realize how worried I had become, and it felt great to be relieved of this concern."Arantxa, that's great. I was really worried about you."

"Jim, thank you for being worried. I appreciate that. I'm so sorry I caused you to be concerned."

"Hey, no problem. But were you, or your friend, able to get any more information from Senora Hernandez?"

"No. Not yet. She is still very fearful. If she knows anything, and I'm not sure she does, she is not yet willing to tell anyone. But I am not quitting. I am going to see her again on Friday. If I learn anything, I'll call you immediately."

"OK. Thanks."

Chapter Thirty-One
SOME CUBAN HISTORY

Now what? There had to be something we could do to move this forward. I couldn't just sit on my hands and wait for the sheriff's department. But for the life of me, I couldn't think of what else to do. We had chased down all of the leads and theories that we knew about. None of them had led us anywhere. All we knew now that we didn't know when we started was that Javier knew something about the cover-up of a murder of an American in Cuba that took place between 1910 and 1914. And, we now believed, that this knowledge may have led someone here on Pine Island to put a bullet through his head to keep him quiet.

But that wasn't much to go on. Was the murdered American connected somehow with Pine Island? There was no way to know that. Especially since we didn't even know who had been killed.

In frustration, I decided to try the Internet once again to see if I could learn anything that might be helpful. Despite my best efforts, I couldn't find out anything about the murder of any Americans in Cuba during that period. But as I stumbled around from website to website, I was able to learn some other very interesting information.

Despite having been, in my opinion, relatively well educated, I found that I really didn't know much about the history of Cuba. The little I thought I knew was that America had freed the Cubans from Spanish tyranny in the Spanish-American War in 1898, generously helping grateful Cubans to enjoy their independence. But a little focused time on the web quickly helped me to see a different picture.

The Cuban War of Independence had begun in 1895. For many years prior to that, Jose Marti had tirelessly promoted the idea of Cuban independence. Marti himself was killed in the very first battle of the war, ensuring that he would enjoy martyr status forever. But the Cuban rebels (never numbering more than 3,000 strong) relentlessly fought the more than 40,000 Spanish soldiers on the island. Despite being badly outnumbered, the rebels were largely victorious. And they were able to achieve these successes even as the US government worked to keep the rebels from winning! For example, on the very day that the war began, the United States seized the three ships that Marti had loaded with weapons and supplies in order to prevent them from sailing from the U.S. to Cuba to reinforce the rebels. Even more amazingly, the US government had immediately notified the Spanish government about what was happening. Over the course of the next two years, the rebels tried on sixty different occasions to send weapons and supplies from the US. But only one of those shipments was able to successfully get through to the rebels. The US Treasury stopped twenty-eight of those shipments, while the US Navy stopped many more. The only shipment that actually made it to the rebels did so only because it was under the direct protection of the British navy. From these actions, it was clear that the United States was actively hostile to the idea of Cuban independence. After all, the rebels in Cuba were largely made up of, and supported by, Afro-Cubans. A revolt by blacks was never going to be popular in the United States, given its own policy at that time of marginalizing its own black population. But despite the impediments presented by the United States, the Cuban rebels were able to defeat the Spanish forces. By 1898, the rebels controlled all of the countryside. The Spanish forces were holed up in the cities, unable to retreat any further. By this time, the population in the Philippines had also rebelled against Spain, and it was widely believed that a rebellion in Puerto Rico would occur next. Spain knew it was defeated, and that it would not be able to hold these territories. The rebels had, in fact, won.

It was at that time, only after the battles had largely been fought, that the United States decided to get involved. In January 1898, President McKinley sent our largest battleship, the USS *Maine*, to Havana Harbor, ostensibly, to protect American lives and property. Three weeks later, that ship exploded under mysterious circumstances, killing 260 US sailors. This disaster gave the United States the excuse it needed to enter the war. With newspaper barons Pulitzer and Hearst whipping the country into a frenzy, the United States declared war on Spain. A few months later the United States signed a treaty with a defeated Spain, agreeing to pay Spain $20 million dollars for control of

Cuba, the Philippines, Puerto Rico, and Guam. While the treaty spelled out Cuba's independence, it was noteworthy that at the treaty-signing ceremony in Havana, no Cuban rebels were allowed to participate. Not only that, but only the US flag was flown. The Cuban flag was not even allowed to be displayed. So much for the dream of Cuban independence. So much for the sacrifice made by the thousands of Cubans who lost their lives fighting the Spanish.

In short order, the Americans pursued their real objective of "developing" the island. The government began to build roads and sanitation facilities, while large American corporations set about buying up as much Cuban land as possible at dirt-cheap prices. It didn't take long for the Cuban peasants to understand that their hard-fought victory meant only that they had exchanged one overseer for another.

In June 1900, Cuba's first elections were held. To vote, one had to be male, over twenty-one years old, a Cuban citizen, be able to read and write, own property worth at least $250 in US gold, or have served in the Cuban army. Consequently, almost none of the actual rebels who had fought the battles could participate in the election. At that time, many in the United States were hopeful that Cuba would be annexed as a state. But by and large, the Cubans wanted nothing to do with this idea. In the elections of 1900, the annexationists were soundly defeated. And despite the roadblocks put in place by the American occupiers, the Cuban National Party, which represented the revolutionaries, was victorious in every major city. Despite these results, as the newly elected Cuban Congress met, the United States demanded that the Platt Amendment be inserted into

Cuba's newly drafted constitution. This amendment required, among other things, that in order for US troops to withdraw from the island, Cuba could not enter into any agreements with any foreign body without the specific approval of the United States. In essence, the amendment was inserted to make Cuba a pseudo colony of the United States. In addition, the United States was given responsibility for the maintenance of "internal tranquility" on the island. America's control of Guantanamo Bay was also formalized. As you might expect, Cuban leaders were outraged. The independence that they had struggled and died for had evaporated in front of their eyes. Now, rather than being enslaved by the crown of Spain, Cuban peasants found themselves working in tobacco fields and sugar plantations owned by American corporations.

Over the next decade, much of the Cuban population grew increasingly unhappy. This was particularly true of Cuba's large Afro segment. Afro-Cubans had made up as much as two-thirds of the rebel forces that had defeated the Spanish. Significantly, at least 80,000 black Cubans had died in the war for independence only to find themselves ignored and marginalized by an American-dominated puppet government. The policy of the American government in Cuba was to minimize the political power of the black population, just as it was at that time in the United States. It did this by restricting the ability to vote. By 1908, the outrage of the black population had reached a boiling point. A new political party—the Partido Independiente de Color—was formed by Evaristo Esteroz and Pedro Ivonnet for the express purpose of representing the interests of Cuba's blacks. Among the white population on the island, this was portrayed as nothing less than a racial uprising. In Cuba, as in the American South, there always had been a terror that the black population would violently rise up against the ruling whites. Now, panic swept the island. In 1909, a law was passed that outlawed any political party that was based upon race. The next year, an increasingly desperate Partido Independiente de Color organized demonstrations across the island, demanding its share of political power. But the demands were ignored, and the unrest continued. In late 1911 and early 1912, additional demonstrations were held. These uprisings resulted in great fear and panic among the white population. In response to several reported murders of whites by blacks, and to the burning of several sugar mills, white vigilante groups began to hunt down, arrest, and kill members of the Partido Independiente de Color. During May and June of 1912, over 8,000 blacks (men, women, and children) were killed, either by vigilantes, or by the government itself. Esteroz was tracked down and killed. Ivonnet surrendered to authorities, only to be killed shortly thereafter "while trying to escape." Once again, the United States sent warships and marines to Cuba. Once again, the purpose of this intervention was supposedly to protect its interests. But in reality, the military force was there to support the Cuban government, and to ensure that the black rebels were defeated. The bid for political power by Cuba's blacks was over. But the resentment remains to this day.

From the information I learned, it was clear that Cuba was a chaotic place when Javier's great-grandfather was there. There was no doubt that America had a strong interest in seeing that its position on the island was protected. I suspected, though I had nothing to base it on, that the Spanish would have liked nothing more than for the Americans to be disgraced. The political intrigue on the island must have been unbelievable. From what I read, it seemed logical that nothing would have suited the Americans and the ruling Cubans more than if the murder of an American businessman could be blamed on a black Cuban fisherman. Maybe the cover-up of the murder that had so incensed Javier's great-grandfather was even used to justify the massacre and suppression of the black population. Was it possible that Javier's great-grandfather's outrage was not so much that one innocent man had been convicted and killed, but that this "crime" had been used to justify the brutal execution of many thousands of innocent people? Was this why he was always suspicious of the United States? Did this explain the Hernandez family's fear that the US government might, even today, be interested in covering up its active complicity in what would now be considered an atrocity and a war crime?

"Shit! Maybe there is something to this idea that the government is involved. If that's the case, our asses are grass!"

Chapter Thirty-Two
A NIGHT AT THE TIKI HUT

I immediately dialed Mike Collins.

"Collins. What you got?"

"Mike, I've just been looking at the Internet. Been trying to educate myself about Cuba back when Javier's great-grandfather was there. I couldn't find any specific information about the murder of an American businessman, but I did find out that the US-backed Cuban government massacred almost ten thousand blacks during that period, and used the supposed murder of whites by blacks as the excuse for this slaughter. Maybe that's what the old man was so upset about. Hell, for all I know, the United States may still be trying to cover up this scandal. I suspect that our government wouldn't want anything to come out now that would make Castro and his brother look good."

"Jim, stop it already. Get a grip. Trust me; our government is not involved in this. Look, if you could find this information on the Internet, it certainly is public information. If there was anything here that could be used, you can bet that Fidel would have used it a long time ago."

"Yeah, I guess. But it is interesting, isn't it? I always thought that we were the good guys back then—kicking the Spanish out of their colonies around the world, freeing the native populations that they had enslaved, and introducing democracy. Now, I find out that it wasn't really like that at all. We basically used the ongoing revolutions as an excuse to do some empire-building of our own."

"You're right. That's sure not what we learned in school, is it?"

"Nope. It's not what I learned. But where does this leave us? Was your intern able to get anything? Or have you been too fixated on her intelligent butt to ask?"

"Look, Jim, if there's one thing I've had to get good at as an employee of an underfunded arm of Lee County government, it is learning to double task. I can certainly do both of those things at the same time. But she hasn't been able to learn anything specific yet. And not for a lack of trying. I was impressed with the effort she put into trying to go back in time. But when she called in, what she had was basically the same stuff you just told me. Clearly, there were a lot of things going on in Cuba back then that we wouldn't be too proud of today. I'm afraid that a lot of the records from back then were destroyed, if they even existed in the first place. She's got the librarians helping her, and they are trying to access some of the databases that the general public can't get into. But even if they can find relevant records from that time, it's going to be a needle-in-a-haystack type of thing. I'm not feeling good that this is going to be helpful. Have you heard anymore from Arantxa?"

"No, not yet. But she's still talking with Senora Hernandez. She's going to meet with her Friday. She'll call me if she gets anything. By the way, thanks for scaring the shit out of me the other day when you dropped her name on me. I bet you thought you were cute doing that, didn't you?"

"Yeah. That was fun! I wish I had been there to see your face. I bet you turned as white as a ghost."

"Yeah. I'm sure I did. I guess my long-standing paranoia about an over-reaching government, the one I developed when I was in college back in the sixties, must have momentarily resurfaced. But where does this leave us? You got anything more?"

"I think it leaves us about where we've been. We still believe that a murder took place in Cuba a long time ago, and that someone in this area is willing to kill to keep that covered up. We now believe that that murder, and its subsequent cover-up, may have been used to falsely convict and execute an innocent fisherman, and to justify the massacre of thousands of innocent people. Maybe that's all the more reason that someone doesn't want this to come out now. Other than that, we've got nothing. Let me know if you hear from Arantxa."

"I will. Talk with you later."

"Now what?" I asked myself. For the life of me, I couldn't think of anything else I could do. With that realization, I decided that the best alternative was to do what we do so well down here—start drinking. I walked upstairs to find Jill, and we quickly made plans to go into town.

One of the unique features about living on an island populated largely by retirees is that the nightlife gets going long before it is actually nighttime. A very good band had been playing all afternoon at the Ragged Ass Saloon. Bands normally start about 2:00 p.m. and play until 5:00 p.m. It's a schedule designed to lure motorcyclists from the mainland out for a day trip. They shut things off early so that the bikers can sober up enough to get home before dark. As the scene at the Ragged Ass was winding down, another band was about to crank things up at the Low Key Tiki. It was scheduled to play from 6:00 to 8:30 p.m. After that, the sidewalks in town begin to roll up so that all the old folks can go home and go to bed. I'm sure younger people might not find this arrangement to be particularly appealing, but Jill and I, and the other old farts in town, find it to be quite reasonable. You hit the bars, listen to some tunes, eat some good food, drink enough to get a buzz on, and then, as the sun is sinking down, go home to enjoy a good night's sleep. A lot of wisdom comes from decades of practice.

And, as they say, practice makes perfect. Consequently, we were soon dragging the bicycles from the garage to make the long ride into town. We did this having consciously decided that the risk of being killed was less than the risk of getting a DUI. I like to let Jill lead the way. I tell her that I like to keep an eye out for trouble. But what I'm really doing is keeping an eye on her as she pedals in front. I love to watch her ride, and I adore seeing her blonde ponytail blowing in the breeze. That's one of the things I've always loved about her look. That and her long, lean legs, and her butt, and…I could go on and on. But she always makes me lead the way on the return trip. Usually, these trips are in the dark, and I think she figures that it would be better if I ran into whatever might be in the way than if she did. At least that's what I accuse her of thinking.

A NIGHT AT THE TIKI HUT

That afternoon, there was a huge crowd at the Low Key. At least, it was huge by Saint James City standards. Fifty or sixty people were crowded around the tiny bar under the thatched roof. The band was an island favorite: Gerry and Keri. This duo is a young married couple that lives nearby. They like to play on the island since they can wrap things up early to get home to their three-year-old daughter. It all works out here on Pine Island. Gerry is the husband—tall, lean, and handsome in a George Strait sort of way. He plays a mean amplified acoustic guitar, and sings with a deep, country kind of voice. He's good, and I'm sure the ladies find him attractive. But as far as I can tell, the real reason everyone comes to hear them is Keri. An admiring musician who we talked with at another bar once said," She's got a set of pipes!" In other words, the lady can sing. Think of Stevie Nicks in her prime, mix in some Susan Tedeschi, and throw in a fair-size helping of Patsy Cline, and you'll be in the ballpark. Without question, she's also good looking, but in a local, down-home, PTA mom, sisterly sort of way. Maybe that's why all the old folks, female and male alike, love her so much.

The place was packed. I have to admit that seeing a bar full of old people takes some getting used to. If you're like me, you probably associate bars with young folks hanging out and trying to meet someone of the opposite sex. I just never thought of bars as being places where your grandma and grandpa go to drink, hang out, and in general, have fun. But that's what you get here. Looking around, there could not have been anyone under sixty years of age in the entire bar, excusing the waitresses and the performers. In fact, most were over seventy. But they were partying down. They were having fun. Most seemed to know everyone else. Jill and I, however, are still relatively new in town, so we only knew about half of the crowd.

One of the guys we recognized was a chap named Matt whom I'd met at Low Key on a quiet night earlier in the year. That night, there'd been no band, so it had been easy to talk. Matt has lived on the island almost his entire life, moving here from Miami when he was three years old. He is easily recognizable due to the scraggily, gray beard that hangs almost to his navel. Matt looks to be at least seventy five years old, but he told me he was only sixty-two. I guess he must have been "rode hard and put up wet" a few too many times. His father had been a commercial fisherman in town. Matt had tried to follow in his dad's profession, but the constitutional amendment in 1993 that banned net fishing in Florida put an end to that dream. Instead, he moved on to working construction—until the recent real estate bust put an end to that opportunity as well. Today, Matt still works when he can, and drinks at the Low Key when he can't. He's pretty much a local institution. I reintroduced myself, and we chatted for a few minutes, catching up as best we could while letting Keri entertain us with her heartfelt songs, her soulful eyes, and the other attractive elements of her performance. I bought us a new pitcher, and enjoyed learning more about Saint James City from one of the old-timers. As we talked, I asked him how many of the old families were still around.

"You know, you'd be surprised at how many of the old families are still here. It's just really hard to leave. When you grow up learning to fish before you even learn to ride a bike and swimming in the sound before you start school, it's tough to give that up. A lot of guys move away when they graduate or quit high school. A lot of them join the service. But eventually, they usually find their way back here."

"Matt, who are some of the really old families on the island? Which families were here a hundred years ago?"

"Shoot, son. That ain't hard. Back then, there weren't that many families that lived out here. Probably less than a dozen at any one time. And most still have relatives here in town. The Darna's were here then. So were the Rodriquez's, the Padilla's, the Sanchez's, the Perez's, the Romero's, the Poppel's, the Spearing's, the Coleman's, the Smith's, and the Watson's. Those are the old fishing families. You want to meet some of their descendants? We could pull together a pretty good-size family reunion just from the guys sitting around the bar tonight. See those three guys sitting down at the end of the bar? There's a Darna, a Coleman, and a Romero. And that's Jesse Rodriquez at that table right behind us. Randy Watson Sanchez is over there, leaning against the door post. She's talking with Ann Spearing. One way or another, they are almost all still around."

"Wow! I had no idea that there were so many of those families still around. Any of them come from Cuba, or have any connections with Cuba?"

"Shoot, just about all of them have some connection with Cuba. All the old fishermen who settled on the barrier islands were originally from Cuba. They were up here looking for prime fishing grounds as soon as the Indians died out. I'm pretty sure the Padilla's were the first ones. They homesteaded out on Cayo Costa. But the Perez's, the Sanchez's, the Rodriquez's, and the Romero's originally came from Cuba, too. All about the same time. Maybe the Darna's, as well; I'm not sure about them. But just about every family on the island has someone who married one of the descendants from one those families, so I guess you could say that just about all of them have some connection with Cuba. How come you're so interested in Cuba?"

"Matt, have you heard about my friend from Spain who was shot here a month ago?"

"Yep. I sure was sorry to hear about that. He was a nice guy. We talked at the bar a couple of times. If I remember right, he bought me several pitchers of beer, too. I liked him. Nice kid."

"Did he ever ask you about Cuba?"

"Now that you mention it, he did. He told me his great-grandfather had once been in the police in Cuba, and he asked me one night what I knew about the families who had come here from Cuba. I told him basically what I just told you."

"Was he particularly interested in any one of the families?"

"No, I don't think so. He wanted to know about all those old Cuban families."

"Was there anything else he was especially interested in?"

"You know, he was very interested in the Punta Gorda Fish Company. He kept asking me about the fish houses. In fact, we went out on the sound in his boat to look at all of the old houses just a day before he was killed. Boy, he sure did like those houses. There was something about seeing them that really excited him. When we got back, he told me how much fun he had had, and gave me a hundred-dollar bill to pay me for show-ing him around. Then, he paid Tricia at the bar for two pitchers of beer for me, and told me to enjoy myself. Like I said, he sure was a nice guy. I hated to see him get killed."

"Yeah. Me too. You got any thoughts about who did it?"

"Not a clue."

"Me either. Look, it's been good talking with you. I appreciate the information. I'll ask Tricia to buy you another pitcher. Thanks."

"Thank you. I'll let you know if I hear anything."

I got up, and moved on down the bar. In passing, I gave Tricia, the barmaid, a twenty, and asked her to take care of Matt for the evening. She grinned, and assured me that she would.

I ducked down the hall, looking for the little boys' room. I was in luck—no line and no one inside. A couple of minutes later, I was walking around the tables outside, looking for Jill. It didn't take me long to find her chatting with a group of the local ladies that she had gotten to know.

"Hey, babe," I said as soon as I could get a word in. "How's it going? You all right?"

"Yeah. I'm good. Honey, have you met Linda? Linda, this is my husband, Jim."

I had not met Linda. But it didn't take me long to learn all I wanted to know about her grandkids back in Minnesota. I excused myself as soon as I could politely do so, and headed back toward the bar, where I found a convenient stool on which to continue to enjoy Gerry and Keri. An hour or so later, Jill put her hand on my shoulder and woke me from my reveries."Hey, big guy! You about ready to head home?"

"Guess we better get going. If we're not careful, we'll break our nine o'clock curfew."

"You lead the way."

Chapter Thirty-Three
A CALL FROM SPAIN

At three o'clock the next morning, the phone by the side of the bed rang. I don't know about you, but it's been my experience that when a phone rings in the wee hours, it's never good news. Usually, someone you know has just died, been in an accident, or one of your kids has been arrested. I don't remember ever getting any good news on the phone at three in the morning.

"Hello," I answered reluctantly, fearing the worse.

"Jim, Jim, Jim, this is Arantxa! I have good news. I am so excited that I have something good to tell you!"

"Arantxa, do you know what time it is? It's very, very early in the morning here."

"Jim, I know. I am so sorry to wake you. It's very, very early in the morning here, too. But I was so excited by the news I have that I couldn't wait any longer to call you."

I knew I'd probably had more sleep than she had gotten, so there was no point in debating how 3:00 a.m. in Saint James City compared to 9:00 a.m. in Madrid. Besides, now that I was wide awake, I was anxious to hear what she had to tell me. "OK. Not a problem. I appreciate the call. What have you learned?"

I went to see Javier's mom again yesterday. We had dinner together at a famous restaurant in Salamanca. It's a lovely place with a great view overlooking the old city. We sat out on the terrace, and had a great meal. We started, of course, with some lovely little tapas—prawns, ham, and cheese. And, of course, we had a lovely Spanish white fino with them. It was just lovely—"

"Arantxa," I interrupted. "I'm glad you had a lovely evening with Javier's mom, but if you woke me up at three in the morning because you were excited about some tapas, I'm really starting to worry about how much partying you are doing over there."

"Jim, stop being so impatient. You Americans. Always in a hurry to jump to the point. Of course, that is not why I'm calling."

"Good."

"I had never been to this restaurant before, but a friend of mine from Bilbao had recommended it. As I said, it was a wonderful place, located in the oldest part of the city, with a patio that overlooks the university. Given my friend's recommendation, I thought that Senora Hernandez might enjoy coming to this place. At first, though, she was very unhappy, and uncomfortable, about being there. As I said, I thought it was a lovely place, and I couldn't understand why she was not enjoying herself. I had thought that if we got out of her house and into a more relaxed setting, that possibly she would be more willing to share information with me about Javier's great-grandfather. But it seemed that I had made a mistake. She became very quiet, and would say little more than yes or no. I was afraid that I had made a big—and expensive—mistake in bringing her to this nice restaurant. I was afraid that my relationship with Senora Hernandez had taken a turn for the worse. I was wondering if we should leave after the tapas. We had had a couple glasses of the wonderful wine when I suggested that if the restaurant was making her uncomfortable, perhaps we should leave. When I said that, she turned her head away, and said nothing. But a few moments later, I heard her crying. I was shocked, fearing that somehow I had made a huge mistake. I didn't know what to do. After a minute, I put my hand on her hand, and said: 'Senora, I am so sorry that you do not like this place. Let me pay our bill, and we will leave. I will take you home.'

"At that point, she turned toward me, gently squeezed my hand, and said: 'Arantxa, I'm sorry, but you do not understand. I do not dislike this place; in fact, I love coming to this place very much. Javier's father and I used to come here frequently. In fact, he and I became engaged at that table over there in the corner. After that, we made it a point to come back here every year on our anniversary. We also, as a family, would come here for other special occasions. It is a place that we loved very much. In fact, this is where we came with Javier to celebrate his graduation from the university. I know you had no way to know this, but the table we are sitting at tonight is the same table at which Javier, his father, and I sat that night. This is like a holy place to me. When we sat down, it all came flooding back. I was overwhelmed by grief, thinking how happy, how proud, and how hopeful we had all been on that night! And, now, dear God, it's all gone. My husband is dead; and my beautiful, gentle son is gone as well. You see, it was more than I could bear to be here sitting again at this very table.'

"I was horrified," Arantxa told me. "I had no idea. I apologized over and over, and then we both started to cry. I don't know, maybe this was the first time that Mrs. Hernandez had cried since Javier had died, maybe not. But it was clear to me that we both needed to release our feelings, and our grief, over his murder. We must have wept together for at least five minutes. We held each other in a gentle embrace. I don't know what the other diners thought, but as far as we were concerned, they didn't exist. To us both, I think, the world stopped spinning for those minutes. Finally, Mrs. Hernandez stopped crying, and I felt her take a deep breath, straighten her back, and lift her head. I said, 'Senora Hernandez, we should go.'

"But she said, 'No, we must *not* leave now. I know now that you were a dear friend of Javier's. Tonight, we are going to stay, and we are going to celebrate the time that we had with him. This was a place that he loved, too. Tonight, we are going to have a party in his honor. And now that I know for sure that you are trying to help find out who killed my dear son, tonight I am going to share with you the rest of what I know about what happened in Cuba.'

"And, party we did, Jim. We ordered the Chef's Menu Tour, which included a little of all of the restaurant's best dishes—there were seven or eight courses of the most delicious food I have ever tasted. And the wine—oh, the wine! We asked the maitre d' to bring a glass of his recommended pairings with each course. He knew his business; he knew it very well. The wines he brought truly complemented the food. I don't know if you've ever experienced wine that actually enhances the food it is paired with, and vice versa. It is not an experience that I have often enjoyed, and Lord knows, I have drunk more than my share of wine. But last night, we had that experience—the pairings amplified each other, almost so much that so that it was as if we had entered another dimension of taste and pleasure. It was truly an amazing experience. And we laughed, and told stories about Javier. She told me all about him when he was growing up. About all the trouble he had gotten into. She told me about the time—I think she said he was five—that he took his little red wagon down into a ravine to load it with rocks. The wagon got so heavy he couldn't pull it back out of the ravine. He tried for hours to get the wagon back up to the road. Finally, his father found him just before the sun was starting to go down. She said that they were not happy with him when he did this. Still, she said that was one of her fondest memories of him as a child. She also told me about his earliest girlfriends. And about how shy he was then. But she also told me about how confident and kind he was with women after he had grown up. They all loved him. I then told her about Javier at the bank. I told her about how respected he was by those who worked with him. I also told her how all the women at the bank loved him, too. She laughed a lot when I told her that. The whole evening was nothing short of fantastic.

"Finally, as we were enjoying excellent coffee with dessert, she got very serious again, and said: 'I know you want to find who killed Javier. I want to know who killed him, too. When we spoke before, I did not tell you everything I knew. I do not know that much. But I know more than I told you before. I certainly do not know who killed my son. I don't even know the name of the person who started all of this back in Cuba so many years ago. The men in the family would not share that information with me—they did not want a woman to be dragged into this ugliness. I really know very little about the facts in this. I think the only thing that I know that may be helpful is simply one thing, and the only reason I remember this is because it sounded so funny when I first heard it. Somehow, the murder in Cuba was connected to something called the Punta Gorda Fish Company. I thought that was funny because in Spanish, *gorda* means fat. I didn't know then if this meant that a peninsula was fat, or whether maybe the fish were fat. I was hoping it was the latter. I know now that Punta Gorda referred to a peninsula in Charlotte Harbor, and that today a fine city exists on that location. And I know that Punta Gorda Fish Company was a business that used to be based in that city. Somehow, this company was connected to the murder that took place in Cuba when Javier's great-grandfather was there.'

"She went on to tell me that when Javier's great-grandfather returned from Cuba, he was a changed man. He no longer trusted the Spanish government. And he especially hated the US government. According to Senora Hernandez, he believed that both governments had condoned the cover-up of a murder, and even more importantly, had used that cover-up to excuse the slaughter of thousands of innocent men, women, and children. He was disgusted by what had happened. But he could not speak out. As you know, he worked for the government. In fact, they made him a hero when he returned. But from that point forward, his relationship with the government was different. No longer was he destined for the top of the Guardia Civil. He was treated with honor, of course, and he was rewarded with prestigious jobs. But I don't think that he was ever again fully trusted. He knew too much. He could do nothing but keep quiet, and pass along the story to the men of his family. He warned them against trying to bring this information to light, since he feared that the embarrassment for either the Spanish or the American governments would be too great. He feared that both governments would be willing to take whatever steps were necessary to keep this story from being made public. He took this secret to his grave, only telling his son, who swore a sacred oath to divulge the story to no one other than his own son at an appropriate time in the future. And that's how this was passed down in the family. Javier's father told him when Javier turned twenty-one. He made Javier swear the same oath that he had sworn, and that his father before him had sworn. As far as she knows, Javier went to his death upholding that oath. But she believes strongly that this secret lead to his murder. She does not know who killed her son. But she would not be surprised if the Spanish government asked the US government to kill him in order to keep him silent. Or maybe someone else killed him for his own reasons. But she believes this secret led to her son's murder—and she wants the killer brought to justice.

"Jim, I don't know if this will help you. But I wanted you to know as soon as possible. I am sure this is all the information Senora Hernandez knows. If she knew anything else, she would have told me last night. We swore an oath to each other to not rest until Javier's murderer had been found, and until justice had been served. We want this with all of our hearts, and I will do anything I can to help her get the satisfaction she deserves. But Jim, you need to be very, very careful. Maybe the government does want this covered up. You may not be able to trust the people in the government who are trying to help you. I don't know. Maybe there is someone else in your town who will kill again to keep this quiet. I don't know, but I do know that your life is in danger. You and Jill need to be very careful!"

"Arantxa, this is great information," Jim said. "Maybe we will be able to use it to identify who was killed in Cuba, and maybe to even find out who killed him. This could be the key to unlocking this whole thing. You have done great work. Please pass along to Senora Hernandez that we are not going to rest either until we have the bastard who did this locked up. Thank you again. I'll keep you posted. Now, you go get some sleep."

Chapter Thirty-Four

THE KNOT BEGINS TO UNRAVEL

I knew it was much too early to call Lieutenant Collins. So I did the next best thing: I woke Jill up.

Now, I don't know about you, but it's been my experience that waking your wife up at four in the morning is normally not a particularly good thing to do. Jill is usually a sound sleeper, and she very much enjoys her nightly eight hours of slumber. So I didn't make the decision to wake her lightly. But I was so excited that we might finally have a clue that I just had to wake her. I couldn't help myself.

To her credit, once she woke up enough to comprehend that the house wasn't on fire or that one of the kids wasn't in the hospital, she reacted to being disturbed at this hour with surprisingly good humor. "Jim, this had better be damned good! You have no idea about how much fun I was having in my dream when you started to shake me. It was a good one! And, no, before you ask, you weren't in it. At least you weren't up until the point when you started to wake me up. I'm really having some very mixed emotions about you right now. So, tell me again, why in the hell are we up at this hour?"

"Baby, I'm sorry to disturb your dream. It was that good, huh? With anyone I know?"

"No. But I wouldn't tell you even if it was. Are we going to talk about my dream, or did you wake me up for some good reason?"

"OK, OK. Arantxa called. She couldn't wait to tell me about some information she had learned from Javier's mom. Bottom line: the murder in Cuba was related in some fashion to the Punta Gorda Fish Company—you know, the old fishing company that built all those fish houses that used to be all over the sound. And somehow this whole thing relates to a cover-up by the governments of the United States and Spain. I think if we can figure out how the Cuban murder relates to the fish company, we may be able to unravel how it ties back to Javier's murder. We need to get started. Now."

"Wow. That's good information. And it's probably a really good thing you woke me up when you did. If that dream had gone on much longer, I'm not sure how I would have felt about you in the morning. You know, you might not have compared very favorably."

"I doubt that. Besides, it was just a dream. It wasn't real. You were probably just having a nightmare."

"Nightmare, my ass. You waking me up from that dream in the middle of the night was my nightmare. But now that we're up, I'll go make some coffee. You go get started on the computer."

A few minutes later, I was downstairs typing "Punta Gorda Fish Company" into a Google search field. A few seconds later, up popped the results screen. It showed 71,400 hits for this subject. Perhaps this was going to take a while.

The first hit, of course, was one of the most useful. Wikipedia had a good summary about the early days of the company. It was founded in 1897 by Eugene Knight and his brother-in-law, Mathew Giddens. They later went into partnership with Harry Dreggers, the company's bookkeeper. The company's creation was made possible because Florida Southern Railroad extended its tracks to the city docks in Punta Gorda. The company supported a network of fishermen in the area. The company then iced the fish, and shipped them by rail throughout the eastern United States. In its heyday, Punta Gorda Fish Company had 250 employees and ran about 140 boats of various sizes throughout its fishing territories in Charlotte Harbor and Pine Island Sound. To support this fishing activity, it built a large number of over-the-water fish shacks throughout the fishing areas. These shacks served as dormitories for the company's fishermen while they fished on the flats. It also built a number of larger, over-the-water fish houses. These centrally located houses served as collection points for the fishermen's catches, and provided cold storage for the fish they brought in. The ice for these fish houses was delivered by run boats from the company's ice plant in Punta Gorda. These fish houses also served as commissaries, providing supplies and groceries for the fishermen and others who lived in the surrounding areas. On return trips, the run boats brought fish back to Punta Gorda for shipment by rail to the markets throughout the eastern United States. The company was very successful. Over time, it was able to absorb most of its direct competitors. The company thrived until 1927. At that time, the newly completed bridge to Matlacha made the network of shacks, houses, and run boats unnecessary. The Great Depression, as it unfolded, also reduced the demand for fresh fish. Nevertheless, the company continued to be one of Punta Gorda's largest employers until well after World War II. After that, the company's business began to decline. It finally ceased operation in 1977.

Most of the other web hits focused on the fish shacks and fish houses that still exist in Pine Island Sound. I noted that the shacks where we had taken Javier were six of the nine shacks that are still standing.

Another site showed a 1947 picture of Harry Dreggers and eight of his employees at the company's dock in Punta Gorda. It was clearly a staged photo, as all of the men in the picture were holding fish by the tail. But looking at the picture, it is clear that Dreggers was the boss, and that the others worked for him. He stood just a little to the side of the group, and he was clearly better dressed than they were. His shoes were shined, while all the others wore scuffed work boots. My impression was that Dreggers was probably not a bad man. In fact, in some ways he resembled my grandfather on my mother's side. Clearly, Dreggers was successful. I'm sure he had worked hard for his money. And I would guess he was probably a little tight-fisted with it. Most successful people are—that's one of their secrets to accumulating wealth in the first place. I would also bet that he was a pillar of the community, and probably was a cornerstone of the local church. That's just the impression I got from the one picture. I didn't think I was looking at a murderer.

Beyond that, the web search quickly turned into a tough slog. Thankfully, Jill arrived about that time with two mugs of steaming coffee. As we shared the warm stimulants, I told her what I had learned, and showed her the picture of the fish company's employees. She agreed that Dreggers looked like an OK fellow. Once the coffee was gone, she directed me to get back to work. She went back upstairs to use her iPad to see what she could find.

I didn't really find much else of use regarding the Punta Gorda Fish Company. There was a ton of information about the fish shacks and fish houses that still survive. These are all now registered with the National Register of Historic Places. But I was able to learn more about the city of Punta Gorda. It was founded in 1882 by Colonel Isaac Trabue, and was originally known as Trabue City. But in exchange for the railroad agreeing to come to the town, he agreed that the town's name should be changed to Punta Gorda. For a while, the town served as the main gateway between the United States and Cuba, with regularly scheduled steamships running between it and Havana. But Trabue got into an argument with Henry Plant, the tycoon who owned the railroad. It is unclear what they argued about. But whatever it was, it must have infuriated Plant. The result was that Plant had the tracks to the steamship lines taken up, leaving only the tracks to the shallow-water fish docks. Apparently due to this argument, Plant decided to make Tampa, and the new hotel that he was building there, the main embarkment point for Cuba. The rest, as they say, is history. I wasn't sure if any of this was relevant to Javier's murder, but it was interesting to learn that traveling to Cuba via Southwest Florida had been common at the turn of the last century.

Try as I might, however, I wasn't able to get much further. Many sites discussed in detail the remaining fish shacks. I learned where they were all located, and who owned some of them. I found a couple of pictures that showed various employees of the company, usually holding fish, unloading fish off of boats, or something similar. I found pictures of the company's run boats, its docks, and even its ice plant next to the railroad. That building still exists, and has been preserved for the public to explore. After several hours of work, all I knew about the men who founded the company were their names, that Harry Dreggers was still alive in 1947, and that he looked to be a pleasant, somewhat aloof, and well-dressed Florida businessman. Beyond that, I had nothing.

Just as I was giving up, Jill came downstairs with more coffee.

"You find anything else?" she asked.

"Not much. How about you?"

"No. I think there's probably a lot of information in the Charlotte County Historical Center about this, but it doesn't seem to be easily available on the web. But I bet if we went up there they would be able to help us."

"Yeah. Maybe that's what we ought to do. Or better yet, maybe we ought to tell Mike Collins, and let him send his professionals up there for a day. If it's there, they can find it."

"I'm sure they can, and I agree that's what we ought to do. But I'm disappointed that we haven't been able to get any further on this. I feel that we're so close. There's got to be something else we can do."

"Maybe you can just go back to sleep, and it'll come to you in a dream."

"Shut up! No reason to get jealous. After all, it was just a dream. See if I tell you anything else about my fantasies."

"I thought I was your fantasy."

"In your dreams, honey!"

With that exchange, I pulled the visor on my cap down over my eyes, and again turned my attention to the computer. But just about the time I started another search, Jill interrupted."Didn't you buy some books about the history of Pine Island? I know you've got one on Saint James City, and there are a couple of others."

"You know, you're right. There's one I've been meaning to read, but haven't gotten around to yet. You remember; it had a funny name. What was that? *Cow Boat? Boat Cow? Boat Horse? Boat Dog?* You remember? What is it called?"

"*Boat Goat!*"

"That's it, baby. Do you remember where I put it?"

"Let me suggest that you try the bookcase. That would probably be a logical place to look."

"No reason to get smart. I did ask you politely. But you're right. I'll have a look."

A couple of minutes later, I returned holding *Boat Goat: Memories of Pine Island Sound, Florida* by Captain J. Kirk Walter."This looks promising. There's a whole section on the Punta Gorda Fish Company. Starts on page 159."A couple of minutes later, I yelled, "Hot damn! Listen to this. Page 161:'Eugene Knight, one of the founders of the company, died under mysterious circumstances in Cuba while transporting a large amount of company funds.'"

This had to be it. It fit together in so many ways. An unsolved murder in Cuba that involved the Punta Gorda Fish Company. This had to be the link that we had been missing.

I couldn't wait to talk with Lieutenant Collins. It was six-thirty in the morning. I knew he wasn't in the office yet, but screw him. I had his cell phone number. This couldn't wait.

He answered on the third ring. "Story, this had better be damned good. I am currently snuggled up tightly against the warm, naked body of one of the Fort Myer's Police Department's most attractive, and well-endowed female officers. And we're working 'undercover,' if you get my drift. Can this wait?"

"Sorry. Call me back later."

A minute later, my phone rang. "She's now in the shower getting ready to go to work. You might say that the moment has passed. What have you got?"

"Mike, I'm really sorry I messed up your deal. But I think I've got something important." I told him about Arantxa's call detailing her conversation with Senora Hernandez.

"That's it?" he growled.

"No. That is not it. I think I know who was killed in Cuba, and why he was killed."

"Now we're talking. How'd you find this out?"

I told him about the story in *Boat Goat*.

"I'll be damned. So we think we've got someone who whacked Knight when he was in Cuba, and took a large amount of funds. Then for some reason, the murder was covered up and used to justify the butchery of thousands of Afro-Cubans. And somebody—or something—doesn't want this information to become public. This is starting to make some sense. Let me get someone on this. We'll check the records in Charlotte County to see if we can verify the date. But even if we can, I don't know where that leaves us. Solving a hundred-year-old cold case in

Havana sounds pretty challenging. But one step at a time. I'll get back to you when we check this out."

"So you're not mad that I called?"

"Hell yes, I'm mad! You don't have any idea how long I've been working on that particular project. And just at the critical moment, the fucking cell phone rings! Yes, I'm mad! I'm just not sure now who I'm mad at. But never mind. You were right to call. I'll be in touch."

Chapter Thirty-Five
A CUBAN CRIME OF PASSION

Jill and I spent the morning as we normally do on the days that we aren't going fishing. After we walked Cody, we enjoyed several cups of hot morning beverages (she likes K-cup coffee; I love black tea). We then embarked on our normal, three-mile walk. I love these walks in the morning. Over the months, we've started to hone in on the patterns of the local wildlife. We know where various osprey nests are located; we've even discovered, after much searching, the location of a couple of eagle nests on our side of town. We can't wait till the spring to watch these spectacular birds rear their hatchlings. That's going to be special.

As I've mentioned before, another of the highlights of these trips is the opportunity to get to know the neighbors. Generally, it's just a quick good morning. But occasionally, there is a chance to stop and get to actually know people. Today, a man who lives down the street was driving his mint-condition 1970s pickup truck by us. As he came alongside, he stopped to say good morning. We carried on a pleasant, five-minute chat right there in the middle of the road. It's not like you have to worry much about traffic in Saint James City. I told him that I liked his truck. He appreciated that. It was obvious that he liked his truck, too. He said he had bought it a couple of years ago from an eighty-six-year-old man up in Punta Gorda who had bought the truck new. He was forced to sell because he no longer had the strength to drive it, since it does not have power steering. All the old guy had been able to do for the past several years was to go out once a week, crank it up, and let it run for fifteen minutes. All he could do was to sit in it and think about how much he loved the truck. When our neighbor bought it, it only had 26,000 miles on it. Our neighbor said he tried to back out of the deal once he saw how attached the old man was to it, but the old man wouldn't let him. He told our neighbor that it was time for him to sell it, and that he thought our neighbor would be a good man to own it. They went ahead with the sale, but they both cried when it was done. We could tell from the conversation that the truck had indeed found a good home.

As we talked further, we learned that our neighbor was a retired crab fisherman. After forty years of pulling traps, his back had finally given out. Now he stayed at home, and lived on a disability pension. However, you could tell by the twinkle in his eye that he was enjoying life, despite his age and his infirmity. After a few minutes, he slowly drove away, and we continued our walk.

"Now, that guy is something," I said to Jill. "He's quite a character. I liked him a lot."

"I liked him, too," Jill said. "He's a neat guy."

Our usual route takes us down by the bay. I love to look at it as we walk. I like to see how bad the chop is, how many boats are about, and just generally what's going on out on the water. That day, there was a pretty strong breeze blowing almost straight out of the North. The water near shore was smooth, since it was in the lee of the island, but further out by Sanibel, I could see that things were getting pretty rough. We could see what looked to be about a thirty-five-foot trawler banging its way up the channel, directly into the chop. It didn't look like any fun to me. Jill and I would definitely not be going out in the boat that day.

As we headed back up the street toward our house, I happened to glance at a brick driveway. I stopped in my tracks."Jill! Look at this." We were looking at what I thought was an owl. At least, it looked a lot like an owl, in some ways. And it looked as if it was asleep, right there in the middle of the driveway. I knew that wasn't right. "What do you think it's doing?" I asked.

"I don't know. Is it sleeping?"

At that point, the bird became aware of us. It lifted its head and spread its wings. But it was clear that it couldn't fly. Obviously, it was either injured or sick. The bird finally just turned away so that its back was to us. It was almost as if it was saying, "I may not be able to fly away, but at least I can try to ignore that you are here." Once again, it tucked its head down, and became still.

About that time, I looked up the road, and saw that our neighbor in the old pickup was coming back from wherever he had gone. I was hoping he might have an idea about what to do with the bird. I waved him over as he approached.

"Well, well, well. Look at that. It's a female marsh hawk. Sure is pretty—for a bird that is. What do you think it's doing?"

"I can't tell for sure, but I think it's injured."

"Yeah, it looks that way to me, too. I don't think she's going to make it if we leave her here. There's too many critters around here that will attack her if she just sits here. But you have to be careful trying to handle these things. That beak and those talons can do a lot bit of damage. Let me see if I've got some gloves in the back. He turned the truck off, got out, and lifted the lid on his storage box in the bed of the truck.

"Heck. I thought I might have had some gloves, but I guess I don't. Let me think a minute about what I can do."

A few seconds later, I saw him pulling off his T-shirt, and then he quietly walked over to the bird. He spread the shirt out, and very gently laid it over the bird. Surprisingly, the bird did not resist, or even seem to mind. I guess it was in bad shape. Our neighbor carefully put his hands around and under the bird, and picked it up.

He said, "I guess I'll just take it home, and see what I can do for it. There's a Wild Bird Rescue Group here on island. I'll give them a call. Maybe they can take her in."

"That sounds like a good plan to me. I appreciate your help with her."

"Heck, this ain't nothing. Besides, I ain't doing nothing for this bird that a lot of other folks ain't doing for me right now. Just seems like the right thing to do. I'll let you know how she gets along."

We walked on down the street. "Wow. This has really been a SJC type of day. It's not every day in most places that you meet a character like him *and* find a wounded hawk in your neighborhood."

"That's for sure. This is quite some place we've moved to."

As we walked into the house, the phone was ringing. I looked at the caller ID, saw it was Mike Collins, and picked it up.

"Mike, what's up?"

"Hey, Jim. I got my intern on the Eugene Knight thing as soon as we hung up this morning. Didn't take her long to find a genealogical site that showed when he died. Care to take a guess?"

"How about late 1911 or early 1912?"

"Right on! October 26, 1911, in Cuba. In addition, she was able to find out that he and his partner in the fish company had taken advantage of the situation in Cuba by buying a very large cattle ranch down there as soon as Americans were allowed in. The purchase had worked out very well for them. He had gone to Cuba a few weeks before he was killed to oversee the sale of that year's crop of yearlings. He was preparing to return to the United States with several hundred thousand dollars in gold when an unknown person shot him in the back of the head, and relieved him of it. The crime was quickly blamed on a black fisherman who happened to be an activist in the independence movement. This guy was quickly captured—and imagine this—killed shortly after, as he 'tried to escape.' But the money was never recovered. This murder, and several others over the next months, were what led up to the vigilante slaughter that took place in May and June of the next year."

"Yeah, yeah, yeah. That's making sense. I can see all of that going down. And I can see old man Hernandez being infuriated with how it was handled. But that doesn't help us know who really killed him. I don't suppose your intern was able to find that out, too?"

Mike laughed. "No. Not yet anyway. I've got her trying to get in touch with the Customs Department to see if there are any records of who might have traveled between Punta Gorda and Cuba around that time. But I'm not very hopeful that those records will still exist. Without them, I don't see any way to fig-ure this out."

"Fuck that! There has to be a way. Let's think about it for a while, and get back together later this afternoon. Thanks for your help, Mike. I think we're getting close on this. I appreciate it."

"Talk to you this afternoon. Give me a call."

Chapter Thirty-Six

OLD BLUE COOLS OFF

"All right, Poirot, what are we going to do about dinner tonight?" Jill asked.

I replied, "You can't just answer a question like that flat out. You have to back into these things. What are we going to do for lunch?"

"Well, I can whip up a sandwich, or there are some brats in the fridge that I can warm up for you."

"No sandwiches! If I see another sandwich this week, I may become unglued."

"I know, I know. When we went fishing the other day we had breakfast sandwiches as we motored out of the canal. Then, as we fished, we had ham-and-cheese sandwiches for lunch. And when we got home, I fixed hamburgers. I understand your point. So, what've you got in mind?"

"How about a salad," I replied.

"OK with me. What do you want to put on it? I could throw some lunch meat and cheese on top, and call it a chef's salad."

"Humor me. You know what sounds really great to me? How about if I went down to the fish house and picked up some smoked mullet? We could have that on a salad, and use the rest to make some dip for later."

"I like it. Why don't you get on your bike and make that happen? When you get back, I'll conjure us up a salad."

What we call the fish house is only a few blocks from our house. It doesn't look like much, but it is a fully operational fish market that services the commercial fishermen and crabbers in the area. While most of their sales are to commercial accounts, they also love it when retail accounts show up with cash in hand. Not only is the retail price significantly greater than what they get wholesale, but I suspect that few, if any, of those cash transactions ever find their way into the official books of the operation.

That's fine with me. What matters to me is that I can pedal my bike a couple of blocks, and buy the freshest seafood you can imagine. You can get fish or crabs literally just off the boat. I also like to take in the sights, sounds, and smells of an authentic piece of historic Pine Island. The prices may be higher, some of the rules and regulations may be different than they were fifty years ago, and the public's taste for various foods may have evolved, but I doubt that much else has fundamentally changed from the way business was done in days gone by. I love going there, just so I can watch.

One of the things I most like to do when I am there is to say hello to the fish house dog, Blue. He is a beautiful, full-blooded, Siberian husky. He's a large dog, and he's starting to get up in years. But he doesn't get in the way, and he doesn't cause any problems when clients show up. He sometimes can be found lying in the shade in a cool spot. But by far, his favorite way to spend the day—I'm not kidding—is to lie on, or in, a large pile of crushed ice. If it's a really warm day, he prefers to be buried from head to toe in the pile. When he's covered in ice, he seems to think that he's in heaven. He will stay there for hours without moving a muscle. I guess he only stirs when he has to answer nature's call. You can see why a trip to the fish house is one of my favorite things to do on the island.

That morning, Blue was on his ice bed, looking as happy as a dog can look. As I walked up, he eyed me momentarily, but quickly seemed to write me off as just a boring retail customer, and returned to his peaceful slumber. I engaged the young fellow who was manning the dock, and told him what I was looking for. He went into the cooler, and returned in a minute with a box of smoked filets.

"How many of these you want?" he asked.

"How much are they today?"

"Eight bucks a pound."

"Well, I'm looking for two fish, but all I brought with me was a twenty-dollar bill."

"Not a problem. I'll fix you up."

He laid the sides from three large, beautifully smoked mullet on the scale. I could see that this sale normally would have cost a little over twenty-two dollars. But not for me that day. I'm sure he had no desire, and probably didn't have the ability, to make change if he'd only sold me two. That worked fine for me. As I left, I said good-bye to Blue; but Blue, still dreaming of life on the tundra, didn't move a muscle. Another treasured moment of life in Saint James City.

A few minutes later, I was in the kitchen, pulling mullet meat off the skin, and separating it from the rib bones. In no time, we had a large Tupperware container full of fat, smoky, delicious fish flesh, ready for Jill's culinary magic. I looked forward to lunch, and to the late-afternoon appetizer.

With that pleasant chore accomplished, I puttered around the house, taking care of various small projects, all the while thinking about Eugene Knight's murder and where the investigation stood. I didn't have a clue about where to go next. I looked forward to seeing what the sheriff's department was able to dig up.

Jill's smoked-mullet salad did not disappoint. There may be better things to eat in the world than smoked mullet, but as far as I'm concerned, it ranks in the top ten. To the mullet, she had added lettuce, a tomato, a couple of hard-boiled eggs, and a nice dressing that featured mayo, Dijon mustard, and some freshly squeezed lemon juice. I suspect that the look on my face, after I had finished eating, was a lot like the look I had seen on Blue's face as he lay in the ice. Absolute contentment.

A couple of hours later, as I was starting to recover from my afternoon nap, the phone rang and the ID showed that Mike Collins was calling.

"Hey, Mike. What'd you learn?"

"I guess I'm getting old. I could have sworn that we would never have been able to find passenger records from steamship trips a hundred years ago. You know, when I was young, it would have taken weeks of digging to find anything like that. But my diligent little intern gets on her tablet, logs onto a historical site, and within an hour has all the records we need. It's simply amazing what you can do these days!"

"Wow. That is amazing. What'd she find?"

"First, there were no passenger ships leaving from Punta Gorda at that time. The only ships that connected the west coast of Florida to Cuba during this period sailed from either Tampa or from Key West. It looks like Henry Plant wasn't kidding when he threatened to turn Punta Gorda into a backwater. But we were able to find that Eugene Knight sailed out of Tampa on September 19, 2011, bound for Havana. The ship stopped in Key West for six hours, and was in Havana the next day. There was no record of him ever having sailed back."

"OK. That makes sense. But what about the other passengers, coming and going? Anything jump out at you?"

"We're still looking, but one thing I noticed was that a Julio Perez embarked in Key West, bound for Havana, a few days after Knight sailed. Again, no record of him having returned by ship over the next twelve months. We're checking this out, but I'm pretty sure that Carl Perez's great-grandfather—you know, the one who had the fish ranch on Cayo Costa—was named Julio. I thought that was very interesting. None of the other names on the lists jumped out at me as being from one of the old families from around the sound."

"That's not much to go on."

"Yeah. You can say that again. First, you had me trying to pin Javier's murder on the Colliers, and now I'm looking at the other most prominent family in Southwest Florida. It's going to take a lot more than this coincidence before I start digging around in Carl Perez's garden. I don't know if you've heard this, but word is that Carl's about to be named by the governor to take the US Senate seat that's currently vacant. There's no way

I'm making any waves for those guys. The sheriff would terminate me before I could even get back to the office. I don't need that kind of trouble."

"But what if he's really the murderer?"

"Yeah. And what if I think the pope's really a Hindu? It's not enough to have a hunch about something. I've got to have proof before I start firing off accusations. And before I fire accusations about Carl Perez, I had better have ironclad, triple-vetted evidence. It's not enough to know that a member of his family might have been in Cuba at the same time that Gene Knight was killed. That crime took place over a hundred years ago. I'm not going to waste time and resources trying to solve that murder when I've got a whole damn book of unsolved murders that took place right here in Lee County in the past few months."

"So, what do we do now? Are you dropping it?"

"Fuck, no! I'm not dropping it. But I'll be honest. Right now, I don't know what else to do. You come up with anything, let me know."

Chapter Thirty-Seven
THE JOY OF FISHING

I hung up, and brought Jill up to speed. Her reaction was the same as mine.

"Shit. That's not good. It doesn't sound like Mike knows where to go next. Frankly, I don't either. What do you think we ought to do?"

"Beats me. But you know, the brain is an amazing thing. It's been my experience that sometimes it'll let you approach an issue straight on and directly reason out an answer to your problem. But other times, when the answer isn't as obvious, it's best to let the brain ponder a problem for a while. It will continue to analyze the question even when you're not thinking about it. Kind of like when we're trying to remember the names of artists who originally recorded the songs that the musicians down at Woody's or Low Key are playing. We think, and we think, and we can't come up with it. But, twenty minutes later, after we've had another drink or two, and we're talking about something else entirely, then, out of the blue, it'll come to us:"Oh, yeah.

Buffalo Springfield!"That's what we need to do now. We need to let this stew for a while."

"So, let me get this straight. Are you suggesting that we go downtown and start drinking?"

"No. Of course not. At least, not yet. What I was suggesting was that we should go fishing. We need to do something to get our minds off of this, and just hope that an answer will eventually come to us."

"OK. That actually kind of makes sense to me. So, why don't you go fishing this afternoon? It looks like the tide is low now. I guess that means that it will be coming in all afternoon. And it looks like the wind has laid down. Should be a good day to fish."

"You don't want to go?"

"No. I love to go fishing with you, but quite honestly, fishing is not really the best way for me to get my mind off something. I think the best way for me to do that is to go shopping. Why don't you go fishing, and I'll go shopping? Then we can meet later—maybe at Woody's—have a few drinks, and see if anything has bubbled up. If it hasn't, maybe we'll just keep drinking until it does."

"I like your plan. See you at Woody's at around six."

It doesn't take me long to get ready to go fishing. I'm just about always dressed for the occasion. Workout shorts, a T-shirt, and flip-flops make up my daily uniform. I wear this outfit when I walk the dog, work in the yard, go to lunch, and when I go fishing. The only preparations I have to make to hit the water are to put some ice in the coolers (I freeze my own ice in Tupperware containers), load the rods, get the keys, and let the boat down off the lift. Ten minutes at the most. I've always got plenty of Gulp shrimp onboard, and anyway, I keep a bait cast net on the boat at all times. I was heading down the canal in short order.

Taking a boat out fishing is a great way to get your mind off what's bothering you. Piloting a boat requires concentration and focus outside of yourself. Simply steering a boat smoothly requires you to look far ahead of your current location. If you don't do that, you'll overcorrect, and the boat will keep wandering from side to side. Looking far ahead allows the brain to calculate more accurately the adjustments required, and you end up pretty much steering in a straight line. Then you need to think about where you want to go and the best way to get there. You need to factor in the wind direction and the tide. And, of course, you need to think about what kind of fish you want to catch, and how much time you have. Then, once you're underway, you've got to pay attention to what's going on all around you. Are there other boats coming your way? What about boats coming up behind you? Will your paths cross? If so, how are you going to pass? There are also a lot of navigation rules to consider when you are piloting a boat. Without question, these are all things that can pull you out of self-absorption for a while.

And if that doesn't do it, just taking a few minutes to look around at the water and the sky should certainly pull you out of yourself. That doesn't even begin to consider the effect of actually fishing—baiting a hook, casting a rod, popping a cork, staring at the water, reacting to the slightest twitch, setting a hook, playing a fish, landing it if it's something you want to keep, or getting it off the hook if you don't, measuring it to make sure it is legal, putting it in the live well, and starting the process all over again. It may not be rocket science, but it requires some concentration, and causes you to focus on something other than yourself. That's what I needed to do. I needed to think about something other than who killed Javier, and how to catch that killer.

I enjoy fishing. I enjoy just about everything that's associated with it. I very much enjoy driving the boat. I like putting a plan together in order to have a successful outing, and I enjoy thinking, if necessary, about how to modify that plan as the day goes along. I enjoy being on the water, and baking in the sunshine. I like watching the birds fly, and watching them feed. I love to observe dolphins doing what dolphins do. All of these creatures are so much better fishermen than we are. I often wonder what the anhinga must think as they watch me flounder around, trying to catch a fish, when all they have to do is dive underwater and grab one. I also like to pay attention to the weather, and try to figure out what is coming next.

In truth, there's really not too much about fishing that I don't enjoy. This may surprise you, but the part I enjoy least is the actual act of fishing. For example, I worry every time I dip a shrimp out of the tank and impale it on a hook. In doing that, I think about the odds of that particular shrimp having been the one that got selected for this horrific end. I worry about how much pain that shrimp felt, and about how much fear it suffered as the net approached, as my fingers grabbed it, and as it sank in the water to await being eaten alive by a hungry predator. But I don't worry enough about this to stop using live shrimp as bait in the cooler months when shrimp are, by far, the best bait to use to catch fish.

When I actually catch a fish, I anguish over that, too. It's one thing to put one in the live well. At least I can justify this by remembering that I'm going to eat it for dinner at some point. What really tears me up is when a fish is too small to keep, but the hook is impossible to remove without killing the fish. I hate it when I have to throw a fish back into the water knowing that it's going to die. I get a twisted sense of being let off my own moral hook when I see that wounded fish scooped up within a few minutes by a hungry osprey or anhinga.

Speaking of which, anhinga really drive me nuts. When I do all I can to make sure that I don't harm the fish that I'm releasing, more often than not, a damn anhinga will have observed the whole process, and will be laying in wait under the boat, ready to grab it. I know that anhinga have to eat, too. But that doesn't mean I have to like it. I hope you won't tell PETA, but I've been known to try to hit them on the head with the end of my push pole, just to let them know that I don't want them around. Usually, if I come close enough with the pole, they get the message, and look for a friendlier boat to stalk. There's probably a law against harassing the damn things, but I'm just not a fan of theirs.

I don't know what the survival rate is for released fish, but I'm betting it can't be much better than 50 percent. It makes me wonder if the fifteen-inch minimum length for trout shouldn't be lowered. It sure seems that with a lower length requirement, I would end up killing a heck of lot fewer fish needlessly. But I'm no ichthyologist. I'm sure they know what they're doing.

Having said all of this, I don't dislike any part of the fishing experience enough not to do it. To me, the pluses outweigh the minuses. Maybe, end of the day, all of this conflict just makes it obvious how weak my character really is. I don't really know. And, at this point in my life, I don't really care. I go fishing. I've always gone fishing, and I probably always will go fishing. If I didn't, what else would I have to talk about in the bar at night?

Certainly all of these activities and thoughts help to keep a person's mind off of his troubles. I'm positive that that's one of the reasons that men, over the centuries, have found fishing to be so therapeutic. I don't think it matters too much if you're fishing with a cane pole in a roadside creek or holding a ten-thousand-dollar rod and reel on a million-dollar sports fishing boat in the middle of the Atlantic. The effect is the same. I'm sure it ties back somehow to the underlying animal in all of us. Clearly, there's something instinctual that makes the act of fishing such an important activity for men. It's not something that any of us really has to do in this day and age, but it is something that many of us want to do—and maybe, at some fundamental level, need to do. We have some basic compulsion to seek prey, to set a lure for that prey, to deceive that prey, and, ultimately, to entice that prey so that we can catch it in our trap or on our hook. In some fundamental way, that's what makes humans, human.

At that moment, just after I popped the cork, I saw it head toward the bottom, and felt the pull of a gator trout. I set the hook, and began to reel in that keeper. And that's when it came to me in a flash. That was how we were going to catch Javier's killer. The popping cork was the deception we would use to lure the monster to our bait so that we could set the hook so deep that he would not be able to escape being caught in our net.

When I finally got that trout to the boat, I gently eased out the hook, and returned him to the sound. Today, I wanted him to live. He had shown me how to catch a killer. He deserved to go free. With that, I pulled up the other line, dipped out the remaining bait, returned the rods to the rack, and headed for Woody's. As I drove south, I was looking, as always, far ahead. But later, thinking back, I didn't remember actually seeing the water. All I remembered was looking into the future, and liking what I saw.

Chapter Thirty-Eight
ON THE DECK AT WOODY'S

To get to Woody's by boat, you motor at idle speed, up Saint James City's main street for a little over a mile. How can you drive a boat on a street? Well, it's not literally a street, of course. But the main center of commerce is a canal that runs right through the heart of town. It's called Monroe Canal. I assume it was named after President Monroe. Regardless, just about every business in town backs up to this waterway. All of the bars and restaurants have places on the canal where you can tie up your boat. The marinas are on the canal, obviously, and so are the boatyards. The crab boats and the shrimp boats all call it home. Heck, even the art gallery and about a third of the houses in town are on the canal. It's the main drag.

The only downside of the canal is that you have to travel through it at idle speed. In my boat, that means letting the engine run at 750 rpm, and moving at about 2.5 miles per hour. I know how fast that is because that's how fast I go when I troll a plug or spoon behind the boat to fish. But that's not how fast I go—or anyone else goes, for that matter— when transiting the canal. I try to move at a little less than twice that rate. At this speed, the wake behind the boat is minimal, but I've still got enough speed to maintain some semblance of steering.

It normally takes me about fifteen minutes to get from the mouth of the canal to Woody's. But it always seems to take forever, especially when the sun's hot, and the wind is at my back. That day, it seemed to take even longer because I was excited to share my plan with Jill. I couldn't wait to talk about how we could put the plan into place, and implement it. I was tempted to jack up the revs to about two thousand and hope that no one would recognize me. But I knew that would not be wise. The idle-speed rule is there for a purpose—the last thing we need in the canal is a wake that bangs tied-up boats against the unforgiving concrete seawall. If it was my boat that was being scratched and scarred due to the action of some inconsiderate lout, I certainly wouldn't be happy. So, despite my impatience, I didn't go faster than my usual speed. In fact, if anything, I may have gone just a little slower. I did not want to draw attention to myself. I wanted to stay as invisible as possible. So I motored very slowly up the canal, hoping that Jill would be there when I arrived.

When I docked and walked onto the deck, however, she wasn't there. The car wasn't in the parking lot. I didn't want to go inside, where I'd have to make small talk with the folks on both sides of the bar. So, when Chesley came out to wait on me, I told her that I was waiting on Jill, and that I would just sit on the deck so that she could see me when she arrived. The fact that this spot was also the most remote part of the bar fit into my plans, as well: I didn't want anyone to be able to hear what we were going to talk about.

As usual, I asked Chesley to bring me a salty dog and a tall glass of water. I really didn't want to start drinking yet, but I find the salt and grapefruit juice hard to resist after a couple of hours on the boat. And I didn't think asking her to make it "virgin" would do much for my image. So I downed the water first, and then slowly sipped the dog as I waited. At least, by my usual drinking standards, I was sipping.

I've never been much of a vodka drinker; at least, I wasn't before moving down here. In the past, I did most of my drinking at night, usually in conjunction with winding down at the conclusion of a stressful day. Being of Scottish descent, and being a banker, my nighttime drink of choice has always been Scotch—the older and smokier, the better. But somehow, Scotch doesn't go so well in the heat of the Florida sun. Hence, my newfound attraction to the salty dog. I occasionally drank these in the past, but they certainly weren't part of my usual routine. But down here in the heart of Florida citrus country, where the heat sucks the salt and the fluids right out of you, salty dogs have a real appeal as an afternoon libation. In just a few months, I learned to like them a lot. And, as is my custom, I've done some research on the origins of the drink's name. I expected to learn that the concoction had a tropical, piratical, seafaring connection, and I was a little disappointed to learn that wasn't the case. It seems that the drink evolved from a simple mixture of grapefruit juice and vodka known as a greyhound. The addition of salt on the glass's rim required a new name, and I guess it just made sense to call that modified version a salty dog. Despite the less-than-romantic source of the drink's name, it seems to fit my new lifestyle. And I like to think that all that salt and all of the citrus juice is good for me. At the very least, I probably won't get scurvy.

Just as I was sucking up the salty remains from the bottom of the glass, I saw Jill pulling up. I asked Chesley to bring a pitcher of Mich Ultra for her, and another round for me. I motioned Jill over to the deck before she headed inside.

As she approached she said, "I glad to see you waited on me!"

"That's exactly what I've been doing. I've been waiting right here, but only about twenty minutes. Chesley's bringing you some beer."

"Thank you. I need that. You wouldn't believe how slow the traffic from Cape Coma has been! I got behind three old farts on Pine Island Road. Apparently, they don't believe in driving more than forty miles per hour, even when the speed limit is fifty. Then, all the way through Matlacha, they poked along at twenty miles per hour in the thirty-miles-per-hour stretch. Of course, when we got to the Center, they all headed south. I was stuck behind them all the way to the American Legion Hall. Damn. It's enough to drive you nuts!"

"Hey, you're on the island now. There's no reason to go fast. Slow down, and smell the roses. Isn't that what they say? Besides, what are those old folks in a hurry for? Most of them have nothing else to do. You need to take a deep breath, and calm down."

"What I need to do is to take a long drink of cold beer."

With perfect timing, Chesley arrived with the goods from the bar."Hey, girl! How're you doing?" she asked.

"I'm good, now that I'm here. You wouldn't believe how slowly some of the old folks drive. It drives me nuts."

"Yeah, I know what you mean. It usually happens to me when I'm late for work. Ya'll want anything else right now?"

"No thanks, Chesley," I answered. "We're good right now, but don't forget that we're out here."

"Don't you worry about that," she said over her shoulder.

"So, babe," I said, turning to Jill. "What did you buy?"

"You're not going to believe all the cute stuff I got. On the way out of town, I stopped in Matlacha at Bert's Gift Shop. You know, that's the store across the street from Bert's Bar. They've got so much cute stuff in there. I got some T-shirts for the kids. But the best thing I got was a couple of pirate flags for the yard. One's got a flagpole that we can mount out front on one of the palm trees, just to irritate the neighbors. And the other one's on a metal stand that we can mount on the dock behind the house. We'll have them covered in both directions."

"I like it. The folks that live around us already suspect that we're not quite right. This should confirm all of their suspicions. I can't wait to put them up. What else did you get?"

"Oh, just some girl stuff. You wouldn't care about that. How was fishing?"

"It was fantastic. I caught one of the biggest trout I've ever caught, and I threw it back! It was even bigger than your record twenty-four-inch fish. Can you believe that? I threw it back!"

"Why did you do that? Are you feeling all right?"

"I'm feeling great!" I looked around to make sure there was no one else on the deck, and said," I think I know how we can

263

catch the killer. That fish gave me the idea. That's why I threw him back. I figured he had earned his release."

Are you sure you're really OK? Have you been in the sun too long? How the heck could a fish give you an idea about how to catch the killer?"

"Well, it's simple, really. I was fishing, just like I always do—drifting over the flats, and trailing a couple of popping-cork rigs baited with live shrimp. I popped a cork, and the fish took the bait. That was it, really. It was that simple."

"What the hell are you talking about? You're drifting along, and you catch a fish. What's so special about that? You do that all the time."

"Exactly. That's what we do all the time. We bait a hook, and then we pop the cork. Why do we pop the cork?"

"Because the fish are attracted to it?"

"Exactly. We pop the cork to create a commotion that sounds like a fish feeding on bait. If we make it loud enough, the fish gets curious, and comes out of the grass looking for food. And then, when it attacks the bait, we set the hook, and then we reel the fish in. That's just what we have to do now!"

"You've lost me. What if the killer doesn't like to fish?"

"No. You don't understand. The killer is the fish. I'm going to be the bait. And, together, you and I are going to pop the cork by spreading the word around town that we know who the killer is. If we can do that loudly enough, he'll come out of the weeds, and attack the bait. When he does, we'll set the hook, and reel him in."

"I think I see what you're saying, but I don't like the idea of you being bait. A lot of times, the fish gets the bait off the hook, and never gets caught. Besides, how are we going to set the hook, and reel him in? Don't get offended, but Doc Ford, you're not. And I'm certainly no Hannah Smith. Hell, you know I don't even bait my own hook! Even if we can find some way to get you attacked, what then? Who sets the hook? Who reels in the killer?"

"You're right. We're going to need some help. I'm hoping that I can talk Mike Collins into this plan—unofficially, at least. With his help, it might just work. You and I need to figure out how to most efficiently spread the word around town that I'm pretty sure I know who the killer is, and that I'm going out to where Javier was killed so that I can talk with Javier's spirit to confirm my suspicions. And as soon as I do that, I plan to go to the *News Press* to announce the name of the killer.

"I'll plan to spend the day out by Punta Blanca, and this is where we'll need Mike's help. I need him to have his best sharp-shooter hidden on the island to cover me. If I'm threatened, I'll give a signal and the shooter can take out the threat. Mike can be standing by with a helicopter in Pineland, and fly in when we need him."

"OK, I can see that working as long as Mike is willing to go along. But I suspect it's not sheriff's department policy to use a civilian as bait. And without his help, this goes nowhere."

"Yeah, I see your point. But what if it's not like that? What if the deputy just happened to be on the island, and just happened to see a civilian being threatened, and just happened to react with force to protect the civilian?"

"Maybe. But you're going to have to work this out with Mike."

THE POPPING CORK MURDER

"Yeah, I know. But assuming that's not an issue, what do you think? Could we spread a rumor?"

"Oh, hell yeah. That would be easy enough. Isn't that what the killer has been doing all along? How did the rumor get around that Javier's death was related to pirate gold? And then, how did the rumor get around that it was tied in to the fortune that Barron Collier buried on Punta Blanca? Someone here was using the island telegraph to spread whatever rumor he wanted spread. There's no reason we couldn't do the same thing. And I think I know exactly how best to do it."

Jill continued, "It would be so easy to do. You would need to tell a few of the guys that meet every afternoon down at the Low Key—Hector, Sammy, Mike, Matt, and Kirk. That should do it. And I would need to tell some of the ladies at Froggy's. I could also tell a couple of the ladies here in town that tend bar. I'll guarantee that, by midnight, everyone in town, including the killer, would know the story. That's the easy part. The hard part is making sure you don't get yourself killed!"

"I agree. And trust me; I really don't want that to happen. If we can't both get comfortable around that point, we don't go forward. I'll get with Mike Collins ASAP."

"Baby, do you actually know who the killer is?"

"No, I don't. And neither does the sheriff's office. That's why I think we have to do something to cause the killer to identify himself. We've got to create enough racket that he swims up out of the grass, and hooks himself. Unless we do something like this, I fear that we'll never know who killed Javier. Even if we make all kinds of racket with this rumor, there's still no guarantee that the killer will take the bait. But look, until today, I have never caught a twenty-five-inch-long trout. And I have popped that cork for years and years. Up until today, I guess that monster trout has just ignored the traps I've set. Our killer may do the same thing. If he simply ignores the noise, he'll be safe. But if the noise is loud enough, and if it creates enough of a threat, he may not be able to ignore it. That's our only hope."

"So, you really don't have any clue about who the killer might be?"

"Here's what I think. The killer is on the island. How else would he have known about Javier, met him, and lured him to his death? The killer is an insider on the island. How else could he have spread the rumors that he's spread? And I think the killer is descended from one from one of the old families on the island, probably a fishing family. Somehow, this ties back to the 1912 murder of Eugene Knight, one of the owners of the Punta Gorda Fish Company. That murder took place in Cuba. So I'm thinking the killer is likely going to turn out to be a Padilla, a Perez, a Darna, a Romero, or a Rodriquez. But who knows? He could turn out to be a descendant of any of the families that were here back then. Maybe he's a Coleman, a Nelson, a Poppel, a Spearing, a Murdock, a Celec, or any of a dozen others. All of them are related to Cubans in one way or another. My gut tells me it's somebody we know. Probably somebody we trust and interact with routinely. So, we've got to be careful that we don't try to set a trap, only to get ambushed ourselves. Whoever the killer is, we know that he's ruthless, and we know that he's smart. We can't let him attack us until we're ready."

"You keep saying 'him.' Do you think the killer is a man?"

"You know, I don't really know. I guess I've basically assumed so, but I've really got nothing to go on. For all I know, it could be one of the girls here at Woody's, at the bank, at Froggy's, or at the real estate office. I don't have a clue. All I know is that once we start the rumor mill turning, we've got to be extremely careful. We want the killer to try to take me out, but not until we're ready. To pull this off will take some planning. In the meantime, we need to keep this to ourselves and to Mike Collins. We need to keep acting as normally as possible. We can't do anything that might alert the killer that things aren't as they seem. In that regard, do you want another drink?"

"Yeah. I guess we better have a couple more. That would certainly be keeping in character!"

"Absolutely! And, babe, whatever happens, I want you to know that I love you very much."

Chapter Thirty-Nine
THE SHERIFF SAYS NO

At 9:00 a.m. I gave Mike Collins a call.

"Good morning, Mike. Hope I'm not disturbing anything."

"Screw you, Story. After your last early morning call, there's been nothing to disturb. I don't think I'm on her approved list anymore. And I hold you totally fucking responsible."

"That's great. Good to know you feel like you owe me, 'cause I'm going to need your help."

"Why do I know that this is going to be special? Since I got involved with you and all the other loonies out on Pine Island, nothing in my life has gone right. I wonder why that is? Jim, why do you think that might be?"

"I don't know, Mike. Why do you think?"

"Jim, here's what I think. I think it's absolutely true what they say about all of you folks out there. You want to know what they say? I'll tell you, Story. Here's what they say: Everybody out on Pine Island is either an idiot, a misfit, a social outcast, a criminal, a drug addict, or some other kind of societal deviant. That's what the fuck they say. I didn't used to believe any of that stuff, but after hanging around you for a couple of weeks, I now know that they're absolutely fucking right. But, unfortunately, I don't get to choose which members of the tax-paying public I serve. As you know, I'm what is known as a public servant. So, Jim, how in the fuck may I be of service to you this fine morning?"

"Wow. I guess sleeping alone hasn't done much for your disposition. Either that, or you got turned around this morning when you were making love with your pillow, and you got out of bed on the wrong side. But as you say, I am a member in good standing of the tax-paying public, and I do need your help."

"What do you need?"

"Mike, have you figured out yet who killed Javier?"

"What kind of idiotic question is that? You know that if I had, I'd have arrested the bastard, and the story would be all over the news by now."

"I didn't think so. Now, do you have a good plan for where you're going to turn next to find out who killed him?"

"You know what we're doing. That's all we've got. We're going to keep looking."

"Mike, you haven't got shit, and you know it. I'm tired of waiting, and the longer we wait, the colder this case is getting. But I think I know how to get the bastard to identify himself."

"I'm listening. The day's young. I haven't heard a good joke yet."

"Mike, do you fish?"

"I'm a healthy, red-bloodied male living in Southwest Florida. Of course, I fucking fish."

"Good. Then you'll know about fishing with a popping cork."

"Of course. That's what the stupid Yankee fishermen do when they get here. They go out on the flats and make so damn much noise by popping a cork in the water that the poor fish hook themselves just to get them to stop making that infernal racket."

"Yeah, something like that. And that's how we're going to catch Javier's killer. Let me tell you how it's going to work."

I outlined my plan.

"Shit, Jim! That's not a plan— that's a prescription for suicide. Even if you're successful in getting the predator to come out of the weeds and strike, how do you figure you're going to keep from getting yourself killed?"

"That's where you come in."

"No question about it. You fuckers out there just ain't right! You're proposing to go sit all day in a boat in the middle of the damn bay, and wait for someone to come by and take a shot at you. And you hope that somehow, I'll be able to keep that shot from killing you?"

"Exactly. I want you to hide one of your sharpshooters on Punta Blanca the night before, so that he will be there in the morning to keep an eye on me. And then, when the killer shows up, I'll give a signal, and your guy can take the killer out before he shoots me."

"Jim, I can't do that. First, you're not a member of the department. I can't just take your word for it that someone is a killer, and then whack him for you. We have to follow something that's called 'due process.' Who knows, maybe you've just got a hard-on about something that someone did to you, and you want him taken out. You get the department to do it for you, so no harm, no foul. Or, what if you're just mistaken, and we end up shooting an innocent person that just happened to stop by to see how the fish are biting? That'll go down well! And I certainly can't go using a tax-paying citizen as bait. Maybe that's how they do it on television, but that's not the way it works here in the real world. We'd look like total imbeciles if you got yourself killed."

"What if you watched, listened to, and filmed the whole thing? Wouldn't that give you what you needed?"

"Jim, even if we had a full confession, there's no way that I can just go ahead and execute someone. And that's what this would amount to. If this went down, the sheriff's department would be run out of the county for being totally inept. This is not how we play the game here in Lee County. Sorry, Story, but this whole thing is a nonstarter with me."

"Mike, I believe this will work."

"I know you do, Jim. And it might. But I can't put the department in this position."

"OK, OK. I see your point. But I'm going to go ahead with this one way or another. I won't involve you directly in the plan. But could you at least have some resources in the area the day after tomorrow, just in case I need you?"

"Yeah. I could do that. Where would you want us?"

"I wouldn't want you close enough so that you'd spook the guy. He's smart, and he's not going to fall for this unless he feels absolutely certain that he can get away with it. He'll be looking at everything for hours before he makes his move, just to make sure he's not being set up. Maybe you could have a boat up by Bokeelia checking registrations or something like that. Hell, they could even be having breakfast and lunch at the Lazy Flamingo—that certainly wouldn't look unusual."

"Easy, big guy! No reason to get ugly just because I said no. How about if we had some plainclothes guys in a flats boat fishing around the back side of Useppa for the day?"

"That should work fine. That wouldn't look out of place, and they could be at Punta Blanca in two or three minutes. How would I contact them should I need them?"

"They'll monitor Channel Sixteen. And I'll give you a cell number to call, as well."

"Mike, I appreciate it. I'll let you know tomorrow if we're on."

"OK. But how do you plan to keep yourself from getting killed?"

"I don't know yet. But I won't go forward with this unless I have that covered."

"I'd appreciate that. The last thing I need is another fucking unsolved murder on Pine Island Sound. Somehow, I don't think the tourism folks out on the islands would be too happy about that."

"I'm going to solve a murder for you, not give you another one to worry about."

"Look, Jim. You won't be solving anything. You're just hoping that you'll be able to whack some guy that you think killed Javier. Do you think that I can just take your word for that? From my point of view, if you actually kill someone out there, I'll be investigating you for first-degree murder. I don't want to have to do that."

"I understand your point. But from my point of view, I will have brought Javier's killer to justice. Mike, I'm sorry, but I really don't see that happening unless I do this."

"Officially, I advise you not to do this. You can't be a vigilante. You go down this path, and I may not be able to help you."

"Understood."

"Story, one other thing. Once you get the word out that you know who the killer is, how are you going to keep safe until you're out in the fishing zone? What's to keep the guy from whacking you on his terms? That's what I would do. I wouldn't wait—I'd hit you the night before, or while you are on the way to Punta Blanca. Maybe I'd put a bomb in your boat. Or shoot you from a distance."

"Yeah. That's something else to worry about. I'll have to work on that. I'll call you tomorrow night."

"I hope so. Be careful."

Chapter Forty
A SOLDIER VOLUNTEERS

"So, what did Mike say?" Jill asked.

"I think he said that he thought I was an idiot. I also think he said that he couldn't do anything to help keep me from getting myself killed. And, he also said that if I went forward with this, he would probably need to arrest me for murder. But more positively, he did say that he could have some guys in the area, just in case I needed them."

"So, does that put an end to this?"

"No. It does not. I'm willing to take my chances with a murder charge, if it means that we can bring Javier's killer to justice. As far as I'm concerned, we'll just have to find some other way to keep me safe. Do we know anybody else that can shoot?"

"There's the guy who runs the gun shop up at Center."

"True. But we don't really know him, and from what I've heard, he's a little 'different.' Besides, for all we know, he may be the killer."

"Yeah. There is that. How about long-haired Mark who hangs out at Woody's? I've heard him talk about guns. He's always talking about teaching ladies how to shoot."

"I've heard his stories, too. But I always wondered if those stories might be more about getting ladies alone in the woods than actually teaching them to shoot straight. Anyway, I think he's from one of the old families. We don't know if we can trust him, either."

"So, you're saying that you think I should cancel the one-on-one concealed carry class with him that I scheduled for next month?"

"Hey, it might be too early to do that. If I get knocked off, you'll be needing someone else to turn to for love and affection."

Jill swatted me. "Stop that! We're not going to do this if there's any chance—any chance—of you getting shot! Now, who else do we know that might be able to have your back?"

"What about Steve Fairchild? He was a ranger in the army?"

She nodded slowly. "That's right. Katie told me that he was leading a Ranger patrol the day he got blown up. But I don't know if he could still do it. He suffered some pretty serious brain injuries, and he has to use a cane to walk around. I know he's better, but I think he's still recovering."

"I know. But all he'd have to do is hide out on Punta Blanca overnight, keep an eye on me the next day, and take a shot if I gave the signal. And I know I could trust him."

"You could, that. He's a good guy. And neither he nor Katie is from around here. Why don't you give him a call and see if he and Katie could come over?"

"You got his number?"

"No, but I've got Katie's cell. I'll give her a call."

She went out onto the porch, and pushed a button on her phone. I heard her carrying on a conversation. In a few minutes, she came back inside.

"They were sitting at the bar at Woody's, watching college football. They'll be here as soon as the ball game is over."

"Good. You want a drink?"

Jill grinned. "Silly question!"

Twenty-five minutes later, we heard steps on the outside stairs, and saw Katie and Steve heading our way. We opened the door, and invited them inside.

"Ya'll come on in. Now, what can I get you to drink?" Jill asked. "Let me guess. Katie, how about vodka, Red Bull, and some cranberry juice? Steve, a beer?"

"Hey, you're good, girl, "Katie responded. "You're right on both counts. So, what's up? Of course, we're glad to see ya'll, but this isn't normally how we socialize. Usually, we just bump into each other down at the bar. Something's up. What is it?"

I said, "You're right. Look, this is a big deal. I need someone to help keep me from getting killed. I was thinking Steve might be able to do that."

Katie was midway to the couch. She turned; her eyes wide. "What in the hell are you talking about? If you need help, you should just call the sheriff!"

"Hey, I know this sounds really strange. But hear me out. Let me start from the beginning and lay this whole thing out for you."

For the next fifteen minutes, I brought them into the loop on what had happened, where the investigation stood, and the solution that I had dreamed up.

"What do you guys think? Is this something you might want to help us with?"

Steve immediately responded, "Hell, yes! This sounds like a lot more fun than spending all day trying to outsmart a stupid damn fish. No offense, Katie, but this sounds like more fun than I've had in a very long time."

"How about you, Katie? Are you OK with this?"

"Yeah. It sounds like fun to me, too. It certainly sounds like it will beat sitting at the bar every night, getting wasted, and listening to everyone lie about how many fish they caught. How can we help?"

"Steve, can you shoot?"

"Shit yeah, I can shoot! You don't get out of Ranger school—with honors, I might add—if you can't shoot the eyes out of Ali five hundred yards away." He accepted the beer that Jill offered. "I may not be able to walk so good anymore, but there's nothing wrong with my trigger finger. In fact, shooting was one of the things they let me do at Walter Reed as part of my rehab. They'd let me spend as much time as I wanted, just about every day, burning up tax-payer bullets. I must have worn out a couple of M-15s while I was there. I'm as good a shot as I ever was. I even have a sniper rifle at the house. It was one of the ones that we used in my unit when I was in Afghanistan. Officially, it was misplaced," he said, taking a pull from the can, "but, somehow, my buddies were able to get it home. Don't ask how they managed to pull that off. They gave it to me as a get-well gift after I got blown up. I've even got ammo for it, too. It's a damn fine weapon—a M24A2 Remington, .30 caliber, with a Leupold sight. It's effective at over a thousand yards. It might be overkill for what we need, but it'll damn sure get the job done. You need someone to cover your back? I'm your man."

"Steve, you need to think about this before you put your neck on the line. You'll need to spend the night on Punta Blanca the night before. And you can't show a light that might alert anyone that you're out there. There's no telling what kind of snakes and other stuff might be crawling around out there."

"Damn, Jim. What the fuck do you think I used to do? I'll guarantee you that there's nothing on that stupid island that's half as scary as what I had to deal with in Iraq and Afghanistan. Snakes were the least of our worries over there. Hell, we used to sleep in the same holes with them. A few critters are nothing compared to a village full of Muslim nutcases that are trying to blow your brains out twenty-four/seven. And, if you're worried whether my legs will let me carry this off, don't. I may not look like much when I walk, but I can get the job done. You know the very first thing I did when I got back to my post in Colorado once they let me out of the hospital? I walked all the way up Pikes Peak—just to prove to myself that I could do it. It took me two whole days, but I got there just fucking fine." He set the can on one of Jill's palm-tree coasters. "I assure you that walking a couple hundred yards in the dark on a little island is not going to be a problem."

"OK. Don't get pissed." I held my palms up. "I'm sorry. Just wanted to make sure you knew what you would be getting into."

"I've got it."

"You also need to consider that if we actually are successful in taking out Javier's murderer, we might be arrested for murder ourselves."

"Jim, are you in?" Steve asked, looking me straight in the eye.

"I'm in."

"Then, I'm in, too. Now, let's get serious. We need to figure out how we're going to pull this deal off."

Chapter Forty-One
PUTTING A PLAN IN PLACE

"All right, Captain. What do you think we need to do?" I asked once Steve and I had moved to the porch to strategize.

"Looks to me like there are five stages in this operation. First, we've got to spread the rumor. Second, we've got to hide you, Jill, and your boat, until the operation starts. Third, we've got to insert me on Punta Blanca. Then, we carry out the ambush. And, finally, if all goes well, we bring in the sheriff to mop things up," Steve said.

"Spreading the rumor is going to be easy. We use Jill, Katie, and me for that part of the deal," he continued. "I'd let Katie work the crowd at Woody's. She's really tight with everyone there. Jill can go down to Froggy's with her girlfriends, and get the news out there. And I'll spend some quality time with the boys at Low Key. I'd guess we ought to get started about five o'clock, and then spend a couple of hours hanging out. That'll give the rumor plenty of time to get passed around. I think there's also a big shindig at the American Legion Hall tomorrow night. By eight o'clock, the news should be well on its way to being distributed all across the island. By then, we'll have to have made sure that you guys are safe."

"Makes sense to me," I said, handing another beer to Steve. "So, how are we going to do that?"

"I'm thinking that Katie and I will book a room at Tarpon Lodge. We'll do that tonight when we get home. We've never hung out down there—it's not really our kind of place—so no one there should know us. Tomorrow afternoon, we'll put our boat on the trailer, and take it with us to the Lodge when we check in. It'll look like we're coming in from Central Florida to go fishing for a couple of days. We'll put the boat in the water there, and have it in a slip, ready to go. Then we'll come back to town and wait until it's time to spread the news. When Jill's done her bit at Froggy's she'll come back here. We'll come by, pick her up, and take her with us to our room at the Lodge. No one will know that she's there, so she should be safe."

"I like that. But what about me?"

"We'll need to make sure that you and your boat are safe during the night. I'd hate it if someone saw you chugging down Monroe Canal or cruising up the sound, and decided to put a slug in you. And we wouldn't want you to turn the key on your boat the in the morning, just to have it explode. Trust me, I've had enough of bombs to last me several lifetimes. You and the boat have to be safely out of the way and well hidden before the rumor mill starts to heat up."

"That makes sense to me," I said. "How do we do that?"

Steve took a sip from the can and then rolled it between his hands while he considered the problem. "Here's an idea. See what you think. You take the boat out tomorrow afternoon—maybe around four—and run it over to Sanibel Island Marina to get fuel. The fuel dock there is open until five. That shouldn't draw any attention to you at all. That'll be well before the rumor mill gets going. It'll look absolutely normal. But after you leave the marina's channel, rather bringing the boat back here, what if you turn to the right, and take it around Sanibel, into the gulf, and up to Captiva Pass? You stash the boat somewhere safe. I pick you up later in my boat, and bring you back to the room at the Lodge."

"I like that—as long as the weather's OK to be out in the gulf. If not, I can run it up Matlacha Pass. But once I get in the sound, where would I stash the boat? I don't think that will be as easy as we think. If I'm right, I expect the killer to start looking for my boat as soon as he realizes it's not on the lift. And I expect that he'll call his friends at every marina in the area and ask them to be on the lookout for it. I don't think it'll be as easy as just renting a slip for the night."

"That's a good point," Steve said. "But why couldn't we just anchor it out in a deserted bay?"

"I don't really feel good about that either. You know, when we go to bed, that's when the commercial guys go fishing. They're out there every night, crawling over every bay in the sound all night long, looking for fish. It seems to me that if they were to find a deserted boat out there, at the very least, they'd alert the authorities. More likely, they might just take it home with them so they could 'salvage' some parts off of it."

"I see your point. So, if we can't put it in a marina, and we can't just leave it in the bay, what are we going to do with it?"

"Steve, try this idea out. You know those beach houses on the south end of North Captiva? The actual houses are on the beach side, but they all have docks on the bay side. I've never seen anyone staying at any of those houses this time of the year. I think the owners only come when it's cooler. What if I tie up at one of those docks for the night? You could pick me up there in your boat after dark."

"That might work," he said. "But I really don't like the thought of trying to get to those docks in the dark. The flats around there are awfully thin, and there's not a marked channel. What would you think about tying it up at one of the fish shacks?

"Huh. I like that. I like it a lot. Those houses are out there in the middle of nowhere. They're too far away for anyone on shore to make out the boat. And, besides, I don't think that a boat tied up at one of the houses would draw any particular attention. That's where the owners tie up whenever they use a house. But they don't use them that often. I think that could work."

We watched a cormorant drying its wings in the sun. "All right, we've got Jill, you, and your boat safe," Steve said. "How do we get me on Punta Blanca?"

"Here's what I'm thinking. Early in the morning, say four o'clock, I take you in your boat over to Punta Blanca. We'll look like a couple of fishermen getting an early start. But we'll need to be quiet when we get near the island. I wouldn't want any curious ears in the area to know what we're up to. I'll drop you off, and then come back to the Lodge. Then, Katie and Jill can take me out to the fish shack."

"Jim, you're directionally correct, but let me suggest one minor modification," Steve said. "You, Jill, Katie, and me take the boat over at 4:00 a.m. Trust me, Katie knows the sound as well as either of us. And she sure as heck can drive the boat better than I can. And besides, I know that she and Jill will be pissed as hell if they can't be involved. Ya'll take me to Punta Blanca, and drop me off. Then she and Jill take you down to the fish shack, drop you off, and then go back to the Lodge. That way, there will only be one trip back to the Lodge. They should be back before anyone else wakes up."

"Yeah, I like it. But we are going to have to be very quiet. I don't want anyone to know what we're up to. That could scupper the whole deal."

"Not an issue," Steve said. "I've got a Honda four stroke on my boat. You know how quiet they are. Sometimes you can't even hear them running when you're in the boat. We'll just run the channel until we clear Useppa. That way, it will sound just like someone going fishing. Then, when we're near Punta Blanca, we'll drop to an idle, and go in very slowly. As quiet as that engine is, no one will be able to hear us do that. And we'll make sure we don't show any lights. Now where do you want me on the island?"

"Here, let me show you on the chart."I unfolded the chart of the sound that I keep on the table by my Adirondack. I pointed to the western tip of the peninsula that circles the mooring basin on the south end of the island. "I think that's the spot. There's good cover for you there. There're pretty thick mangroves at the shore, and there're lots of Brazilian peppers trying to smother the gumbo limbos, and some palms and figs. I would think you could easily hide in there so that no one could see you, even if they were right on top of you. Hopefully, you will be able to find an opening for a clear shot."

"Don't you worry about that. If I need to, I can create an opening. How do you think we should come in? It looks as if there's a channel all the way around the south end of Punta Blanca. The chart shows deep water right up to that point," he said, studying the chart.

"There is. But I don't know about that. I just have a funny feeling that you ought to not make yourself seen on that side of the island. I know not many folks live on Cayo Costa, but I'd like to have Katie drop you off on the eastern side, directly opposite where you want to go. There's an old marine railroad track there that leads down into the water. It's left over from Collier's days. I'm betting that the bottom there has a gentle slope, so she should be able to just bump the boat in, and drop you off almost on dry land. And the moon's almost full, so you should be able to walk over to the western end of the point with no problem. I think this approach will be simpler, with less risk of running aground and less chance of someone seeing us. How's that sound to you?"

"I'm good with that."

"Then, Katie takes me down to the fish shacks. It's only a couple of miles to the south. She drops me off, comes back to the Lodge, puts the boat in the slip, and then she and Jill just wait, and stay out of sight. About nine o'clock, I'll bring my boat up the channel, around the south end of the island, and anchor west of the peninsula. The spot where Javier was killed is only about two hundred yards due west of where you'll be hiding. Take a look at the chart. Here's where I'll be anchored. From there it looks to be maybe a quarter of a mile over to Primo Point on the east side of Cayo Costa. South of Primo Point, there's Primo Bay. There's an old canal there, and there's an old house on that canal, but nothing else."

Steve studied the chart. "Good. That should give me a clear path to shoot into without having to worry too much about what might get in the way of a stray bullet. Is there anything else out that way?"

"Only one thing worries me. This spot is one of the best anchorages in Southwest Florida for gunk holing on sailboats. Look at the chart, there's at least eight feet of water around the south side of the island, and almost all the way from where I'll be anchored to Primo Point. If there are any boats anchored in there, that could screw up the whole deal. I don't think our friend will want any witnesses, and we sure as hell won't want to shoot a sailor. But there's nothing we'll be able to do about that. We'll just have to see how that plays out when we get there."

"Got it. So, tell me this—how am I supposed to know who to shoot? I know we're expecting the killer to come see you, but what if instead, a fisherman just stops by to see what you're doing out there all by yourself? Don't suppose you want me to shoot him."

"No. We'll need to have some kind of signal. What about this? If you see me wave my left hand, that'll be your signal to fire. But it'll be my left hand—not my right. I'm right-handed, and I'll likely be waving at people during the day with my right hand. You do know your right from your left?"

"Yeah. That C-4 scrambled my brain up pretty good, but I can still make out left from right. You wave your left hand, I take out who ever is close by. Just make damn sure you don't wave it by mistake."

"Got it."

"Now. When we need to, how will we contact the sheriff?"

"I've got the VHF, and I'll take my cell phone. If we get the killer, I'll call Mike Collins, and tell him to get his ass out there ASAP. He said he's going to have some of his guys fishing in the vicinity. You better take your phone, too, in case I don't make it."

"Don't you worry about that. OK, what happens if we sit out there all day, and no one shows up. Then what?"

"I plan to stay out there until five o'clock. If nothing's happened by then, I'll come by and pick you up where we dropped you off. But, you know, if he doesn't show up, I'm in fucking trouble. I'll go to the *News Press* anyway, tell them about this whole plan. I'll ask them to run a story to make it clear that I really don't know who the killer is, and that it was all just a ruse to lure the killer into a trap. Hopefully, they'll do that. But even with that, I don't think we could ever feel safe living in Saint James City again. If this doesn't work, we'll just find somewhere new to live."

"I hear you. Let's hope this works."

"Yeah," I said. "Now, what are we forgetting?"

"What about the weather? And how about the tides?"

"Good point. Let's take a look." I turned on Jill's iPad and pulled up am marine weather site. "It looks like the weather's going to be perfect. The winds are going to be light and generally out of the east all day tomorrow, and tomorrow night. That'll be perfect for running out in the gulf. If that pattern holds the next day, it should put the bow of the boat toward where you'll be sitting. You won't be able to get a better shot than that. Looks like we've got a high tide early in the morning, with a low around lunchtime. That's all perfect. Should help to keep us from getting stuck while we're running around out there in the dark."

"Cool. Now what about a weapon for you? You got anything?"

"Shit no, Steve!" I laughed, and said "Jill won't let me have one. She's scared I'd hurt myself with it. And she's probably right."

"I've got a little nine-millimeter Beretta you could take. You could put it in your pocket, just in case."

"I appreciate the offer, but I really wouldn't know what to do with it. I'd rather just rely on you."

"That's all right with me. I think we've got a plan that can work."

"I agree. Steve, I want you to know that I appreciate you agreeing to help with this. But, really, you don't have to do this."

"I know. But, like I said, this is the most fun I've had in a very long time. My military career was over the instant that bomb went off. I spent the next year doing sheet time at Walter Reed as they tried to figure out what was left of me, and then put those pieces back together. The person I am today is not the person I was before that bomb went off." He leans towards me, looks me in the eyes, and in a lower voice says, "learning to live with this new person hasn't been easy, for me or for Katie. Trust me. This helps."

"OK. Now look, as I see it, we've got nothing to do until about noon tomorrow. You want to go fishing in the morning?"

"Damn straight!"

"Be here at seven, and I'll have the boat ready to go."

***

Steve showed up as the sun broke the horizon, and we were underway as planned. Twenty minutes later, we were drifting the south side of Red Light Shoals, our lines in the water.

"Steve, are you still OK with our operation?"

"Yep. And, Katie's on board, too. She's excited, and glad to help."

"Good. Jill's pretty worried about what could happen to me. She really feels better that ya'll are with us."

"Hey, Jim, when do the fucking fish start to bite? I've been popping this cork to beat the band, and I haven't had a single bite. I can't even lose my shrimp! It's like there's nobody home."

"Yeah," I said glumly. "Let's just hope that doesn't happen tomorrow."

We fished for a couple more hours, pretty much in silence. When it was time to go in, there wasn't a thing to show in the live well. I hoped that wasn't an omen.

Chapter Forty-Two
A LATE-NIGHT PIZZA PARTY

At four o'clock that afternoon, I put the *Pulapanga* in the water, and headed down the canal. *Pulapanga* is what I named my boat. I've observed that people tend to name their boats in one of three ways. Most, it seems, try to name their boat with some clever play on words. For example, down the canal, one guy has a boat called *Playing Hooky*, and another guy named his boat *Fuelish Pleasure*. I like that kind of thing. I'm just not smart enough to come up with something really neat. A second type of boater seems to want to use the boat's name to publicize his occupation and/or his success. I recently saw boats on the sound called *Severance Package* and *Diversified*. I'm not really a fan of that naming convention. The third group, and the one I like the best, are those who name their boats after loved ones. And, in a way, that's the path I followed. I decided to name my boat after my late father. Or, more precisely, after an old joke that he loved to tell.

He had grown up on the creeks and rivers that flow through the Gulf Hammock cypress swamps on their way to the gulf.

He was a quarter Creek indian, but given an ample helping of other dark-skinned genes, he looked like that percentage could have been even higher. Every time he took a new group out on his boat up in the Hammock, he loved to tell them this story. As they headed down the Wekiva, a body of water that looks for all the world like something right out of a Tarzan movie, he'd start to talk about the different types of birds and other wildlife they'd see along the banks of the river. For folks who had never spent any time in a Florida swamp, this trip downriver could be a pretty unnerving experience. Of course, he'd tell them that they needed to keep their eyes peeled for gators and water moccasins, since they could pop up at any time. That would always get their attention really focused on the surroundings. Eventually, when he judged his passengers to be sufficiently apprehensive about whether they were going to survive, he'd start a discussion about the legendary "pulapanga," warning them that this was the only bird that the ancient people native to these swamps actually feared.

This large bird lives only in the gulf's coastal swamps, he'd say, and it eats only one thing—a fiery, hot pepper pod that grows there. This pepper is over twice as hot as the Scotch bonnet on the Scoville Heat Scale. It's so hot, in fact, that after a pulapanga eats one of these peppers and subsequently takes a crap, it has to fly backward at an extremely high rate of speed to cool off its rear end. And, of course, when it flies backward, it can't see where it's going. Consequently, there is always a serious risk that one of these unguided missiles could fly right into you. And, should one hit you, you'll be in serious trouble. You need to watch out for pulapangas, he'd say with a straight face.

As a kid, I must have heard him tell this story a hundred times. Off course, he would never let on that it was a joke. When he told it, he would never break a smile. Some, especially those from the South, knew better than to believe him. But more often than not, people from the North would buy into his story and ride the rest of the way downriver with their heads down.

Anyway, I decided to name my boat in my dad's honor. He was a great fisherman and a great boater. I hoped that some of his skill and luck might rub off. As I idled away from the house, it occurred to me that over the next twenty-four hours, we were going to need a lot of that luck.

Once I cleared the no-wake zone, I put the boat on a plane, and headed south toward the Sanibel Causeway bridge. Ten minutes later, I was tying up to the fuel dock at the Sanibel Island Marina.

"Hey! Long time, no see!" Tim called. "I was beginning to worry that you might have sunk that thing."

"Hey, you should know better than that. I just can't afford to run it much, given what you're charging for fuel. That must be liquid gold you're selling!" I called back. What are you getting now? Five bucks a gallon?"

"You're in luck," he said. "We just dropped the price. It's now only four dollars and eighty-three cents. How much you want?"

"Wow! At that price, I better fill her up."

"You got that right. What've you been up to?"

"Oh, you know. Same old stuff—trying to fool some fish into coming home with me every once in a while."

"Looking at how clean your boat is, I'd say you haven't been doing too well with that," Tim said, laughing.

"Looks can be deceiving. I just always clean her up good when I bring her in. I've actually had a couple of pretty good weeks. Got the freezer pretty full."

"That's good to hear. Hey, it really is good to see you. It's been pretty quiet around here since our pirate buddy left town. Word has it that you might have had something to do with that."

"Oh, I don't know. I think there a lot of people that had had enough of his antics. What do you hear about where he is now?"

"Last I heard, he was in Marsh Harbor, out in the Abacos. But, who knows? By now they may have gotten tired of him, too."

"Wouldn't surprise me. Hey, Tim, things must be going good for the marina. Looks like you put some new boards on your fuel dock since the last time I was here."

"Yeah, we sure did. Ain't they pretty? And we painted the whole place. She's looking sharp now. Course, it's hell trying to keep the birds from shitting all over everything. Old Frank has a heck of a time mopping all that poop off every night when we close down. But it gives him something constructive to do, and I tell him it certainly helps him enjoy his evening beer. He likes to remind me that he always enjoyed it fine, even with the old dock."

"Well, it looks good. Have things started to pick up for the season yet?"

"No. Not much, yet. I expect that we won't see it pick up until late October. But that's fine with me. I like to enjoy the peace and quiet while I can."

"I hear you. OK, looks like she's about full—I can see some bubbles starting to come out of the overflow. Damn, that's sure a quick way to kill a couple of hundred bucks!"

"Just be glad you've only got one of those bad boys bolted to your stern. I see the guys that have two or more three-hundred-horsepower jobs weighing down the back of their boats a lot more than I see you. So, you heading out fishing?"

"No. I just needed to fill up. But it's such a nice afternoon, I think I might ride over to the lighthouse, watch the sunset, and then just head on home."

Tim tore a slip of paper off the printer. "Here's your receipt. Enjoy the sunset."

"Thanks. See you in a couple of weeks."

I left the marina's channel, and hung a right. The Sanibel lighthouse sits on the southern tip of the island. It's picturesque as hell, and it sure sells a lot of postcards. But I didn't go by this afternoon to get a close look. Instead, I stayed well away from shore, worked my way around the island's tip, and then went out into the gulf. Fortunately, there was only a slight chop as the incoming tide met the easterly breeze. I ran offshore about a mile, and then turned north. Four barrier islands make up this part of the Lee County shore: Sanibel, Captiva, North Captiva, and Cayo Costa. My plan was to run north past the first three, and then come back into the sound via Captiva Pass, which separates North Captiva from Cayo Costa.

As soon as I got in the lee of Sanibel, the run north was smooth and peaceful. The water was almost as calm as a lake, with just a slow swell coming in from the west to remind me that I was in open water. I'd have loved to have been able to move closer to shore and try to scout out some daisy-chaining tarpon along the beach. But I couldn't do it that day. About then, it occurred to me to hope that I'd still be alive the next day. Maybe I'd be able to hunt tarpon in the future.

By this time, it was after five, and the other parts of the operation would be underway. I knew the girls were looking forward to what they were going to do. Jill had told me how they planned to pull it off. She was going to Froggy's to meet the women who rendezvous there most every night. They had been inviting her to join them for a while, and this was the perfect opportunity. She planned to look extremely worried, and when asked why, she'd explain how worried she was about me because of what I knew, and what I was planning to do the next day. She thought she might even need a tissue or two as she worked through this story. I gathered that Katie had a variation of that strategy in mind for her role at Woody's. She was going to ask Anna if she had noticed how worried Jill seemed, and from there, launch into why Jill was concerned. I thought everyone would buy that story pretty quickly. I wasn't exactly sure what Steve had in mind, but I knew he would get it exactly right.

I wasn't in a hurry to go into the sound to tie up at the fish shack. I figured the less time the boat was tied up there during daylight, the better it'd be. So, to kill time, I ran further north. Once I reached the Boca Grande channel, I turned around, and just let the boat idle back toward the south. I hung a couple of rods off the rod rack, and trolled some spoons behind, just to look less suspicious should I encounter any curious fisherman. I actually was hoping I wouldn't catch anything. I just wasn't in the mood. But I guess, when it's your day, it's your day.

Bam! Whizzzzzzz. I was jarred out of a near nap by the sound of something slamming the heck out of one of the rods. "Shit," I said. "Why can't you guys give me a break?" But this fish clearly wasn't paying any attention. He was headed far away from the boat, and he was in a hurry to get there. If I wanted to have any line left on the reel, I needed to deal with this situation. I knocked the throttle lever into neutral, and grabbed the screaming rod. I could have just cupped the thing, and broken the line, but I really didn't have anything else to do, so I figured I might as well just try to fight the thing. Heck, it might be the last fish I would ever catch. The drag on the reel had been set with a light level of resistance, since all I normally catch are trout. I figured there was plenty of room to tighten the drag without breaking the line. So I gave it a couple of turns while I kept the rod nearly vertical. That increased resistance gradually slowed the progress of the fish. He was still taking line, but I could tell that he was starting to tire. A couple of minutes later, I could feel him stop running away from the boat. Instead, he was now swimming parallel with the boat. I figured he was taking a break, trying to gather his strength for another run. But I couldn't let him do that. As soon as he stopped taking line, I began to lever the fish in, raising the rod and then winding line onto the spool as I slowly let the rod drop toward the fish. When I had gotten as much line in as I could without letting the fish pull directly on the reel, I stopped winding, and pulled the rod back toward a vertical position, slowly dragging the fish toward me in the process. Then I'd repeat these steps, always taking care to never let the line slacken. I'd probably managed to bring the fish toward me by ten yards, when the fish caught onto what I was doing. In an instant, he took back that ten, and about twenty more. But then he stopped, and I knew that was about all he had left. So I started the pumping process all over again. This time, I got back all that I had lost and about twenty yards more before the fish gave it another try. This time, all he could get back was about ten yards. The fish and I repeated this drill a few more times, and soon, all he had the strength to do was to run sideways. I knew he was tiring, but I also knew that the fight was far from over. If I gave him any slack at all, he'd feel it in an instant, shake his head, and probably throw the hook out of the hole in his lip that I knew was getting larger and larger as the fight continued. And if he couldn't do that, I knew he would do everything he could to position himself so that he could try to cut the leader against his gill plates. I figured that was pretty likely, since all I used for inshore fishing was thirty-pound fluorocarbon.

The game was on, and all either of us could do was play it out to see how it would end. And that day, as luck would have it, it was my day to win. Ten minutes later, I had a fifty-pound king mackerel next to the boat. Normally, a fisherman would have gaffed that thing, thrown him in the cooler, and headed home to the grill. But that day was that fish's day, as well. I reached down with a pair of needle-nosed pliers, and eased the spoon's hook out of the king's lip. Then, I stood and watched him swim away—slowly at first. Then, as soon he realized that he was free, he checked out. I was pleased that he didn't appear to be damaged by our encounter. I truly did wish him well.

By now, the sun was nearing the horizon. Watching the sun go down on a clear evening from a boat in the gulf is a sight you'll never forget. When you watch the sun higher up in the sky, you can't really tell it's moving. But as it nears the horizon, a large orange ball sinks toward the water at a surprisingly rapid rate. For some reason, the closer it gets to the horizon, the faster it seems to move. It's almost as if the sun is in a hurry to get to a new day in another part of the world.

All I could think about was whether this was the last sunset I would ever see. The sun may have been eager for this day to end, but I wasn't. I paid close attention as it set, willing it to slow down, and trying to soak in every detail.

As the last of the orange sphere disappeared, it was time for me to head into the sound. I wanted to tie up to one of the fish shacks just as it got dark. I put the boat in gear, brought it onto an easy plane, and headed toward the entrance of Captiva Pass.

Fifteen minutes later, I tied up against the dock of the southernmost of the Captiva Shoal fish shacks. I had been glad, as I approached the houses, to see that none appeared to be occupied. I'm sure that all the owners know each other, and probably try to look out for each other's places. If any of them had been there, and had asked what I was doing, it would have been a challenge to explain why I was there. Fortunately, I didn't have to do that. In another fifteen minutes it would be pitch dark, and I would be in the clear.

Fortunately, that darkness came quickly. While I was waiting for my ride to the Lodge, I made a point of putting a small piece of clear tape over the seam between each hatch door and the deck surface of the boat. I figured that if someone showed up in the middle of the night to plant a bomb, he wouldn't likely notice a small piece of clear tape, and, therefore, I should be able to tell in the morning if anyone had been on board.

Once I had a piece of tape over each seam, I climbed onto the deck of the fish shack to wait for my ride. In the dark, I was amazed at how much I could still see and hear. The only real light was from the moon, but once my eyes adjusted, I could see remarkably well. It was nice to see the sound like this. But listening to the noises coming across the water was nothing short of amazing. Sound travels remarkably well over water, with nothing to muffle or interfere with the sound waves. Noises from miles away sound like they come from nearby. With the gentle easterly breeze pushing the sound my way, I could even hear folks talking and laughing at the Lodge. That had to be at least three miles away.

And don't ever let anyone tell you that fish don't make sounds. In fact, at night, they make all kinds of racket. Of course, there are the sounds that you hear all the time, such as dolphins breathing or mullet jumping. But you can hear all kinds of other stuff going on, as well. A snook crashing into a school of bait can be frighteningly loud when it happens just a few feet from you. And, surprisingly, you can even hear noises being made under the water. There's a reason some fish are called "grunts."And, there's a reason some belong to what is known as the "drum" family. During the day, you normally can't hear all this racket. But on a still night, if you're quiet, you can hear all kinds of sounds. It's absolutely amazing.

Occasionally, I would see the lights of boats going through the Pass, or running the sound. Folks who haven't spent time around boats wouldn't know what they were looking at. All they'd see would be different colored lights that appear to move randomly in one direction or another. But to a knowledgeable boater, there is logic to what those lights are doing. Small boats are required to show three different lights when they are underway at night—a red light on the port bow quadrant, a green light on the starboard bow quadrant, and a white light toward the stern. Knowing this, it doesn't take much practice to understand what the boat on which they are mounted is doing. For example, if you see a boat showing both a red and a green light, you know that the boat is coming straight toward you. If you only see a white light, then you are looking at the stern of a boat moving away from you. If you see a green light, then you are looking at the starboard front quarter of a boat crossing your path from left to right. To avoid a collision, you'd need to turn to port, in effect putting your green light toward the green light of the boat in front. As long as you continue to see its green light, you won't run into the boat in front. Likewise, if you see a red light, you know that you are looking at the port front quadrant of a boat passing in front of you from right to left. With a little practice, it's simple to understand what you are seeing. And sitting on the quiet deck of a fish house in the middle of Pine Island Sound creates a great opportunity to practice understanding how the navigation lights on boats work.

Fortunately, I didn't see any green/red combinations coming toward my fish shack until about nine thirty. I figured that would be the right time for Steve to be coming to pick me up. It was.

I was able to recognize his boat while it was still a good ways away. That was a good sight to see. Until that moment, I hadn't realized how tense I had become. Once I recognized him, and saw him wave at me, I could feel myself exhale and relax. As he idled toward me, I walked to the dock and motioned for him tie up against the side opposite of where the *Pulapanga* was tied.

As I grabbed the dock line, he said, "Hey, dude! How've the bugs been?"

"Thankfully, they haven't been bad at all. I'm guess I'm too far away from shore for the mosquitoes to smell me out here. How are things with you?"

"Things are going great! Katie and Jill are safely in the room at the Lodge. And, if I do say so myself, I think we all did a great job getting Saint James City stirred up about you having solved the murder. There's no question that the whole town's buzzing right now. There were five or six guides hanging out with me at the Low Key, and, to a man, they were all worried to death about you tomorrow. They all wanted to come up this way, and just hang out by Punta Blanca to keep an eye on you. It took all I could do to convince them that you wouldn't be able to communicate with Javier's spirit if they came up here and disturbed his karma. But, I wouldn't be surprised if one or two of them came by any way, just to check on you."

"I guess I should be flattered. But I hope they don't scare off our friend."

"Yeah. I know. How about the anchorage up at Punta Blanca? Did you go by there to see if there were any boats holed up there?"

"No. I didn't think to do that. I just wanted to get tied up here, and keep quiet. Maybe we should ride up that way when we go back."

"Yeah. We ought to do that. Hop in."

A couple of minutes later, the fish shacks were to our east, and we were heading north up the sound. We soon cleared Cabbage Key, and when we had enough deep water, we veered off toward the south end of Punta Blanca. We didn't have to go far to see that the anchorage was not empty. There were two, separate 360-degree, white, masthead lights showing, indicating that a couple of sailboats were anchored there for the night.

"Shit. We're damn sure not alone," Steve said. "Where does that leave us?"

"All we can do is hope they are transients. Maybe they'll pull up their hooks after breakfast, and move on. I suspect there's a good chance they'll do that."

"I hope so. I sure would hate for them to spoil my fun."

"Yep. Me too. Let's head back to the girls."

The channel from the sound to Tarpon Lodge is twisty, narrow, and, in places, shallow. The flats that surround the last half mile have only a foot of water on them at low tide. From what I have read, the channel was dug by hand back in the 1920s. Later, the labor leader John L. Lewis, who owned a home next to the Lodge, helped the owner deepen the channel by bringing a group of union coal miners down from West Virginia. Reportedly, they used dynamite to blast a deeper path through the sandstone. But despite their efforts, there's still little room for error when you run this channel—especially at night. You need a good spotlight to illuminate the markers that keep you from veering off into the shallows. Fortunately, Steve had thought of that, and we were able to get to the dock without incident.

Tarpon Lodge is a very nice place to stay. It was originally built as a single-family dwelling, but after the original owner's death, it was converted into a small hotel. Over the years, it was expanded with the addition of a wing of modern rooms. And, now, there's a sizeable marina and dry storage facility right next door. It's a great place for folks to come who want to fish, but also want a little luxury at the end of the day. The Lodge has a great restaurant and a friendly, cozy bar.

But luxury and fine dining weren't what we were about that night.

Soon enough, we had the boat in its slip, and quietly walked toward our room. To help ensure privacy, Katie had requested a room in the new wing, rather than one in the house. But from what I could tell, no one paid any attention to us anyway as we walked up from the dock. When we reached the room, Steve gave the prearranged, double-secret knock, and we were soon inside. Jill gave me a big hug. She was smiling, but I could see that she had been crying. I looked around the room, and noticed the two queen-size beds. I was glad to see those. It's been a long time since I've slept on a pallet on the floor.

"So! How'd it go, ladies?"

Katie went first. "I haven't had this much fun since we short-sheeted the camp counselor's bed when I was thirteen. All the regular Woody's girls were there. I started with Anna, and, of course, Chesley. It didn't take long before all the other ladies were coming up to me to ask what was going on. I think the whole garden club was there, too. Most of them had gotten to know Javier, and they were all excited to hear that you had figured out who killed him. As time passed, I noticed many of them pulling out their cell phones, and making calls. I suspect that they were telling everyone they knew that the murder had been solved. Trust me; the Woody's angle was covered."

"Fantastic! How about you, babe?"

"I had to go about things a little differently. Since I didn't really know the bartender or the wait staff, I had to work on the girls that I had gone there to join. I went kind of slow because this was the first time I had been invited to be part of their drinking group. But after a half hour or so, I started to slip into my worried act. You've seen it often enough when I do it for real, Jim, so you know how it looks. I started to get real quiet, and let the lower lip get a little pouty. It didn't take too long before one of the girls asked me what was wrong. From there, I was off to the races. In no time, they were all patting me on the back, hugging me, you name it. They bought it, and were really worried. The best news is that most of them left Froggy's to go to some kind of big shindig down at the American Legion Hall. They wanted me to go with them, but I begged off, explaining that I wouldn't be very good company, and that I needed to go home and be with you. I'm pretty sure that, by now, the news has been spread around. I don't think it could have gone much better."

"That's great. Steve told me that Low Key was handled, too. I think we're in business. If the killer's ears are as attuned to what happens on the island as we think they are, he'll hear the news tonight, for sure. I'd bet he's heard it already. I hid the boat at the fish shack. That went without a hitch. But let me tell you what happened out in the gulf while I was waiting for the sun to go down. You should have seen the kingfish I caught. It was huge!"

"You bastard!" Jill said. "You let us do all the work while you went fishing! Why am I not surprised?"

"Hey, babe. It was all part of the plan. I couldn't just sit out in the middle of the gulf and twiddle my thumbs. That would have looked really suspicious. To keep from looking strange, I had to go fishing! So I just trolled some spoons around for a while. Is it my fault that I'm a great fisherman?"

I could tell that Jill wasn't totally buying it. But she wasn't really all that upset, either. And it was a big fish. I just wish I had thought to take a picture.

Jill had ordered Domino's delivery, and it showed up about that time. That was a good thing, because we were all starved. Thankfully, she had also remembered to bring a cooler full of beer, and a bottle of Scotch. For the next hour we ate, drank, and talked happily. If you didn't know better, you would have thought that we were just getting ready to go fishing the next day. But when Steve pulled out his duffel to do a last-minute check of his equipment, the mood became a lot more somber.

To break the chill, I said, "Hey, Captain, you got your bug spray?"

"Damn right, I've got that. That was the first thing I put in the bag. I never go anywhere down here without that."

"How about bullets? You didn't forget those, did you?"

"What do you mean bullets? All I'm going to need is one."

That comment didn't do much to lighten the mood. "Do me a favor, Steve. At least take a couple. Just to be on the safe side," I said.

Don't worry. I've got three ten-round magazines in the bag. Ammo's not going to be a problem. I've got a few other goodies in there, too. Just to be safe."

At a little after ten o'clock, we set the room's alarm clock for 3:00 a.m., and Katie and Jill set the alarms on their cell phones. We turned off the lights. We knew we'd all need to be as fresh as possible in the morning. The boat ride, Scotch, and pizza, had worked wonders on me. I was dead to the world in no time at all.

I think it probably took Jill a little bit longer to get to sleep. After all, she was worried that the next day I might really be dead to the world.

Chapter Forty-Three
AN EARLY START

Three o'clock in the morning is one a hell of a time to get up. My body's internal clock rebels at that kind of abuse. Even when I'm out of bed and moving around, most of my being can't yet accept the fact that this is for real. I guess that's why they invented coffee. Fortunately, our room had a programmable pot, and the fragrance of a freshly brewed, high-end coffee promised to improve our conditions.

It's often said that wisdom comes with age. Maybe there's something to that. All I know for sure is that Jill and I were very gracious guests and insisted that Katie and Steve use the facilities first. Of course, that gave us the opportunity to immediately have second cups of coffee. And when Steve and Katie had finished, and come back into the bedroom, we had another freshly brewed pot waiting for them. So, I guess it worked out OK for them, too.

A little before four, we all walked out together carrying rods, a tackle box, and a cooler. We weren't actually planning to fish, but we wanted to look as authentic as possible, just in case anyone was paying attention. The cooler, though, was full of water and ice. I knew I'd need it on the boat if I was going to sit out in the hot sun all day. Steve would have to make do with a canteen.

We climbed into the boat. Katie got behind the wheel, inserted the ignition key, attached the dead-man clip, and started the engine. She made sure the water pump was sending its stream of water out the motor's side, and then turned on the boat's navigation lights. Steve took his spot on the bow. Together, he and I quietly untied the dock lines and secured them on board. Katie backed out of the slip, and eased out the channel. Steve was ready with the spot light to locate the next markers. But, thankfully, the moon was bright, the night clear, and we didn't need to use the light. We could see the markers that outlined the channel almost as clearly as if it were daylight. We were underway.

I'd had some questions in my mind about how well Katie would be able to handle the boat. I guess I may still be a little sexist in how I view some things. But, honestly, it has been my experience that ladies are often challenged when it comes to seamanship. Jill, for example, refuses even to take the wheel of our boat unless it's moving no faster than idle speed. When we're on the boat, her preferred spot to sit is wherever it is most advantageous for her to work on her tan. Even when we're fishing, she pays attention to that. I guess we each have our own priorities.

But I realized very quickly that I had no reason to worry about Katie's boat-handling skills. It doesn't take long to understand whether someone knows what they're doing when they are at the controls of a boat. A skilled captain feels the boat, feels the water, feels the wind, and anticipates how all of those things will come together to accomplish what needs to be done. Katie calmly, quietly, and efficiently spun the boat around, and got underway. It was clear she knew what she was doing.

We idled for the first half mile, just to make sure we didn't wake anyone up. Then, she brought the boat onto an easy plane, running it just a little over twenty miles per hour. We slid past the darkness of deserted Part Island, and then negotiated the tight turns that the channel makes around that island's north tip. As you round the north end of this island, your inclination is to turn directly for the channel that runs between Useppa and Mondongo islands. But it is absolutely critical that you do not do that. Instead, you need to run several hundred yards further to the south, and another couple of hundred yards to the west before you head for the main channel. A very shallow sand shoal lies in wait of any boater who is not paying close attention to the chart. Fortunately, Katie was paying attention. I was impressed.

Once we had cleared the sandbar, she brought the boat back to a northerly heading. Soon, we were between Useppa and Mondongo. Useppa is a private oasis for the well-heeled, with at least fifty large, luxurious, old-Florida-style "cottages" around the perimeter of the island. It seems strange to me that these rich folks want to be so tightly packed together on a relatively small island. I'd think they'd get on each others' nerves pretty quickly. But maybe I just don't understand what it's like to be rich.

But whoever owns Mondongo Island clearly doesn't like to be crowded. This is a true private island, with just one large main house, a guest cottage, a boat house, and a dock. If I were wealthy, that's the kind of island retreat I'd want.

As we ran the channel between the two, it didn't look to me like anyone on either island was awake. At least, I didn't see lights on in any of the houses. All appeared to be quiet.

A minute later, Katie throttled back, let the boat settle, and turned toward the south end of Punta Blanca. We coasted toward our chosen landing spot. The southern tip of Punta Blanca is not more than four hundred yards off the main channel. Everything there appeared to be quiet and still. Seen like this, it was hard to imagine that at one time this place had been a bustling, active community. Now, it just looked dark, deserted, and slightly spooky—a tropical ghost town. Having seen it in the daylight, I knew it was overgrown with Brazilian peppers, and covered with dead trees that I presumed were left over from when Hurricane Charlie plowed right over it in 1994. Even in the daylight, it looks foreboding. I was glad I wasn't the one who was going to have to walk into that jungle in the dark.

"Look!" Katie whispered. She pointed at the lights clearly visible on the masts of the two sailboats that were still moored in the deep water on the south side of the island.

"We know. We saw them last night. We're hoping they're just transients, and will move on this morning. Nothing we can do about them. We just don't want to make any noise that would let them know we're here."

Steve laughed softly, and whispered, "I bet if I fired off a couple of rounds in their direction, they'd move on pretty quickly."

"Yeah. I bet they would. But I don't think the sheriff would appreciate that."

"Heck!"

It was good to see that Steve was relaxed, and in a good mood. He was going to have a long day ahead.

Katie bumped the boat in as close as possible. Where we were coming in, the bottom is firm sand that slopes gently upward to the shore. She was able to let the bow touch the bottom, while the foot of the tilted motor still had enough depth to operate. Perfect. Steve would only have to walk a few feet through the water.

Steve leaned around the console, and gave Katie a kiss. In return, she stood up, and gave him a long embrace.

He said, "All right guys. It's time to get this show on the road." He went back to the bow, sat on the gunwale, and swung his legs into the water. When he stepped down, I noticed that the water only came up a little past his ankles. I also noticed for the first time that he had belted a large knife, which was stowed securely in its camouflaged scabbard, to his calf. I also noticed that he had a semiautomatic pistol in a holster attached to a belt around his waist. He reached back into the boat, picked up his duffel, and slung it diagonally over one shoulder and across his back. He clearly had done this before. Finally, he reached one more time into the boat, and grabbed his walking cane.

"Hey, Captain," I whispered. "Take care of yourself."

"Ya'll better not forget to come pick me up this afternoon," he answered. "See you later."

He began walking toward the shore. Katie slipped the transmission into reverse. As we backed away, we could see him wade onto the shore. Then, without looking back, he headed into the bushes, a soldier intent on the job at hand. As soon as we had enough depth, Katie lowered the engine, spun the boat, and idled toward the channel. No one said a word. We could tell that this was starting to get serious.

Once the sonar showed deep water, Katie brought the boat onto a plane and headed south. This time, we went along Useppa's west side. Still no lights to be seen. We continued past Cabbage Key. No lights there, either. As I had noticed before, Katie knew what she was doing. At the south end of Cabbage Key, the channel bends sharply to the west, and then back again to the south. While these turns are well marked with red and green beacons, in the past I have noticed that folks often get confused at this spot. But Katie smoothly steered the required course with no drama. Once beyond that point, the channel is a straight shot, pretty much running down the middle of the sound. As we headed south, we saw no other boats. From what I could tell, we were alone.

A mile further down the channel, Katie began to steer to the east. I knew she was following the GPS tracks that Steve had laid down the night before. The fish shacks are built on top of a long sand shoal that runs north to south. From a distance, it looks as if you could drive straight up to them. But there's not enough water to get there that way. You have to run about five hundred yards to the south to get around the shoal's southern tip. Then, you can head back to the north, taking care to stay in a narrow channel along the shoal's east side. Inside that channel, there's plenty of water. Katie carefully eased the boat toward the shack where the *Pulapanga* was tied. From what we could see, everything looked to be in order. At least the boat was still there. I thought that was a good sign.

Katie gently laid her boat alongside the *Pulapanga*. I tied the two together.

I swung the cooler and a small bag onto my boat. I checked to make sure that I had the boat's keys.

"All right, babe," Jill said. "What's the plan from here? You want to crank it up and make sure it runs before we leave you?"

"No. I don't think so. I'm in no hurry to get up to Punta Blanca. I think I'll just wait here until the sun starts to come up. I'd like to have enough daylight to look it over good before I try to start it. I may be being overly cautious, but I'd rather be safe than sorry. And at this point, there's no reason to be in a hurry. Assuming all's good with the boat, I'll ease out into the sound as soon as I've got good light, and then, just hang around out there for a while. There's no reason for me to be in place at Punta Blanca before nine o'clock. If for some reason there's something not right with the boat, I'll give ya'll a call on the phone, and you can come back to pick me up."

At that point, I think we all realized that we had reached a critical juncture. Jill and I looked at each other; neither of us said a word for several moments. I'm not sure what she was thinking, but I know I was hoping that this wasn't going to be the last time we were ever together.

Finally, she broke the silence. "I guess we'd better get out of here so you can get to work. You be careful. I'll see you tonight."

Yeah, I'll be careful. Ya'll better get back to the Lodge. Love you, babe."

"I love you, too."

We gave each other a hug and a kiss. Then, I climbed over the gunwale into my boat. I untied the dock line, and handed it back to Jill. Katie turned the key to crank the Honda, and quietly backed away into the darkness. Seconds later, the boat faded into the night, and all I could see was its white stern light as it retraced its path to the south. I could tell when the boat turned west around the bar's tip, as the white light disappeared, and was replaced by a green glow. I heard the motor throttle up and its tone change as the boat accelerated onto a plane. Moments later, Katie banked the boat to the northwest, heading back toward the main channel. A minute later, all I could see was the white stern light receding into the darkness. I could see the light move as the boat swung through the curves south of Cabbage Key. I finally lost sight of it altogether when it disappeared behind Useppa. I sure hated to lose sight of that light. As soon as it was gone, I really started to feel alone and vulnerable.

It was almost time for me to be bait.

Chapter Forty-Four
A SURPRISE

When I had been waiting on the shack's dock for Steve to pick me up the night before, the sound had been active. Now it was just quiet and still. I thought about trying to sleep a little, but I knew I was too amped up on coffee and fear to do that. Besides, the boards on the dock looked awfully hard. I was also tempted to start the boat and ride around for a while, just to relieve the boredom. But I knew that really wouldn't be a smart move.

Fortunately, Jill had packed a thermos of coffee, and put it in my pack. I didn't really need more caffeine, but I sure did need the warmth, smell, and taste of something good. Maybe it wasn't Starbucks, but in that setting, it was fabulous.

As I savored the Joe, I tried to imagine how the day's events might unfold. I was torn between fearing that no one would appear and being scared that someone would show up. Finally, I decided that the outcome I dreaded least was facing the killer. I knew Steve had my back.

I also realized that sitting on the dock was a far sight better place to be than being where Steve was sitting. All I had to worry about was being shit on by a passing pelican. I didn't like to think about what Steve might be dealing with. I knew there would be plenty of bugs in those trees and bushes. I hoped his repellant was up to snuff. I assumed there could be snakes, too. I hate snakes! I had read that back in Collier's time, nearby Patricio Island was infested with rattlesnakes. I hoped that none had ever swum over to Punta Blanca. I hoped Steve was going to be OK.

Eventually, I could see the eastern sky beyond Pine Island begin to lighten. Shortly after that, I could see a pink tinge start to form on the bottoms of the clouds way out on the horizon. With these first hints of daylight coming, I knew that in quarter of an hour, I would have enough light to inspect the boat. With that encouragement, I poured myself the last cup of coffee from the thermos. Finally, I was beginning to get excited about what was to come.

Once I had enough light, I climbed down into the boat, and had a look around. Nothing looked amiss. Next, I started at the bow and began to inspect the pieces of tape that I had placed on each hatch cover. The one over the anchor locker was in place. So were the pieces over the bow storage locker and the small locker that serves as a step onto the bow fishing platform. The forward bait well's tape was in place, too. I moved to the stern, and saw that the tape was undisturbed on the battery compartment, the rear bait well, and the live release well.

I was beginning to feel comfortable that no one had discovered the boat during the evening. Normally, when I'm toward the rear the boat, I'll reach down, rotate the master electrical switch from the off position, and turn on one or both of the boat's batteries. I reached down to do that. But just before I touched the blue handle, I froze, realizing that I hadn't yet checked the tape on the openings in the center console.

First, I looked up at the electronics locker that sits over the steering position. The tape there was good.

Next, I looked down at the two doors that cover the center console storage compartment. And my heart stopped. The tape that should have stretched between these two doors was only attached to one side.

What did this mean? Had it simply come undone? Or had someone been on board during the night? I tried to remember if I had locked the console when I left. I used to do this religiously. But, lately I had slacked off on this, reasoning that there was a lot of other stuff to steal on the boat that wasn't locked up, so why bother securing this compartment. As I thought back, I was pretty sure that I had not locked it. Damn! I had made it way too easy for someone to plant a bomb on my boat.

All of the boat's electrical switches are mounted on the upper surface of the center console, facing the pilot. It occurred to me now that all those electrical connections would present an easy opportunity to wire in a bomb's detonator. It also occurred to me that I sure didn't want to open the doors of that console.

If the bomber was sophisticated, he probably would have rigged his device so that opening the console's doors would set off the bomb. But, for the life of me, I couldn't figure out a way to look inside the console without opening the damn door. If I'd had my tools, I might have been able to take off the door's hinges. But, of course, the boat tools were inside the console. I considered trying to remove one of the instruments on the dash, but they are all secured from the inside to discourage theft. And I didn't have anything with me that I could use to pry one off.

Finally, there was nothing to be done except open the damn door. I learned a long time ago from a good man who used to work with me that when something unpleasant needed to be done, no good would come from putting it off. It was best just to get the unpleasant task done as quickly as possible. I reluctantly concluded that looking inside the center console definitely fit in the category of unpleasant tasks.

But the question remained. How should I open the door? Should I ease it open? Should I jerk it open? Was there any way to open it remotely? Was there any way that I could shield myself as I opened it? After considerable thought, I decided that there was no way I could open it from a distance. And besides, if there was a bomb on the boat, its explosion would likely demolish not only the boat, but the fish shack as well. There were not a lot of things to hide behind out there. Finally, I decided to open the door as gently as possible. If it blew up, it blew up. At least I'd go out with a bang. Somehow, though, that wasn't much comfort.

So I very carefully depressed the button that locks the console's doors. I was right; the lock had not been locked. Then, holding the port-side door in a closed position, I began to swing the starboard-side door open as slowly as possible. I was relieved that I didn't feel any resistance. And I didn't hear any sound. In fact, the door seemed to open normally. So, I pulled it open a little further. Again, nothing. I opened the door another inch. And then another. At that point, I decided that there wasn't a bomb detonator wired to the door, and went ahead and opened the door all the way. I was still alive.

Then, still holding the port door closed, I stuck my head inside. Shit! There it was! Sitting right on top of the coast guard's required throw-able floatation device, was what I assumed was a hunk of plastic explosive with what looked to be a detonator sticking out of it. The detonator device appeared to be simply wired to the boat's main electrical circuit that leads to the ignition switch. If I had turned on the boat's main power breaker—ka-boom! Thankfully, I hadn't. And, thankfully, it looked to me like this bomb was going to be easy to disarm. As far as I could tell, there was nothing tricky about it. I couldn't see any motion detector to worry about, nor could I see anything fancy about the detonator. I'm no expert, but I've watched enough episodes of *CSI Miami* to suspect that if I cut the wire leading to the detonator, it should be disarmed.

Just to make sure, I carefully inspected every inch of the inside of the console. I looked at the wiring over and over again. I made sure that there was nothing that looked complicated or tricky. Finally, I decided that it was, in fact, as simple as it seemed: an electrical circuit between the power line to the ignition switch and the bomb's detonator.

I carefully removed the onboard tool kit from under the pouch that holds the boat's life vests, and laid it on the deck outside the console. I pulled the pair of cutting dykes out of the case. I inspected them carefully, all the while breathing deeply. What I was inspecting them for, I really didn't have a clue. Upon reflection, I concluded that I was just delaying the inevitable. And, given my friend's rule, I knew I needed to get started. So

I stuck my head back inside the console, and placed the wires that lead to the bomb between the blades of the pliers. I took a very deep breath, closed my eyes, and squeezed. Snip. I actually heard a snip! I didn't know if you would have time to actually hear a bomb explode. Probably not. But I knew that only hearing a snip was a very good thing!

Next, I very gently lifted the bomb from the cushion, and carefully maneuvered it outside, making sure that I didn't bump it into anything. And then, ever so slowly, I laid it on the dock. I thought about just leaving it there, and getting away from the damn thing as soon as I could. I could call the sheriff's office to have his bomb squad come pick it up. But I didn't want that kind of law enforcement commotion out of the sound today. On the other hand, I didn't just want to leave it on the dock where anyone might come along and pick it up. Finally, I decided that the best thing to do would be to drop it into the water by the dock's ladder. I didn't know what effect saltwater might have on the explosives or on the detonator. But I figured it would probably be OK for a day or so. I eased it into the water.

Shit! Who knew that C-4 floats? I needed a new plan.

I picked it up, put it back on the dock, and reconsidered my options. From what I've heard, without a detonation cap it's practically impossible to get C-4 to explode. I even remember seeing an episode of *Myth Busters* on which the hosts tried to cause C-4 to explode without using a blasting cap. They even tried to shoot it with a high-powered rifle. Despite several direct hits, it wouldn't explode. Armed with this wealth of knowledge, I concluded that I probably ought to pull the blasting cap out. If

I did that, I figured it would be safe enough to take the plastic explosive with me in the boat.

It looked simple enough to do. So I slowly and very gently eased the cap out of the plastic. That seemed to go OK. Then, I placed the C-4 in the boat, setting it on top of the leaning post's cushion. But I wasn't about to carry the blasting cap in the boat. Ever so carefully, I tied a six-foot length of fishing line to it, secured the other end of the line to the dock's ladder, and carefully placed it in the water. It slowly sank to the bottom, and lay there. Good enough for me!

I hoped I would be alive later to tell the sheriff where to find it. I'd hate for the shack's owners to show up one day, find something tied to their dock, pull it up to look at it, and then have the damn thing go off in their hands. I wouldn't want that on my conscience. I have enough regrets already without adding another one on what might possibly be my last day on earth. So just in case, I pulled out my phone, and sent a text message to Mike Collins, telling him exactly what had transpired. But I asked him to stay away from the shack for the rest of the day.

Next, I wrapped the C-4 in a couple of boat towels, and stashed it in the radio locker. I sure hoped that what they'd said on *Myth Busters* was true. I'd hate to find out that a radio transmission would set the stuff off. But if you can't trust *MythBusters*, what can you trust? I took one last, long look around the interior of the console, just to make sure I hadn't missed something. Everything looked good. I closed it up.

I then inspected the whole boat again, opening each locker to make sure there were no hidden surprises. There weren't.

Finally, I felt like I could breathe again. I knew I must have been breathing for the last twenty minutes. But honestly, if I did, I couldn't remember it. I took a deep breath, savoring every precious element of it. Only then did I notice how badly my hands were shaking. Shit! Somebody really was trying to kill me!

I've never been in this situation before. But I can tell you, having that realization will absolutely focus your attention.

For a moment, I considered whether I should just pick up Steve, call the whole operation off, and then get Jill and me as far away from Pine Island Sound as possible. But soon enough, I discarded that idea.

I couldn't run away from this fight. Some sorry bastard had killed a great friend of mine, and I wasn't going to let him get away with it. I was going to find him. And when I did, one of us was not going to walk away. Maybe this would be the day that would happen. Maybe not. Regardless, I was not going to stop searching for him until I found him.

With that resolve, I walked to the stern area, and rotated the main battery switch so that both batteries were engaged. I immediately heard the radio squeak, and saw the GPS fire up. Absolutely normal. I turned the ignition switch to light up the Yamaha. It started quietly. Just like it always does.

Round one to the good guys!

Chapter Forty-Five
KNEELING AND PRAYING

I untied the *Pulapanga*, and quietly motored down the channel that runs by the fish shacks. My plan was to head out into the sound, find an out-of-the-way fishing spot, anchor, and kill time until a little before nine o'clock. No one would pay much attention to someone fishing early in the morning. Once the time was right, I'd reel in my lines, pull up the anchor, and motor toward Punta Blanca. It'd look like I was simply hunting for a more productive spot to fish. And, in a sense, that would be exactly what I would be doing.

I worried about Steve being out on that overgrown island all by himself, and hoped that he had gotten through the night with no issues. But, truthfully, I was glad it was Steve and not me. As badly as I had been scared by the close encounter with being blown to kingdom come, I still preferred being where I was to having to stay on Punta Blanca in the dark. I hoped he was OK.

I started to text him to see how he was doing. But we had agreed to not contact each other unless it was critically important. I concluded that simple curiosity really wasn't a critical issue.

At ten minutes to nine, I reeled in the two un-baited popping-cork rigs that I had put out to look like I was fishing, punched the "up" button on the Talon shallow-water anchor, and started the Yamaha. It was show time.

I idled out of the manatee zone and into some deeper water. Once I checked to make sure that the engine tilt was in its lowest position, I fed in the throttle. With only one person on board, and with the live wells empty, the boat leaped out of the water, and was quickly on a plane.

The morning was gorgeous, with just enough small ripples to remind me that I was on the water, not sliding across the biggest mirror in the world. It was a great day to boat on the sound. The sunrise had been spectacular, with its rays spreading multicolored reflections through anew thunderheads out over Lake Okeechobee. Pelicans were diving almost everywhere I looked, creating geysers of spray as they dropped onto unsuspecting schools of bait. Dolphin were active, breaching periodically as their pods eased along, searching for breakfast. A truly great day on the sound—unless you were bait.

And of course, that's exactly what I was planning to be. My job was simply to hang out, dangling myself like a shrimp on a hook, and see what showed up to try to eat me. Given all the commotion we had created last night in Saint James City, and given the surprise I had discovered this morning on the boat, there was no doubt that I was, in fact, being stalked by an unseen predator. And since the bomb had failed to satisfy the killer's appetite, I had to assume that he was still hungry, and that he was still stalking me. I guessed I'd find out soon enough.

As I headed north, toward the spot where the channels intersect, the sound was coming alive with other boats. Fishermen in flats boats were flying south, impatient to get to their first fishing spot of the day. Sailors were raising their sails and pulling anchors, as they prepared to head toward their next gunk hole of choice. And large, sports fishing boats, sedans, and trawlers were throwing up huge wakes as they hurried toward their next dock and fuel pump. Another day on the sound.

I took it easy heading north. No reason to hurry, and I needed to go slowly to negotiate the wakes of the larger, faster-moving motor vessels. On any morning, it's hilarious to listen to the radio chatter on Channel Sixteen as captains still at anchor squabble with those underway who are, in their opinions, creating too much wake in a no-wake zone. Conversations can get testy in a hurry.

But, that morning I wasn't paying attention to the radio. I had other things on my mind.

Cabbage Key, Useppa Island, Mondongo Island, and Punta Blanca Island are close together. I'd guess that there's less than a half mile between any two, and most are closer than that. Patricio Island, Collier's garden island, lies just to the east of Mondongo. When you're out there in a boat, it's easy to understand why Collier purchased all of these islands: you can easily row a boat between any of them in just a few minutes.

As I eased past Cabbage Key, I didn't notice any large boats tied up at the inn's main dock, but it looked as if a couple of the cottages were rented, since there were boats at the docks in front of them. I could also see a couple of flats skiffs bobbing next to the resort's seawall, their impatient captains waiting for late-rising clients to finish breakfast. Otherwise, Cabbage Key was quiet. The lunch horde wouldn't start to arrive until a little before noon. But once the stream of diners began, it would continue for three or four hours. Sometimes it's a real circus at the dock at lunchtime. It can be a lot of fun to watch—unless, of course, it's your boat tied up at the dock and about to be gouged by a rented boat piloted by someone who obviously has done it before in his life. That can be a stressful experience for all concerned.

Cabbage Key is really a great place. We always take our houseguests up there. Not only do they get to experience a unique part of Florida history, but they get to see almost the entire sound during the boat ride. But it's a lot better to do it on a weekday rather than on a weekend. Take my word for it.

Useppa lies directly across the channel from Cabbage Key. It's a private island accessible only by member and their guests. The only exceptions are passengers on the local tourist ferries, who, as part of their excursion fees, get to eat lunch at the Useppa Club. I guess it's a safe-enough way to defray the overhead of maintaining a truly first-class kitchen for a privileged few. As I eased by, I told myself that if I survived, I was going to go to take the ferry to Useppa one day, and have lunch there.

I noticed that the island was starting to come to life. The dock masters were washing down the white planks of the dock to get rid of any stains deposited overnight by pelicans and seagulls. The docks were nearly full of beautiful motor yachts. On a few, crew members were hosing down the decks, or wiping dew off cabin windows. I also observed a couple of fishing guides who were idling their skiffs out of one of the two channels, transporting clients toward fishing spots of choice. Everything looked absolutely normal..

As I started to slow, I glanced toward Mondongo. Despite its strange name, which, I have read, means hog intestines; this is a very pretty island. I believe that, at one time, it was owned by the Lykes family, of meatpacking fame. They must have liked the name! The island still looks like something out of the 1920s, but I have no clue who owns it today. To me, it looks like the kind of place that everyone would dream of owning. That morning, as usual, I saw no sign of life.

As I took all of this in, I throttled back, and turned toward Punta Blanca. I idled in between the south shore of the island on the right and the old pilings on the left that used to support the large Punta Gorda Fish Company ice house. At one time, this complex was comprised of three separate structures—an ice house for fish awaiting transport to Port Charlotte, a residence and office for the house's manager, and a warehouse for supplies that would be sold to fishermen and to the residents of the neighboring islands. The entire complex burned under mysterious circumstances in 1993, on the very night that the state of Florida's gill-net ban went into effect. It was rumored, but never proved, that the fire had been set by mullet fishermen angry that their way of life had been legislated out of existence.

Now those old pilings looked kind of lonely, and maybe just a little unhappy that they hadn't burned when everything else did. But the pelicans and anhinga that were resting on them, digesting their breakfasts, didn't seem to care one way or the other. They just kept a suspicious eye on me as I slid past. Clearly, I was the one who was out of place.

A channel with about eight feet of water stretches around the south end of the island. It was dredged out by Collier's crews back in the twenties. They did a good job; it's still useful today. Lots of overnight boaters drop anchor there. As I motored in, I was glad to see that one of the sailboats that had been anchored there was already gone. I guessed it was probably one of those boats that I noticed heading south as I motored up the sound. I was glad it was gone.

Unfortunately, the other boat was still there. And I was disappointed that I couldn't see any sign of life on board. I had been hoping that I would see people cleaning up after breakfast in preparation to weigh anchor. But that was not the case. I guessed that the occupants were just sleeping late, probably after drinking a little too much rum the night before. It happens. It's happened to me on more than one occasion. Still, I hoped they would be underway soon. As I went past, I couldn't help but admire the boat. It had to be at least fifty feet long. Its lines were beautiful and classic. The hull was painted a deep, ocean blue, with red bottom paint. Its cabin trim was bright white. I like those colors on a boat. It was rigged as a ketch, having a mast smaller than the main located aft of the steering post. I've always admired ketches. This rig's small trysail in the rear of the boat comes in very handy. It can keep the boat from swinging at anchor, and, in a storm, it's a lot easier to handle than trying to reef the main. The boat's fore-sails were divided into a cutter rig. When the winds pick up, this sail plan gives you the option of using a foresail smaller than the large Genoa jib up front. If you've ever had to replace a large jib with a smaller one in the middle of the night during a raging storm, you can appreciate a cutter rig on a sailboat. I couldn't help but notice, as I went past, that all of the sails featured roller furling. Not only did the boat have an extremely functional sail plan—one that would give the crew a lot of options for dealing with the wind—but the electric-roller furling capability meant that the boat could easily be handled by a small crew, or maybe even one sailor. The boat was equipped with a full complement of electronics and solar panels to power them. This was a serious boat, equipped for serious voyaging. And, I noticed, it also was equipped for fun when it got to wherever it was going. A paddleboard, a surf board, a scuba rack, and an inflatable dingy were securely lashed down to deck. One could take a boat like this just about anywhere in the world, and easily live aboard. I had once hoped to have a boat like that.

But, then, as I slid past, I caught a glimpse of the name on the stern. It was a shock. In bright gold letters was the name "The Spanish Princess," with a home port of Marsh Harbor displayed underneath. No way that this could be a coincidence. Did this mean that Big Ed had returned from the Bahamas to play out more of his fucking pirate fantasies? This was certainly not whom I had anticipated meeting today.

I steered along the channel toward the western tip of the island. Despite the deep channel coming in, you still have to take care in this area. As you make the turn to the west, the channel has silted in. At one time, Collier's channel ran all the way around the peninsula and into a secluded basin open to the wind only to the west. That basin is still there, and it still has good depth on its south side. It would make a first-class hurricane hole. But it's not easy to get in there now.

That morning, I wasn't planning to go that far. As I got to the shoal area, I veered west into slightly deeper water. A hundred yards further, I came to an area with a solid eight feet. I knew from the chart that this deep water stretched almost to the shore of Cayo Costa. Carlos and some of the other guides have told me that there's good fishing where the flats drop off into this kind of pocket. Unfortunately, Carlos also told me that this was the exact spot where Javier was killed.

I dropped anchor in the eastern edge of the deeper water. In seafaring class, you are taught to let out your anchor rode in an amount equal to seven times the depth of the water in which you are anchoring. This amount of scope (that's the ratio of line to depth) will ensure that the pull your boat puts on the anchor will be roughly parallel to the bottom. A parallel pull will keep the anchor digging in. If there's less scope, in waves or swells the boat will exert an upward pull, tending to lift the anchor out of the bottom. That's obviously not a good thing, especially in a storm, when you need the anchor to hold. If you have room for the boat to swing, and if you're expecting a blow, even more scope is better. But I wasn't planning to stay past sundown, and I wasn't expecting wind stronger than a gentle breeze. So I only let out about forty feet of anchor line. I guessed that with ten feet of depth at high tide, a four-to-one scope would be sufficient. Besides, I didn't want to get any farther away from Steve than was strictly necessary.

The morning shore breeze was blowing directly out of the east. That allowed the bow to point directly at the tip of Punta Blanca where, I hoped, Steve would have a clear shot at anyone stepping onto the *Pulapanga*. I planned to sit all day on the cushion that forms the seat in front of the center console. With this setup, there was no way that Steve couldn't put a bullet where he needed to put a bullet in order to protect me. He claimed to be able to hit a six-inch target a thousand yards away. I wasn't more than 250 yards from Punta Blanca's tip. No way would he miss his target when the time came to shoot.

Once in place, I figured that now was the time to put on a good show. I needed to convince anyone who might be observing that I was a grief-stricken man who had come to Punta Blanca to talk with the spirit of a friend who had breathed his last breath exactly where I was now anchored. If I could do that in a convincing fashion, the predator might be enticed to strike. Whenever you're fishing, presentation is important. I needed to make it look good.

Sitting in the same location on my boat as Javier had been sitting on his when he was shot, I bowed my head, and brought my hands together in the universal sign of prayer. I'm not a religious guy, but I figured, what could it hurt? In truth, I was damn glad to have narrowly avoided being blown to smithereens a couple of hours earlier. Saying thanks to whoever might have been responsible would not be out of line. Besides, I wanted this to look good. I couldn't see anyone watching, but somehow I knew that others were paying attention. I just hoped that one of them was Steve.

After I had "prayed" for about ten minutes, I moved to the fishing deck on the bow. There I knelt, and bowed at the waist as deeply as my plump thighs would allow. I held that position for a couple of minutes, and then straightened up, raising my face to the sun. As I came to this position, I extended my arms out to each side with my palms facing upward. I closed my eyes, and silently counted to two hundred.

I was doing my best to make it appear that I was seeking divine guidance from on high. I haven't had too much experience actually doing this, so I wasn't sure how I should go about it. But I remembered from going to church as a child that bended knees were an important element. When I got to two hundred, I repeated the ritual five times. I figured that, by this time, if anyone was watching, this display should have been convincing enough. Besides, my arthritic knees were beginning to ache. I needed to take a break.

I stood up, stretched, and looked around. Nothing. The sailboat was still were I had passed it earlier, about five hundred yards away; and there was no sign of life on board. That seemed kind of strange. Neither was there any sign of Steve. But that was OK. I didn't expect to be able to see him. As I looked all around the bay, there was no sign of anyone. It began to dawn on me that this was going to be a long day. I walked to the cooler in the back of the boat, and grabbed a bottled water. I took my shirt off—heck, might as well get some sun while I was being bait—and returned to my seat in front of the console.

I decided that I had done enough praying. Now, I wanted it to look like I was thinking. I assumed the classic "thinker" position—chin supported by my palm, elbow resting on my knee. From afar, one would have to conclude that I was deeply in thought. And in truth, I was. I was now fairly certain that I knew who the killer was. But I wanted to carefully review in my mind every aspect of what had led me to form this conclusion. So, for the next hour, I just sat, waiting for him to strike. I did some thinking about that, too.

After an hour, just to break the monotony, I repeated the prayer ritual. I was pretty sure that I was putting on a good show. If I had been the one looking, I think I would have been convinced. But this time, when I returned to the seat at the console, I varied the thinking posture, trying to appear to be more agitated. Occasionally, I even talked out loud to myself.

Then, at the conclusion of this next repetition, I took out a pad of paper and a pen from my pack, and began to write. I wanted it to appear to anyone watching that I was writing out the story I intended to give to the *News Press*. I wrote for nearly an hour. And, in fact, it was what I intended to give to the paper.

As I wrote, I occasionally looked up, appearing to stare into space for inspiration. But, in fact, I was keeping an eye on what was going on around me. After some time, I guess it must have been almost eleven o'clock, I noticed that the neighboring sailboat was finally underway. It was too far away for me to clearly make out who was at the wheel, but it appeared to be a man. A man of average height, with a longbeard. It certainly wasn't Big Ed, and it wasn't anyone that I recognized. I know a lot of guys in Saint James City who have long beards, but I'm pretty sure that none of them owns a beautiful, brand-new, fifty-foot-long ketch. In fact, I'm not sure that any of those guys actually owns much of anything.

I watched the ketch head east, hit the deep water of the main channel, and then turn toward the north. I assumed it was probably heading to Tampa. Or maybe to New Orleans. Or Houston. Who knows where it was headed? A boat like that could go anywhere. Now, I was just relieved that it was leaving. I was also glad that it didn't appear to be Big Ed Lowder's boat. A boat liked that shouldn't be owned by a low class asshole like him.

I watched the masts of the boat for as long as I could, but soon they were out of sight behind the trees on Punta Blanca. I silently wished the skipper a good voyage, and returned to the bow of the *Pulapanga* for yet another round of meditation.

Hopefully, all this kneeling was going to do some good. One thing was for sure: I would probably be too sore to walk in the morning. I hadn't done this much kneeling since the last time Jill and I went to a Catholic wedding.

Chapter Forty-Six
JALAPENO VIENNA SAUSAGE

Those who know me well know that I hate to miss lunch. Something about an empty stomach makes me grumpy. The little bit that I had eaten back at the Lodge had long since faded away, and I was getting hungry. Despite all of our careful planning, I had somehow forgotten to pack something to eat. I guess I had assumed that by this time, the situation would have played itself out, one way or the other. But that had not happened.

Fortunately, I remembered that I had left a can of Vienna sausage in the radio console a few weeks earlier. I don't know about you, but I am a fan of Vienna sausage. When I'm on the boat, I'd much rather eat a can of these little wieners, maybe with some cheese and crackers, than chow down on a sandwich and a bag of chips. It just makes me feel better. Back when I was a kid, Vienna sausages only came one way. But now, there all kinds of different flavors from which to choose. In addition to the standard variety, you can get barbecue, jalapeno, cheese, chipotle, and who knows what other varieties. The can that I had stashed on the boat was my current favorite—jalapeno. They're tough to beat, but you'd better have something cold to drink to wash them down—preferably a beer. I just had water that day. Nonetheless, they were delicious.

About the time I savored the last morsel, I noticed what looked to be a flats skiff coming around the south end of Cabbage Key, heading in my direction. OK! Finally, some action.

I stowed the sausage can and the water bottle, and looked around the boat to make sure I was as ready as I could be. I mentally reviewed how I would alert Steve that he needed to shoot to kill—I would wave my left arm. There was nothing else for me to do other than make sure that I acted like the most attractive piece of bait possible.

The skiff continued to head toward me. Then, it veered to the west for a couple of minutes, before turning back to the north, and heading toward me again. I assumed that this deviation had been necessary to avoid the oyster bars that litter that part of the bay. The guides will tell you that in order to learn where all the shallow spots are, you need to get out on the water when the tides are negative low. The only way you can really learn where the water is thin is to see it for yourself from behind the wheel of your boat. You need to have that sight picture etched in your mind so that when you need it, you will be able to draw upon that knowledge base. The other thing they'll tell you is that not only do you need to know where it's shallow, but you better make sure you know whether it's shallow because it's a sandbar or because it's an oyster bar. You run up on a sandbar—it'll just be embarrassing; you run up on an oyster bar—it'll also be expensive! At the very least, if you hit oysters, you'll need a new prop. But if you're going fast enough, you'll probably need a whole new lower unit. That can get expensive quick!

The person piloting this skiff obviously knew what he was about. I watched him wind his way through the shallows and up the eastern shore of Cayo Costa. There was no way I would have felt comfortable going that way at that speed. I guessed that whoever killed Javier had known his way around, too. How else would he have been able to come in and get out without anyone noticing him?

I could sense my blood pressure starting to rise. Maybe this was it! I hoped that Steve was ready. I wanted to call him just to make sure he was awake. But I knew that wouldn't be necessary. And it wouldn't have looked right. I really needed to look like bait.

I watched the boat get closer and closer. Now he was in the deep channel about eight hundred yards away, heading toward me, and closing fast.

You're OK, I told myself. Take a deep breath! Keep calm! Stay focused! I sat down on my console seat, and waited, watching the boat get closer and closer.

When it was four hundred yards away, I could see a steering station mounted on top of the boat's T-top. But whoever was steering was sitting behind the center console. Still, the boat was coming directly at me. Shit! What if he just stopped a couple of hundred yards away and took a shot at me? I had to assume that Steve wasn't the only one who knew how to shoot around here! And there was no way that Steve could take a shot at him until after he'd shot at me—probably not until he'd killed me.

We hadn't thought about that. Once he had shot, Steve might be able to take him out. But that wasn't going to help me too much! At least, he'd know who had killed Javier.

The boat was continuing to head my way. I still couldn't tell who was driving it. But gradually, the boat started to look familiar. It was a little larger than most flats skiffs, and there was a deeper, more pronounced, flair to the bow than what you see on most shallow-water boats. And this one was painted battle-ship gray, which was unusual. It certainly looked a little menacing. I told myself again to stay calm.

Shit! Now I recognized who this was. Piloting the boat was Hector Sanchez—the fishing guide who lives in my neighborhood. A really nice Cuban guy. He was the guy who, along with his wife, had come to tell me that Javier had been killed. He couldn't be the killer—could he? No way! The sheriff had checked out his alibi and cleared him. He had been out fishing with a client that day. Hadn't he? There was no way that Carlos could be coming to kill me. Heck, he's just too nice of a guy! But what if he and the client had been in it together? Could they have vouched for each other? Could they have set up the trip just so they would have the chance to kill Javier? Would this explain why no one except them had seen Javier on the day he was killed? Had he set the whole thing up? He did come from an old Cuban fishing family that had been here forever. Crap!

By now, Hector was only a hundred yards away. He throttled his Mercury back, and let the boat settle gently in front of its wake. Once the wake had moved past, he slipped his engine into forward, and began to idle toward where I was anchored.

As he approached, he didn't say a word. But knowing Hector, that wasn't out of character. He never says much.

Fifty feet out, he knocked the engine out of gear, and let the boat coast in my direction. He picked up his right hand and waved. Still, he didn't say anything.

I exhaled, and tried to relax. I started to wave back. For just a moment, I picked up my left hand to wave, but caught myself in time. I waved back with my right.

"Hector, how you doing? What are you doing out here?"

"Jim, I was just passing by. Wanted to scout out this area to see if there are any redfish schools feeding up here. You know, sometimes this is one of their favorite spots to hang out. I've seen them so thick in here that you can't stir 'em with a stick! But I haven't seen many yet. How about you? You seen any fish up here?"

"No, Hector. I haven't seen a single tail sticking up so far. Kind of a long ways up here for you to come scouting, isn't it?"

"Oh, hell no. I do it all the time."

I didn't say anything. I just looked at him.

"Shit, Jim. I might as well tell you the truth. I was just worried about you. We all heard last night from the captain about what you were going to do today. I told him that I didn't like it. I was scared that something might happen to you, just like it did to Javier. He told me not to worry about you, that you needed to be out here by yourself, and that I needed to stay away. But I didn't like you being out here by yourself. So I just figured I'd hang out in the general vicinity. I've been fishing all morning over in Captiva Pass. That's only a couple of miles from here.

I figured that was far enough away to not disturb your karma. Hell, there's been at least six other boats fishing there all morning, too. I figured that if they weren't going to mess you up, that I wouldn't either."

"Hector, I appreciate your concern. I really do. But I notice now that you're not actually fishing in Captiva Pass. Unless I'm hallucinating, it looks to me like you and your boat are up here by Punta Blanca."

"No. You're not seeing things. I'm here. Truth is, the tide's started to slow in the pass, and the fish have stopped biting. And, the slower they bit, the more worried I got. Finally, I couldn't stand it anymore. I just had to come up here and make sure you were OK. And, besides, I wanted to give you my gun. I always keep a .45 automatic in my console, just in case I need to kill a shark. But I figure that today you might need it more than me. Let me get it out for you."

"Hector," I yelled. "Stop! I don't want your fucking gun. Please, do *not* take a gun out of the console!"

"Are you sure you don't want to borrow the gun? I won't mind a bit."

"Yeah, Hector. I'm real sure. I appreciate the thought, but I don't want a gun. Now, look, it's been very quiet out here. There's nothing going on. I've just been sitting here all morning thinking about what happened to Javier, and trying to make sure I know who killed him. I know it sounds strange, but in a fashion, Javier and I have been talking. I'm pretty sure I have this almost all figured out."

"Damn, Jim. That's good! But do you really think it's a smart idea for you to be out here all by yourself? If I know you're out here, there's no reason that whoever killed Javier won't know that, too. And, if you know who he is, what's to keep him from killing you just to keep you quiet?"

"Hector, trust me, I'm really not worried about that. But in order for me to know for certain who killed Javier, I need to be here—and I need to be alone—in this exact spot where Javier was shot. I'm sorry. But, you can't be here."

"OK. I'll buy that. But what if I were to go fish over by Cayo Costa and just keep an eye on you from there?"

"Carlos, I appreciate the offer. I really do. But I would know you were there, and I'm afraid that might screw up my ability to communicate with Javier's spirit. I feel weird enough trying to talk to a ghost, without knowing that someone is watching me do it. Look, I desperately need to be able to talk with Javier today. It just won't work if you're around. I need you to promise me that you'll go somewhere else to fish."

"Jim, I want you to know that I think you're fucking nuts putting yourself out here in this position. I wouldn't do it, that's for damn sure. If I were you, I'd just pull up your anchor right now, head on back to one of the bars around here, and start to drink heavily. That's the only way I've ever been able to communicate with any goddamned spirits."

"Hector, I appreciate the advice. And if I get through this today, that's exactly what I plan to do. But now I need you to get out of here. And please, promise me that you won't try to keep an eye on me. Trust me, that would really mess things up."

"OK. I'm going to run up and fish off the east side of Bokeelia. But I'm going to stop back by here on my way to check on you. I hope to God that I don't find you like I did Javier, with a fucking hole in your head. Good luck, Jim. I'll see you later."

"Thanks, Hector. See you later."

I watched him crank up and head east. I listened to his engine's note as he ran around Mondongo. From what I could hear, he was keeping his word.

In a moment, the bay was once again deserted, and once again quiet.

Chapter Forty-Seven
A MATTER OF FAMILY PRIDE

Every time I come to this area, I can't help but think about what it must have been like in Collier's day. Looking at the desolation that is Punta Blanca today, it's almost impossible to imagine what it would have looked like back when the south end of the island was crowded with buildings, machine shops, boats, and people. Then the island was abuzz, not only with the activities of Collier's folks, but with boats of all sizes coming from and going to the big fish house around the corner. Back then, this place was truly alive with human activity. Now it's just plain quiet. It reminds me of that old English poem, the one that comments on the Egyptian monuments sitting out in the desert, covered in sand. Kind of the same thing here. Once this place symbolized wealth, power, and human endeavor. Now it's just quiet.

I know this sounds crazy, but when the wind out here is just right, I swear I've sometimes heard the squeals, screams, and laughter of little kids echoing out across the south end of the island. I figure that the happy ghosts of a few of the kids who went to school on this island are still hanging around out here. It wouldn't surprise me if this is where those folks were happiest when they were alive. It would have been a great place to be a kid. Maybe, once they died, they decided to come back here so they could play again, this time to their hearts' content.

That day, however, I didn't hear a damn thing. Guess they must still have to go to class sometimes.

Another hour went by. And, quite frankly, I was getting bored. Even the novelty of waiting to get shot starts to lose its excitement when you've been sitting in the sun for hours on end. About the only exciting thing that had happened to me since Carlos left was that the wind had changed direction.

When I had anchored in the morning, the wind was out of the east. In the absence of a frontal system, that's normally what you get here in the morning. It's called a shore breeze—where the wind comes from the mainland, and blows toward the water. It's caused by the different rates at which land and water heat and cool over the course of the day and night. Normally, the land cools off faster at night than does the sea. This differential cooling rate causes the air over the land to settle, creating a gentle breeze blowing toward the warmer waters of the gulf. That easterly breeze had kept the *Pulalanga's* bow pointing toward Punta Blanca in the morning. Now the reverse process was underway. The land mass of the Florida peninsula had soaked up the sun's warm energy all morning, and now it was heating at a faster rate than the sea was. This thermal heating was causing the air mass over the mainland to rise, and in the process, sucking in air from the gulf. Consequently, in the early afternoon in this part of Florida, the prevailing wind direction is out of the west. The shift usually takes place shortly after noon. Now the bow of the *Pulapanga* was pointing toward the west.

The only problem with this, of course, was that now my back was to Punta Blanca, and to Steve. If someone were sitting in front of me on the bow of the boat, Steve might not have a clean shot at him. I would be between Steve and his target. We really hadn't anticipated this. I guess we had both expected this thing to have played itself out long before the wind changed direction.

But it hadn't. I was still sitting in the middle of the bay. And, thus far, the bait had not been touched. But the sun had started to do a number on my skin. Shortly after Carlos left, I had pulled my shirt back on. I had even sprayed a little sunscreen on my face, neck, and ears. Having been in Saint James City all summer, the rest of me is now pretty impervious to the sun, but the skin on my face is just too thin to take much solar abuse. Regardless, there I sat.

I was bored. I had already written down what I believed had happened to Javier. I didn't feel like doing that again. But it was important that I continue to look like I was dealing with Javier's murder. I wanted to give this my best shot. It was my only shot, so to speak. So I kept up the kneeling and praying, and the sitting down and writing. But this time, rather than writing down who I thought had shot Javier, I started to write songs.

Writing songs has always been a fun thing for me to do. Back in my teen years, unsurprisingly, I always wrote love songs. Now, not so much. I had to laugh about what I was writing that day. I had titled it "Retirement Blues." One of my favorite verses was:

I made a lot of money,
But I pissed it away!
Now I'm living on a pension,
But I'm fishing every day!
For a chorus, I wrote:
Retired, retired,
It's the life that I choose.
Retired, retired,
Sweet chicks, cheap booze.
Retired, retired,
Nothing to lose.
Just a really good case
Of the retirement blues.

It kept me occupied and entertained. In fact, I had almost forgotten why I was out in the boat, and I was starting to enjoy myself a little bit. I had just laughed at one of my lines when I looked up and noticed a paddle boarder heading south out of Pelican Bay.

Pelican Bay lies between the north end of Punta Blanca and Cayo Costa. It is, without doubt, the most popular gunk hole for sailboats on this stretch of the coast. Every sailing cruiser on the west coast of Florida whose boat draws less than five feet has probably spent quality time anchored in Pelican Bay. It offers 360-degree shelter from the wind, and it is large enough so that you can usually enjoy adequate privacy. In addition, the anchorage is close to the state park's dock, so it's easy to dingy over for a trip to one of the best beaches on Florida's west coast. This beach usually is deserted, especially in the late spring and early fall. Consequently, it's not unknown for beachgoers on Cayo Costa to take off all of their clothes and soak in the rays. It's a nice place, indeed, to hole up for a while.

But, now, I was paying attention to the paddle boarder. He seemed to be poking along the shore of Punta Blanca to the northwest of my position. He might have been fishing.

I have only tried to paddleboard once. That was at Daytona Beach, where I rented a paddleboard for an hour, just to see what it was like. It wasn't that hard to do, but when my hour was up, I was absolutely whipped. You really use a lot of core muscle strength trying to stand upright and paddle. In my younger days, I use to surf—a lot. And I used to water ski—a lot. Back then, we didn't have paddleboards. Back then, people would have thought you were nuts if you tried to stand up on a board and paddle the dang thing. Now it seems cool. I might try it again someday. Hopefully.

One day, a couple of months ago, I was fishing a little north-west of Demere Key, at least two miles from shore. Despite that, a guy on a paddleboard paddled right by me, heading west. I never will forget that as he passed, he told me that he had seen a school of very large redfish on the sandbar next to the key. I thanked him for the information. Last I saw of him, he was heading toward Captiva.

I also know that my literary hero, Randy Wayne White, is an avid paddle boarder. I mention all of this just to say that it's not all that unusual anymore to see paddle boarders in the area. They're getting to be pretty common. So I didn't get too alarmed with the boarder who was slowly heading my way south from Pelican Bay. It made a lot of sense to me that a sailor had probably anchored there, and was out on his paddleboard to get a little exercise, and to enjoy the scenery. I'd have done the same thing. It looked like fun.

For the next twenty minutes, I occasionally checked him out, as he explored the mangroves, all the while slowly heading in my direction. He finally got to where, if he had continued to follow the shore, he would have paddled into the basin. But rather than follow the shore behind me, he changed direction, and paddled straight toward me. I assumed he planned to go around, and then explore the south side of Punta Blanca. I concluded that he probably was going to spend the afternoon circumnavigating Punta Blanca. Consequently, I hadn't paid a great deal of attention to him.

That changed when I heard him hail my boat.

"Ahoy! Ahoy, *Pulapanga!* Request permission to come aboard!"

Now, I looked more closely, and I recognized who was on the board. It was none other than my friend, Carl Perez, the Realtor who had sold us our house. I gave him a big wave, taking care to use my right arm.

"Carl, come on over. Damn! It's good to see you. Tie that thing off on a stern cleat, and climb on in."

Carl paddled alongside, and tied a neat cleat hitch to the boat's starboard aft cleat, using the board's quarter-inch bow line. As he made his board fast, I noticed that he was dressed in a shorty wet suit with what looked to be a waterproof waist pouch fastened around his midsection. He sat on the gunwale, and then swung his legs on board.

"Carl! What in the hell are you doing out here? Come on up on the bow, and sit down."

"Jim, hell, everyone on the island knows that you're out here today. Since I was in the area anyway, I just thought I ought to come on out here and check on you."

"What do mean while you were in the area? This is kind of off the beaten path, isn't it?"

"Not really. I own a little place over on Cayo Costa. It's actually the old family homestead. It's where my great-grandfather had his fish ranch when they first came over from Cuba. We were able to get it grandfathered as private ownership back when the state acquired the rest of the island. It's the only place on the whole north end that's not owned by the state now. I like to come up here when I need to get away. Tomorrow, the governor's going to announce the Senate appointment. So I thought this would likely be the last time I'd get to come out here for a long, long time. Besides, it's a really beautiful day."

"Well, as you can see, I'm fine. But Carl, it looks to me like paddling that board is kind of hard work. I tried it one time, and it really tired me out."

"Well, once you get the hang of it, it's not too bad. You've just got to stop fighting to maintain your balance, and kind of let your subconscious make the adjustments for you. Once you figure that out, it's really a piece of cake. I guess it's a lot like learning to ride a bicycle. Whenever I'm on Sanibel, I usually try to paddle every afternoon. But now that you mention it, paddling in the sun in this wet suit has heated me up pretty good. Any chance I can bum something off of you to drink?"

"Sure. But all I've got is water. That OK?"

"Perfect."

I got up, and went to the cooler to get us each a bottle. When I turned back toward the front, I instantly knew that my suspicions had been confirmed. Carl, comfortably seated on the lower step to the fishing deck, had pulled what looked to be a compact, nine-millimeter semiautomatic pistol from the pouch around his waist. It had what I assumed was a silencer attached to its muzzle. The gun was pointed right between my eyes.

"Jim, please don't do anything silly. I'd appreciate it if you would open my water bottle, and slowly hand it to me," he continued calmly. "I really am hot and thirsty. Once you do that, I would appreciate it if you would return to your seat, and open your bottle. Then, I'd like us to have a little chat."

I don't know why I didn't try to jump overboard right then. I probably should have. Instead, I did exactly as he requested. I opened his water bottle, put it in my right hand, and then placed it in his left hand. All the while, he had that evil-looking little weapon pointed right at my face. I have to admit that I was petrified. But despite my fear, as I gave him the bottle, I pretended to stumble. To help me regain my balance, I waved my left arm. I knew it was important that it appear to Carl that I really had lost my balance. At the same time, I hoped it was not so realistic that Steve wouldn't recognize it as the signal that it was meant to be. I didn't know if I would ever have another chance to wave my arm to alert him.

"Jim, be careful! I wouldn't want you to hurt yourself."

"Is that right, Carl? You could fool me with that damn gun pointed at my face!"

"I didn't say that *I* wasn't planning to hurt you, did I Jim?"

I took my seat, and looked Carl in the eyes.

"Carl, I've been expecting you. I was going to be disappointed if you didn't turn up."

"Is that right? I didn't know if you had actually figured this out, or not. But I really couldn't take a chance that you had. And, if you hadn't, one more mysterious death wouldn't matter that much."

I laughed. "It might matter to me!"

"Yeah. But not for long."

"I would hope not."

While I was laughing with Carl, I was trying to figure out how to keep him talking long enough for Steve to take his shot. I knew he would only need one.

"Jim, if you're thinking that your friend on the island is going to save you by shooting me, I'm afraid that you are going to be disappointed. You see, that was me in the sailboat that left here about eleven o'clock this morning. I had been keeping an eye on you and your friend all night. When I motored by the other side of Punta Blanca, I dropped off an acquaintance of mine, who swam over to the island. His job was, shall we say, to neutralize your 'backup.' You know, Jim, it's really too bad that Captain Fairchild's legs are injured. I'm sure that he wasn't able to run as quickly from my acquaintance as he might have otherwise been able to do. I'm sure it would have been a much more sporting proposition if he had been healthy. But I can't worry too much about how fair the fight may have been. And I'm sure that my acquaintance enjoyed himself anyway. I just hope that Steve didn't suffer too long, or too much. Lord knows, he's suffered enough already. You know, Jim, I really like to support the brave men and women who serve our country to keep our nation free.

Veterans' issues are going to be one of the key things that I focus on when I'm in Washington. They all really need our support."

"Carl, that's touching. And I'm sure it'll play well with the voters. By the way, that's a hell of a boat you were in. I liked it a lot. And, that name and port on the stern was really cute. "

"Thanks, Jim. I like it, too. I bought it about a month ago. My acquaintance has been living on it down in the Keys. Just keeping it ready to go, should I ever need it. If things had gone south, so to speak, I could have been on it in a matter of hours, and then off to who-knows-where? And I have enough money stashed offshore so that, if worse comes to worse, I'll never have to worry about having sufficient *dinero*. But I don't think I really need to worry about dealing with this concern too much anymore. In fact, I don't see any reason why I won't be able to deal with you just like I dealt with our young Spanish friend. You know, no one really pays the least bit of attention to a guy on a paddleboard these days. With Javier, I simply paddled over from my cabin on Cayo Costa and back again, and no one saw a thing. This time, I knew I needed some help. So I had the boat brought up. We stayed the night on it, watching you and your friends run up and down the sound. Then we got a good night's sleep, and enjoyed a very leisurely breakfast. Once I had seen all I needed to see this morning, I got under way. And, I'm really glad that you appreciated the name I put on the boat. I would have been so disappointed if you had missed the significance of that. I had it done down in Key West, using vinyl letters. Tonight, as soon as I get out in the gulf, I'll pull those off and The Spanish Princess will disappear forever. I thought it was kind of cute to resurrect the specter of our modern day Jose Gaspar. And, it certainly couldn't hurt to cast a little more suspicion at our unpleasant little friend. You really can't have too many red herrings. And, I hope you enjoyed my beard. It was left over from my costume for last year's Pirates Ball at Bert's Bar. I was the honorary king of the pirates in recognition of my many, many civic contributions. That party is really a hoot. You get all the ladies dressed up like pirate tarts, get a little rum in them, and you can't believe what you can get away with! You should try it this year. Well, then again, that might not actually be possible for you. Pity. But I digress. After I dropped my friend off for his swim, I put into Pelican Bay, and went for a casual cruise on my board. And once I'm through here, I'll just paddle back to Pelican Bay, lift the anchor, sail back around to the south, and pick up my friend, who'll swim out to meet me. And then, we'll be off to sea. I would think that we will be gone long before anyone even notices that anything is amiss with you. I do so much appreciate you telling everyone not to disturb you. That will be very helpful. Once we're in the gulf, we'll head south along the islands. And, tonight, once it's dark, I'll paddle in to Sanibel, just like I do two or three nights a week. No one will think a thing about it. I think it'll all work fine. By this time tomorrow, I will be sworn in as the newest United States senator."

"Carl, that sounds like a pretty good plan. But before you waste me, can I ask you a question?"

"OK, shoot. Oh, I'm sorry. I couldn't resist saying that. And I don't know that I'll ever have that opportunity again. Go ahead, ask me your question."

"How did you find my boat last night? And how did you get the explosives?"

"Good questions, Jim. I'm glad you brought that up. I've actually been wondering how you managed to avoid the little surprise I left for you. I had been so expectant that I'd see you dropping in—so to speak. I kept waiting to hear a boom this morning. I was really very disappointed when I saw you show up here in one piece. Why don't you answer my question first?"

"OK. I was worried that someone might find the boat, and try to do something to it. So I simply put pieces of clear tape over all of the locker seams. When I saw that the one on the console was out of place, I knew that someone had visited the boat during the night. Your turn."

"Good for you! I never thought to look for that. Even with my little light, it was too dark out there to pick up on that tape. My bad."

"So, how'd you find my boat?"

"Oh, that was just pure coincidence. A friend of mine actually owns one of the fish shacks out where you hid your boat, and I've got a key to it. My buddy doesn't know it, but I've got a space up in the rafters where I keep some of my special toys—like this cute little pistol I'm holding. I needed to stop by and pick it up. When I found that your boat was not on its lift in Saint James, I came up here. But, by the time I got here, you had already tied your boat up and gone. I'm sorry that I missed you. The C-4 was just something I had at my house in Sanibel. When I had it built, they had to use quite a bit of explosives to deepen the water under my boat house. When they were through, I simply bought a little from the guy who did the blasting. Just in case I might ever need it. You never know when something like that might come in handy. As you could obviously tell, I don't really have much expertise in this area. But I think it would have worked all right if you hadn't left your tape."

"Yeah. I think it would have done the job just fine. While we're chatting, do you mind telling me why the hell you killed Javier? That guy never hurt anyone in his life!"

"Granted. And I really hated to have to do that. I really did. I guess that by now you've figured out that my great-grand-father, Julio, killed Eugene Knight in Cuba, and stole the gold Knight had gotten from selling his Cuban cows. From what I've always been told, Julio hated old man Knight with a passion. He thought that Knight was a cheap bastard, and that his company was always cheating him on the price of mullet. Supposedly, he was convinced that he was being shorted a penny a pound on his catch. And he really didn't like the prices he had to pay for salt, coffee, and the other necessities they had to buy at the fish house store. I don't know how he heard about Knight going to Cuba for the big cattle sale, but somehow he did. So he took his boat down to Key West, bought a ticket on the steamer, and went over to Havana a couple of days after Knight did. After he had killed Knight, he stole a fishing boat, sailed it up to Key West, sold it at the docks, and then sailed his own boat back up here. When he got back, he never said a word about it to anyone. Not until just before he died.

"Apparently, he came home with all that gold, and just hid it. But every couple of years, he'd pull out a coin or two, and use it to buy up a few acres of land on Sanibel or Captiva. Eventually, by the time he died, he owned most of both of those islands. I guess he figured that these transactions were kind of like what today we would call money laundering. Of course, he couldn't say anything about that land. He had to keep it to himself. All he could do, and I think all he ever really wanted to do, was just keep on fishing. I suspect that he was happy just knowing that he had gotten even with old Gene Knight. He only told his son where he'd hidden the deeds on the day he died. With the deeds, he had placed a note that explained what he had done, and why. Needless to say, my grandfather was flabbergasted. But at that point, my granddad figured that there was nothing to be gained by saying anything about it. If my grandfather had come forward, the family's reputation would have been destroyed. He and the whole family probably would have had to clear out, and go back to Cuba. I'm sure he'd have had to turn over all the property to the Knight estate. I guess he figured that it was better to just keep quiet about it. Once the property had been conveyed to my father, he concocted the myth about how his hardworking grandfather had acquired it. The murder and the theft were kept quiet. At least, they were kept quiet until Javier showed up."

"What did he want you to do?"

"He came over to Sanibel, met with me, and suggested that I should come clean in the press. I told him that I needed time to think it through. Then I called him and asked him to meet me here to talk through how it should be done. He agreed. I guess he figured that I was an honorable man, and that it would be safe enough. I guess he trusted me to do the right thing. We talked. He asked me to go with him to the newspaper, and tell the whole story. But he said that if I didn't go, he planned to tell the story anyway. He said that if I went with him, I would come off looking like an honorable person who came forward once I had been told where my family's wealth had really come from. But I told him that I couldn't do that. Instead, I offered to make him a wealthy man if he would keep the story to himself. I offered to deposit five million dollars in his name in a Cayman bank account—no taxes, no record. But he said he couldn't do that."

"Carl, that was quite an offer. Did Javier say why he wouldn't take the money?"

"He said that for him, his father, his grandfather, and his great-grandfather, it was a matter of family honor. He said he had no choice but to do what he was doing. So I told him that I, too, had no choice. And I shot him."

"Carl, why didn't you do what Javier suggested? It really would have made you look good."

"Jim, I couldn't do that. You know why? In Florida, my family's name means something. My family built one of Florida's greatest fortunes—we built it from nothing. I couldn't let that legacy be destroyed. For me, too, this was a matter of family pride."

"Carl, I think there's a difference between honor and pride. The legacy that you are so proud of was really just a lie. Your family's fortune was not built; it was stolen."

With that, Carl raised the pistol, steadied it with his left hand, and pointed it right toward the bridge of my nose. I guessed that what I was seeing now was the last thing that Javier had seen. I knew that I damn sure wasn't ready to die, but I didn't see that I had much choice.

Ka-bammmmmmmm!

It wasn't Carl who had fired. Instead, I turned to see that his paddleboard had almost been destroyed. The bow of the board was still tied to the *Pulapanga,* but parts of the aft section were now drifting in the wind toward Punta Blanca.

I turned back toward Carl. His face had gone as white as the proverbial sheet. That high-powered rifle shot could mean only one thing. And we both knew it. His friend had failed in his mission to take out Steve. Steve was watching what was going on. Now, there was no way that Carl could kill me, and escape. Even if he shot me, Steve would kill him. Carl might try to hide, but there was no way that he would be able to pull in the anchor and start the boat without being shot. And even if, by some miracle, he was able to avoid being shot, Steve would still be able to tell the authorities what had happened. Carl was trapped. He dropped his hands so that the pistol was now lying across his lap.

But as I looked Carl in the eyes, he once again gripped the pistol, slowly raised it, and pointed it toward my head. There can't be a sight more terrifying than looking down the bore of a loaded weapon that's pointed directly at you by a person intent on ending your life. I've never looked into the eyes of a cobra waiting to strike, but it can't be any more frightening. I was staring straight into the face of death.

"Jim, I think it's time. Don't you?"

I didn't answer. Even if I could have spoken, I didn't think it would matter in the least.

"I should have done this earlier. We have spent way too much time talking. It's time for this to be over. Jim, I'm sorry it's come to this. I've always liked you and Jill. But you should never have come to Pine Island. If you had not come, none of this would have happened."

I could see the tendons on the top of his right hand flex. I knew that he was gripping the pistol tighter, getting ready to shoot. I also knew that, at this distance, there was no way he could miss. Unfortunately, there was also no way that Steve could get a clear shot at Carl with the boat's center console and my head in the way. If Carl was intent on killing me, and I had to assume that he was, it didn't look good for the home team.

"Jim, let's get this over. If you like, you can shut your eyes. It might make it easier on you, and it will make it a lot easier on me."

I thought about doing that, but concluded that it would have been a coward's way out. Every good person whom I'd ever seen being shot in the movies had kept his eyes open. And, besides, apart from the drama playing out on the bow of my boat, it was truly a gorgeous day on the sound. I wanted to take in as much of that as I could before I would never see it again. At least, that's what I told myself I was going to do. But as soon as I saw the muscles in Carl's jaw start to tense up, and his trigger finger move, I closed my eyes as tight as they would go.

Ka-bammmmmmm!

Chapter Forty-Eight

BEING DEAD IS NOT SO BAD

Being dead must not be much different than being alive. I remember that being the first thing I thought after I heard the shot. Granted, my ears hurt from the noise, and I could smell the acrid odor of the spent ammunition. But, otherwise, I still felt pretty good. I guessed that being dead must really be OK.

Eventually, though, I got up enough nerve to open one of my eyes. What I saw was not at all what I had been expecting.

Carl's body had fallen to his left. He now lay face down on what had once been my sparkling, white, fishing deck. It wasn't white anymore. His right arm was limply extended next to his right leg, and the pistol lay on the deck of the boat. The right side of Carl's temple appeared to have a small hole in it. But the left side of his head, which I couldn't see, must have had a significantly bigger hole, given the amount of blood and other stuff that was draining out on what had once been my spotless deck. It didn't look like a shot that Steve could have made.

All I could do was to stare. My mouth was open, and my hands were on the sides of my face. I think I was breathing. I must have been breathing. But I can't really remember breathing.

Just then, I heard music playing. It sounded far away. What was this? Were these the angels of heaven or their supporting band? No! I didn't think so. This wasn't really an angelic sound. It sounded more like a blues refrain. Maybe God liked the blues as much as I did. That kind of made sense. But as I continued to listen, I realized that what I was hearing was repetitive. Just a few bars of music. The sound would pause, and then start again. In my confused state of shock, I really had no idea what I was hearing. Finally, it dawned on me. It was my cell phone ringing! I had stored it in the boat's radio locker. My ring tone is an old blues riff. I slowly got up, stiffly moved around to the boat's leaning post, reached up to the radio locker, and opened it. I picked up the phone, and answered the call.

"Jim, are you OK?"

"Yeah, Steve. I'm fine. How about you?"

"Yeah. I'm fine, too. But from here it looks like old Carl's not doing so good."

"Yeah. I think his paddle boarding days are over."

"Guess so, unless that's what they use to cross the River Jordan."

"Could be, could be. But, damn, Steve! That was close."

"Tell me about it. I never could get a clear shot. Your head was right in the way. I was hoping that you might think to lean over, so that I could get a shot off."

"Shit. Why didn't I think of that? I just sat there like a damn bump on the log, waiting to get my head blown off."

"I was going to risk taking a shot anyway. I knew that it would be tricky, and that I'd have to come within an eyelash of the side of your head to get to him. I was just starting to squeeze the trigger when I saw what he was really up to. At that point, I just let him do his own thing."

"What about the guy who swam to the island?"

"He's taking a nap. And he's kind of up a tree—so to speak. I'll tell you all about it later. Why don't you call Mike Collins?"

"Yeah. I will. And I'll have him send some of his guys over to get you and your friend. I'll just stay here until they arrive."

"Talk to you later."

"Thanks, Steve."

***

"Story, what the fuck is going on over there? It sounds like a goddamned war zone. Are you OK?"

"I'm OK."

"We headed your way as soon as we heard the first shot. Our guys in the flats boat should be there in a minute or so. That is, if they could tear themselves away from catching fish. They reported right before we heard the first shot that the fish were really starting to bite!"

"Sorry to mess that up. I know what it's like to wait all day for something to bite, and then have to go in just at the wrong time."

"Speaking of catching fish, did you catch what you were fishing for?"

"Yeah. But he's not in the live well. In fact, he's ready to go on ice. Get here fast and I'll tell you about it. Have one of your boats stop at the southeast tip of Punta Blanca to pick up Steve Fairchild. He's got one of the bad guys up a tree, whatever that means."

"We're on the way."

As I hung up, I could hear an outboard heading rapidly in our direction.

I called Jill.

She answered immediately. "Are ya'll all right?"

"Hey, babe. Yeah, we're both OK. But Carl Perez is dead. He shot himself on the boat right before Steve could take him out. And Steve's got one of his accomplices tied up and waiting for the sheriff. Mike Collins and his guys are on the way. In fact, I see them coming around the corner of the island now."

"We have been so worried about ya'll. Katie's chewed her nails down to the quick, and I've worn a path in this expensive carpet, just pacing up and down, waiting to hear something. When we heard the shots we both screamed, and started to cry. We were so worried."

"Sorry, babe. But everything is good now."

"We're going to come out there right now. Katie's already standing at the door with the keys to the boat in her hand."

"Baby, I don't know if that's such a good idea. The sheriff's guys probably aren't going to want ya'll getting too close. They are going to have a lot of work to do out here. Besides, it's not really a pretty sight. I suspect that we're going to be tied up for at least a couple of hours."

"Fuck you, and fuck the sheriff, too. We're on the way."

"Love you."

"I love you, too."

Chapter Forty-Nine
PROCESSING THE SCENE

A fishing skiff with three men aboard slid around the corner of the island. It had to have been going at least forty miles per hour. While there were a lot of fishing rods sticking up in the boat's rod holders, it was clear that these guys weren't here to fish. I think it was the two military-style, semiautomatic, twelve-gauge shotguns pointed in my direction that convinced me they weren't here to look for a redfish. The boat squatted from its plane, and coasted in my direction.

"Lee County Sheriff. Put your hands in the air—NOW!"

I did as I was told. The boat idled closer.

"I'm glad to see you guys. Hope I didn't disturb your fishing."

"Keep your hands in the air. What is going on here?"

I explained the situation, and mentioned that Steve was on the island with a bad guy tied up. I also advised them that Steve was armed with a very high-powered rifle that was probably carefully zeroed in on one of them as we spoke, and that it would be a very good idea if I defused this situation by getting Steve to stand down.

"Please do that, sir."

I turned toward the island, and gave Steve two thumbs up.

"Do you have a weapon on board your boat, sir?"

"The only weapon on board is the pistol that this guy used to kill himself. It's lying on the deck. And the two filet knives in the seat under the leaning post."

"Sir, I want you to sit down, and stay there, until we have additional resources here to secure the situation. Please don't move about in the boat until I tell you that you can."

"Not a problem."

As we spoke, I could hear other boats coming in our direction. I knew it wouldn't be long before the scene was secured.

A couple of minutes later, another boat slid around the corner. It, too, was going at high speed, but this time there was no mistaking that it belonged to Lee County. I could see Mike Collins standing on the bow.

"Damn it, Story. Don't you have anything better to do that just sit around here all day?"

"I've got a hell of a lot better things to do. But your associates have suggested that I should take a rest until they knew more about what was going on."

"Yeah, well, I appreciate your cooperation with their request. Now get off your ass, and help us tie off against your port side."

He then directed his attention to the three deputies in the first boat. "I've got the situation here in hand for the time being. I need you to go over to the sandy shore on Punta Blanca's southeast corner, and assist a Mr. Steve Fairchild. I believe that he may have a person of interest tied up in a tree. You will need to arrest this person, and assist Mr. Fairchild in any way that he may require. And I would advise you to not piss Mr. Fairchild off. He's a really big, really bad dude. You will want to keep him on your side. Now, take off."

I took the dock lines from the patrol boat, and secured them to the cleats on my boat's port side. Lieutenant Collins took a long look at the scene, and directed the deputies with him to photograph every part of the boat.

"Jim, why don't you start by telling me how all this went down?"

I started from the beginning. I told him how Jill, Katie, and Steve had spread the story, and went on to detail everything that had transpired since then. I told him about the bomb, and that I had a pound of C-4 sitting in the radio console. I told him about the blasting cap. I described how all of the day's events had transpired. I told him about Carl's boat, and his plan. I told him about our conversation. I told him how the tables had turned on Carl when it became obvious that Steve still had my back. I told him about staring down the barrel of Carl's pistol waiting to be shot, and about my surprise when I realized that he had blown his own brains out instead.

"Story, do you buy lottery tickets?"

"Sometimes."

"Well, I'd suggest that when we're through with you, you need to stop by the Quick Serve, and buy some. Today, you are one very, very lucky guy!"

"I know. I know."

"Why don't you get your phone, and come on over to my boat. We're going to need to process your boat. That's going to take some time. You probably won't be able to use it to go fishing for several days. You know this story is going to get real big, real fast. Every prime-time reporter will be salivating all over this. Your life is going to get really difficult for a while. You might want to skip the country for a while!"

"Yeah. I hear you. Are we free to go?"

"Ya'll don't need to stay here in our way. But I'd like you to be close by, just in case we want to ask you anymore questions. Can we take ya'll somewhere to wait this out?"

"There are going to be two very beautiful, but very worried, ladies showing up here in a couple of minutes, demanding to give Steve and me passionate embraces. How about if you release us into their custody? We'll go over to the bar at Cabbage Key, and wait to hear from you. I'm sure you won't object to us charging a couple of their nicer guest rooms to the Lee County sheriff's account. That seems to be the least you can do in return for us doing all your work for you."

"Watch it, Story. With that kind of attitude, you might just find yourself sitting over on Punta Blanca with the chiggers and the sand gnats for a couple of hours."

"Just joking, just joking."

Just then, Mike's radio crackled. "Collins, Collins, this is Boat Sixty-Three. We've got a little situation here."

"What you got, Sixty-Three?"

"We've got two fired-up ladies in a boat demanding access to the scene. They're starting to get pretty belligerent. Should we take them into custody?"

"No. Don't do that," Mike said, glancing at me. "We've got enough to handle here without having to deal with a couple of crazy wildcats. Just send them my way."

"OK, Jim. Ya'll go pick up Steve, and then head on over to Cabbage Key. Keep your phone nearby in case we need you."

"Will do. But I'm not promising that I'll be able to hear it. You know how loud it can get in the Piano Room when a roomful of drunks start to carry on in there. And I'm pretty sure that there are going to be four drunks in that room pretty damn quickly."

"Enjoy yourself."

"You want us to bring you something?"

"Fuck off, Story! Ya'll get out of here now before I revert to being a standard-issue law-enforcement asshole."

Chapter Fifty
IN SEARCH OF A LITTLE PEACE

With Steve on board, and Katie at the controls, we headed toward Cabbage Key. The sun was sinking toward the horizon, casting a golden glow over the Key and its buildings. Jill and I have been to Cabbage Key dozens of times. It's the one place we always try to take our island visitors. Everyone always seems to appreciate the scenic boat ride and the adventure of having drinks and a meal at such a charming "Old Florida" type of destination. We've never had anything but happy times when we've visited. But I assure you that the happiness of all of those visits combined could not begin to equal the near-giddiness we felt as we turned out of the main channel and slowed to enter the Key's entry channel. Jill and I sat beside each other on the bench seat in front of the console, enjoying the warmth of our thighs pressed together. I had my arm around her, and she leaned her head on my shoulder. We both knew this was a very special moment, and one we would always remember.

Katie raised the dock master on Channel Sixteen, and once on a working channel, negotiated a premier spot at the main dock to tie up her relatively small outboard. Negotiated may not be a good description of how the conversation actually went. The dock master there usually reserves the premier dock spaces for much larger boats, and requests that smaller outboard boats, like the one we were in, simply bump bow-first into the sandy beach and throw out anchors. The only problem with this arrangement is that some, if not all, of the passengers usually have to wade a few feet to dry land when they disembark, and again when they get back on board. None of that for us tonight.

There must have been something in Katie's voice. In no time, the dock master was assisting us as we tied up at the north side of the main dock. We explained that we would be in the Piano Room should any law-enforcement officers need to find us. Understandably, he didn't appear to know exactly how he should take that comment. But once the others were walking toward the inn, I took him aside and filled him in on what had just gone down.

"There's been a shooting over by Punta Blanca. We were involved. The sheriff's office suggested we come over here and wait, in case they need to question us further. We'll likely be staying the night. By the way, you should know that in a few hours, the Key is going to be descended upon by an absolute horde of media. You're probably going to need some help on the dock. By the way, thanks for the slip."

I joined the others in the bar. They were already seated at the only table in the room, and a round of drinks was on the way. I was delighted to hear that Jill had ordered me a double

Glenlivet on the rocks. She knows me well. It sounded like a great way to start the evening.

I went to find the manager, explained what was going on, and requested two rooms for the evening. The inn only has seven small rooms in the main house, and that number of quaint cottages scattered around the island. Fortunately, a couple of the rooms in the house were available. We were set for the night.

I also advised him about the likely influx of out-of-town reporters.

"What makes you think this is going to be such a big deal?"

"You know Carl Perez? That's who killed himself on my boat. He's also the guy that murdered Javier Hernandez out here about a month ago."

"Oh my God! I see what you mean! This is going to be huge! I'd better get as much help in here as I can. I'm sure the Lodge is going to need to do the same. I'll give them a call. But you guys won't want to be here when the media shows up."

"Yeah, I know. We're going to have few drinks, and relax. Then we'll have dinner, and try to get a few hours sleep. With the sheriff's permission, I'd like us to get out of here before things get too busy. I'd appreciate it if you could let me know as soon as you hear about any reporters heading this way. We really don't want to face that."

"I understand. I'll let you know as soon as I hear anything. By the way, your dinner and drinks are on me. Just let me know when you're ready to eat."

"Hey, man. I really appreciate that. But you may not understand how big your bar bill is going to be. It's not every day that you survive being killed—twice. I've got some meaningful celebrating to do!"

"Enjoy yourself. You've earned it. And, besides, I'm not too worried about the bar tab. You're already well through the only bottle of single malt on the island. Another couple of rounds and you'll be relegated to drinking a cheap blend."

"Another couple of drinks and I'll be too far gone to care what I'm drinking. Thanks again."

I rejoined the group, and told them the good news about the rooms, and about our tabs being comped. I also told them that we were probably going to want to get out of Cabbage Key before daylight.

"Mike Collins said we might want to skip the country to avoid the media scrum that's going to take place. I'm not sure if he was serious or not, but I actually think that's a good idea. Ya'll up for that?"

Steve said, "I'm up for going anywhere there is no one trying to kill us—as long as they have lots of rum when we get there."

"I know just the place. Give me a minute." I stepped outside, pulled out my phone, and clicked on Mike Collins's cell phone number. "Mike, you going to need us anymore?"

"No, Jim. Everything's lining up with the accounts that you and Steve gave. I'm not going to need you tonight."

"We're going to take your advice and get way out of town— if that's OK with you."

"I'm fine with it. How can I get you if I need to?"

"I'll have my phone. How about my boat?"

"We'll clean it up for you when we're through, and I'll have someone put it up on your lift. Just don't check the engine hours too closely. We may have to do a little fishing on our way back down the sound."

"Be my guest! Call me if you need me."

Next, I delved into the contacts list on the phone and found an international number that I had saved for a special occasion. I dialed it.

The voice on the other end said, "Peace and Plenty, how may I help you?"

"Annette! Damn, it is great to hear your voice. This is Jim Story. You know, Jill Story's husband."

"Of course I know who you is! 'Tis long time since you reach. When you and Miss Jill coming to see us?"

"Annette, that's why I'm calling. Do you have a couple of suites available for a week, starting tomorrow?"

"We do. You know it's slow down here this time of the year. Too damn hot for most folks. So, ya'll coming tomorrow?"

"We're coming. They'll be another couple with us. What airlines are flying into Georgetown these days?"

"Jim, it still be the same. Either the American Eagle from Miami or Gulfstream out of Fort Lauderdale."

"I'll check with Gulfstream. Fort Lauderdale's closer to us than Miami. I'll let you know if I can't get us on. Otherwise, you can count on us being there."

"If you're flying Gulfstream, you must be feeling lucky!"

"Annette, you don't know just how lucky I am feeling."

"OK, then. I'll have Luther waiting for you at the airport. And Doc will put some extra Kaliks on ice. I know how much Jill loves her Kaliks."

"You got that right. And lay in some extra rum, too. I think a case or two of Pusser's ought to just about do it."

"We got plenty of dat. I member last time ya'll was hear. Drank us completely out of tequila. There wasn't a bottle left on the whole damn island. And we was out for a whole month since de supply boat run aground. But rum? Dat's not a problem. We never run out of dat. We're so glad you coming back. We've missed seeing you."

"Not near as much as we've missed seeing you. Can't wait to be there. Good-bye."

A few more minutes on the phone, and we had four tickets booked on a flight into Georgetown, leaving Fort Lauderdale at 12:30 p.m. the next day.

I walked back into the bar. I guess it was the smile on my face that gave me away.

"OK. What did you do? I haven't seen a grin that big on your face in years."

"We need to be in Fort Lauderdale at eleven in the morning. That should give us plenty of time to catch our flight. We're all going to the P&P for a week!"

Everyone seemed to really like the idea. We agreed that we would need to leave Cabbage Kay at five in the morning. We would take the boat over to Tarpon Lodge, check out, and get our stuff. Katie and Jill would drive the car back to Saint James City, while Steve and I would go down by boat. We figured that should give us plenty of time to pack.

"Ya'll got passports?"

"Yes. We're good."

"Jill. What about the dog?"

"Let me call the pet sitter, and see if she can help us out."

We excitedly began talking about Exuma, and about how much fun we were going to have there. As a result, for the next twenty or thirty minutes, our minds were totally off of what had transpired earlier. But, soon enough, our attention returned to the day's events.

"Steve, how was your night on the island?" I asked.

"It really wasn't that bad. I had a good moon, and could see pretty well. It's hard to spot this from a boat, but the middle of the island is all sandy, and it is actually quite barren. I simply found a nice sandy spot to sit, and waited for the sun to come up. As soon as I had enough light, I looked around a little bit, and then went over to the west side to find a good spot to keep an eye on you. Everything was pretty uneventful, actually."

"Uneventful, my ass! What about Carl's buddy who tried to kill you?"

"Well, you know the second thing they teach you about conducting a successful ambush in ambush school, don't you?"

"No, what's the second thing they teach you in ambush school?"

"Make sure you don't get ambushed yourself. So, once I had my operation site established, I started to explore the island more thoroughly. In a few minutes I found a tree, a strangler fig, that was perfectly located for keeping a good eye on the island without being seen. And, fortunately, it was easy to climb. I guess it was still growing around its host palm. The fig's trunk had formed what looked almost like a latticework pattern around the palm. It was really easy to use all those nooks and crannies as hand- and footholds to climb up the tree. It really wasn't any harder than climbing a ladder, even for a guy like me. Once I got up to about thirty feet, I had a great view all around the island, and with the fig leaves and the palm fronds, there was no way that I could be seen. My spot was high enough so that I could see over the peppers and the mangroves. I just sat up there with my rifle most of the day, and kept an eye on things. But, quite frankly, there wasn't that much going on. I saw Hector stop by, and I kept an eye on him, but I never figured him to be the guy we were after. The one thing that worried me, though, was that damn sailboat. It just didn't look right. There should have been people in the cockpit, drinking coffee, taking a piss over the side, fishing, or something. But there was nothing. That wasn't right. So, when the guy finally emerged, hauled anchor, and motored off, I made sure to keep my eyes glued to that boat. I saw the dude slip into the water, and start to swim toward the island. At that point, it was clear what was going to take place. So, I slipped down from the tree, and went to a spot where I knew the guy would have to pass. All the space near the shore is totally crammed with the trunks, and limbs, of dead trees. And all of that is completely overgrown with Brazilian peppers. I had found that there was only one decent path through that maze. I knew that unless he was very good, this dude would come up that path. I found a good-size Australian pine beside the path. All I had to do was stand behind that trunk, wait for him to pass, and then take him out. As I figured, the guy really wasn't that good. He came right up the path, and walked right past me. My only question was how to take him out."

"So, how did you do that?"

"The rule that I always follow is to use the simplest, and most reliable, method at hand. So in this case, when the dude walked by, I simply tapped him on the back of his skull with the head of my cane. He fell like a sack of rocks."

"You only tapped him?"

"Well, truth be told, I may have hit him a wee bit harder than that. You know how it is; sometimes your adrenaline just takes over. I don't think he actually woke up until just before the deputies came to get him. And, even then, he wasn't making too much sense. After he went down, I dragged him over to a nearby palm, and put his back against the tree. Then, I extended his arms back around the trunk and taped them together, using the roll of duct tape I'd brought with me in my pack. I also taped his mouth shut to keep him quiet. Next, I put a strip across his forehead and around the tree, just to make sure that his head stayed upright so he could breathe. Finally, I taped his ankles together, just for good measure. If he had come to, I didn't want him to get any ideas.

"Once he was out of the way, I knew that our target would be coming from Pelican Bay. I just wasn't sure how he would be arriving. Then, when I saw the guy on the paddleboard, I knew that it was show-time. I probably should have just gone back up my tree. But I wanted to be closer to Jim, so I went back to the original spot that I had selected to operate from. As it turned out, I could see everything clearly from there, but, once Carl was on board and sitting down low, I didn't have enough elevation to be able to shoot cleanly over the console. Once I recognized the issue, I didn't think I had enough time to relocate. I've got to tell ya'll, at that point I was worried. And then, once Carl pulled his pistol out, and I saw you wave, I knew that I had to do something. I kept waiting, just hoping that the boat would swing to one side so that I could get a clean shot at Carl. But that never happened. Finally, I had to do something, or you were going to be a dead man. So I blew up his fucking paddleboard."

"From that point on," I said, "he knew he was done. But I still thought that he was going to kill me anyway."

"It looked that way to me, too. But I just couldn't get a good shot. I stood up to try to get enough elevation, but it just wasn't enough. I tried to ease to the side, but every time I did that, I swear, the wind would veer just enough to keep the boat's stern lined up directly toward me.

"When he pointed that gun toward your head I knew I had to go for a shot. I was actually squeezing the trigger when I saw him point the gun at his own head. At that point, I decided I'd just let him do my job for me. That's all there was to it. I really didn't do that much."

"What are you talking about? All you did was save my life!"

"Yeah. Maybe. But I'm really sorry I wasn't able to put one through Carl's head. That would have made me feel more like I'd done something for Javier."

"Hey, my man. You did plenty."

"Thanks. But, tell me Jim, when did you figure out that it was Carl that had killed Javier?"

"Truthfully, I wasn't a hundred percent certain until he pulled out that pistol. But, I strongly suspected he had done it. Once I knew why Javier had really come down here all the pieces started to fall into place. And, then, when we learned that Eugene Knight had been killed in Cuba, and that Carl's great-grandfather might have been there at the same time, it made even more sense. And, finally, today on the boat, I remembered that Anna had said that Javier had been excited about having been to Sanibel, and accomplishing something that his family had never been able to. It wasn't proof, but it sure narrowed down the list of suspects. I was pretty sure that it would be Carl who would show up today. But, I've got to tell you that when I saw the name on that boat's stern today, it really confused me. I was about ready to throw up my hands in frustration at that point. But, when Carl pointed that pistol between my eyes there wasn't any doubt."

I don't think that either Jill or Katie had realized, until that moment, just how close a call this had been—for both of us. At this point, both ladies got real quite. I ordered another round of drinks. And, then another. Thus fortified our thoughts eventually moved on from the day's events, and we began to talk instead about how much we were going to enjoy the Bahamas . More drinks were followed by a great dinner, and then, we were off to our rooms. Five o'clock was going to come early.

Chapter Fifty-One

A PARTY IN SAINT JAMES CITY

We didn't drink up all of Exuma's rum supply, but we damn sure put a dent in it. There may not be any place in the world more peaceful—and more fun—to spend a week than the Club Peace and Plenty in Georgetown, Exuma. It may not be much to look at by modern standards, but it more than makes up for lack of glitz and glamour with old-school charm and out-island friendliness. When we weren't on the beach, fishing for bonefish, playing ring toss, or dancing by the pool, we were at one of the club's two bars. And the very best part of the week was that there wasn't a TV in the whole place. Consequently, we were able to totally miss all the media drama concerning the death of Carl Perez. It was perfect!

By the time we came back to Saint James City, all of the reporters had left town, and moved on to other stories. I later learned that the day before we returned, a prominent local businessman had gone missing, along with twenty million dollars of his investors' funds. Like I say, in Florida, there's never a shortage of entertaining news. Our answering machine was at capacity, mostly with urgent messages from reporters who desperately needed to talk with us. Some were polite; some, not so much. Regardless, we deleted them all.

But there were some calls that I did need to make. The first was to Arantxa.

"Hello, Jim. I've been expecting your call."

"So you know? We got the bastard."

"Yes. We heard on the news. Are you OK?"

"Yeah. We're all fine. We just took off for a week to hide from the press. Does Senora Hernandez know that we got him?"

"Yes. I called her as soon as I saw the story on television. She was very relieved when I told her. She was happy that not only had Javier's killer been found, but that the whole story about what had happened in Cuba had also been uncovered. She said that General Hernandez would finally be resting in his grave knowing that this story had been told. She asked me to pass along her thanks to you, and to your wife, for everything that you did to help avenge Javier's death. And she would like it very much if you would come to visit her in Spain, so that she can thank you in person."

"I'm just glad we were able to help. I do hope that she will be able to find some peace now. And I hope she thanked you, too. Without your help, we would have gotten nowhere."

"Yes. She understands that. Will you come to Spain?"

"No, Arantxa. I don't think that we'll ever go back again to your beautiful country. We've pretty much already traveled the world. Now, all we want to do is stay here in our quiet little fishing village. Speaking of which, when are you going to come to visit us and go fishing?"

"Jim, you know that I hate fishing. And I hate quiet, too! You go to bed about when I am ready to go out in the evening. Twenty-four hours down there, and I would be—how do you say?—crawling the walls! Sadly, I'm not a village kind of person. I much prefer the city. But I will miss you. Please say hello to Jill."

"I will. And Arantxa, thank you again for your help. And please say hello to all my Spanish friends."

Next, I dialed Frank Tranh's number.

"Do you have that bottle of Glenmorangie ready?"

"You bet. It's sitting here waiting for you to come and share it with me. But I've got to tell you, it's been begging me to go ahead and open it. I'm not sure how much longer I'm going to be able to resist. When will you be coming to help celebrate?"

"How does this weekend look?"

"Done. Let me know when to pick you up at the airport."

"Will do."

"Hey, Jill," I called upstairs after I got off the phone. "Frank Tranh's coming down this weekend to help us celebrate."

"That'll be perfect. I just got off the phone with Katie. She was talking with Anna down at Woody's. They want to have a special party Saturday night so that the whole town can celebrate, too. It'll be perfect for Frank to be here and be part of that."

***

Saturday night (if you can call six thirty in the evening "night") Frank, Jill, and I pulled into Woody's parking lot. Actually, the parking lot itself was already full, so we had to park along the street. It looked like the whole town was already there. And I could hear music coming from inside. It sounded like the tunes were coming from the west coast of Florida's most politically incorrect roving minstrel, Jay Crawford. Everyone likes to joke that Jay has been playing the bars in Saint James City so long that he once entertained Ponce de Leon. And there may be some truth to that. But no one ever gets tired of his songs. They are designed to poke fun wherever fun needs to be poked. He's as much a comedian as he is a musician. And he's a damn fine musician. He's really a town favorite. I was delighted that he was on board that night. He always earns a shot of good whisky on my tab whenever he performs, but that night, he was going to get more than one. I just hoped that he wasn't planning to drive back to his home on Anna Maria Island after the gig. If so, he was going to need to rethink that plan. But it wouldn't be the first time: He often jokes about how many nights he's slept in Woody's parking lot.

As we walked toward the door, I told Frank about how Javier had come to love this place, and how the bar's patrons had come to love him, too. We paused outside the entrance so he could take in the full-size channel buoy that sits next to the door. It is painted to resemble the famous marker in Key West that proclaims it is the "Southernmost Point in the Continental US." But this buoy proclaims that Saint James City is the "Drunkenmost Point in the Continental US." We got a laugh about that. And, as we went inside, I pointed out another sign to Frank. This one warned that "Saint James City does not have a town drunk—we all take turns." I had a feeling it might possibly be my turn that night, but I noticed that a few others seemed to have jumped the line, and had a head start on me. As we entered the main room, Jay Crawford led everyone in singing "For He's a Jolly Good Fellow!"

We looked around. The place was packed with our friends, and with the friends that Javier had made in Saint James City. I noticed that Katie and Steve were at their customary spots at the bar. I was surprised to see Mike Collins sitting at the end of the bar. He was in plain clothes. I hoped it was his night off. He raised his glass in a salute as our eyes met. I gave him a thumbs-up.

At this point, everyone descended upon us, patting us on the back, and shaking our hands. I looked at Anna behind the bar. She already was handing me what I knew would be a Johnny Walker Red and water, in a tall glass. And Jill was already drinking her Mich Ultra, with a full pitcher sitting on the bar. I gave Frank my drink, and motioned to Heather for another. She happily obliged. I watched her pouring some more smoky smoothness into a tall glass. Normally, when you ask for a drink in a tall glass, you do it so you'll get more water with your liquor—the strategy being that you can drink longer without getting drunk. But Anna always crosses me up by giving me liquor in an amount proportionate to the size of the glass. Consequently, despite my best intentions, I usually end up getting really drunk. But I guess, in some ways, that's not all bad.

As soon as we had our drinks, I asked Jay if I could borrow his microphone. When I had everyone's attention, I thanked them all for coming to celebrate this remembrance of Javier's life. I then introduced Frank to the crowd, noting that he and

Javier had worked closely together for many years, and that his help had been vital in unraveling the mystery about who had killed Javier. The crowd gave him a round of applause. Next, I asked for Jill, Katie, and Steve to join me. I described to everyone the roles they had played, and personally thanked each of them. The crowd again applauded enthusiastically.

Next, I asked Mike Collins to join us. I told the crowd about how diligent he had been in making sure that Javier's killer was brought to justice. I asked the crowd for a cheer for him, to which they responded, "Fuzz, fuzz, fuzz, fuzz, fuzz."

Next, I thanked everyone, not only for all of their help and support, but also for being such good friends to Javier. I also passed along Senora Hernandez's special thanks.

And, finally, I thanked Adam, the manager of Woody's, for organizing this tribute. With that, I gave the microphone back to Jay, and requested that he sing us something particularly off-color. He growled that that wouldn't be a problem, and began to sing something about cats in the chow mein down at the local Chinese restaurant. Everyone roared with approval. I could see the garden club's executive board lined up, ready to take their turns in leading the crowd in chanting "You Bitch, you Slut, you Whore!" Life was starting to return to normal in Saint James City.

I grabbed Jill, gave her a great, big kiss, and we began to dance right in the middle of the restaurant, all without spilling a drop from our glasses ,which Anna had so thoughtfully refilled during my speech. Dozens of couples spilled out to join us. Jay kept the music playing. Anna and Adam kept the beer and the booze flowing. I noticed that one of the garden club girls had grabbed Frank, and they were dancing enthusiastically. The other two appeared to be trying hard to get Mike Collins onto the dance floor. Over toward the side, I could see that Sea Tow Sammy was having a great time, dancing with his wife. And I noticed the fishing guides huddled up in a corner, presumably talking about where the big ones were biting. Saint James City is a special place!

Jill gave me a hug, looked me in the eyes, and said, "I'm so glad we live here." I kissed her again, and said, "Me too." I knew that we looked forward to spending the rest of our lives here, in this "quaint little fishing village with a drinking problem," a place where nothing ever much happens.

NOTES ON VISITING PINE ISLAND AND SAINT JAMES CITY

Pine Island, and Saint James City, are real places. My wife and I love it here. In some ways it really is like a place that time has forgotten. The pace of life seems slower, and the residents are definitely friendlier. But, while there is plenty to do, the island is definitely not for everyone. For starters, there are no beaches. Further, the lodging, dining, and entertainment options are limited. And, it's not too much of an exaggeration to say that the sidewalks here (if there actually were any sidewalks) roll up early. If any of that doesn't sound like what you're looking for, then you should probably stay in Sanibel/Captiva, or Ft. Myers Beach. But, if immersing yourself in a quaint, quiet piece of Old Florida sounds like fun, then come on out to the island.

The following chapters provide additional information about life in Pine Island and Saint James City. I hope you find this to be of interest.

Mosquitoes and Thunderstorms

We bought our house in the spring. The temperature then was pleasant, the skies were clear, and there were no bugs. It seemed like paradise. We moved in midsummer. What a difference. We immediately learned that summer in Saint James City is characterized by three things: heat, rain, and mosquitoes. Ninety degrees may not seem that hot to you, but when it is combined with near-saturated humidity, you start to sweat the moment you walk outside. I tried a couple of strategies for dealing with this perspiration. I tried showering in the morning, and at lunch, and again before dinner. But despite all this bathing, for most of the day I was still soaked in sweat. Eventually, I just accepted the inevitable and enjoyed one long, luxurious shower in the evening once the day's work was complete.

Another reality here in the summer is that it rains every day. The normal pattern is for there to be a thunderstorm at about three thirty in the afternoon. A local joke is that you can set your watch by them. But quite honestly, that pattern doesn't always hold—you can have thunderstorms here at any time of the day or night. You may wake up to rain, it may storm at noon, it may rain in the afternoon, or it may rain all night.

Did I mention that there are thunderstorms? That is to say, it doesn't just rain. Not for nothing is Southwest Florida known as the lightning capital of the world. Rain in this part of the world is usually accompanied by the most amazing displays of lightning and thunder you have ever seen or heard.

Now, all of this water that falls from the sky has to go somewhere, right? That leads to several other things we quickly learned about Saint James City. First, we observed that in the summer, the ditches are always full of water. Not only do they have water in them, but—I'm not making this up—the water level is actually impacted by the tides. I guess that gives you an indication of how low the elevation level here actually is. And if you don't believe that, as we were driving from Birmingham, we occasionally looked at the GPS display in our car. One bit of information that we took special notice of was the elevation reading—it was close to a thousand feet in Birmingham. As we drove further south, this reading steadily fell. By the time we went through Tallahassee, it was down to only a couple hundred feet. When we went by Tampa, it was nearer to thirty feet. As we drove out Pine Island Road toward our new home, Jill started to laugh. She pointed at the display and said, "I guess we're getting close."

I looked at the GPS. The reading was zero! I kid you not. Sea level takes on a whole new meaning here on the island.

Now all this water has an especially nasty consequence: it creates great breeding conditions for mosquitoes. These demons from hell need standing water in which to breed, and the summer rainfall had created the perfect environment for mosquito reproduction. As soon we got out of the car to walk into our new home, we were attacked. What we had envisioned to be a romantic, hand-holding period of gazing lovingly at our life's final residence quickly turned into a face-slapping race to be the first inside. So much for romance during mosquito season in Southwest Florida.

We quickly learned that you can't go outside early in the morning or late in the day during the summer without first covering yourself from head to toe with industrial-strength bug spray. Deep Woods Off seemed to do the trick. Then, once appropriately protected, we were able to cope. After a few days, this morning application even started to seem "normal." Just goes to show you what amazing capacity human beings have for adaptation—and for self-deception. We soon learned to love the sound of planes and helicopters making low-level runs to dispense insecticides to keep the demons knocked down. What's a little cancer, twenty years down the road when you're being eaten alive on a daily basis? We really loved those planes.

Island Life

Gradually, we began to develop our new daily routine. Not only were we learning to live in a new location, we were also having to adapt to life as retirees. Just about everything we had ever done up to this point in our lives together was different. Trust me; this takes some getting used to. An adaptation of this magnitude is not without stress. More than once, we both came close to cracking. But understanding that we didn't really have much choice, we persevered, and got on with organizing the way we would live in our new town.

Since we have a pet, the morning's ritual starts with walking the dog. I've found over the years that it's better if I let Cody tell me where she would like to walk. So, I let the dog lead the way. And I'm happy to do this since I'm sure that each morning's walk is the highlight of her day. As a consequence, we usually put in a good tour of the neighborhood. One of the first things I learned about these walks is that we were not alone. If you go out at about 7:00 a.m., you're going to run into a host of neighbors doing the same thing. Saint James City is a very dog-friendly environment. Interestingly, most of these early morning walkers appear to be female; only a few couples and one other solitary male make up the poop-patrol regulars.

Generally, we'll also encounter a number of bicyclists and quite a few walkers. I've observed that most people appear to know each other. Often they'll stop and bring each other up on the latest happenings in their lives, and, I guess, the doings on the island. Even the woman who delivers the morning paper will sometimes stop her car in the middle of the street to chat with the folks she knows. There is no worry about other traffic at this time of day; there simply isn't much. And what traffic there is will sit patiently and wait until the conversation is over. Things are definitely different here. We like it.

Early on, as we were setting up the house, we would have lunch and dinner at one of the local restaurants. Normally, we'd go to the Waterfront for lunch. I found out quickly that Carl was not really right about the grouper sandwich. While the one he had recommended was very, very good, it was not the best. The best grouper sandwich in the whole world can be found at the Waterfront. You can trust me on that. I'll pass on another tip: try the triggerfish sandwich. I love grouper, but triggerfish may actually have it beat. And if you don't want a sandwich, the kitchen will grill up whatever fresh fish it has and put it on a killer salad. It doesn't get much better than this. Jill, however, would take exception. She absolutely loves the Waterfront's fried conch and grouper basket. She's ordered that so often that now the servers just ask if she's having the regular.

The Waterfront is really a great little place. But we only go there for lunch. The Waterfront does not have a liquor license; it only serves beer and wine. While this would not trouble Jill in the least, it does create a problem for me. I simply don't like to drink beer. It makes me feel bloated and puts me to sleep. This is not to say that I don't drink. To the contrary, over the years, I've found that I usually need several Scotch whiskies in the evening. Badly. To get that, we have to head down the street to Woody's—another excellent institution where you can get excellent food and drinks.

Woody's backs up to a canal and features a great, thatch-covered, outside patio. During the cooler months, this place is usually packed—particularly if there is live music on the deck. This is a great boating destination for folks coming out of Cape Coral and Fort Myers. After a couple of hours on the boat, you're ready for food, libations, and fun. You can get all three at Woody's.

The tavern was named for the owner's dog—a large, loving Labrador that, unfortunately, is no longer with us. But his spirit lives on, captured in a great photo that appears on the menus. It shows Woody curled up asleep, with a large can of brew between his paws. As I mentioned, beer is an important element of life for most that live in Saint James City (excluding me). Apparently, this holds true even for the dogs.

Another personality that no longer patronizes Woody's is a life-sized, poster-board likeness of Joe Paterno. When we first moved to town, that image occupied a prominent corner of the bar area. Woody's owner is a Penn State football fan. But we all noticed that the cardboard Joe Paterno in Woody's went missing about the same time as the real one in Happy Valley, Pennsylvania, was undone by a sex-abuse scandal.

You can drive from one end of Saint James City to another in about five minutes—by bicycle. There are three restaurants and a couple of bars. There are two boat-repair facilities where you can get anything fixed, a marina, a fishing tackle store, a very small hardware store, a couple of churches, an auto repair shop, a produce stand, and a couple of mom-and-pop-type motels. Those are all of the commercial establishments in Saint James City.

I should also mention that there is no serious crime in town. With only one bridge on and off the island, criminals tend to avoid Saint James City, lest they can't make good their getaway. And, because everyone here knows each other, there simply are no local criminals. Consequently, no one here even bothers to lock his door.

Note that I indicated above that there was no *serious* crime. We have noticed, however, that the consumption of marijuana does not appear to fall into the category of "crime." It appears that several members of the community do, from time to time, enjoy this form of relaxation. We have even heard mention that several of the town's most senior members may have helped with the import of this commodity in times past.

For many, this place may be too small and too slow. But for us, it feels great. We love it here.

Pine Island Sound

The economy of Saint James City revolves around the water. It sits at the south end of Pine Island, which is sixteen miles long and roughly a mile wide. Saint James City was first developed as a fishing resort in the late 1890s as a consequence of a national frenzy created by media reports of the first tarpon ever to be caught with a rod and reel. The fish had been landed at the mouth of what is now known as Tarpon Bay. The spot where the fish was hooked is less than half a mile from Saint James City. But at that time, Saint James City could only be reached by boat. As a result, the resort never prospered. In the early 1900s, the city saw another boom period as it was selected as the location for a sizeable rope-making operation. A large factory was constructed here, and the whole south end of the island was devoted to the cultivation of hemp. But after about a decade, the production of rope moved offshore, and the works was abandoned. Since then the community has seen periodic real-estate booms and weathered roughly the same number of busts. Now, despite 120 years of economic development efforts, the permanent population of the town is not much larger than one thousand hardy souls. During the "season" (roughly November to April), however, the population easily triples as "snowbirds" fly south to escape the cold.

The town fronts the intersection of San Carlos Bay and Pine Island Sound, which together flow into the Gulf of Mexico less than a mile away. Given its proximity to the gulf and the sound, there are few locations in the world more blessed with great fishing. The area is renowned for inshore fishing—with tarpon, snook, redfish, and speckled trout abundant in nearby waters. Excellent offshore fishing can also be found only a short boat ride into the gulf. As a result, the town is almost totally focused on meeting the needs of boaters and fishermen. Saint James City is laid out around a series of canals that were dredged out of the mangrove swamps over the past century. Almost every home in town either faces the bay or backs up to a canal, and features at least one boat lift, davit, or boat slip. It would be impossible to recreate this type of community today, given current ecological concerns. But it does exist, and if you don't mind being relatively isolated from the modern world, it is an almost unique place to enjoy Florida the way it used to be.

Pine Island Sound is a truly special body of water. It runs north to south for almost twenty miles, separating the coastal barrier islands of Sanibel, Captiva, North Captiva, and Cayo Costa from Pine Island. At its broadest, the sound is only a couple of miles wide. It flows into the gulf at its north end via Boca Grande, and at the south via San Carlos Bay. It also flows into the gulf through several passes that separate the barrier islands. The northernmost pass is Captiva Pass, which separates Cayo Costa from North Captiva. Further to the south is Red Fish Pass, which separates North Captiva from Captiva. Blind Pass, which is further to the south, lies between Captiva and Sanibel.

Inside the sound are a large number of smaller islands, only a few of which are inhabited. Two of the most famous are found at the north end of the sound. Useppa Island was once the grand home of one of the country's wealthiest men, Baron Collier. But today it is a very exclusive private resort. For some reason, it seems to be especially popular with Germans. Another famous nearby island is Cabbage Key. This island originally was the home of the son of a famous American mystery writer, Mary Reinhart Roberts. Today, however, it's a "must-visit" restaurant and bar for anyone visiting Southwest Florida. However, since it can only be reached by boat, visitors need to either rent a boat or use one of the local ferries that stop at the Key. Most weekends, despite the challenge of reaching the island, you'll have to wait for a table for lunch. During the season, it can be an absolute circus. Even so, it's one of those places you have to say that you've been to at least once if you either live in or visit Florida.

A Mango Tango

"There are a lot of places on the island that sell the mangoes they actually grow. Two of the best are the Mango Factory in Bokeelia and Pine Island Fruit and Vegetable, located just a couple miles north of Center. Trust me; you haven't eaten a mango until you've eaten a Pine Island mango."

My experience with mangoes has been limited to what we've bought in the grocery store. They always look great, but somehow, when I actually eat one, they leave me just a little disappointed—not quite what I expect from something that's supposed to be the "king of fruits."

There are over a thousand different varieties of mangoes grown around the world. But, these varieties can be grouped into two main types of the fruit—one type originated in Southeast Asia. The varieties of this type tend to be lighter in color and milder in flavor and smell. The other type originated in India and Pakistan. Fruit of this type is slightly darker in color and more intensely flavored and scented.

A few weeks after arriving in Pine Island we were lucky to attend a mango tasting at Pine Island Fruit and Vegetable. Our host said that his farm had about fifty varieties under cultivation, all grown organically. But they only had twenty-five varieties available for tasting today, since not all types ripen at the same time. His assistants then uncovered twenty-five different trays of sliced mango. Our host invited the crowd to line up and enjoy a sample of each. His assistants provided sheets of paper and pencils for taking notes about which varieties we liked best. And, of course, he mentioned that all of the fruit that we would taste would be available for purchase, once the tasting was complete.

Soon we were moving through the line, armed with toothpicks for securing the slices of fruit. We were trying our best to keep notes about which varieties we preferred. Simply stated, most of the varieties we tasted were nothing like the ones that you find in the grocery store. It seems to me that the varieties in the store have a somewhat thin taste and an off-putting smell of turpentine. And sometimes, there are strings throughout the flesh.

But what we tasted was different. "Delicious.""Wow." "Oh, my God.""Heavenly." "I can't believe that." "I've never tasted anything like this." These were just a few of the comments we heard from our neighbors as we munched our way through the tasting line. And, of course, we were making the same kinds of comments. The flavors were like nothing we had ever experienced. Some were sweet; some tasted distinctly like lemon; some tasted like coconut; and some tasted like nothing we had ever experienced before, but certainly wanted to taste again. On and on. We couldn't get enough. When we got through all twenty-five, we looked at each other and said, "Let's go though again!" We did.

Finally, we compared notes and agreed to take the following types home for further exploration: Doc, Lemon Saigon, Carrie, Pickering, and Valencia Pride. We also agreed that the variety you find in stores, Tommy Atkins, is best left for those who don't have mango orchards nearby.

For the next month, we ate mangos with just about everything. I started every morning with freshly sliced mango and a pot of tea. Lunch frequently featured a mango salsa paired with something. And at dinner, it was not uncommon to find a dish that is a particular favorite of mine: seafood, mango, onions, and lime juice all baked together in foil. We even bought an ice cream churn so that we could enjoy homemade mango ice cream before we turned in for the night. Mango vanilla, mango banana, and mango coconut were just a few of the ice cream concoctions we enjoyed. Unfortunately, mango season is short, and by September all of the island's mangoes were gone. But they were great while they lasted!

Boating on the Sound

We love our new island home, and enjoy showing it off to visitors. In addition to fishing, we like to boat over into Tarpon Bay and visit with the pod of manatees that lives there.

Up until the mid 1980's, Tarpon Bay was home to a successful marina. But, then the US government made it, and most of the surrounding area, into a Federal Wildlife Refuge. It's a beautiful area.

One reason it is one of my favorite places is that this is where the author Randy Wayne White once lived, and worked as a fishing guide. When you read his books, it's clear that Tarpon Bay is the setting for the home of his protagonist-my hero- Doc Ford. In the books, he lives on a body of water called Dinkins Bay. There happens to another body of water a mile of so up the sound that is called Dinkins Bayou. But, there's no mistaking where Doc Ford really lives- he lives on Tarpon Bay.

We enjoy taking the boat throughout the sound. There is always something to see, or experience. And, there are a number of great restaurants and bars to visit as you explore. Places such as the Green Flash, Teen Waters Inn, South Seas, Tarpon Lodge, and Barnacles are all worth a visit. And, if you want to run the whole sound, make sure to visit Cabbage Key for lunch, dinner, or drinks. And, if the weather allows you may even consider going into the Gulf outside the barrier islands, and heading up to Boca Grande. It makes for a great day to come in through that pass made famous by Gasparilla, dock in the town to have lunch at one of the great restaurants, and then spend the afternoon exploring that splendid village. I love to walk its quiet streets, and try to imagine where Jose Gaspar's pirate headquarters was located.

You may also enjoy running your boat to the south, crossing San Carlos Bay, and entering Matanzas Pass. This really makes for a quick trip to Fort Myers Beach. Maybe twenty minutes by boat, versus almost an hour by car. One of our favorite things to do on a Sunday afternoon is to take the boat over to Doc Ford's Rum Bar (of course), have a great lunch on the waterfront deck, and listen to one of the great bands that play there on the weekends. If you go, make sure you have at least one serving of that restaurant's fantastic "Yucatan shrimp," a large bowl full of boiled jumbo shrimp swimming in a sauce of melted butter, garlic, cilantro, and hot chili sauce. Trust me- it doesn't get much better. Just make sure to dip pieces of the restaurant's freshly baked Cuban bread in that sauce. It's heavenly.

The Fish Shacks

The story of the fish shacks is one that makes this part of the world so interesting. In the late 1890s and early 1900s, commercial fishing was the most important economic activity in these parts. Fish were extremely abundant throughout the sound and relatively easy to catch using large nets. The difficult part was getting the fish to market. In the early days, fishermen from Cuba established fishing ranches on the barrier islands. But they had no way to get fresh fish back to Cuba. All they could do was to dry and salt them.

In the early 1900s, however, the railroad was extended to Punta Gorda. That offered the opportunity to ship fresh fish to the markets of the Eastern United States. But at that time, there were no engines available for smaller boats that would allow fishermen to quickly and reliably get their catches from the fishing grounds to the rail head. To solve this problem, fish companies devised a relatively efficient, four-stage process for harvesting, storing, transporting, and shipping fish. The process started at the companies' headquarters, located in towns that were both on the water and, critically, at railroad stations. The most important of such towns in Southwest Florida was Punta Gorda. At their headquarters, the companies established ice-making plants, commissaries, and warehouses. The second stage of production involved large steamers, and later, diesel-powered boats known as "run boats." These boats made the run between headquarters and the fishing grounds. Throughout the fishing grounds, in strategically important locations, the companies built what were known as fish houses. These houses served both as ice houses to store the fish that had been caught and as commissaries to supply the fishermen. On the outbound runs, the run boats carried ice for the fish houses and supplies and mail for the fishermen and their families. On the return run, the boats were loaded with iced-down fish. The boats would return to the rail head, where the fish would be loaded onto refrigerated railcars for shipment north. Another important role of the run boats was to ferry passengers from the outer islands to and from town.

The companies' fish houses were typically built on pilings next to deep water where it was easy for the run boat to access the house and to dock. One side of the fish house was a heavily insulated warehouse designed to hold ice and store fish. The other side typically comprised the living quarters and office for the manager of the fish house. Normally, there was another wing of the house that was used as a store house and commissary.

The final production stage involved the fishermen who actually caught the fish. They typically lived in small, stilt houses built over the water near the fishing grounds. These houses were referred to as "fish shacks." Since the fishermen had no efficient way to travel for long distances, they essentially lived on (literally, above) the fishing grounds. At day's end, they would row or sail their catches to the fish house, and then return to their fish shacks to sleep and eat. Their lives revolved around the tides and the behavior of the fish. It was not uncommon for the fishermen to spend months at a time fishing and living in these shacks. Normally, a fisherman would work exclusively for one fish company. In many ways, this process was similar to the company towns in mining communities around the country, only all of the activity took place on the water rather than under the ground.

Today, the term "fish house" is used generically; no distinction is made between the facilities that were used for buying and storing fish versus those used as dormitories for fishermen. Most of the houses have been destroyed by hurricanes or neglect, or occasionally, on purpose. With the advent of efficient and fast gasoline-powered boats, and with the building of the bridge onto Pine Island, it was no longer necessary for fish companies to maintain the elaborate production process that required the use of remote buildings out on the water. Consequently, shortly after World War II, almost all of the fish houses were abandoned. In some cases, they were given to the fishermen in the area, who tore them down and used the lumber to build houses on the surrounding islands. In other cases, they were simply abandoned. In the early 1960s, the Punta Gorda Fish Company, which over time had become the dominant fishing company, began to sell off its remaining fish houses to anyone able to buy them. Many local families pooled their resources and purchased one to be used as a weekend retreat. As time went on, the state of Florida became concerned that these houses posed threats to navigation and created environmental pollution issues, as the residents used the bay as a sewer. The state seized a large number of these houses and simply had them burned. Eventually, however, a few of the remaining owners successfully challenged the state in court and were able to halt the destruction of the fish houses. Through this action, the houses that still existed were declared to be of historical significance. Today, only nine of them remain in the sound.

Cabbage Key

Cabbage Key is a truly magical place. This small restaurant, bar, and resort sits on an island that can only be reached by boat. It was originally constructed as a private residence for the son of Mary Reinhart Roberts, who at the time was one of America's most popular mystery writers. Today, it's a very popular destination for those boating on the sound. It's only drawback is that in 'Season' it can be too popular, making it sometimes difficult to find a place to dock. But, don't let that deter you. This is a place you have to visit.

The staff that works on the Key lives on the island for weeks at a time. I've been told by some folks around town that this really isn't a bad deal. Typically, they work breakfast, lunch, and dinner shifts every day they are there. The upside is that since there is nowhere to go and nothing to buy, there is no temptation to spend any of the money they make while they are out there. Every time we've gone, we tend to see the same folks waiting tables. So I guess it must be true that it's a pretty good gig.

I can't really recommend the fish sandwich here, unlike those sold at most restaurants on the sound. It's always a piece of previously frozen mahi-mahi—nothing to get excited about. But I can speak enthusiastically in favor of ordering a pound of peel-and-eat shrimp. I'm pretty sure they are fresh. And Jill swears by their cheeseburger. I'm also a fan of a salty dog from the bar. It's probably just the boat ride, but every time I have one there, it seems colder than usual and it goes down really, really well. I'm a fan. But two is my limit.

I'd be remiss if I didn't note the dollar bills pinned to the walls of the restaurant. Apparently, the habit of writing your name on a bill to document your visit to the island started a long time ago. Now it's a rite of passage for anyone visiting the island. The bills, stuck on the walls, the ceiling, and everywhere else you can imagine, have to be inches deep. It really is something to see. Once a year, management strips off the layer of bills, and donates them to local charities.

Getting There

Pine Island is located in Lee County, Florida. There is only one road onto the island- named, appropriately enough, Pine Island Road. Once you leave the mainland, and head west onto the island, I swear that you can actually feel the pace of life start to slow down. I can always also feel the pressures of the world start to lift from your shoulders. In many ways, when you head to Pine Island you are leaving civilization behind.

The first town you come to is Matlacha (pronounced Mat-la-shay). At one time this town was a simple fishing village. But, today it's the home to artists, musicians, and a large number of other assorted island characters. As you drive through you'll also find a multitude of colorful shops that cater to the souvenir needs of our winter visitors. You can find some pretty cool stuff there.

Continuing west, you'll cross Little Pine Island. No civilization here. Instead, it's a wildlife sanctuary, where you commonly see bald eagles, ospreys and other birds soaring overhead. You can also frequently see tourists doing three sixties in order to return as quickly as possible to civilization, having decided that there can't be anything worth seeing further out Pine Island Road. That's OK with me.

A couple of miles further along you'll come to a four-way stop. This is Pine Island Center, located as you might expect, in the middle of the island. Turn right to go to Bokeelia; left to go to Saint James City. The main road on Pine Island is called Stringfellow Road, named after the county commissioner who years ago was able to get the road built. It runs north to south. Bokeelia is almost eight miles north of Center; Saint James City about eight miles to the south. And, there's nothing much to see along the road heading to either location. Going north you'll see palm groves, mango orchards, and other agriculture. To the south, it's mostly undeveloped land that has largely been set aside as parks and wildlife refuges.

As you come into Saint James City, Froggy's is on the left, just before the town's only bridge. Ragged Ass Saloon is on the right, immediately past the bridge. A few hundred feet further along, on the right, you'll see Low Key Tiki, with the Monroe Canal Marina next door. The marina is immediately followed by Woody's. The Waterfront is at the end of the road, maybe a half mile further along.

I hope you'll come pay us a visit. I'll be keeping an eye out for you. But, your best bet to find me will be to stop at Woody's, go inside, and look for an old guy with a pony tail, and gold hoop earrings. It's possible that there may be several folks there that match that description. If so, I'll be the one drinking a Salty Dog.

ABOUT THE AUTHOR

Mitch Grant is a retired banker, race-car driver, and an aspiring buccaneer. He is a seventh-generation Floridian, having grown up in Polk County, where, when not attending school, he worked in the family's groves and ranches. He also spent summers and vacations in the wild swamps of Gulf Hammock, located on Florida's remote northwestern gulf coast. There, he learned boating, fishing, and other cracker skills. After graduating from Stetson University, he served his Uncle Sam as the leader of one of the US Army's finest field artillery units. In recognition, his uncle paid for further education at the University of South Florida, where he earned a master's degree in business administration. He used this degree to secure employment in the commercial banking industry, where, for the next thirty-five years, he helped to lead banks in Florida, Georgia, and Alabama to success. During this time, he also pursued his passion for sports-car racing. Now, having raced for over twenty-five years, he is one of the nation's most experienced and best-known amateur drivers. Upon retirement from banking, he and his beautiful wife, Sherry, moved to Saint James City, Florida, a quaint Florida fishing village, where he began to pursue another dream—writing fiction. His writing is modeled after that of his hero, and Sanibel Island neighbor, Randy Wayne White. Now, when not writing or fishing, he is helping to educate his four grandchildren in the ways of Southwest Florida's legendary pirates.

Made in the USA
Charleston, SC
03 February 2015